MESSENGER OF LOVE

"Why do you not ask me anything? Don't you want to know about me? Aren't you interested?" Kathleen looked up at Dawson, her blue eyes serious.

Dawson smiled the lazy smile and reached up to push a long strand of hair from her shoulder, gently placing it behind her ear, "I don't need to ask you anything. I know all I need to know about you."

"Just how could you know all about me, Mister Dawson Blakely? Why you only met me tonight! What could you *possibly* know? Some men think me quite mysterious." She snatched the blond curl and pulled it back over her shoulder.

"My dear Kathleen, I'm sure you are. Here's what I know about you. I know you are the most beautiful girl I've ever seen. I know you never tire of asking questions. I know that tomorrow night I am taking you for a long carriage ride in the moonlight." Dawson leaned close and once again pushed the blond curl behind her ear. "And I know that you will fall madly, helplessly in love with me."

KATHLEEN'S SURRENDER

BY
NANCY
HENDERSON
RYAN

ZEBRA BOOKS
KENSINGTON PUBLISHING CORP.

ZEBRA BOOKS

are published by

KENSINGTON PUBLISHING CORP.

475 Park Avenue South
New York, N.Y. 10016

Copyright © 1983 by Nancy Henderson Ryan

Printed in the United States of America

One

Life was gracious and tranquil for the inhabitants of Natchez, Mississippi, the richest city in the country's richest state. Plantation owners in ruffled shirts and lace cuffs ruled over their households and vast cotton empires with a firm hand and relaxed authority that rarely made it necessary to raise the whips they carried jauntily. No perspiration from labor ever soiled their custom-made suits and no calluses ever appeared on their soft-palmed hands. As long as the pink and white blossoms of the cotton plants burst open every spring, their pleasing color stretching as far as the planter's eye could see from the balustraded captain's walk atop the hipped roof of his stately mansion, all was right with his world. He could continue to live a life matched only by royalty in its splendor and grace.

He was respected and feared by the Negroes that worked the fields and called him master. The planter owned them body and soul, just as he owned the cotton, the mansion he lived in with its priceless furniture from France, English glassware, Italian marble, first editions of classics, master paintings and art objects, blooded racehorses imported from Kentucky, and the fair lady dressed tastefully in tight-waisted gowns and billowing skirts. All belonged to him and were instrumental in allowing him to live in the best of all possible worlds this side of Paradise.

In the most magnificent mansion in all Mississippi, Louis Antoine Beauregard, one of the wealthiest cotton planters in the South, stood in his sun-filled bedroom, being assisted with his jacket by his faithful manservant, Daniel. Daniel was smiling sunnily, white teeth splitting the black face, happy with his task, pleased to be of service to the white man he had loved and respected for the entire forty-five years Louis Antoine Beauregard had lived. Daniel was only a boy of nine when Louis Beauregard was born in this very bedroom on a cold winter day in 1809.

Louis put his long arms into the jacket Daniel held out for him. He stood at the tall windows and looked over his estate, shimmering in the hot afternoon sun. The fertile land that had been in his family for generations spread out below him and the big house with its many rooms, gleaming columns, circular stairways, high ceilings, imported carpets, broad porches, and priceless treasures was far grander today than when it was built a half century ago in 1804. His burgeoning riches made refurbishing, upgrading, and beautifying the old estate, inside and out, every few years, as effortless as the snap of his long, slender fingers.

In front of his beloved Sans Souci, acres of rolling green lawn sloped down to the terraced gardens of azaleas and roses, camellias and wisterias, interspersed with lush green hedges. Huge trees, a century old, cast their welcome shades at intervals around the vast garden. Thick green vines climbed the white latticed summer house in the distance where three young girls in their white summer dresses chattered in hushed tones, passing the lazy afternoon on the long white settee under the octagon-shaped roof, glasses of cool lemonade in their hands.

Louis turned and gazed down on the long rows of cotton plants, bursting with white, almost ready for the harvest, their delicate bolls facing the sun in all their glory, mature and ready to be pulled by hundreds of nimble black fingers, tossed in long sacks, loaded onto wagons, taken to the gin. The soft white cotton would then be turned to the color of money, bringing new riches to the master of Sans Souci, new frocks and jewelry for its mistress, new party dresses and

6

dancing slippers for the master's young daughter, new trinkets and gifts for the black hands that picked the cotton, and a respite from their labors. Frolicking and celebrations spread throughout the quarters where they lived at the back edge of the big plantation. It was the best time of year for Louis Beauregard, the master of Sans Souci, and for everyone and everything he owned.

Abigail Howard Beauregard, Louis' attractive blond wife, a soft-spoken, elegant lady, reserved in manner, delicate of features, high born and bred, remained coolly detached from the running of the estate, preferring to leave it in the capable hands of her adoring husband and the trusted servants he had placed in command. Not wishing any care ever to crease the high, fair forehead of the grand, blue-blooded beauty he'd been married to for over seventeen years, Louis was careful to guard her from anxiety. He made it clear to his staff of house servants that their mistress was to be pampered and respected above all else and no discouraging words should ever reach her shell pink ears. Her world was as pleasant and carefree today as it had been when she was a young girl in her father's home. Her husband had taken her as a young bride, determined to spoil and shield her from the world in a grander manner than her father before him. The white bolls of cotton at Sans Souci had made it possible and Abigail had never in her thirty-five years wanted for anything. Life was as easy for her as fluttering her thick lashes over big blue eyes and expressing her latest desire in a voice barely above a whisper.

Abigail was in the room adjoining her husband's. Hannah was hooking up the tight-bodiced dress while Abigail stood, her hands on her small waist, studying her reflection in the mirror. A hint of a frown was on her pale face and the small mouth was turned down slightly at the corners. Hannah raised her eyes from her mistress' back and saw the look of displeasure on Abigail's face. Hannah, tired from a long day's work, weary from climbing the winding stairs time and again throughout the long, hot day, her bulky weight bearing down on tired, aging legs, was not concerned with her own misery, but with the clouded blue eyes of her mistress.

"Now, honey, what troublin' you?" Hannah moved back a step and put her chubby black hands to Abigail's small waist.

"Hannah," Abigail sighed, "this gown does nothing to become me. What shall I do?"

Hannah rushed to the big dressing room filled with frocks of assorted colors and fabrics. Soon she was sashaying back, grinning, a sky blue satin gown over her arm. "Look here, chile, this'll make yo' pretty blue eyes sparkle lak saphires."

"Perfect, dear Hannah. Get this terrible dress off me." Hannah laid the blue dress on the bed and rushed to unhook the rose cast-off that had displeased her mistress.

"I think I shall die of boredom," Kathleen Diana Beauregard sighed loudly. The usually high spirits of the young mistress of Sans Souci were sagging badly and the hot, sticky air of the late August afternoon weighed down her slim shoulders like an unbearable burden she could no longer carry. She raised her bare arms up to the heavy blond hair laying limply around her neck. With both hands, she jerked the thick tresses up off the glistening nape and held it high atop her head, her features contorted, a pout covering the mobile face, heavy lids drooping over the big blue eyes. "Don't you think this has been the most impossible summer you've ever seen? Not one exciting thing has happened for months!" She leaned further back on the white settee, lowering a hand to fan at the still air. A pesky mosquito determined to make her life ever more miserable.

Kathleen was flanked by her two closest girlfriends. The three were inseparable and spent every long, hot day of summer at one of their homes, usually Kathleen's. Becky Stewart, a tall girl, slim to the point of being skinny, was lethargic today, too. The heat sapped what little strength there was in her thin frame, but she was not as bored as Kathleen. "I don't think it's been so bad," she grinned lazily down at Kathleen.

"Oh you," Kathleen scolded, "you're so smitten with Ben Jackson, you don't know if you're coming or going. You're absolutely no fun at all anymore, Becky. Ben's all you ever talk about. I don't know what you see in him."

The satisfied grin never left Becky's slim face and she giggled suddenly and said, "There's a lot you don't know about, Kathleen Beauregard!"

Kathleen looked at her friend, studied her face carefully, trying to understand what delicious secret Becky was hiding. Becky's smile gave nothing away and Kathleen turned to the tiny girl on her other side. Julie Horne, at five foot one was even tinier than Kathleen. A gentle girl with chestnut hair and big brown eyes, Julie possessed a sweet disposition and a calm nature and rarely complained about anything. Shy around boys, she nevertheless was well liked by the young men of Natchez who found her demure and daintily pretty. Not as pretty as Kathleen, few girls were, but quite fetching. Always optimistic and congenial, Julie looked at Kathleen fanning herself in bored irritation and said, "Kathleen, I think it's been a nice summer. Why, we've had lots of parties and picnics and . . ."

"Oh pooh," Kathleen said in a huff. "They were all dreadful. You're as bad as Becky. I know you are sweet on Caleb Bates, but I warn you, you'll have a long wait if you've dreams of being his wife. His father is dead set on Caleb finishing college before he marries and by that time you'll be an old lady."

Julie nervously twisted a chestnut curl and bit her lip. Just the mention of Caleb's name was enough to set her heart to beating a little faster and the thought of becoming his wife brought color rising to her cheeks. "Kathleen, don't tease me. Caleb doesn't know I'm alive. I don't see why you persist in accusing me of fancying Caleb. Really, I don't know where you got that idea, I just think he's nice and mannerly and . . . well, he is very nice looking.'' Her eyes grew dreamy as she discussed him.

''You don't fool me for a minute, Julie Horne! I see the way your eyes light up whenever Caleb is around. And I'd say by the way he develops a stammer and turns red as a beet when he asks you to dance, he must feel the same way.''

Raising up on the settee, Julie grinned broadly, ''Do you really think so, Kathleen? Oh, if only it were true.'' She wanted reassurance.

''Don't be a goose, Julie. You know very well Caleb likes you.''

Still smiling, Becky agreed, ''Don't worry, Julie. I think he really likes you; he is just not as forward and worldly as my Ben.''

The last sentence caught Kathleen's attention and she felt some of the lethargy slipping away, replaced with curiosity. Turning her attention from Julie and her constant, irritating mooning over Caleb Bates, she caught Becky's arm and asked, ''How forward is Ben?'' The big blue eyes widened as she looked with interest at Becky's face and waited for an answer.

Looking like the cat who had just swallowed a juicy canary, Becky closed her eyes tightly and simpered, ''Wouldn't you just like to know,'' and settled back on the settee, determined to keep all her secrets safe from her inquiring friend.

Kathleen's fingers tightened on Becky's slim arm and she said, ''Becky Stewart, you just open your eyes and look at me this instant. You're hiding something and I want to know what it is. Has Ben, has he . . . kissed you?''

Becky's eyes flew open and she pitched forward on the settee, jerking Kathleen's hand from her arm. She said indignantly, ''That's a terrible thing to say, Kathleen. Do you really think I would let Ben do anything like that? Why, I'm

10

mortified that you would think such a thing," but the green, catlike eyes gave her away and the mock horror at her friend's probing question didn't fool Kathleen for a second.

"I knew it, I knew it, you did let Ben kiss you," she turned excitedly to Julie. "She's let Ben kiss her, Julie. Ben has *kissed* her!"

Julie's big brown eyes grew even bigger and her tiny hand went to her mouth as she gasped, "Is it true, Becky?" and leaned out to look at Becky's face, the hand still at her mouth.

"When," Kathleen questioned, "when did Ben kiss you? Did you like it? Was it like you expected? Please, Becky, quit acting coy and tell us about it. I think you're terrible for not telling us right away. Aren't we your best friends?"

The smile had finally left Becky Stewart's thin mouth under the furious questioning of her girlfriends. Embarrassment replaced the self satisfaction of a moment ago and she found her throat dry and had trouble finding her tongue as she looked at the shocked expression on Julie's face and the excited, piercing blue eyes of Kathleen. Girlish guilt mixed with feelings of betrayal. She had told Ben she would never tell a soul and swore him to secrecy. Ben had assured her wild horses could never drag it out of him and she knew he spoke the truth because Ben was the most honorable man she had ever met and would never compromise her. Finally she spoke, looking from Kathleen to Julie. "If either of you ever tell, I shall never speak to you again and I mean it!"

"We won't," both girls promised in unison. "Tell us about it. Oh, I knew it," Kathleen rubbed her palms together, forgetting the sultry heat and the boredom of the day.

Becky coughed and cleared her throat, "I suppose you both think I'm awful, but remember, I'm already sixteen, a year older than you. Lots of girls are married by the time they are my age. You know I love Ben; I have for ever so long. He's been coming over to call on me all summer and bringing me flowers and holding my hand any time he got

11

the chance."

"Yes, so go on," Kathleen prodded.

The smile was returning to Becky's face and the green eyes softened. "Exactly two weeks and four days ago, Ben came over to take me for a buggy ride. I packed a lunch and Mother said since it was the middle of the day she saw no harm in us going on a picnic alone as long as we didn't stay more than an hour or so, just long enough to eat our lunch. She told us to take our fried chicken and go over to the park and cool ourselves under the old trees there while we ate. We said we would do just that and she waved goodbye as Ben lifted me up to his carriage." Becky paused for effect. "And then, instead of going to the park, Ben headed out to the Bayou country."

"You're joking," Julie was shocked anew.

"Be quiet," Kathleen frowned at Julie, "let her finish. Then what, Becky?"

"I put up a terrible fuss and told Ben to just turn the carriage right around, that I wasn't going anywhere with him but to the park in Natchez proper, but he just smiled at me and kept right on going. That made me mad and I folded my arms across my chest and rode all the way in a huff, swearing I would never speak to Mister Ben Jackson again as long as I lived." Becky sighed contentedly and began again. "But even as I tried to be angry with him, I . . . I just couldn't make myself and, by the time we reached the country, I found myself *so* excited to be alone with him, no matter where he was taking me. I slipped my hand under his elbow and he smiled at me in an impish way and I just had to smile back. He pulled the carriage up and helped me down and nodded to a shade tree. He said, 'This is a much shadier spot and I really think we'll be cooler here, don't you agree?' Before I could answer he had the picnic hamper out of the carriage and he was propelling me toward the tree. He was so commanding and sure of himself, I went along asking no further questions. He set the basket down and spread a blanket

12

on the ground. He held out his hand to me, I took it, and we sat down together. He dropped my hand and looked at me and his eyes seemed to be questioning me, searching mine for an answer. I grew flustered under his steady gaze and turned quickly to the picnic lunch. I took out the fried chicken and without a word he took it from me and set it aside. When I reached for the basket again, he stopped my arm. He raised my hand up to his lips and kissed it, then he leaned close to me, still holding my hand, and he said very softly, 'Becky, I've been seeing you all summer and I've yet to be alone with you. We're finally alone now and I want to kiss you.' Well, of course, I was shocked and told him in no uncertain terms that I would not allow it. I tried to pull my hand away, but he refused to let it go. Instead, he pulled me closer and put his other hand on my cheek. . . .'' Her voice trailed off.

"Becky Stewart, if you don't finish the story, I will choke you with my bare hands,'' Kathleen's eyes were dancing.

"Please,'' Julie begged, "what happened then?''

"Ben looked right into my eyes and said ever so sweetly, 'Becky, please say yes,' and I couldn't resist. I looked into those intense brown eyes and 'yes' just rose to my lips automatically. He leaned over and kissed me right on the mouth! I thought that would be the end of it, but he kissed me twice more after that.''

"Oh, that's the most romantic thing I've ever heard! Did you like it? Did you want him to kiss you three times?'' Kathleen questioned.

"I liked it plenty,'' Becky answered without hesitation, "I love Ben, I swear I do. Kissing is very, very nice when you're in love. But you'll both find out soon enough.''

"I shall never find out! Nobody has ever tried to kiss me,'' Kathleen lamented. She turned to Julie, "You've never been kissed, have you?''

"Don't be foolish, Kathleen, you know very well I haven't.'' Her small face reddened as she thought, "I wonder what it would be like to kiss Caleb," and her face turned redder still.

"Oh, my life is so hopelessly dull! I don't think anything exciting is ever going to happen to me. I will die a dried-up old maid just like the Hamilton sisters, getting a little skinnier and crazier every year I live," Kathleen said unhappily.

"Such silly talk," Becky shook her head at Kathleen. "You can have your pick of any of the boys in Natchez and you know it. You are too particular, Kathleen. Why, every time there is a party, you're the most sought after girl there. There's a dozen different boys you could have if you just snapped your fingers."

"I don't want any of them, they're all clods and not a good dancer in the lot. They bore me with their mindless prattle and their silly compliments. I want someone dashing and exciting. Someone worldly and wise and big and handsome. I want someone to sweep me off my feet, thrill me with his daring, and . . ."

"You want a dream, Kathleen!" The soft spoken Julie shook Kathleen from her girlish reverie. "You want Prince Charming on a white horse to take you off to his castle. That's in storybooks and if you insist on hunting for something that doesn't exist, you *will* be an old maid. Get your head out of the clouds and look around you; you'll find there are some really nice boys that you'd like a lot if you just gave yourself a chance. Right, Becky?"

"She's absolutely right, Kathleen. Look how happy I am; you could be that happy, too."

Kathleen sighed heavily, "Maybe you're right, I guess I'm longing for something that doesn't exist."

"Well, hunt yourself a beau tomorrow night at the party. There'll be plenty to choose from," Becky reminded her.

Kathleen felt depressed, reluctant to give up her hopes for the perfect sweetheart, but sighed and said, "I had forgotten about the party, but I suppose I'll have to be there since it's at my house. Oh, my life is so hopeless!"

Two

Dawson Harpe Blakely stood in the drawing room of his spacious mansion on the bluffs in Natchez. One of the few places built directly atop the bluff's edge, he had known for years he would own the place. He had to own it. He could walk out the heavy mahogany door right now, across the acres of lawn, through the flower-laden gardens beyond, and look over the bluffs. Look down on the place where he was born, where he spent the first twenty years of his life. Natchez Under the Hill. Down Under. Hell Under the Bluffs. Lower Natchez. All names given to the patch of soft earth at the Mississippi's muddy banks, little more than a mile long.

Dawson Harpe Blakely was born in Natchez Under in a two-room shack perched precariously on stilts at the water's edge twenty-seven years ago tonight, the son of a riverboat gambler down on his luck who'd drifted into Natchez in 1826. James Blakely was a tall, swarthy, black-haired man with flashing dark eyes, a way with women, a weakness for the bottle, and an ace up his sleeve. He married a comely redhead with dark brown eyes and creamy skin when she was no more than fifteen years old. The daughter of a poor family of the violent lower classes, Elizabeth Harpe fell quickly in love with the tall, dark gambler. She loved him completely for the two tempestous years she lived with him and never complained when he was gone for days or weeks at a time. James Blakely's homecomings were always happy occasions and Elizabeth ran to his arms when he walked in the shanty door. Always cheerful and smiling, he would present her with some small trinket he'd bought her and, if he'd been lucky, he would grin and stuff a roll of bills down the bodice of her dress and bend down for the sweet kisses he knew were coming. When their love produced a beautiful baby boy, Elizabeth Harpe Blakely worshiped the cuddly toddler and felt her life was complete.

Her world came apart one cold January night when a knock on the shanty door roused her from a deep slumber. A tall black man stood in the door and gave her the news that James Blakely had been killed in a knife fight at a gambling den on Silver Street. As Elizabeth raised her hands to her face and screamed, she looked down at the small replica of her handsome husband, who tugged on her gown. "Daddy," Dawson said, and cried with her. Elizabeth Harpe Blakely continued to exist for ten more weary years, but the heart inside her died the night James Blakely was caught holding one too many kings.

"I've come a long way from where I started," Dawson Blakely thought as he knotted his black silk tie. "And tonight I'm going even farther. I can't believe it, I'm going to a party at Sans Souci, the home of Louis Antoine Beauregard. I'm finally going to meet his beautiful young daughter." Dawson felt his hands shake when he thought about her. He was almost obsessed with her, had been since the day he had seen her riding by in her father's big carriage on her way home from Mass. It had been three months ago and he hadn't been able to get the vision of the enchanting charmer out of his head. The silky blond hair shining in the sun, the big blue eyes rimmed with thick black lashes, the skin as white and pure as alabaster, the curvaceous little figure in her blue ruffled dress. He wanted her the minute he saw her, could think of nothing else. He had only seen her that once, though he'd looked for her every time he went out. He'd lived that day in his mind over and over. It was stamped indelibly on his memory and would remain there.

It had been the first week of May and Dawson was in town with his attorney, Crawford Ashworth. They sat in Dawson's big carriage in front of Parker's Hotel on Main street. They talked idly before going into the hotel dining room for Sunday lunch. It was a perfect day, the sweet, humid air not yet heavy with the blazing heat of summer. A carriage turned the corner of Pearl Street and came down Main, passing directly by Dawson's. The grand carriage was drawn by six snow white chargers which drew the attention of the two men. Inside the carriage, a handsome middle-aged couple sat talking, both dressed grandly, the lady with a dainty parasol held over her head. They were saying something to the young girl sitting across from them and Dawson's eyes fell on her and never left. He watched, enrapt, and when she turned after they'd passed to look over her shoulder at something, he tried to catch her eye but failed. She looked right through him, never realizing he was there. He watched the back of her blond head as the grand carriage went out of sight. He sat quiet and stunned when he could no longer see her.

"Dawson, old man, I can read that look in your hooded eyes," Crawford Ashworth was shaking his head.

"That is the most beautiful girl I've ever seen, Crawford. I've got to find out who she is," Dawson said.

"I know who she is and you don't want to know her, believe me."

"You know her? You must introduce me. I've got to meet her, to see her again."

"Dawson, that girl is the daughter of Louis Antoine Beauregard. Ever hear of him?"

"The name's familiar, but it means nothing to me."

"Well, keep it that way, son. Come on, let's go have some lunch," Crawford started to step from the carriage, but Dawson pulled him back.

"Why should I keep it that way? What kind of man is

he?''

"Oh, Louis is all right. I like him and I've done some business with him, still do occasionally. I mean, you wouldn't want to know him if you've designs on that lovely daughter of his. She is the apple of his eye. He wouldn't let you near her.''

"Maybe he won't have any choice. Besides, what could he do? I've got to meet her, Crawford. Find a way. You know him, introduce me.''

"Dawson, my boy, haven't you made love to the most beautiful women of Natchez, New Orleans, London, and other points of the compass? Do you really need to borrow trouble by chasing after some child whose father protects her and would kill any man for even having impure thoughts about her?'' He frowned at Dawson, trying to convince him to drop the idea. "Look, Dawson, as your attorney and as your friend, let me tell you that you would be better off taking his land, his slaves, even his old estate, Sans Souci, than you would be touching one golden hair on Kathleen's head.''

"Kathleen,'' Dawson smiled, "Kathleen Beauregard, what a lovely name. It suits her.''

"Damn it, Dawson, listen to me! I'm serious. Like you, Louis Beauregard is the successful veteran of many a duel. One night at a Fourth of July ball about ten years ago, a militia captain danced with Louis' wife, Abigail, in a suggestive manner that Louis didn't quite fancy. That captain is now up in Rosemond, fertilizing the daisies.''

Dawson threw back his head and laughed. "Crawford, I can take care of myself. I'm not afraid of Mister Louis Beauregard and I don't want to harm his precious Kathleen. I want to meet her and you're going to make it possible. Look, as a state senator, I'm sure you've been invited to parties at Sans Souci, haven't you?''

"Yes, I've been to Sans Souci on a number of occasions, but . . .''

"And you'll be invited again, won't you?''

18

"I suppose so, but . . ."

"Good. It's settled. The very next time you are invited there for a party, you are taking me along as your guest. Understand?"

"Now, Dawson, I don't think . . ."

"Senator, are you forgetting the money I gave you for your campaign?"

"That's not fair, Dawson. You know I haven't forgotten and I'm grateful to you, I always will be, but . . ."

"I don't want your gratitude, Crawford. I want an invitation to Sans Souci. I'm going to meet Kathleen and there's nothing Louis Beauregard or you can do about it, so you may as well help me. The very next time you're invited, I mean it."

"All right, all right, now can we have lunch?"

"A great idea, I'm starved," and Dawson Blakely wore a devilish grin throughout the meal.

"Tonight I'm finally going to meet the fair-haired child of my dreams who's made all others pale by comparison," Dawson said aloud. "Ah, my sweet little Kathleen, tonight your life will change forever and you are not even aware of it." Dawson laughed to himself, pulled on his black evening jacket, and went to the carriage to meet Crawford Ashworth for the ride to Sans Souci.

"I don't even want to go to the party, Hannah! Why don't you tell Mother I'm sick," Kathleen stood fretting while Hannah hooked up the yellow organdy dress.

"Now, honey, don't talk lak that. It gonna be a nice party and lots of young folks comin'. You have a good time and you look so pretty," Hannah tried to jolly her.

"What's the use of looking pretty? There's not anybody I want to be pretty for." Kathleen stuck out her lower lip in a

19

pout.

"Now, chile, jest stop you whining and get on downstairs. I'se out of patience with you, miss."

"Very well." Kathleen flounced out of the room. She could hear voices in the big ballroom and rolled her eyes upward, but plastered a smile on her young face before she entered. She sashayed in and quickly mingled with the guests, charming all with her beauty and sweetness.

A sudden summer rain had blown up and was now pelting the tall windows of the ballroom. Kathleen stood near the windows, whispering quietly to Becky Stewart. The room was alive with people, all dressed in their finest, ladies in gowns and jewels, the gentlemen whirling them around the polished marble floor while an orchestra played waltzes. Ben Jackson had gone to get punch for Becky and Kathleen and Becky was telling Kathleen it was getting more serious with Ben every time they were together. Kathleen was half listening and nodding when she noticed a stir; the double doors swung open.

Kathleen watched as her father extended his hand to Senator Crawford Ashworth and a dark gentleman. The stranger stepped beneath a chandelier and Kathleen's eyes widened. A compelling figure, he towered over her father and the men in the room. Heavily muscled yet lean, he had coal black hair, a face brown and handsome, a sleek mustache above full lips. Her father said something amusing and the stranger's mouth parted in a smile, exposing white, even teeth. Vaguely aware of Becky talking to her, Kathleen did not respond. Her eyes never left the dark stranger and when she saw her father leading him across the room, her heart rose to her throat.

Dawson spotted Kathleen the minute he entered the big room. More beautiful even than he'd remembered, his throat grew dry and he found it hard to follow the conversation. He laughed over some anecdote Louis told them, but had no idea what the story was about. He kept looking at

Kathleen and thought of touching her silky blond hair, of pulling it across his mouth and nose, losing himself in it. The big blue eyes were looking at him and he could hear his pulse drumming in his ears. She wore a pale yellow dress, tight around the waist, the low ruffled neck going around her shoulders and dropping down in front, her young bosom pushed up in a most temptingly sensuous way. Dawson cursed himself for what the sight of that white young breast did to his reserve.

The men reached Kathleen and Louis introduced her. Dawson's eyes never left her and, when he spoke, his voice was a warm baritone that suited him perfectly and made Kathleen feel nervous and shy. They stood in awkward silence for a short time and when a youth came to their circle to ask Kathleen for the next dance, without even looking at him, she said, "I'm sorry, I've promised the next dance to Mister Blakely."

They were on the dance floor and Kathleen found herself almost swallowed up in Dawson Blakely's arms. The top of her pretty head reached only to his chest. Dawson didn't bend and whisper silly compliments into her ear like the boys her age, and he didn't carry on mindless chatter. He said not a word, but his eyes never left hers and his arm held her tightly, his big hand clutching hers in a firm grip. It was as though he didn't realize there was another person in the room besides Kathleen.

In the white lattice summer house in front of the old estate, Kathleen set out to find out more about Dawson. The rain had stopped and he took out a clean white handkerchief and spread it out for her to sit on before taking a seat beside her on the white settee. She questioned him in a sweet childlike manner that enchanted him, though he gave only yes and no answers to her frank questions. Yes, he owned a plantation. Yes, he owned racehorses. Yes, he was born and raised in Natchez. No, he wasn't married. No, he never had been. Yes, he had traveled. Yes, he had been to

21

Europe. Yes, he liked to dance. No, he didn't want to go back inside.

Kathleen asked question after question and this strange, handsome man smiled lazily at her and seemed not to mind at all. How refreshing it was. And how exciting he was. And how good looking. And how irritating that he asked no questions of her.

"Why do you not ask me anything? Don't you want to know about me? Aren't you interested?" Kathleen looked up at him, her blue eyes serious.

Dawson smiled the lazy smile and reached up to push a long strand of hair from her shoulder, gently placing it behind her ear, "I don't need to ask you anthing. I know all I need to know about you."

"Just how could you know all about me, Mister Dawson Blakely? Why you only met me tonight! What could you *possibly* know? Some men think me quite mysterious." She snatched the blond curl and pulled it back over her shoulder.

"My dear Kathleen, I'm sure you are. Here's what I know about you. I know you are the most beautiful girl I've ever seen. I know you never tire of asking questions. I know that tomorrow night I am taking you for a long carriage ride in the moonlight." Dawson leaned close and once again pushed the blond curl behind her ear. "And I know that you will fall madly, helplessly in love with me." He laughed and watched her face as the blue eyes flashed fire.

"If you are not the most conceited, egotistical, rude man I've ever met in my life. I wouldn't go anywhere with you if you were the last man on earth!" She was off the settee, running across the lawn, her blond hair flying wildly around her head, the yellow dress billowing around her. She could hear his easy laughter behind her as he remained in the gazebo, not even trying to stop her or come after her. Infuriated by his brash words, but madder still that he did not try to stop her, she turned when she got to the edge of the garden to look back at him. He sat with his legs stretched out in front of

22

him, lighting a cigar, making no effort to move. And he was still laughing.

The next day, Kathleen learned more about the strange and dashing Mister Blakely. Her girlfriends sat visiting with her in the summer house and they were full of gossip they had heard from brothers, cousins, and friends. Dawson Blakely had turned twenty-seven years old just yesterday. He was born below the bluffs at Natchez Under. His middle name was Harpe. He was a descendant of the murderous group of bandits from Kentucky who had terrorized the old Natchez Trace over fifty years ago. His father was a gambling drifter and his mother was a Harpe, an uneducated girl from a family of poor white trash. Dawson Blakely had spent most of his life at Natchez Under and was cunning and smart and had made money from all kinds of business schemes. Some were not the kinds of things gentlemen should be involved in. He was a notorious ladies man, having women both above and below the bluffs. He was a gambler, probably got that from his worthless father. He could hold more liquor than most men. He had a mean temper and had been in many duels, some of them over women.

Kathleen listened, fascinated, while Becky and Julie told her all they had heard about this dashing man. Then she smiled and rose from the settee, pushing her hair up onto her head. "Dawson Blakely is even more exciting than I thought. He's coming to take me for a buggy ride in the moonlight tonight," and she laughed at the shocked expressions on the faces of her girlfriends. "I have to go in now, I must take a long hot bubble bath before Dawson arrives. See you tomorrow."

At eight o'clock sharp, Dawson pulled into the estate road and came up the drive to Sans Souci. Dressed impeccably, he

23

shook hands with Louis and kissed Abigail's hand. He made easy small talk with them both and waited for their daughter to come down. She floated into the room at last and Dawson couldn't take his eyes off of her.

"Why, Mister Blakely, I didn't know you were here," she looked at him coyly. "How nice to see you again."

"I'm pleased to see you, Miss Beauregard. It's such a lovely evening, if your father will give me permission, I would like to take you out for a buggy ride. That is, if you are agreeable."

Kathleen smirked and shrugged her shoulders, "Well, it is rather warm tonight and I suppose going for a ride would be better than doing nothing." She walked to her father, kissing him on the cheek, and said, "You don't mind, do you, Father? I won't be gone long; I'm really rather tired and listless tonight."

"Go on, Angel, if you really want to," Louis smiled at her.

"Oh, I don't particularly want to. Mister Blakely was quite presumptuous in coming over without an invitation, but now that he is here, I don't want to be as rude as he."

Dawson smiled his lazy smile and rose to his feet. "Good night, ma'am," he bowed to Abigail. "Thank you, Mister Beauregard, I'll have your daughter home early," and he walked to Kathleen, took her elbow, and ushered her to the door. He walked her to his carriage without a word and helped her up. The driver coaxed the horses and drove out into the country.

As soon as they were out of sight of Kathleen's home, Dawson pulled her close and said, his black eyes flashing, the smile never leaving his lips, "If you ever act like that again, I shall pull you across my lap and spank your luscious little bottom. Do I make myself clear? You wanted me to come tonight, knew very well I was coming, and spent at least an hour making yourself as lovely as possible to tempt me. I know why you acted that way; you did it because I frighten

24

you. You are afraid of me because you are as attracted to me as I am to you. My guess is by now you've found out all you possibly can about me, for I've never seen anyone that loves to ask questions as much as you do. I don't try to hide what I am or anything I've ever done, so if you want to know about my lurid past, you're welcome to ask me. You don't need to be wary of me; I will never do anything to hurt you. Quite the contrary, I intend to shield you from the world and take care of you and I assure you no one can take better care of you than I can. And when I told you last night that you will fall helplessly in love with me, I wasn't joking. But my dear, beautiful child, I shall be just as madly in love with you. You'll find loving me most pleasant and more fun than anything that has ever happened to you. So, from now on, kindly don't play any of your foolish games, for it irritates me greatly. Relax and be your sweet, charming self and put all pretenses away. Remember, Kathleen, I'm not a boy; I'm a grown man and nothing you can do will fool me. It is I who could fool you, but I will never do it. I have plans for you, Kathleen Diana Beauregard. Now give me a big smile and tell me you knew I was coming and couldn't wait until I arrived.''

Kathleen looked at him, unbelieving. She had never met anyone like him, but for some reason, she was not mad. She liked what he had said to her. She looked up at him and smiled and said softly, ''Can I ask you a question, Dawson?''

Dawson threw back his head and laughed happily. ''That's my little Kathleen. Yes, darling, ask anything you like.''

''How long do you think it will be before you fall helplessly in love with me?''

Three

The party was at Becky Stewart's and Kathleen knew Mister Paul Stewart, Becky's father, meant to announce the engagement of Becky to Ben Jackson. Kathleen envied her girlfriend. To be engaged, how wonderful! Kathleen thought of Dawson as Hannah finished buttoning up the pink cashmere dress she had chosen for the party. She had visions of herself in a long white gown, coming down the aisle to meet Dawson, handsome and proud, waiting for her at the altar, eager to make her his wife. Mrs. Dawson Harpe Blakely! A delicious chill went up her spine as she mulled the scene over in her mind. She had completely lost her heart to the dashing charmer and couldn't wait until he popped the question. If he ever meant to. She had to admit to herself the romance was not progressing as fast as she would have liked. She had met Dawson on August eleventh. Here is was almost Thanksgiving and still he had made no effort to kiss her, though she would have been more than willing. There had been a time or two when he pressed her hand tightly and looked at her in a strange, unsettling way and she was certain he was going to bend and kiss her. Then he would pull away and talk rapidly, the moment's magic gone.

Kathleen frowned when she thought about it. Dawson was truly exasperating at times! Any of the young boys who came to the parties would have loved the chance to steal a kiss from her, though she would never let them. But Dawson was not a boy at all; he was twenty-seven and had surely kissed ladies before. So why not her? She knew he found her attractive, wasn't he always telling her how pretty she was? And at the parties, didn't he always remain at her side throughout the evening, reluctant to leave her even for a moment's conversation with the other men. His hand stayed protectively at her waist even when they were not dancing and he never danced with any girl but her, though she could see in their eyes they were all green with envy and would be thrilled and flattered to have a dance with him. Didn't this prove she was his sweetheart, the only girl he cared about? But if so, why in heaven's name hadn't he kissed her? Kathleen heard voices downstairs and the huge front doors being opened. Dawson's clear baritone floated up to her and she smiled at the sound of his rich, enchanting voice and vowed silently to herself, "Tonight I will make him kiss me!"

The engagement party was a gala affair and Kathleen was quite breathless from dancing. She stood beside Dawson, his hand at her waist, talking with the other guests. A gentleman she had not met until this evening, Mister Charles Byner, had approached them and, after being introduced, had apologized to her and said he must have a few words with Dawson. Dawson told the man politely he couldn't leave Kathleen alone, but to speak freely. Not interested in what the two were discussing, Kathleen let her eyes roam around the room. She smiled when her eyes met Becky's. Her friend looked so happy and prettier than she had ever been before. Her adoring Ben stood with his arm around her, obviously very much in love. Becky smiled and winked at Kathleen and Kathleen raised her glass of punch in a toast before letting her eyes slide further around the grand ballroom. Julie Horne sat alone in the corner. Caleb Bates walked up to her. Kathleen watched as Caleb bent down awkwardly and said something, his face a bright shade of red. Julie rose immediately and Kathleen knew Caleb had finally found the nerve to ask Julie for a dance. She read Julie's lips as she shyly looked up at the tall, skinny boy and said, "Why, Caleb, I'd love to." Kathleen smiled to herself; they were both so painfully shy she didn't see how they ever got together, but somehow they had managed and Kathleen suspected they would follow Becky and Ben to the altar in a few months. Leaving only her. Unmarried. Not even engaged. An old maid.

"The repairs were completed tonight. You can have your men load her in the morning if you like," Dawson was saying to Mister Byner.

"Splendid, Mister Blakely, we'll start at first light. That will work out fine."

"Sorry for the delay, but it couldn't be helped. She's as good as new now and ready for the trip."

"Thank you, Mister Blakely. Now if you'll excuse me. Ma'am," Mister Byner bowed to Kathleen and disappeared into the crowd.

"What will be ready in the morning, Dawson?" Kathleen looked up at him.

"A steamboat," he smiled, returning his full attention to her.

"A steamboat? You own one?"

"Yes, Kathleen, several," Dawson answered, matter of factly.

"You have more than one?" She peered up at him, surprised.

Dawson laughed, "Yes, dear, what's so strange about that?"

"Dawson Blakely, you never told me you owned any boats, much less more than one." The blue eyes widened as she looked up at him.

"I never thought you'd be interested, Kathleen. It's part of my business. They aren't pleasure boats, they're cargo vessels, packet boats. I'm afraid there's nothing very exciting about them."

"But it is exciting, Dawson. Oh, I want to see one of your boats. May I?"

"Sure you can, honey. Now, would you like to dance, they're playing a waltz."

"No, I don't want to dance! I want to see your boat, Dawson Blakely. You said I could."

"You mean now," he laughed at her and jerked a blond curl playfully. "Dear, I didn't mean tonight. This is a party; I thought you loved parties and dancing. And it's cold out, remember. You can see it another day."

"No," Kathleen reached up to his lapel. "Please, Dawson, take me to see your boat *tonight*. It would be so exciting and I won't be cold. Oh, please."

"Kathleen, your father would horsewhip me if I took you down to the river tonight and you know it. I want to please you, honey, but you are being foolish." But the thought of being alone with her intrigued him greatly.

She saw the look in his dark eyes and pressed him. "Oh, Dawson, no one need know. Father will never find out; he'll think we are still at the party. And it's so crowded here, no one will miss us." She fluttered the thick black lashes at him and put as much honey into her voice as possible.

Finding her utterly irresistible, Dawson agreed against his better judgment. Smiling and leaning close, he whispered in her ear, "How can I refuse you. Get your wrap and let's be off."

They were in the back of Dawson's big carriage, the chill November wind stinging their faces. "Are you cold, pet?" Dawson was gracious as the carriage left the bluffs and headed for the river.

"Not at all. Really." Kathleen was too excited to feel the cold. She wanted to see Dawson's boat and was also thrilled at the prospect of going to Natchez Under at night. Kathleen had heard all the stories of the things that went on down there and could hardly wait to see for herself.

They reached the bottom and already she could hear boisterous laughter and shouting and was eager to get to the scene of all the merriment. The driver turned the carriage down Silver Street and Kathleen looked out in wide-eyed amazement. Yellow-skinned barkers stood on the street and shouted out the pleasures to be found on this main street, the toughest in all Mississippi. She saw drunken men staggering along the wooden sidewalks and she gasped when she saw half-naked women leaning out of windows calling to them. Loud piano music drifted to the carriage along with high feminine laughter. Kathleen saw the dregs of humanity all gathered together in a hell she could never have imagined. It was all terribly shocking and fascinating to Kathleen Diana Beauregard and she stared in horrified wonder at the scenes they passed. Most shocking of all to her was that all the men under the bluffs were not river rats, boat crewman, Negro musicians, or white trash. She gasped audibly while, practically leaning out of the carriage for an unobstructed view of the sinful place, she saw a sleek, well-dressed gentleman slap the rear of a passing gaudily painted female. Shrinking back inside the carriage immediately, she tried to digest what she had seen. A queasiness filled her stomach when she realized that many of the men seeing their pleasures down under were the blue-blooded gentlemen dwelling in the pillared mansions above.

"I should never have brought you here," Dawson said softly, looking down at her frightened face. "I'm sorry, honey," he slowly raised his arm and brought it around her shoulders. She settled back against him, unable to speak for a while. Frightened, stunned, her teeth chattering slightly, she nestled closer to him in the security of his arm.

She put her hands on his chest and looked up at him, "Dawson, are we in danger?"

Dawson couldn't help himself; he had to laugh at the absurd question, though her blue eyes were terrified. Then he remembered she was only an innocent young girl, barely sixteen years old. Pulling her closer, he covered the tiny fingers on his chest with his own brown hand. "Honey, do you think I would ever let anything in this world happen to you? You are as safe as a babe in her cradle, I assure you. I was raised down here, remember?''

"Oh, Dawson, it must have been awful! How did you survive it?''

Dawson shrugged his massive shoulders. "I knew nothing better then, it seemed only natural to me. Now I know there's a cleaner, more beautiful way of life and I want to be a part of it, to belong.''

"You belong,'' she assured him, then grew silent for a moment. Peering up at his face, she said, "Dawson, can I ask you a question?''

"Anything, pet.''

"Have you ever, that is . . . did you . . . I mean . . .'' She couldn't finish.

"What, honey?'' Dawson's voice was soft, "what do you want to know?''

Kathleen moved her hands from under his and put them in her lap. Her face grew crimson as she whispered, "Have you ever been to one of those houses?''

"One of what houses, Kathleen?'' Dawson teased, making her squirm.

In a flash, her haughty spirit returned and her childish curiosity overcame her embarrassment. "You know what I mean! I want to know if you have ever been to one of those . . . those loose women!'' The blond head jerked up quickly to look at his face.

The smile on Dawson's face did not change at all and she could read no answer. He spoke, but he didn't tell her what she was longing to know. "Kathleen, for a young lady of high birth and social standing unparalleled in all Natchez, do you really think it proper to be discussing such things? Your breeding warrants tact and it's really terribly rude to ask such crass questions, don't you think?'' His throaty laughter made her want to bite her tongue off. She ducked her head, seething at him for laughing at her. He quit laughing and pulled her close again and her anger disappeared when she

31

felt his lips on her ear and he whispered ever so softly, "I'm sorry, honey, don't be angry." She smiled again and looked at him. She still did not get the answer to her question.

By the time the carriage reached the river wharf, Kathleen had forgotten the squalor and gaudiness of Silver Street and was eager to get on board Dawson's boat. The carriage stopped on the pier at the water's edge ad Dawson helped her up the gangplank. "Sam," he shouted, and almost immediately a tall, powerfully built black man appeared on the hurricane deck above them. Bigger even than Dawson, Sam leaned over the railing and smiled. White teeth flashed as he responded to Dawson's shouts, "Yes, Cap'n Dawson, right here, suh."

"Good, Sam, I have a young lady with me and she's dying to take a look around."

Sam moved from the railing and came down the gangplank reaching for Kathleen's hand, bowing grandly. Dawson said proudly, "Sam, this is Kathleen Diana Beauregard."

"Pleased to meet you, Miz Beauregard," Sam nodded and the huge black hand took hers and gently pulled her up the gangplank.

"Honey, this is Sam Jones, the best riverboat pilot on the Mississippi." Releasing Kathleen's hand, Sam grinned and glanced down at his shoes.

"Sam, I'm happy to meet you," Kathleen said politely, but she sank further back against the security of Dawson's large frame, looking up at the black giant of a man in front of her.

"Is she fired up, Sam? I'd like to take Kathleen for a little ride."

Kathleen's face brightened and she spun around and put her hands to Dawson's chest, "Oh, could we, Dawson? It would be so wonderful to get out on the river."

He smiled down at her, "I can refuse you nothing, my pet. If a short ride on this old riverboat will make you happy, you shall have it." He winked at Sam over her head.

Sam turned immediately and started shouting orders to the crew. Black men scurried from their card games on the boiler deck. The firemen, roustabouts, and deck hands soon had fires glaring in the long row of furnaces. Sam went up the ladder to take his position in the pilothouse.

Kathleen stood on the hurricane deck with Dawson, breathlessly watching and listening to all the excitement. Soon a man was shouting, "Let her go," and the boat was leaving the wharf. The bell was clanging loudly and the engines started up, shooting plumes of steam high in the air. The paddle wheels churned up white foam about the stern as the vessel backed away to head for the river.

The boat slid past the long rows of other vessels moored at the pier; timber rafts, broadhorns, tiny trading scows, coal barges, and other riverboats. Sam stood at the wheel coaxing her safely past, his big hands firmly on the wheel, his eyes staring alertly in the darkness, looking fore and aft, wheeling her a little to this side then a little to that, until they were on the river.

Kathleen watched the blinking lights of Natchez Under the Hill and Natchez on the Bluffs, her bright blue eyes aglow with the excitement and giddy laughter escaping her happy lips. "Oh, Dawson, this is every bit as thrilling as I expected. Thank you for bringing me."

"Come, I'll show you the pilothouse." Dawson led her up the companionway to the pilothouse. Inside the glass enclosed room it was dark, no lights were burning, and the stove was cold with no fire built in it. Kathleen's eyes moved around the room as Sam smiled to both of them before turning back to stare straight ahead at the river.

"Dawson," Kathleen whispered to him, "why has Sam got the lights turned off and why doesn't he build a fire?"

Dawson smiled and explained, "It's very dark tonight, honey. Sam keeps it this way in the wheelhouse for safety. If he had the lights blazing and a fire burning brightly, he wouldn't be able to see the river clearly and that could prove dangerous. Now, dear, would you like to take the wheel for a while?'' Kathleen peered up at him not knowing whether he was teasing or not. Dawson's black eyes were crinkling at the corners and he laughed and said, ''I'm serious, darling. Would you like to try?''

''Oh, Dawson, may I? Do you think Sam would mind?''

Dawson put his arm around her waist, ''Let's ask him. Sam, Kathleen is just itching to take your job away from you.''

Sam smiled broadly. ''Yes, suh, Cap'n Dawson. She look lak she be a good sailor.'' He relinquished the wheel.

Not certain she was up to the challenge, Kathleen hung back. Dawson took her arm and pulled her to the wheel, laughing, ''Come on, pilot, you said you wanted to steer. She's all yours.''

''Are you sure it's safe, Dawson? I wouldn't want to wreck us.''

''Just do as I tell you and it will be fine.''

''Okay,'' she said, putting both hands to the wheel, ''but you won't be far away, will you?''

'Miss, do you take me for a fool? I just got this boat repaired today. I'm not planning to let it get wrecked. Now, I'm going to stand right behind you, so you have nothing to worry about.''

Kathleen stood steering the boat, the blond head barely able to peer over the wheel, the long pink cape blowing softly in the wind. Dawson stood directly behind her, saying, ''Now just hold her steady, okay, turn just a bit, now straighten her out. You're doing fine, honey.''

''I've mastered it,'' she laughed gaily and felt giddy and exhilerated, her blue eyes dancing. They made their way slowly down the Mississippi and Kathleen loved every minute of her adventure. Dawson stood quietly behind her, smiling to himself, happy with her pleasure.

Around the bend of the river, a bright light suddenly came

into view and Kathleen felt her hands tighten on the wheel. "Dawson, it's another ship, what shall I do?"

"Blow the whistle to signal him."

"How, I don't know . . ."

"Here it is," Dawson pulled the rope closer to her. "Now, pull on it a few times."

She jerked the rope with all her might and jumped at the loud noise of the whistle blowing loudly. The oncoming vessel sounded a reply.

"Now what, Dawson?" She put both hands back on the wheel.

"Just keep right on your course and you'll have no problems."

The lights were growing close and Kathleen was growing nervous. She wished Dawson were steering, wished he would take the wheel, relieve her of her duties. As though he had read her mind, Dawson stepped a little closer to her and she could feel his hard chest touching her back, his chin brushing the top of her head. Slowly Dawson's hands covered her shaky grip and she smiled and leaned back, safe again, no longer frightened with him so near. They passed the lighted ship to starboard with only a few feet to spare.

The crisis past, Kathleen relaxed. After a few minutes, Dawson leaned down and whispered, "I think that's enough steering for your first time, matey."

"I agree," Kathleen said, willing to give the wheel back to Sam. He stepped up, smiling, and took over from her. Kathleen lifted her skirts daintily and started down the companionway, saying, "Dawson, where's your cabin?"

"Below the wheelhouse."

"Good, show it to me."

"Dear, there's nothing to see. It's just a small cabin, large enough for me."

They were on the hurricane deck and she turned and said, "Please, Dawson, I want to see where you stay when you go out on the boat. Sam called you the captain, didn't he? Well,

I want to see the captain's quarters!'' Dawson smiled and led her underneath the wheelhouse, down a few steps to the cabin door. Taking a key from his pocket, he opened the door while Kathleen leaned forward eagerly, ''Oh, Dawson,'' she said, starting inside, but he put his arm across the door to stop her.

''No, Kathleen, we aren't going inside.'' His eyes were strange and cold. Barely giving her time to glimpse the spacious room with its heavy desk and chair, mahogany paneled walls, oversized master bed neatly made, long leather couch, crendenza with framed pictures on top, thick, rich carpet on the floor in a deep red shade, he was once again locking the door.

''Dawson, I want to go inside and look around and see what . . .''

''Miss, I don't think you have any business being in my cabin.'' Dawson meant it. His voice softened and he smiled at her, ''Let's go up to the bow and feel the spray on our cheeks.'' Kathleen's face brightened and she quickly agreed, but she was still puzzled about why he wouldn't take her inside his cabin.

Together they walked to the very front of the boat. Kathleen put her hands on the railing and breathed in the cold night air. Her long blond hair whipped around her face and she shivered. Dawson saw her shake and stepped up behind her. His hands clutched the railing in a wider arc than Kathleen's, encircling her in his arms.

''Dawson, I want to ask you something,'' Kathleen said, looking out over the cold river.

''If it's about going into my cabin I . . .''

''No, not that. Why do you have a black pilot on your boat? All the men on your boat are Negroes, aren't they? Why do you use slaves to run your ship?''

He laughed and leaned closer, ''Kathleen, Sam is not a slave, none of my crew are, they work for me. Sam would be hurt, darling. He's a proud man and a very experienced

36

riverboat pilot. He's been standing his own watch for years. I admire and respect him."

"But the others? They aren't slaves?"

"Kathleen, I own no slaves."

She whirled and looked up at him. "What about the Negroes that work your plantation? I don't understand."

"No, they all work for wages." His jaw tightened and he looked straight at her and there was a fierceness in his black eyes that frightened her. "I don't believe in one man owning another, Kathleen."

"But, Dawson, Father owns hundreds of slaves. Everyone does."

"Not everyone. I don't and never have. Sam is my friend, an equal."

"Dawson, why do you feel so strongly about something that . . ."

"Kathleen, there is more than one kind of slavery, all unpleasant. I know too well."

"I'm sorry, Dawson." Her lips began to tremble, afraid he was upset.

He said, "Let's forget it. Don't you love the river at night?" They turned back around to look out at the water.

"Yes," she answered dreamily, happy his mood had passed. She watched the lights of Natchez Under slide past her view and sighed, "Isn't it romantic out here?"

"Yes, it is, love," Dawson kissed the top of her blond head.

She murmured, "Dawson, what's the name of your boat?"

"*The Nighthawk*," he answered, his lips still on her hair.

"But I thought ships and boats were feminine, that you were supposed to give them women's names. Why don't you name it after a woman you care about?"

"Have anyone in mind?" he teased.

"Yes," she said, a broad smile lighting her face, "I think you should name it after me."

37

"My girl, the name will be changed tomorrow morning before she leaves port. From now and forever more, the name of this little vessel shall be *Diana Mine*."

"Oh, Dawson, thank you," she said, very pleased. Then the thought struck her that he must surely love her; he was going to name his boat after her, that would prove it to the whole world. If he loved her, then he surely must want to kiss her. Shyly she turned to face him. Dawson didn't move, looked down at her tenderly, his arms still encircling her. She raised her hands to the black cloak covering his broad chest and looked up at him. His black eyes were studying her, the swarthy handsome face intent, thick black hair blowing softly in the wind, the sleek black moustache shiny above his full mouth. "Dawson," she said coquettishly, "you know, I've never kissed a man with a mustache."

He threw back his head and laughed loudly, his white teeth flashing. She frowned as she watched him and when finally he stopped laughing and spoke, he raised a hand from the railing and put his fingers under her chin, "Kathleen, you've never kissed any man, with or without a mustache."

"How dare you, how do you know who I've . . ." The sentence was never finished. Dawson's black, laughing eyes grew serious and he bent and covered her mouth with his, barely brushing her lips for a second.

"I'm glad you've never kissed a man before, honey, and if I have my way, you will never kiss any other but me." Again his lips covered hers. He kissed her tenderly and the kiss lasted longer and slowly the hand gripping the ship's railing came away and went to her back.

When he pulled away a little, Kathleen's eyes were closed and she looked radiant. Slowly her lashes fluttered open and she looked up at him. "Oh, Dawson," she whispered and her arms went around his neck. He pulled her even closer and she could feel his hard, muscled chest as he crushed her to him. Again he bent to kiss her and this time his demanding mouth parted her trembling lips. She grew faint and thought perhaps the motion of the boat was making her dizzy. He kept kissing her and when finally he raised his head, she gasped, "Dawson, I'm weak, I'm going to faint, to fall."

His strong arms tightened around her and she could feel the violent trembling of his body as he stood against her. "No, you won't, my darling, I've got you. I won't ever let you go." The old riverboat continued to slice through the icy waters of the Mississippi as the two lovers stood embracing in the cold night air.

Four

Dawson came to Sans Souci the next evening and when Kathleen heard him coming in the doors, she flew from the library to greet him. Mindless of her parents sitting just inside the drawing room, she threw her arms around his neck and kissed him on the mouth.

"Kathleen," he whispered, gently pushing her away and looking around, "can't you wait until we're alone; what will your father think?"

She laughed and kissed him again and said in a voice loud enough for the entire household to hear, "Darling, Father knows I'm crazy about you, so I'm sure he's figured out by now that you've kissed me and will do so again, so why not here in my house?"

Still unnerved, Dawson gently drew her arms away, cleared his throat, and walked with her into the drawing room.

"Daddy," Kathleen laughed, "Dawson's afraid you won't like it if he kisses me. Tell him that's foolish."

Dawson's swarthy face turned red and he looked at Louis to read his reaction. Louis Beauregard smiled, "Relax, Dawson, you know you're always welcome here even if my beautiful daughter does insist on kissing you in the foyer of my home. Can I fix you a drink?"

Dawson returned the smile. "Thanks, no, Mister Beauregard, we really need to be getting on our way. We're going to a party at a friend's home and we're late already."

"I see, then you'd better run along. Do come back when

you can stay longer. Why not come over tomorrow night for dinner? Abigail and I would love to have you, wouldn't we, dear?''

''Yes, indeed. We would greatly enjoy your company, as well as that of Kathleen. We don't seem to see her much since she met you.'' She smiled at Dawson.

''Thank you. I'll be happy to come over for dinner. Now, Kathleen, let's get your coat and be on our way.''

Kathleen ran into the hall and came back carrying a long beige cape. She handed it to Dawson and he slipped it around her shoulders. She went to her father and kissed his cheek. ''Goodnight. We'll be back early and thanks for being such a darling father. You're the best on earth.'' Louis' face broke into a broad grin and he watched her walk out with Dawson, blowing a kiss to them over her shoulder.

As soon as they were out the door, the smile on Louis' face vanished and was replaced with a look of pure hatred. ''The thought of that man being in this house, much less kissing my daughter, makes my blood boil.''

''I know, dear. I feel the same way. Why don't you do something about it? When he's here, you act like you're pleased he's escorting Kathleen. Why, you even invited him over for dinner. I don't understand you; why don't you put a stop to it? I'm afraid Kathleen is growing too fond of him. He is coming over more often all the time. I think it's time you had a talk with her. Tell her how we feel about Mister Dawson Harpe Blakely.''

''Abigail, that wouldn't be smart. If I forbid her to see him, she will only get upset with me and I couldn't bear that. She's just a child; she's had crushes on boys before and gotten over them. She'll get over this infatuation, too. You know how easily she gets bored with beaux when they stay around for a while. She's always been that way. A new toy never entertained her for very long when she was a baby and it's the same thing now. He's a toy to her, but she'll soon tire of him and toss him aside without a backward glance. We

41

will just have to endure her whims for a while longer. I'm sure within a few weeks she'll forget all about him.''

''Perhaps you're right, dear, you usually are, but I still don't see why, if you won't forbid her to stop seeing him, you couldn't have a talk with Blakely. Let him know how we feel about him calling on her.''

''It's too risky. He would probably tell her and then she would be furious with me. I do not intend to lose the special relationship with my daughter over some Under the Bluffs scoundrel. She'll tire of him soon and then she'll just be Daddy's little girl like she's always been.''

''You embarrass me, Kathleen Beauregard,'' Dawson said when he got her out the door.

''Good heavens, why, Dawson?'' she smiled up at him.

''Look, Kathleen, I want your parents to approve of me. I've gone out of my way to reassure them I'm a gentleman with you and would never do anything out of line. Then you run into my arms and kiss me with them sitting in the next room. You bluntly tell you father that I've been kissing you when actually last night was the first time, though he'd never believe that now. How am I to make a good impression on them if you insist on misbehaving?''

''Dawson, you're so silly. My father loves me and he wants me to have everything I want. He has always spoiled me. It's that simple.''

''Yes, Kathleen, but what you want now happens to be me and I'm not so sure he wants you to have that.''

The party was at the manse of a friend Dawson had known for years. Kathleen had a good time and all who met her were charmed by her beauty and wide-eyed innocence. Dawson proudly introduced her and politely turned down dance invitations extended to her with a casual smile and a shake of his dark head. He was standing with his arm around her while she chattered and ask innumerable questions about everyone at the party. The party's host approached them, smiling to Kathleen. "I hope you're enjoying yourself, my dear, so glad Dawson brought you."

"Thank you, Mister Carpenter, I'm having a lovely time," she smiled at him sweetly.

"Dawson," Chuck Carpenter turned to him, "I hate to ask you, but I really need to have a word with you."

"No problem," Dawson smiled, "what's on your mind?"

"Well, actually, it's rather, well it's business. Kathleen would be bored. I wonder if I could borrow you for just a few minutes?"

"Certainly. Go on, Dawson, I'll be just fine."

"Look, Chuck, couldn't this wait? I don't want to leave her."

"Dawson, it's important, I have to talk to you. Here comes a special guest, she'll be happy to keep Kathleen company while you're gone."

A tall, fair-haired girl approached them and smiled. She had overheard the last part of the conversation and said to Dawson, "Go on, Dawson, Kathleen and I haven't had the chance to do any gossiping because you never let go of her. Let us catch up on a little girl talk." Reluctantly, Dawson let himself be propelled into the other room, looking back over his shoulder at Kathleen as he went.

She smiled at him and said "I'll be fine." The two women made small talk, but were interrupted shortly by a tall blond man asking for a dance with Kathleen. "No, thanks, I don't think so," she said, smiling.

Persistent, the young man said, "I'm Dan Logan and I refuse to be turned down. I've been watching you dance with Dawson, you love to dance and I do, too. Come on. Just one," and he took her arm and led her to the floor.

The music was a slow waltz and the blond man pulled Kathleen close and pressed his cheek to hers. She followed his

43

easy lead and enjoyed the dance. "Dawson is a lucky man," he said, looking down at her. "Not only are you beautiful, you dance divinely, too. What more could a man want?" She smiled and her blue eyes dazzled him.

Dawson entered the room just as Kathleen was smiling at Dan Logan and Dan was pulling her closer. He wore a relaxed, lazy smile. When the music stopped, Dan walked Kathleen back to Dawson and said, "She's a marvelous dancer, Dawson, and she's a real beauty, too."

"Yes, she is," Dawson smiled down at her. "I think we'd better be going, dear, it's getting late."

"All right," she said and they went to get their wraps.

When the big front doors closed behind the departing couple, the smile left Dawson's face and his eyes turned cold. He took Kathleen's elbow without a word and pulled her down the long walk. His grip was so tight it hurt her arm. She looked up and saw the strange expression on his face and was puzzled. "Dawson, you're hurting me," she said. He gave no answer and didn't loosen his grip on her arm. He shoved her up into the carriage and climbed in beside her.

"What's wrong?" she said, cringing at the look on his face. He didn't turn his head to look at her. "Dawson, look at me. What is wrong with you? You're acting so strange, you frighten me. I've never seen you like this."

He turned at last and snarled at her, "You know very well what's wrong, so stop acting coy." He turned and stared straight ahead.

Stunned and confused, she reached up and put her fingers to his face. He drew her hand away and placed it in her lap. "Dawson, please," she begged, "tell me what has happened. Did the man you had a meeting with give you some bad news or did . . ."

All at once, Dawson whirled on her. "I leave your side for five minutes and you're in some other man's arms. And you're smiling up at him and flirting and . . ."

"Dawson, the man's your friend. You took me to the

party, remember? He asked me to dance and I accepted because he is your friend. Why are you mad at me? I didn't do anything wrong, I didn't.'' She started crying, tears overflowing from the hurt blue eyes.

He saw the tears and it touched his heart; he was immediately sorry for making her cry. His dark eyes softened and his arm came around her and pulled her to him. He put his fingers under her chin and raised her face to his. Sad tears streamed down the fresh young cheeks and he wanted to bite off his tongue for hurting her. "Oh, darling, I'm so sorry. Please don't cry. I'm so mean and selfish, it's just, well, when I saw you in Dan's arms, I couldn't stand it. I wanted to run to you and tear him away from you. I'm a jealous fool, but I can't help it. I can't stand any man's hands on you but mine. Please forgive me." He wiped the tears from her eyes and leaned down to kiss the trembling lips. Her arms came around his neck and she whispered, "You frightened me, Dawson, you looked so mean and I didn't know . . ."

"Oh, darling, I know and I'm sorry. I don't ever want to frighten you, I would never, ever hurt you, you know that."

"Well, I just don't understand why . . ."

"Because, Kathleen Diana Beauregard, I lose all logic when you are around. I'm crazy about you, honey, and I can't stand to share you with anyone else. The thought of another man touching you makes me insanely jealous." Dawson lowered his voice to a faint whisper and put his lips to her ear. "You see, darling, I'm completely obsessed with you. You're all I ever think of, all I ever want. The only reason I take you out to parties is because you're young and pretty and I know you like to dress up and go out where there's fun and gaiety. If I had my way, I'd never share you. I'd take you to my big house where there would never be anyone to dance with but me." His lips dropped from her ear to the pulse in her neck. He softly kissed the faint throbbing there and felt it speed up. "I'm sorry I scared you, honey, I promise I never will again," and his mouth stayed on her neck.

45

Softly, she sighed and murmured, "Oh, Dawson, it's all right. I wasn't really frightened." Her eyes closed. He smiled and raised his head. He put his hand up to the shiny blond hair, stroked it, and gently pushed her head back against the carriage seat. Her eyes fluttered open as his mouth came down on hers. He kissed her tenderly, lovingly, barely touching his lips to hers. Between kisses, he continued with the thrilling confessions she loved to hear.

"You're so beautiful, it makes me lose all reason; I don't even like anyone else looking at you. I've been meaning to tell you that I don't want you wearing those low cut dresses any more except when you are alone with me. I don't want other eyes seeing the beauty of the soft white skin that belongs only to me."

"Dawson, I didn't know you felt that way, I thought you liked my dresses, I . . ."

"I love your dresses, darling, but they show too much of you to the world. I want you covered up when others are around because when I see another man's eyes go to that sweet bosom, I can barely control my rage. I want to rip his eyes out of his head." His lips again moved to her throat, then up to her ear.

"Oh, Dawson," she sighed and pulled him closer.

"You are mine, Kathleen, only mine. I want you to remember that always. I would kill any man who ever tried to take you from me. You belong to me, every sweet square inch of you. Don't ever forget it." His mouth moved back to her lips. He kissed her and said, "These lips belong to me, they will never kiss another."

"No, Dawson, never."

He pulled back a little and put his hand around her neck, held it there for an instant, then let it slide slowly down over her throat to the soft flesh of her breast. "And this belongs to me," he said, his fingers tightening slightly on the bare skin, "no one else will ever look at it again, much less touch it, do you understand?"

46

"Oh, yes, yes, it all belongs to you."

"Good," he said, moving his hand down to her waist and kissing her again. He then leaned back on the seat and she rested her head on his broad chest.

"Dawson," she looked up at him, "can I ask you one question?"

Dawson laughed happily and looked down at her, "Yes, darling, what is it?"

"Does this mean that you have fallen helplessly in love with me, like you told me you would?"

Chuckling still, Dawson said, "Not yet, but I'm on the way."

Five

The glorious days of the following year flew by, and yet they seemed to drag for Dawson because he had fallen in love with Kathleen. They flew by because every day Kathleen was a new delight for him, his love for her changed the most routine meetings into magical interludes. Everything about her enchanted him. The way she tilted her head when she asked one of her countless questions. The smile on her lovely face when he surprised her with some sentimental little present. The trust in her sweet face when he stood at the wheel of the "Diana Mine" with her beside him, she certain he was the best pilot on the river. The thrill he felt when she told him she wanted to steer the boat again, but only if he stood behind her with his hands on hers. The love he felt for her when he came up the steps of Sans Souci and she ran to him and covered his face with kisses, even with her parents near. The respect he had for her, making it pleasantly easy to restrain his kisses from ever getting too heated, so afraid he was of doing anything that might frighten or upset her. The pride he felt when he took her to dances and parties and saw the envy in the eyes of other men, their open admiration for the beauty of the young girl who loved only him. The anticipation of the day when she would be his wife and share every minute of each day and night with him. All these things made the love-filled days fly by for Dawson.

The days also dragged as they never had before. Each day became a new, exquisite torture because he was near Kathleen, but could not possess her completely. He ached to take her in his arms and know the full wonder of her love. He longed for the day when they were married and he could carry her away to his house, far from prying eyes and parental rules. He prayed that nothing would ever happen to come between them and break his love-filled heart. He cursed himself for the passion that made him almost ill with desire. He fantasized guiltily about kidnapping her, whisking her away from home and family and holding her prisoner, locked safely away where no one could ever be near her. He yearned for the moment when he could at last unclothe the sweet body and let his thirsty eyes drink in her youthful beauty until he got his fill. He lusted after her in an animal way that made him want to hurt her, ravage her, shock her, devour her. He loved her so much he wanted to touch her tenderly, awaken her slowly, teach her patiently, worship her openly, be her slave for life. He feared that he would wake up to find she no longer loved him, that she would send him away to live the rest of his days in lonely agony without her.

For Kathleen, mere hours, not days, flew and dragged. The hours she was with Dawson went too rapidly; his very nearness was enough to make her happy. Everything about Dawson thrilled and pleased her. The way he always said, "I love you, honey," when he saw her, even if he'd only been gone for a few hours. His smile, so sensual and easy, lighting his handsome face whenever she entered the room and remained as long as she was at his side. The trust he inspired in her by his self-assured, take-charge manner, making her feel safe and secure when she was with him. The thrill she got when he took her in his arms and held her close, promising to love her forever. The love she had for him was so deep that it scared her with its intensity. The respect she had for him as a man, for in her eyes he was above reproach and the most brilliant person she had ever known. The pride she had in him when he took her out and she saw the envious eyes of girls and ladies when they looked at her tall, good-looking escort. The anticipation of becoming his wife someday was delicious and fun and made her heart pound at times in a pleasant, exciting way.

The hours dragged only when he was not by her side, but she experienced none of the agonies of aching, longing, yearning, lust, or fear her sweetheart endured. She was much too young, naive, and spoiled to be plagued with the complex problems that disturbed the sleep of her anxious lover. Kathleen slept like a baby, happily drifting off into uninterrupted slumber with nothing on her mind but the memory of his goodnight kisses.

Love changed the personality of both and affected the other lives they touched. Dawson became so obsessed and distracted with Kathleen that he could think of little else. Always a stickler for details, he had ruled his plantation with an iron hand. Under his watchful eye, it had become one of the most profitable cotton plantations in Mississippi. His overseer discussed all problems, plans, and profits with Dawson and Dawson was acutely aware of everything that went on at his property. Nothing got by his eagle eyes and never had.

He had been the same way about the small fleet of cargo boats he owned. He knew where each one was at every hour of the day and night and nothing was ever loaded or unloaded without orders from Dawson Blakely. He signed complicated documents with the flash of a gold pen and made profits rise miraculously with his keen business sense. There were times he would have eight to ten different business schemes going at once and was never mixed up or confused on any of them.

Even with a head full of valuable knowledge and hundreds of people looking to him for answers and decisions, he still found time to be a ladies' man. He remembered what particular weakness each lover had and knew just how to please them. After hours spent wooing and thrilling a half dozen ladies, juggling them successfully, keeping them all happy and feeling like they were *the* special one in his life, Dawson still found time to gamble often in the joints at Natchez Under. The sun came up many mornings before Dawson Blakely headed for his waiting carriage for the ride to his mansion on the bluffs.

Then Dawson saw Kathleen Beauregard and he fell in love for the first time in his life. He became a different man. The overseer at the plantation found Dawson had lost interest in hearing about the latest ideas for the future. When he could catch Dawson for a much needed meeting, which wasn't often, Dawson said little. He would merely nod and say, "Whatever you think's best, Brody," or "Buy it if you need it," or "Sorry, I don't have any more time."

Sam had the same problem; getting a word with him was next to impossible. When he needed to talk about the boats and the cargo they carried, all he got was, "You handle it, Sam, I trust you," while Dawson grinned lazily and walked away.

The women in Dawson's life were confused and upset. He disappeared from their worlds without a word of explanation and more than one hopeful heart was broken by his sudden lack of interest. They had no idea what had happened. The last time they had seen him, he was charming, attentive, and promised to be back soon, leaving them glowing from his warm parting embrace.

Dawson even quit drinking and gambling. The gentlemen, and men who were not gentlemen, who had enjoyed his companionship at the dice tables or the drinking taverns, missed him and found it hard to understand how he could give up his favorite vices without a backward look.

Dawson Blakely was a man in love. Totally, completely, everlastingly in love, and anything that did not involve Kathleen Beauregard left him bored and impatient. There was no longer room in his head or his heart for anything but the golden-haired charmer he adored.

Kathleen was changed by love, too, though in different ways. Her mother found her more respectful, less argumentative. Her father found her less willful, more eager to please, better-mannered. Hannah found her kinder, more considerate, less bossy. Her girlfriends found her more fun to be with, less jealous of their happiness, possessed of a sweeter disposition. All of them found her more beautiful than ever as the fires of love put a new brightness in her blue eyes, new color in her white cheeks, a new radiance about her that came from within. The haughty, high-tempered, selfish young girl had turned into a more placid, easy-going, giving young lady.

When they were together, Dawson and Kathleen displayed the changes wrought by the mysterious magic of love in opposite ways. Dawson was unaware of anyone but Kathleen. He would sit in the drawing room of Sans Souci, his arm around her, looking only at her. If Louis Beauregard tried to engage him in intelligent conversation, he answered in polite, short sentences. He had little interest in anything or anybody but her and cared not at all who knew it. Including Louis Beauregard.

Kathleen on the other hand grew more talkative than ever, bending over backwards to act interested in what everyone had to say. She was animated and lively, spending endless hours discussing subjects that had never inspired more than a bored yawn from her before. Dawson listened to her endless chatter with adoring ears and one would have thought he was sitting at the feet of Plato, hearing pearls of wisdom from the master's lips, instead of the giggly conversation of a sixteen-year-old girl. Everything she said or did amused and pleased him; she was amazed and puzzled that she did. She was totally in awe of her handsome, intelligent lover and found it almost unbelievable that he was in awe of her, too.

No two people were ever more in love than the innocent, beautiful Kathleen Beauregard and the reformed, handsome Dawson Blakely.

The night of November 10, 1856, was damp and cold in

Natchez, Mississippi. Dawson stood in the foyer of Sans Souci in a long gray cashmere cloak, shaking off the chill of the evening. Daniel had let him in and was taking his cloak when Kathleen came down the stairs to meet him. Dawson looked up at her and drew in his breath. She wore a deep rose velvet dress with long, tight sleeves and the molded bodice was pinched in at her small waist and buttoned discreetly up to her chin. The ten-yard skirt billowed out and rustled over matching crinoline petticoats. Her blond, silky hair was tied up in a rose velvet ribbon and loose tendrils of its golden beauty escaped the ribbon and hung around her small face and on her neck. She was smiling at Dawson, holding up her skirts prettily and coming down to him. Dawson looked at her, smiled, and decided in that instant he couldn't wait much longer to marry her. He had been patient long enough, he must have her soon or he would lose his mind.

"Darling," she stood on tiptoe to kiss him.

"Hello, sweetheart," he smiled, "are your parents home?"

"Yes, they're in the library, shall we go in?" Kathleen took his hand and led him into the big room.

Louis and Abigail were gracious as usual to Dawson and their warmth made it easy for Dawson to tell Louis he had something on his mind.

"Mister Beauregard, I would like to have a meeting with you tomorrow, sir, if it's convenient."

"Certainly, Dawson, anytime you say," Louis smiled and offered the young man a drink.

Dawson declined politely. "Then I shall come out at 2 P.M. tomorrow, if you are agreeable."

"Fine, Dawson, I'll be looking forward to it. We'll have the place all to ourselves. The ladies are planning a shopping trip, I believe, aren't you, dear?" He looked at Abigail.

"Why, yes, we are. Kathleen and I are going into town for lunch. Then we intend to do a little early Christmas shopping, as well as look at some new winter frocks."

"Mother, this is the first I've heard of it," Kathleen looked at her mother, puzzled. "I'd rather stay here if Dawson is coming out." She squeezed Dawson's hand.

"Now, dear, I need your help. I want you to go with me and besides, Dawson wants to *talk* to your father."

"Where are we going tonight, Dawson?" Kathleen leaned close to him in the back of the carriage.

"Darling, tonight I'm taking you some place you've never been before," Dawson smiled mischieveously.

"Where, where?" She loved surprises.

"You'll see," he said, refusing to tell her. It was a short ride across town and when the carriage pulled up to a stop in front of his big mansion, Kathleen was as excited as a child.

"Dawson Blakely, your house! But, why? I've asked to see your home at least a hundred times and you never would bring me here. Why have you changed your mind?"

He didn't answer, just smiled broadly and helped her out of the carriage. The doors were swung open by a smiling, short black man who said, "Good evening, Miz Kathleen, Mistah Dawson."

"Kathleen, this is Jim. He's been with me for years and takes good care of me," Dawson handed his cloak and Kathleen's cape to the smiling servant.

"Pleased to meet you, Jim, but how did you know my name?" Kathleen held out her hand to him.

"Oh, Miz Kathleen, Mistah Dawson, he tell me all bout you. I feels lak I knows you already." He laughed and disappeared with the wraps.

Kathleen turned and admired the huge hallway, its floor of black and white mosaic marble, which served as an art gallery with original paintings of masters dotting the walls, along with gold leaf mirrors. Dawson beamed and drew her into the large dining room on the left. Furnished in rosewood, it contained silver by Tallois of Paris, rare china, and crystal.

"Dawson, it's lovely, I can't believe it." Kathleen's eyes were big and full of wonder.

"Come," he said, taking her arm and drawing her back across the hall and into the double drawing rooms. Kathleen admired the handcarved woodwork, ceiling rosettes of hand-made plaster of paris, French hand-blocked wall paper, painted window shades. The furniture of rosewood was upholstered in antique blue brocade. There were Windsor chairs, a French piano in the corner, Aubusson carpet covering the floors. Venetian and Waterford chandeliers lighted the room. Kathleen drew in her breath and looked up at Dawson, "Darling, it's absolutely beautiful. I had no idea your home would be so luxurious." Dawson smiled and led her into the big library adjoining the drawing rooms. Gothic bookcases shelved thousands of books in the big room. "Dawson, have you read all these books?" Kathleen was impressed.

"Not quite," he laughed. "I don't seem to have time to read since I met you." He took her arm. Behind the library, he showed her a card room with green felt tables scattered around and a long bar covering one entire wall. "I don't use this room anymore, but we used to have poker games here often . . . before you came into my life."

Dawson led Kathleen up the mahogany stairway, the most unusual one she had ever seen, its beauty outstanding. Down the long corridor, Dawson told her, "These are just bedrooms, guest rooms, I suppose," and pointed to the many doors they passed. At the far end of the hall, he opened a massive door and took her into a gigantic sitting room. A roaring fire blazed in the room furnished in heavy mahogany furniture. The walls of the sitting room were of the same blue brocade she had seen downstairs. Dawson dropped her arm and walked to the double doors that connected the sitting room to his bedroom. He drew back the doors and invited her inside. It was the biggest bedroom Kathleen had ever seen. Another large fireplace directly across from the over-sized master bed burned brightly. The room was filled with heavy furniture and tall windows covered two walls of the corner room. Blue brocade drapes were open, giving a breathtaking view of the lights below the bluffs and the Mississippi river.

"Dawson Blakely, this room is unbelievable. You can sit in your bed and look out at the river while you have your breakfast. I love it, it's so, so . . ."

Dawson smiled and walked to the big bed and sat down. Kathleen stood at the windows looking at the lights below. She turned to smile at him and said, "Aren't you going to put on some lights so I can see the room better?"

Dawson patted the bed beside him, "You can see the room well enough, the fireplace gives off plenty of light. I wanted a romantic atmosphere for what I have to say. Come here."

Shyly, Kathleen walked to the bed. Dawson took her hand and pulled her down beside him. "What are you going to say, Dawson?" Kathleen was wide-eyed.

Dawson tilted her chin up, "Darling, I love you, I've loved you since the first moment I saw you. I want to marry you, I want you to be Mrs. Dawson Harpe Blakely." He bent and kissed her lips tenderly.

Her arms went around his neck and she said, "Oh, Dawson, when? I love you, too; when do you want to marry me?"

"As soon as possible, sweetheart. That's what I'm going to talk to your father about tomorrow. And that's why I brought you to my house. It's going to be your home now, so I wanted you to see it and start thinking about what changes you want to make. You can do anything you like with it. I want you to be happy." He stroked the blond hair falling around her face.

"Dawson, I wouldn't change a thing! It is the most beautiful home I've ever seen. I can't wait to live here," her eyes roamed around the big room, picturing how it would be to spend her days in the big mansion with him.

Dawson laughed, "Honey, I'm sure there's some things you'll want to do. The house is rather masculine. If you like, you can make this your room and do it over in a way that will suit you." He pushed a strand of hair from her neck and kissed her.

"Darling, I want my room to be your room. I don't want separate bedrooms. I want us to share everything."

Dawson raised his head. "I was hoping you'd say that because I never want you out of my sight, my love. It's settled. This will be our room and we'll spend all our nights in this big bed." He smiled and kissed her lips. Her arms tightened around his neck and slowly he eased her back and down into the softness of the massive bed. "My darling," he whispered hoarsely as his lips moved to her throat. His hand left her waist and slowly moved up to the fullness of her breast. His fingers trembled as he caressed its curve through the soft velvet of her dress. Kathleen sighed and arched her body up. "I wish we were married now," he breathed against her neck and pulled her closer. "I want you so much, my darling."

"Oh, Dawson," she murmured and pulled his mouth to hers again. Dawson felt himself losing control as her sweet mouth responded to his kisses and the room around them started spinning. Abruptly, he sat up. Her eyes flew open and she looked at him, puzzled. "Darling, what's wrong?"

"It's time for us to go, Kathleen," he said shakily and rose from the bed. He ran a brown hand through his disheveled hair and looked down at Kathleen, her arms spread out on the bed, her breath coming fast. A smile came to his full lips as calm returned and he put out his hand to her. "Come on, darling, and remember, the very next time we are in this room, you'll be my wife and we can stay right here forever if we choose."

She rose and smiled. "You're right, darling. And don't you dare change a thing about this room, I like it just the way

57

it is." She walked to the door and Dawson followed, nodding his agreement.

"Hannah," Abigail called, "we're ready to go into town, where are you?"

Hannah appeared at Abigail's door, "Miz Abigail, I knows I promised to go with you and Miz Kathleen, but I'se feelin mighty porely today. I wonders if I could stay here and rest?"

Abigail looked at Hannah's tired face and said immediately, "Hannah, dear, of course you may stay home. Now go to your room and lie down. You stay right there until we get back, promise?"

"Well, sho, honey. I jest stay in my room and take a nap. You have a nice trip and I sees you when you gets back." She ambled off.

When Abigail kissed her husband goodbye, Kathleen was already perched in the carriage waiting for her. "Louis, Hannah is sick and she asked if she could stay home. But don't worry, you will not be disturbed, she's promised to stay in her room all afternoon."

"All right, dear. Take care." Louis kissed his wife's cheek. Abigail went to join Kathleen in the carriage. Daniel coaxed the horses and they left, Louis waving after them.

At precisely two o'clock, Dawson rode up to Sans Souci on a big, black stallion. No one was there to meet him, so he tied his horse to the fence and came up the long walk.

"Dawson, come in," Louis answered the door himself.

"Hello, Mister Beauregard. Did Kathleen and her mother go on their shopping trip?" He smiled winningly at the older man.

"Yes, we're quite alone, Dawson. Come into the library, please." Louis' face was stern as he closed the double doors behind them. "A drink, Dawson?" He poured one for himself.

"No thanks, Mister Beauregard. I'll come right to the point," Dawson smiled and stretched his hands out to the fire. Louis walked to the fireplace and stood looking at Dawson. "I love your daughter very much, as I'm sure you know. I want to marry her. I promise to take excellent care of Kathleen and cherish her forever. I hope you'll give us your blessing."

Louis took a long swallow of whiskey and looked into the fire, his eyes dark and cold. At last, he raised his head and looked straight at Dawson. "Mister Blakely, you are not about to marry my daughter!" He drained the whiskey glass and waited for Dawson's reaction.

"Mister Beauregard, I don't understand, surely you must . . . what are you saying?" Dawson was taken aback, stunned at Louis' harsh words.

"I'm saying you are crazy if you think I would ever let my precious daughter marry you. Can I make myself any plainer?" He looked at Dawson defiantly. At a loss, Dawson looked at the older man and struggled to find his tongue. Speechless, he just stared. "You are not fit to marry Kathleen, Mister Blakely. You won't marry her, I forbid it!"

"How can you forbid it? Your daughter is in love with me; you must have known we were planning to be married." Dawson's words came out in a rush. "You have made me welcome here, willingly let Kathleen see me. What has happened to change your mind? You aren't making any sense."

"I never wanted you here, never. I've tolerated your presence because my willful daughter was fascinated with you. I thought she would surely get over it, but it seems that isn't going to happen. She fancies herself in love with you, much to my dismay."

"What have you got against me? What have I ever done to

displease you? I love and respect your daughter, you know I do. All I care about is making her happy."

Hannah lay on her bed upstairs, her tired eyelids drooping sleepily. She heard faint noises downstairs and opened her eyes. Voices grew louder and Hannah sat up. She strained to hear and wondered who was talking. She slowly rose and went to her door and opened it a crack. Puzzled, Hannah shook her head. No one was supposed to be home. Abigail had told her just before she left for town that Mister Dawson was not coming out today, that something had come up and the meeting had been postponed. So who was downstairs talking? Quietly, Hannah slipped down the stairs and what she heard when she neared the closed doors of the library shocked and hypnotised her. Hannah pressed close to the door and listened to the unmistakable, angry voices of Louis Beauregard and Dawson Blakely.

"I want my daughter to be happy, too, Mister Blakely, and that's precisely why I'll never let her marry you."

"But why, for God's sake? What have I ever done but please her?" Dawson was terribly upset, his voice raised to a shout.

"Will you lower your voice, please! Mister Blakely, my daughter is above you, can't you understand that? She is descended from the throne of France on my side of the family and from the throne of England on her mother's. We are aristocrats and members of our family never marry beneath themselves. If you want to better yourself by marrying into a family with an impeccable background, you've come to the wrong place. I won't allow it."

"I'm not trying to better myself and you know it. I don't care about your background. I love your daughter. Nothing else matters to me."

"Well, it does to me. I know what you came from and you are not good enough for my daughter! Your middle name is

60

Harpe, Mister Blakely, and the entire South is well aware of what kind of people the Harpes are. Robbers, murderers, the scum of the earth; mean, ruthless, the dregs of humanity!''

"Mister Beauregard, I'm not like that. Can I help it if my ancestors were Harpes? What has that got to do with me? I'm a decent man and you know it.''

"I don't care. You're a Harpe and I won't have Kathleen marrying into that family. You are trash, Blakely, you were born and raised under the bluffs. Your mother was a Harpe and your father a worthless gambler. The Harpes are notorious! People still tell of the unspeakable things they did. They were animals; they hacked people to death, they killed whole families, they disemboweled helpless victims and filled their empty stomachs with rocks. So despicable were they that one of them even bashed the brains out of his own child! That's what you came from! Do you have to ask why I refuse to let you marry my daughter?''

Dawson's face grew darker with rage. "I know everything about my family and I refuse to apologize for any of it. Maybe their lives were not easy like yours has always been. How do you know what it's like to have nothing and have to make your own way? Everything has been handed to you on a silver platter. I was born under the bluffs, but I alone struggled to better myself and get out. No one ever helped me, *ever*. I did it on my own and I'm proud of it. If you had been born there, you would probably still be down there, powerless to do anything but feel sorry for yourself! My mother was a sweet girl, she never did anything wrong in her life no matter what her name was. I never knew my father, but if she loved him he must have been special. I'm not ashamed my middle name is Harpe; I'm proud of it and I'm proud of what I've made of my life, regardless of what you may think of me.''

"Be as proud as you like, but you will not marry my daughter!''

"Yes, I will. I love her and she loves me. I'm going to

61

marry her right away and there is nothing you can do about it!''

''Ah, you're wrong. There is something I can do about it and I will.'' Beauregard's face broke into a slow smile and he continued, ''I have spent many long hours deciding how to keep you from marrying Kathleen. I've come up with a fool-proof solution. I intend to publicly challenge you to a duel, Blakely.''

Dawson laughed in Louis' face, ''Good Lord, man, do you really think I'm afraid of you? I'm a Harpe, remember? As you said, we're all murderers. There's no doubt in my mind I could kill you easily in a duel.''

''Exactly,'' Louis smiled at him. ''You would almost certainly kill me. And if you did, do you think my daughter would still love you? I think not; she would hate you for killing her father. I've got you, Blakely. It's simple. I will challenge you to a duel. If I kill you, you lose and if you kill me, you lose. Either way, you don't get Kathleen! If you really love my daughter, there is only one thing for you to do. Go away. Get out of her life and leave her alone. Go, because I know your pride and arrogance will not allow you to refuse to duel.''

''She won't stop loving me and, if I tell her what you've said, she'll marry me at once.''

''You aren't going to tell her. She wouldn't believe you and I would deny it. You aren't going to see her again. You are leaving, Mister Blakely, and the sooner the better. If you stay, I intend to challenge you publicly; you'll kill me and she will hate you forever. So why not go? I've won, Blakely; she'll never be your wife. I love her enough to give up my life to prevent her marriage to you.''

''I could take her away with me, never let you know where . . .''

''I would hunt you to the ends of the earth and you know it. The results would turn out the same, one of us kills the other and you lose. She will never love a man who killed her father. She loves me, too, remember?''

A feeling of helplessness came over Dawson as he listened to the determined man threatening him. He was powerless to do anything. Kathleen's father wasn't bluffing and Dawson knew it. He shook his head, trying to clear his thoughts, to come up with a solution, but he could think of none. The thought of Kathleen hating him was more than he could bear. There was no way out. If he took her against Beauregard's will, this cruel man would indeed track them down. If he told Kathleen about this meeting, would she believe him? Her father had never been anything but nice to him, acting like he was more than pleased with the prospect of Dawson for a son-in-law. He'd cleverly concealed his true feelings from Kathleen all this time. Would Kathleen believe that he really hated Dawson and refused to let her marry him? No, she loved and trusted her father. Her father would convince her it was he, Dawson, who was lying. There was nothing he could do but give her up. He loved her too much to ruin her life. If her family felt this way about him, there was no way it could ever work. It would be best to get out of her life; it was the only answer. She would get over him, forget him. For her happiness, he would become Louis Beauregard's unwilling ally.

''I'll leave. I love her and the last thing I want is to make her unhappy. You've won. I suppose you intend to tell her I never really loved her and that I ran away?''

''That's exactly what I'll tell her. She'll cry a little at first, but she will soon forget you. If you love her as much as you say, you are doing the right thing. It's best you leave Natchez at once. When do you think you can go?''

''I'll leave tonight,'' Dawson answered sadly. ''I won't see her again. I'll go to my boat as soon as I wind up things at home. I'll be gone before the night is over.''

''Good. That's just fine. If Kathleen asks, I'll say you never came here today, that I heard you were leaving town.''

Dawson swallowed and said, ''As you wish.''

Louis smiled, "Now if anything unforseen happens and Kathleen should find you before you have a chance to leave, you are to tell her that you don't love her, you never did, and you're going away. Understand?"

"I understand." Dawson moved to leave and Hannah quickly left her place just outside the door, moving quietly along the wall to the back of the house and out of sight. Her heart was pounding in her chest. What she had overheard made her violently ill and she held her big stomach with both hands, her body trembling. Kathleen's father was sending her true love away and it was going to break the poor girl's heart. What should she do? How could this be happening? It was too terrible. Oh, what should she do?

Dawson reached the doors and opened them and Beauregard called after him, "Also, Mr. Blakely, I want you to take her name off that boat immediately!"

Dawson whirled and his eyes flashed fire. "Your daughter may belong to you but, that boat is mine and it will keep the name *Diana Mine* for as long as I live. Don't push me, I would just as soon kill you right now as look at you." He rushed from the house and to his horse. He galloped away from Sans Souci at breakneck speed, cursing the demon who called himself a loving father. He spurred the big horse on and flew down the streets, his face contorted with rage. It had taken all the control Dawson Blakely possessed to keep from killing Louis Beauregard with his bare hands.

Six

Kathleen was brimming over with happiness and excitement while she dressed for the most important evening of her life. She stood humming a Stephen Foster song while Hannah hooked up the soft blue velvet skirt. She grinned at herself in the mirror, thinking it was a shame she had to cover up the dainty batiste camisole she wore with a blouse. Delicately pretty, it was sheer and soft, a blue satin ribbon at its top tied in a small bow at the center. Tiny straps over her shoulders had the same blue ribbon running through them. Kathleen put her hands to her waist and turned around, imagining Dawson seeing her this way, without her blouse. She blushed, realizing that in a few short weeks he would see her in less than the camisole.

Hannah picked up her new white blouse and Kathleen put her arms into the long sleeves. She pinned the small cameo left to her by Grandmother Howard onto the collar. Dawson had given her the blouse and she thought it the most exquisite one she had ever seen. His taste was excellent and he found unusual clothes for her, delighting in giving her pretty things, though her father told her it was not proper for a gentleman to give clothes to a young lady. She had laughed at her father and assured him it was quite proper because Dawson was in love with her and intended to make her his wife and buy all her clothes.

It was turning dark out and Kathleen assumed the important meeting between Dawson and her father had gone smoothly. Dawson was to be here by seven-thirty for dinner and they would all drink toasts and celebrate the coming event. Dressed and eager for her handsome fiancé to arrive, Kathleen left her room and skipped down the stairs still humming. She hurried into the drawing room to join her parents, but found only her mother there. Abigail looked up when her daughter entered the room and smiled to her.

"How lovely you look, dear," Abigail said sweetly.

"You, too, Mother." Kathleen went to Abigail's chair and kissed her cheek. "Where's Father? Isn't he dressed yet?"

"Your father isn't home. I don't know what could be keeping him. I told him we would be having dinner around eight, shortly after Dawson arrives."

"You mean, Father hasn't been at home this afternoon?" Kathleen was puzzled.

The words were hardly out of her mouth when the front doors opened and Louis came in. Kathleen ran to the hall to meet him. Daniel was helping him take off his heavy cashmere overcoat.

"Daddy," Kathleen threw her arms around her father's neck, smiling. "Did you see Dawson?"

"Sweetheart," he disengaged himself from her arms, "can't I go in and get warm before you bombard me with questions?" He walked to the fireplace in the drawing room, nodding to Abigail, "Good evening, dear." His wife smiled and watched him stretch his hands to the fire.

Kathleen followed him to the fireplace. "Father, did you see Dawson? Did he have the talk with you today?" Louis stared into the roaring fire, reluctant to meet his daughter's eyes. "Father, answer me! Where's Dawson? He was to come over here today at two o'clock, remember? Didn't he come? Something's wrong, tell me."

Slowly, Louis lifted his eyes to Kathleen's. "Dear, I haven't seen Dawson today; he never showed up. I'm afraid I have some bad news for you. I was in town and heard that Blakely is leaving Natchez tonight. I'm sorry."

Kathleen stared at her father, then laughed nervously. "Father, you have lost your mind! Dawson will be over here any minute for dinner. He was to meet with you today and tell you we are getting married."

"Oh, darling, I don't know what happened, but I do know Dawson's leaving."

"This can't be. Dawson promised, he . . ."

"Sweetheart," Louis put his arm around Kathleen's shoulders. "I waited and waited for Dawson, but he never arrived. I'm as puzzled as you are. I'm so sorry, Kathleen."

Kathleen pushed her father away and shouted, "You're lying, you've got to be lying. Dawson loves me, he wants to marry me, I know he does. It's a mistake, it's all a mistake."

"Kathleen," her mother rose to comfort her. "Your father wouldn't lie to you. Dawson fooled us, too. Please, don't be so upset, there will be other young men."

"Stop it, both of you. He loves me, do you hear me! He's going to marry me!"

Abigail looked helplessly to her husband and his face had grown stern as he looked at Kathleen. "Now, I want you to stop all this foolishness right now. Dawson Blakely is leaving tonight and there's nothing we can do about it."

"No," Kathleen was screaming now, "he can't go. I won't let him!"

"Kathleen, please let me . . ." her father began.

"Don't touch me! You're lying! I'm going to him." Kathleen ran into the hall, jerked the closet door open, and swept a long blue wool cape around her shoulders. Her parents rushed after her, her mother now wringing her hands, saying, "Louis, do something, you must stop her."

"Kathleen Beauregard," Louis shouted, "you're not going anywhere. You're making a fool of yourself. He's probably already gone, he was going to his boat and . . ."

"The boat, the "Diana Mine"! I'll go there and stop him. It's a misunderstanding, I'll talk . . ." Kathleen was near hysterics.

"Young lady, you are not leaving this house!" Louis Beauregard took her arm."

Kathleen pulled her arm free and ran to the door, whirled around and shouted, "I'm going to Dawson! No one is stopping me." The blue eyes blazed and she flung the door open and ran out into the cold night.

"Daniel," Louis was shaking with wrath. "Hurry, you must go with her!"

"Yes, suh, Mistah Beauregard, I go with that chile," and he followed Kathleen down the steps without stopping to get a coat.

"Why did you let her go, Louis?" Abigail was crying softly as her husband closed the heavy front doors.

"There, there, dear. Don't worry. Come back in by the fire," he coaxed her.

"But, Louis, what if . . ."

"I've taken care of everything, I assure you. Dawson's probably already gone, but even if he hasn't, he'll be gone by tomorrow and he won't be marrying our daughter. If Kathleen finds him, he will turn her away and in a few weeks she'll forget all about the scoundrel, so don't worry your pretty head about it." He kissed her and smiled, "Now, why don't we go in and have our dinner. I'm quite hungry, aren't you?"

Kathleen sat in the back of the carriage, fear clutching her heart, her mind totally confused, tears streaming down her cheeks. "What is happening? Why is Dawson leaving? He loves me, I know he does. It's a mistake, it can't be true." But the fear refused to leave and she knew something was very wrong.

The carriage had hardly come to a stop on the wharf near the *Diana Mine* before Kathleen jumped down and ran for the gangplank. Sam heard the footsteps and came to investigate. "Miz Kathleen, what is you doin . . . ?"

"Sam, Sam," she said, taking his big hand. "Where's Dawson? Is he here?"

Sam looked very grim and answered, "Miz Kathleen, he be here, but sompin be wrong with the cap'n. He be in terrible black mood and he shout at me, say we leaving tonight. He starts drinkin and he throw things and he cuss and he . . ."

"Where is he, Sam? I must go to him."

"Oh, please, Miz Kathleen, I don't think you better, he not be hisself, he be real mean. He might hurt you."

"Sam, is he in his cabin?"

"Yes'um, but I don't thinks you . . ."

Kathleen dropped Sam's hand and ran across the hurricane deck and down the steps to Dawson's cabin. Hurriedly wiping tears from her eyes, she knocked loudly on the door.

"Go away, Sam!" Dawson shouted from inside.

Kathleen took a deep breath and pushed the door open. She stepped inside and closed the door, leaning back against it, breathing shallowly. There was one dim light aglow on the big desk and it cast an eerie pattern of shadows over the spacious room. Steamer trunks and suitcases were scattered around, some half open. Dawson sat behind his desk, his face in the shadows, his big hands on the desk, clutching a glass and a half empty bottle of whiskey. Kathleen looked at him for what seemed an eternity and slowly he leaned up to the desk and into the dim light. His face was hard and cold, his black hair disheveled and falling over his forehead. His white ruffled shirt was wrinkled and open to the waist, exposing his hard brown chest matted with thick black hair. He looked at her coldly and wearily rose from his chair. Dawson came around the desk and stood in front of it. He looked at her as though he had never seen her before.

Finally, he spoke. "What do you want, Kathleen?" he said coldly.

Kathleen took off her cape and threw it to the leather couch, then took one step forward and said, "What do I *want?* I want to know what's going on! Why are you doing this to me, Dawson?''

"I was not aware I was doing anything to you, Kathleen. I've just been here in my cabin on my own boat. I've bothered no one."

"Dawson, what is wrong? Please tell me." She was crying again. She came to him and put her hands up to the open white shirt. "Darling, what has happened? You must tell me."

"Nothing has happened; I just decided I'd like to get away, there's no law against it, is there?"

"Dawson, you're not making sense. You love me, we're going to be married. You can't go away." She was shouting now.

"Don't, Kathleen. I've a terrible headache."

"Headache? Have you lost your mind completely? You . . . you're drunk. That's it. You're very drunk and you don't know what you're saying."

"I'm not drunk, Kathleen, though I'm working on it and plan to get that way real soon."

"Dawson, darling, I . . ."

"Kathleen, I want you to go. I didn't invite you here and I would like to be alone."

"Dawson, please, I love you and . . . you love me."

"No," Dawson said coldly, "I don't love you, Kathleen. You amused me for a while, but not anymore. You see, women are like champagne. Fresh champagne is bubbly and it tickles your nose and makes you giddy. But then the champagne goes stale. Our relationship has gone flat, Kathleen. It's over." Dawson removed her hands from his shirt.

She was terribly hurt and confused, but she would not give up. She moved closer to him, stood on tiptoes and whispered, "You love me, Dawson Blakely," and kissed him on the mouth. "I know you love me." Her lips traveled over his hard brown face and came back to his full mouth. She pressed against him and prayed his strong arms would come around her. Dawson's teeth stayed tightly clenched and his cold lips moved not at all under her trembling mouth. She looked up at him and his eyes were still dark and cold. In desperation, she threw her arms around his neck and pulled his head down, kissing him wildly, whispering his name. Still she got no response. His arms remained at his sides and his body stayed completely rigid.

"Please don't Kathleen. It won't work," he said in a tired voice.

Undaunted, she moved her arms from around his neck and put her fingers to the white shirt front. She slowly pulled the shirt apart and leaned to him and kissed his brown chest, murmuring, "You love me, you do, say you love me." She couldn't see Dawson's eyes softening. Nothing else about him changed. Slowly, Dawson raised his hands and jerked her away, pushing her back a step or two.

"It's no use, Kathleen, you're wasting your time. I don't love you, I never did, really." He pulled out a straight-backed chair and sat down, his feet apart, arms folded across his chest. "Why don't you leave?"

Kathleen stood looking at him, hurt and unbelieving, bewildered and shocked that her kisses meant nothing to him, did not arouse him at all. Perhaps he doesn't love me, I should leave, that's what he wants. He wants me to go. But she couldn't, she loved him too much. "It can't end like this, I won't let it."

Slowly, Kathleen raised her fingers to the brooch at her neck and unfastened it, tossing it on the desk. "I will make you love me," she said defiantly and started unbuttoning the top buttons of the white lace blouse. Dawson's eyes never left her, but he said, "Don't do it, Kathleen."

She continued unbuttoning the blouse and looking at him. He tried to lower his eyes and found it impossible. "She's teasing me, she'll stop in a minute," he thought. She did not stop. She unbuttoned the last button at the waist, took off the blouse, and threw it on the desk. She stood before him in the sheer batiste camisole with its dainty blue ribbon and Dawson's breath caught in his throat.

"For God's sake, Kathleen, don't shame yourself. Stop it; where's your pride?"

"Pride?" she looked at him sadly, tears now overflowing from the big blue eyes. "I have none left. I love you and I will not let you go." Her shaking fingers untied the little blue bow at the top of the camisole and then the top hook was opened.

"Stop," Dawson shouted, "I mean it!"

Kathleen paid no attention to his command and continued to look him in the eye. She undid the last three hooks and stood with the camisole seductively open.

"Please," he whispered hoarsely, but she let the camisole slide down her arms and to the floor. Still looking straight at him, she stood bare to the waist before him and finally saw the change come into his dark, brooding eyes. He looked at her, not speaking, drinking in her beauty.

Dawson felt his heart completely stop for a minute as he stared at her. She was the most temptingly beautiful creature he had ever laid eyes on and he loved her and wanted her beyond all reason. When her hands went to the waistband of her skirt, he slowly reached out and took her arm. The touch of his hand turned her quiet tears to sobs.

In slow motion, Dawson pulled her between his legs and sat her down on his left knee. He held her close against him and stroked her hair until her sobs subsided. Then he kissed her tenderly and whispered her name. Her lips were warm under his; he tasted the salt from her tears and the heart inside him began to pound. He looked into her eyes and felt a lump forming in his throat. His dark, agonized eyes rolled up briefly and he moaned, "God forgive me," and slowly bent his head down to her. His fevered lips sought the soft white skin of her bosom as all logic and reason left him and nothing existed but the sweet closeness of his beloved. Kathleen looked down at the handsome dark head bent over her. She felt the fiery kisses covering her sensitive skin and was filled with a new emotion as yet unknown to her. She raised her hands to the dear head and leaned down to kiss the thick black hair.

"You do love me, darling, you do," she whispered.

"I worship you," he murmured against her tingling flesh and continued to press his burning mouth to her breast. He rained kisses all over her torso, her bare shoulders, the valley between her breasts, the hollow of her throat, the sides of her sensitive neck. Carefully avoiding the tempting pink tips of her breasts, he wisely held himself in check. He didn't want to do anything that might spoil the shared closeness of the minute, because he had come to the unconscious decision to take what she was offering him.

"Dawson, please tell me . . ." Her words were swallowed as his mouth once again took hers. He ran the tip of his tongue around her trembling lips until Kathleen felt as though her mouth were a circle of fire. He teasingly bit at her full bottom lip, kissed the corners of her mouth, and finally plunged his tongue inside. Kathleen's arms slid around his back and she kissed him frantically, her tongue meeting his, exploring, melding, savoring the hot, slow kiss that was making her weak and faint.

His mouth left hers at last and moved to the velvety texture of her smooth, pale cheek. The soft skin under his lips was flushed and warm and the sweet voice calling his name was breathless, high-pitched. Dawson's hand moved up to her breast, letting it fill his hand, his thumb going to the taut tip, to circle it lazily while he continued to kiss her cheeks, her eyelids, her neck. He traced the contour of her small ear with his tongue and whispered huskily, "Kathleen, my own. I love you, darling. No one is going to have you but me." All thought of the morrow departed. There was only one thing Dawson Blakely was positive of; he loved this beautiful girl as he'd never loved another human being and he was going to make her his. He was going to love her the way he'd always wanted. He was going to unclothe her lovely body and take all her sweetness, taste all the delights he'd been craving, drink from the draught of love until his thirst was quenched.

"Dawson," she said tremulously, "tell me that you didn't mean what you said earlier. Tell me you're not tired of me, that you . . ."

"Sweetheart," he murmured, kissing her neck, "I'll show you how I feel about you." His mouth claimed hers again and Kathleen reeled and clasp him tightly as he pulled her against him. His bare, furry chest was crushing her tender breasts and she gloried in the feel of him. She consciously pressed herself closer while his hot mouth continued to plunder hers as he kissed her in a way he'd never kissed her before.

Dawson's hand slipped under her knees and, with his lips still on hers, he rose from the chair. His lips lifted from hers and she buried her face in his brown, smooth throat while he carried her to his big bed. Gently standing her beside the bed, Dawson again kissed her before turning her to face away from him. His big, eager hands went to the waistband of her velvet skirt and deftly unfastened it. Like a small child, Kathleen stood dutifully still and quiet while Dawson pulled the skirt, petticoats, and underwear down over her hips and legs. Offering her his hand, she took it and stepped out of her shoes and the billowing garments, while Dawson stooped, picked them up, and placed them on a chair. He stood behind her and put his hands to her shoulders. While the blood pounded in his temples, he looked down at the bare, beautiful body so close and had to restrain himself from jerking her around to face him. He desperately wanted to look at her, to have her turn round and round while he beheld and admired her loveliness. He bent his head and tenderly kissed the side of her neck and whispered, "Kathleen, Kathleen" as he started to turn her slowly.

Suddenly shy and frightened, Kathleen twisted from his grip and quickly got into bed, nervously pulling the sheet

74

up to her chin, giving Dawson's searching eyes barely a glimpse, but it was enough to make the blood surge through his veins. He bit his lower lip and cautioned himself to go slowly, very slowly.

Knowing the sudden sight of his nakedness would further frighten her, Dawson sat on the edge of the bed and removed only the open white shirt and black boots, leaving the tight black trousers on. He moved closer to her, remaining in a sitting position, and put a hand on either side of her trembling body. "Love," he whispered, "open your eyes and look at me. Kathleen."

Her eyes opened tentatively, but her small hands continued to clutch at the sheet, holding it tightly in place just under her chin. She gazed up into the dark, smoldering eyes which looked down at her with more love and tenderness than she'd ever seen before. "Dawson," she whispered shakily, "I . . . I . . . love you, but I . . . I'm afraid."

His hand went to the side of her head, his long fingers raking through her silky hair. "My darling," he whispered, "don't be. It's Dawson, darling. Your Dawson. You don't have to be frightened of me. I love you. Oh God, how I love you."

His lips descended slowly to hers and her lips parted in invitation. She loosened the grip on the sheet, relaxing a little. His mouth was warm and moist and undemanding as he kissed her tenderly, slowly, starting over from the beginning, as though it was the first time he'd ever kissed her. She sighed as he placed sweet little kisses on her lips and soon she was raising her head from the pillow, longing for the kisses to last longer, wanting him to kiss her deeply, passionately. Dawson continued to take only soft quick sips from her eager lips, purposely making her crave more. Soon, she was nervously nipping at his bottom lip and plunging her tongue into his mouth. Her arms had come from under the sheet to clutch the nape of his neck, pulling him down to her, trying desperately to draw him closer.

"Dawson, Dawson," she sighed through fevered lips, "please . . ." Her lips traveled over his brown face, as in a frenzy of desire she licked at his jawline, kissed his chin, bit at his ear.

Only then did Dawson claim her mouth in a deep hungry kiss of passion. Sighing with gratitude, Kathleen kissed him wildly, her hands pulling at the dark hair of his head while her open mouth twisted under his and welcomed the penetrating tongue seeking out the honeyed recesses of her mouth. So lost in his fiery kiss was she that she hardly noticed when Dawson's big hand unobtrusively pulled the sheet slowly down, stopping only when it lay at her waist.

When the kiss ended, Kathleen's eyes were closed and her lips were swollen, her face hot. Dawson took her limp arms from around his neck and placed them beside her. Snuggling down into the softness of the bed, Kathleen smiled and opened her eyes just as he bent his head to her breasts. She made no move to stop him when his lips went to a rosy peak. She sighed her approval and Dawson opened his mouth and began gently to suck. He ran his tongue around the circle of it and raked his teeth over it, taking care not to hurt her. Kathleen's eyes widened and she swallowed and arched her back as new and wonderful sensations shot through her and incredible heat engulfed her.

"Dawson," she gasped in amazement and twisted her hand in his hair. "Dawson," she moaned, as she licked her lips and clutched at the bed with her free hand. Dawson didn't raise his head; he continued to draw the erect sweetness into his mouth while his dark eyes closed with passion and his kisses became greedy as he tried to inhale all her delicious warmth.

For a long, long time, Dawson did nothing more than kiss her mouth and her breasts. When finally she was writhing on the bed, her rounded hips beginning to move seductively under the sheet covering her and her blue eyes glazed over with passion, Dawson peeled the sheet down from her stomach and thighs, whispering endearments to her throughout. The sheet was at her knees; he stopped and let his hand go to the flatness of her gleaming stomach. His long fingers raked over her and she trembled at his touch. Still wearing his tight trousers, Dawson stretched out beside her and again was kissing her, while his hand stayed on her stomach, carressing, tickling, arousing.

His drugging kisses continued and Kathleen was lost in them, in the strange new waves of feeling rippling through her hot body. Dawson's hand had moved down to her hip and then slid to her thigh. Slowly, he let it go up to the warm inside, caressing, gently touching. Kathleen moaned and tightened her arms around his neck.

"Dawson," she cried against his lips, "Oh, Dawson . . ."

Moving his mouth to the softness just under her ear, he pressed burning kisses there and murmured, "Let me love you, darling. Relax here in my arms and enjoy it."

"I can't . . . I don't know . . . I . . ."

"Yes, you can, I'll teach you. I'll help you, Kathleen. Trust me, sweet."

He continued to stroke and caress her until her small body was burning and her throat was dry, her eyes wild. She clung to him and moved her hips sensuously against his loving hand, longing to be closer, wanting more, straining against him, no longer frightened. She wanted him, she wanted all the love he could give her, she wanted the heated pleasure of his hands, mouth, and body. She wanted him to possess her completely, to make her his own, to become a part of her.

While his lips roamed restlessly over her warm, beautiful face, Dawson reached down to the buttons of his trousers, quickly flicking them open. With the grace of an animal, he was off the bed, freeing his painfully aroused body from its confines. The trousers on the floor, Dawson stood above Kathleen and felt a groan starting deep inside his broad chest.

Kathleen's eyes opened just a slit and she looked up at him. Her gaze slid over his powerful, fully aroused brown body. Her hand raised to him and she murmured excitely, "Love me, darling."

The groan inside him surfaced and Dawson fell on the bed beside her and gathered her into his arms. The touch of her sweet, bare body pressed to the naked length of his made his heart pound anew and he was momentarily terrified that he could wait not one second longer. At that instant, Kathleen kissed his chin and whispered again, "Love me, Dawson. Please, please love me."

Gently placing her on her back, Dawson parted her legs with his knee and shifted his weight partially onto her. Looking deep into her trusting eyes, he whispered, "I love you, Kathleen, more than life itself. I will love you until the day I die."

"I love you, Dawson," she whispered. "I will never love another."

Smoothing an errant lock of blond hair from her cheek, he said huskily, "Kathleen, it will hurt this one time. I'm sorry, darling. You know I never want to hurt you." He moved atop her, his face above hers, so close he could feel her warm, sweet breath. He lowered his lips to hers and kissed her passionately, lovingly, deeply. When he raised his head, she was radiant, flushed, inflamed. While her tiny hands clung tightly to his broad shoudlers, she whispered breathlessly, "I love you, I love you." Dawson thrust into her, his dark eyes full of love and concern for the innocent young girl whose soft, pliant body had never known a man. When she cried out in pain, Dawson's love for her soared and he kissed her and murmured soothingly, "My darling, I'm sorry, so sorry."

Tears coursed down her cheeks from the white hot pain tearing at her insides, but Kathleen tightened her arms around Dawson's neck and when she felt his warm mouth on her cheeks, tenderly kissing away her tears, she breathed softly, "Dawson, my love."

Held tightly in his embrace, the pain subsided and soon Kathleen's pleasure was not only recaptured, it was more intense than before, as Dawson kissed her mouth, her neck, her throat. He slowly began to move within her. Her innate sensuality made Kathleen's hips move with his, bringing so much heightened pleasure to Dawson that he had to bite the inside of his jaw to distract himself lest he come to the pinnacle of passion immediately. Eyes smarting from self-inflicted pain, his lean, hard body ground against the sweet softness of hers and his mouth dipped to hers, searing her lips with flaming heat.

Wave upon wave of wild, new pleasure rippled through Kathleen's aching, anxious body as she pulled Dawson frantically to her. She could feel a tenseness building deep inside, radiating heat, graduating in intensity, screaming for release.

Dawson's lithe frame moved more rapidly as he speeded the pace and his deep voice urged her to cast off inhibitions, to yield to desire, to abandon all restraint.

She began to moan in uncontrollable passion as she quivered beneath him and started the assent to the summit. Dawson lovingly guided her to the top and when the frightening, glorious, earthshaking release claimed her with such turbulent tremors that her eyes flew open in surprise, Dawson kissed her dry, trembling lips and her climax became his own. He moaned in unbelievable elation, as physical pleasure combined with spiritual. His satisfaction was just as new and frightening as it was to the sweet young girl clinging to him, because for the first time in his life, Dawson was in the arms of a woman he truly loved.

When the last tiny tremors finally stopped and Kathleen let her tired arms fall away from him, Dawson moved to her side and gathered her limp, damp body close to his. Kissing her softy, he whispered, "I never knew such bliss existed."

"Nor I," she murmured and trustingly laid her head on

his broad chest. Dawson stroked the long, touseled hair, pushing it from her face, kissing the crown of her head. He sighed and held her close, fitting her small soft body to the length of his. For a short, happy time they lay in silence, the only sound that of their breathing as their pulses began to slow to normal and their respiration became regular once again.

Refusing to think past the moment at hand, Dawson wanted nothing more than to lay with Kathleen encircled in his arms while the boat underneath them gently swayed and rolled in the smooth water of the port. For just a while longer, he wanted to be closeted here in the warmth with his precious love while the storm outside heightened, turning the world cold and frigid. He wanted only a few more minutes to hold her, to let his eyes roam at will over the pale, satiny body, so fair and white contrasted with the darkness of his. He knew deep inside that he must carefully memorize every tempting curve, every silky inch of the beautiful body laying against his that had given him such pleasure. He slowly ran his hand over her, gently caressing the full, high breasts, the slim, small waist, the flat, velvety stomach, the long, slender legs. His chest began to ache dully and he knew that the happiness would soon end; he couldn't hold back time.

"When Dawson?" Kathleen said softly.

"When what?"

"When will we be married? I don't want to wait, do you? Let's get married tonight." Kathleen lay with her head on Dawson's chest, his arms around her. She felt his body stiffen and slowly he took his arms from around her, gently pushing her away. Raising himself up, he put a pillow against the headboard of the bed and leaned back. "Dawson, what's wrong? What is it?"

"Kathleen, this doesn't change anything."

"You can't mean that, Dawson, you . . ."

"I mean it. I'm going away," and he looked away from her toward the porthole.

She sat up and said, "Dawson, you can't, you love me, I . . ."

He looked back to her and said steadily, "No, I don't love you and I'm leaving." Kathleen watched his lips moving, knew he must be talking, but it was impossible to comprehend what he was saying. The words seemed to be coming from far away, like someone shouting against the ocean's breakers. There was a loud roaring in her head and his voice could hardly be heard above it. She shook her head trying to stop the awful roaring so she could hear him. "I'm leaving tonight, just as I told you before."

All at once, she was pounding on his chest and screaming. Dawson tried to stop the flailing fists, but her fevered frenzy made her hands move so rapidly he was almost helpless against the barrage. "Liar, liar," she screamed and beat on him, tears streaming down her face, her eyes as wild as an animal's. "I hate you, I *hate* you! It can't be true, you love me. You told me you did. Told me you worship me. Say you're lying!"

Dawson was finally able to grip the flying fists and subdue her. He pulled her down, still struggling, trying to jerk away, pulling with all her strength. He held her arms pinned behind her back, breathing heavy from exertion. After several wild minutes, her strength ebbed away and she collasped against him, unable to fight any longer. She lay on his chest, her hair falling over her face and onto his body, her eyes red and anguished, her tears wetting his chest. So weak she could no longer move against him, Dawson slowly released her arms. They fell limply from her back, lifeless. She lay on him staring with unseeing eyes, the tears drying up. He lay completely still under her, not moving or speaking, not offering any words of comfort. They both lay not moving a muscle for the next half hour, suspended between saneness and insanity.

Slowly, Kathleen raised up and wearily got off the bed. Like a sleepwalker, she went to her clothes and began dressing while Dawson's dark eyes followed her. Still he remained silent. The blue velvet skirt and white lace blouse back on at last, she walked to the couch and picked up her cape. She put it around her shoulders and tied it under her chin and walked to the door. With her hand on the doorknob, she turned back to look at Dawson. He had not moved and was looking directly at her. She studied the face she loved so much, the dark, sultry eyes, the black mustache above the full lips. Then her eyes dropped to the brown, lean body and she felt her heart breaking.

"I do not know you, never knew you," she said softly, "you no longer exist." Then her anger rose suddenly and she raised her voice slightly, "I shall hate you to the grave and beyond." She went out the door and Dawson heard her tiny feet going down the gangplank to her carriage.

Slowly, Dawson got up and pulled on his black trousers. He went to the desk and pulled out the middle drawer. He took out a small blue velvet box and popped it open. He took out the diamond engagement ring and held it tightly in his palm. He opened the cabin door and went up the steps.

"Cap'n Dawson," Sam came hurrying down the companionway, "Is you okay? I hear Miz Kathleen scream and then she run out crying and . . ."

"Get out of my way," Dawson shoved the concerned black man.

"But, Capn' Dawson, you'll freeze out here with no clothes, why you is barefooted. . . ."

Dawson paid no attention, walked to the front of the hurricane deck, shouting over his shoulder, "Fire her up, let's get out of here."

Dawson reached the railing in time to see Kathleen's carriage just before it pulled out of sight. She turned to look up, saw him, and jerked the blond head around instantly. But he saw her hands come up to her face and the head bow down

82

and he knew she was crying.

Dawson stood gripping the railing in the exact spot where he'd stood with her the first night he brought her to his boat. The night air was freezing now, but he was not aware of it. A few snow flakes were falling, sprinkling his dark head with white crystals, but he didn't notice. The boat was now slowly gliding through the water, heading for the river, but Dawson didn't know they were in motion.

He was aware of only one thing. After tonight, he loved Kathleen Diana Beauregard more than ever and he was never going to see her again. With eyes as dead as his dreams, he looked straight down. Slowly, his hand went out over the railing and his fist opened. He looked down at the engagement ring he'd bought for her. The diamond was as black and lifeless as his heart, for there was no light left for it to reflect off of. He spread his fingers and let the ring drop into the icy waters of the Mississippi. It was over. Everything was over.

Dawson Harpe Blakely clung to the railing, trembling, but not from the cold. While the *Diana Mine* gently sliced through the water, he lowered his dark, weary head. And he cried.

Seven

At Sans Souci, Louis paced the floor. He had been since ten o'clock. It was well after midnight and Kathleen had not returned from her meeting with Dawson Blakely. Her father had been expecting her since before nine and his mind raced with every conceivable bad thing that could have happened to keep her away. Had Dawson told Kathleen about their talk? Surely not, the man was no fool and he knew he meant every word that he had said. He wouldn't dare disclose to Kathleen what had really happened. So why wasn't Kathleen home?

Had Dawson Blakely said nothing of the meeting, but stupidly talked Kathleen into going away with him? "If that has happened, I'll trace him to the ends of the earth. He couldn't get far enough away that I wouldn't find him. And I'll kill him the minute I capture him." That couldn't be it. Maybe she never found Dawson, maybe he had already gone by the time she got to the boat. But if so, where had she been all this time? Where was she now? Louis poured himself a bourbon and walked to the fireplace. He turned up the glass, then looked down into the fire. "Oh how she would hate me if she knew what I've done. She loves that flashy, worthless scum, though how she could I don't understand. I thought she would get over him after a few months, but instead she grew more fond of him. And Dawson Blakely is clearly in love with her." Louis shook his head. "It doesn't matter, I did the right thing. I did it for her because I love her and I'm glad I did. The man is beneath her, not fit to come into this house, much less marry her. It would never have worked; she will see that someday. Someone deserving of her will come along and she'll forget she ever knew Dawson Blakely and he can sink back into the slime he came from. And I won't have to look at grandchildren that have Harpe blood running through their veins." The thought made him shudder.

"I should have stopped her, should not have let her go to him," he thought. "But she would never have held still for that, she would have hated me and that would defeat my whole purpose. I wanted her to find him, so he could turn her away and convince her he doesn't love her. Which is exactly what he'll do, if he has any sense. Then she can never blame me and she'll hate him. I'm sure that's what happened, but if so, where is she?"

The sound of horses' hooves snapped him from his thoughts and Louis eagerly ran to the front doors, setting his bourbon glass aside. He threw open the doors and saw her coming slowly up the walk. He ran out in the cold to meet her and when he reached her, she collapsed in his arms, sobbing loudly.

"Oh, darling, darling, don't cry." He put his arm around her shoulders and led her up the walk. The look in her eyes terrified him; there was pure misery written on her face and it broke his heart to see his lovely daughter so unhappy.

"You were right, Father," she sobbed, "Dawson doesn't love me, he never did. He told me he doesn't want me."

"Oh, my poor baby, I could kill that man, he's the most despicable cad I've ever heard of. Come on, sweetheart, let's get inside and warm you by the fire."

Louis led the sobbing Kathleen into the drawing room and helped her remove the long blue cape. "Here now, Angel, I'll take care of you." He pulled a footstool up to the fire's warmth and gently helped her down to it. He sat on the floor beside her and took her hand. "Kathleen, I'm so terribly sorry, it's so hard to understand. I thought Dawson Blakely was in love with you. He fooled me and I know how he fooled you. Tell me, darling, what happened, what did he say to you?''

Kathleen looked tiredly into the fire, ''He said I no longer amuse him, that he is tired of me, that our relationship is over.''

''The nerve of that worthless scoundrel! To toy with your affections the way he did. He should be strung up. I was so worried about you, darling, you were gone so long. What happened, why were you away for such a long time? Did you have trouble finding him, is that it? You've been gone for hours.'' His face showed deep concern.

Kathleen drew her hand away and gave him no answer. Finally, she rose from the footstool and said in a cold, flat voice, ''Nothing happened. He's gone. It's that simple; it's over and I never want to hear his name again for as long as I live. I'm going to bed,'' and she left her worried father looking after her as she went from the room and wearily climbed the stairs.

Louis breathed a sigh of relief when she was out of sight. It was over. He had nothing more to worry about. His plan had worked perfectly. He had read Dawson Blakely correctly. The poor fool loved Kathleen so much he was willing to give her up. Everything was going to be all right. His precious baby was safe. Blakely was out of her life for good. He had his daughter back at last. Everything would be wonderful again. His eyes clouded a little as he poured himself another bourbon, ''But why was she gone so long?''

Eight

Kathleen went to her room and, without illuminating it, stripped the clothes from her tired body and got into bed. Her head ached and her eyes were swollen from crying. She wanted to die, wished she would just never wake up. Dawson didn't love her; he was going away. She would never see him again. Oh, but she hated Dawson Blakely. He was mean and cruel. How could she have ever loved a man like that? He had fooled her. He had made her think he loved her all this time; he had told her over and over again how much he loved her and how she belonged to him. Told her he wanted to marry her. "I despise Dawson Blakely. I'll despise him until the day I die."

Kathleen repeated these declarations to herself over and over. It didn't work. It was no use. Bitter tears streamed down her cheeks as the face of her lover refused to disappear no matter how tightly she closed her eyes and commanded him to go. Her body arched up in her bed, still feeling his burning lips on hers, the knowing hands caressing every part of her, thrilling her with ecstasy. She relived how the lean, brown body had taken hers, possessing her completely, raising her outside the realm of earth, taking her away with him to float on the clouds of heaven, until finally they shuddered as one body while the crescendo of their love consumed them totally and produced a bond between them that could never be broken. "I hate him," Kathleen cried into her pillow and longed for him in a way she had never known was possible before tonight.

* * *

In her small room at the back of the house, Hannah lay awake far into the night. She heard Kathleen come in, heard the lies her father told her. She heard Kathleen's sobs and felt the heart inside her own big body breaking for the young girl. Should she go to her, tell her what she had overheard? Should she tell her Louis Beauregard was lying? Hannah shut her eyes tightly and tears rolled down her cheeks. How could she live with this terrible secret inside? Louis Beauregard would kill her if she told. Hadn't he told Dawson he was doing it for Kathleen's sake? He loved his daughter very much. He must think he's doing the right thing. Hadn't he always been kind and understanding, a good man? But what of Dawson Blakely? His heart was broken. Should I tell Kathleen and help her go to Dawson? Maybe Dawson Blakely isn't good enough for Kathleen. He is poor white trash, though he's done well and is such a nice, good-looking young man. Will she soon have forgotten all about him? I can't tell her. I can't tell no one. Won't be long before she'll be okay and, with Dawson gone, she'll forget all about him.

Doubts continued to nag Hannah and it was a long time before she slept. When she did sleep, the slumber was interrupted by strange and frightening nightmares. Kathleen appeared in her dreams and she had turned into a withered old woman with snow white hair. Her blue eyes had faded and were dull and lifeless. She was shouting at Hannah, "It's all your fault, your fault! You've ruined my life; I shall never get over him and now he's gone. You knew and you let him go. I hate you, Hannah, I hate you." Hannah awoke at dawn and shuddered and felt as though she had not rested at all. And that she would never rest well again.

"Louis, I'm so worried about Kathleen," Abigail said to her husband at the breakfast table. "That man has been gone for over three weeks and she still doesn't seem to be any better. She's so pale and she's lost weight. It has really broken her heart. What are we going to do?''

"Abigail," he patted her hand, "I'm worried, too. I knew she would take it hard at first, but it's time she started getting over it. I've tried to talk to her, but it doesn't do any good. She sits and barely listens, no matter how hard I try to make her understand that she is better off without him and she'll soon forget. I've begged her to come down for her meals, but she refuses. I just can't seem to reach her.''

"I know. I tried to talk to her several times, too, but she paid no attention to me. Becky and Julie have been over to visit and she won't even let them come up. She refuses to see them and we have to send them away with no explanation other than she isn't feeling well. Perhaps we should get a doctor.''

"I've thought about that, but what could we tell him? That our daughter is dying of a broken heart over a worthless man she's well rid of? No, we can't do that. We'll just have to give her more time. She's young, she will get better. Let's just not push her, let her snap out of it on her own. And she will. After all, she's our daughter, isn't she? Nothing will keep her down for long. Now, try not to worry, darling.''

"All right, dear. You know best.''

"Hannah, please take that tray out of here. I told you, I'm not hungry.'' Kathleen frowned at her mammy. She sat in a chair by the fire, mesmerized by its flames. She still had not dressed, though it was mid-morning. She had no intention of dressing, saw no reason to do so. In fact, she saw no reason for living.

"Now, Kathleen honey, you gots to eat sompin, you lookin' bad. Please eat jest a little,'' Hannah pleaded with her, clearly concerned for the health of the wan girl staring into the fire.

"Why should I eat? I don't care if I look bad or not. What difference does it make?"

"You don't mean that, Kathleen Beauregard! You always cares how you looks, let me brush yo' hair for you, then you put on a pretty dress and go downstairs for a while. It'll make you feel better."

"I'm not eating and I'm definitely not going downstairs. Can't you get it through your head that all I want is to be left alone? Can't I even have that? Is it asking too much for you and everyone else to quit nagging me?" Her blue eyes never left the fireplace.

Tears cames to Hannah's eyes and she looked down at the young girl. "No, honey, that ain't askin' too much. I'se sorry, I'll leave you alone." Hannah raised the corner of her apron to wipe her eyes and sadly left the room. The tray beside Kathleen remained untouched.

The pattern continued and no one in the house could reach Kathleen. She refused to leave her room. She went days without ever changing out of her nightclothes. Louis and Abigail became more concerned with each passing day. The strain on Abigail became too much and she took to her bed for several days. Louis was clearly worried and silently questioned whether he had done the right thing in sending Dawson away. He was afraid his daughter might have a nervous breakdown or that her health would be permanently damaged from not eating properly. Time and again, he went to her room only to be turned away by her cold, blue eyes and her pleadings to be left alone.

"Cap'n Dawson, let me in." Sam knocked on the cabin door.

"Go away," Dawson shouted and threw an empty whiskey bottle at the door. It broke and shattered loudly. Sam shook his big head and sadly turned to go. Dawson had been in his cabin for days. He refused to leave and when Sam asked him where he wanted the *Diana Mine* to go, Dawson hollered, "Just stay on the river. I don't care where you go." The cold black eyes never looked up. He sat at his desk, the small cameo pin in his hand. He looked at it by the hour and when he fell tiredly to sleep at night, the cameo was clutched tightly in his palm. He never shaved, he didn't change clothes, he would hardly eat. The only thing he would do was drink. Sam never heard anything from him except when he ran out of whiskey. Then he would come to the cabin door, fling it open, and shout at the top of his lungs, "Sam, I'm out of whiskey! Bring me a bottle!"

"Cap'n Dawson, we ain't got no mo' whiskey, you drunk it all," Sam would respond as soon as he was called.

"*I want whiskey,*" Dawson's eyes glared at the big black man.

Sam would pull the *Diana Mine* into the next port and send a crewman out for more liquor. Knocking at Dawson's cabin door, Sam would hold out the bottle and say, "Cap'n Dawson, I thinks you should quit drinkin', you lookin' bad, you needs to eat sompin."

Dawson would glare at him, greedily grab the whiskey bottle, saying, "Mind your own business and leave me alone. I pay you to steer this boat, now get up there and do it," and the door would slam in his concerned friend's face. Sadly, Sam would return to the wheelhouse and steer the boat aimlessly up and down the Mississippi river.

"Sam," he heard Dawson calling to him one morning at dawn, "Sam, come down here." Sam hurried down the companionway, dreading the fact that he would have to tell Dawson they had run out of whiskey again. The door to the cabin was open when Sam got there and Dawson stood staring out the porthole. He turned when Sam came in and Sam saw immediately that Dawson was sober for the first time in weeks.

"Sam," Dawson said in an even voice, "where are we?"

"Cap'n Dawson, we is 'bout ten miles nawth of New Orleans."

"Good. Take her into port."

"Yes, suh, does you want to stop and buy mo' whiskey?"

"No, I'm going to get a ship in New Orleans, Sam. I've decided to go to Europe."

"But, Cap'n Dawson, what 'bout yo' plantation? What 'bout the boats?"

"What about them?" Dawson looked at him, bored.

"Wal, I means, what does you want me to do, I don't . . ."

"Sam, I don't care what you do. You're in charge of the boats. Operate them. Sell them. Sink them. I really don't give a damn."

Sam's big eyes looked hurt and Dawson regretted that he had been short with the gentle man. "Sam, I'm sorry. I'm not myself, I know I've been a monster. Please take care of the boats while I'm gone. You know as much about the business as I do. I trust you and your judgment. And Sam," Dawson paused and sighed, "when I get back, I promise I'll be better. I loved her, Sam, I really loved her."

"I know, Cap'n, I know."

Six weeks had passed and Kathleen still had not left her room. Hannah pushed the door open and saw her still lying in her big bed. She looked sad and miserable, but there was something else about her. Kathleen looked up at Hannah and the blue eyes held a pleading, frightened look. Hannah set the tray down and went to the bed. "What is it, honey?" Hannah knew she was different this morning.

Kathleen's hands flew to her face and she covered her eyes, "Oh, Hannah, Hannah," she sobbed. "I've got to talk to you, you've got to help me."

"Sho, honey," Hannah sat on the bed beside her, "I do

anything for my baby, you knows that. Now, look at me and tell me what to do.''

Kathleen's hands came away from her eyes and she looked at her mammy. ''Hannah, I . . . I . . . oh, what am I going to do?''

''Honey,'' Hannah was puzzled, ''I knows you miss Mistah Dawson sompin awful, but you is goin' to get better soon as . . .''

''No, Hannah, you don't understand, it's more than that. Hannah how do you . . . when can you tell . . . oh, Hannah, I think I'm pregnant,'' and Kathleen threw herself into the arms of the big black woman.

''Oh my Lawdy, honey,'' Hannah's big arms came around the frightened girl. ''Oh, my po' chile, my little gal.'' She rocked Kathleen while Kathleen clung to her and cried in desperation. Waiting until the girl's sobs subsided, Hannah held her gently and stroked her hair, saying, ''Hannah gonna help you, honey. Don't be afraid. Ol' Hannah gonna take care of my baby.''

At last, Kathleen quieted a little and pulled back. She wiped her eyes and said, ''Hannah, do you know . . . is there someone in the slaves' quarters who would . . . Hannah, help me, I've got to get rid of this baby, I can't have it, I can't.''

Hannah's dark eyes blazed and she grabbed Kathleen's shoulders and shook her hard, ''Don't you ever talk lak that! You ain't 'bout to do sompin lak that. Does you think I would allow it? It's dangerous. Ain't nobody gonna touch you, you hear me?''

''Yes,'' Kathleen answered sadly, ''but what am I going to do?''

''Honey, you jest quit that cryin'. I'll think of sompin. We gonna face this together. Now, the first thing you gots to do is start eatin' right. If you gonna have a baby, you gots to take care of yoself.''

''Hannah, will you help me run away? I can't face Mother

and Daddy, I just . . ."

"You jest stop that foolish talk. I tol' you, I is gonna help you and I is. Jest give me some time to think. Now, you eats all that breakfast."

"All right, I'll eat, but we must think of something soon."

"We will, honey, we will."

As Hannah left the room, Kathleen sat dutifully eating her morning meal. Hannah closed the door and her big body swayed against the wall. "It's my fault," she thought, tortured by the hidden secret in her breast. "I done ruined that po' chile's life. It's my fault, I shoulda tol her. I be responsible. I shoulda tol' her, spite of Mister Beauregard. That po' baby loves Mistah Dawson and Mistah Dawson loves her, too. Now what that po' baby gonna do, oh Lawd, what she gonna do?" She straightened at last and went sadly down the stairs, a new burden weighing down upon her.

Not an hour had passed before Hannah flung Kathleen's door open and came hurrying in. She slammed the door behind her and lumbered to the closet. "Honey, get yoself out of that bed. I'se found the answer. Now hurry and I'll get you dressed!"

"What is the answer you've found, Hannah?" Kathleen looked at her hopefully.

"There's a young doctor downstairs."

"Oh, Hannah, I don't want to see a doctor. That's the last thing I want. Do you want everyone to know?" she was exasperated.

"No, honey, I don't mean lak that. I mean Doctor Rembert Pitt's downstairs and he's got his nephew with him. He's handsome, nice, young and unmarried. He be jest right fo' you. He jest happens to be a doctor, too. Now come on, he be tall and blond and good-lookin'. He the answer, now hurry!"

Slowly Kathleen rose and dressed for lunch.

Nine

The chill December wind blew Doctor Hunter Alexander's thick blond hair around his high forehead. He stood, his hands folded in front of him, looking down at the two graves not yet eight months old. His slim body was motionless, his head bowed slightly. Having come alone to the tiny cemetery on the plantation that no longer belonged to him, he quietly said goodbye to the two people resting there, vowing silently to himself to find a cure for the dreaded disease of yellow fever that had taken them from him within a week of each other. Hunter would never be free of the sight of their suffering.

It had been a June they had all looked forward to, his last year of medical school. He would be returning to Vicksburg, a full-fledged doctor at the age of twenty-four. Proud of their brilliant son, William and Judy Alexander had looked forward to his return to the plantation and the evening of his arrival was a festive occasion for the family and scores of friends took part in the celebration. Doctor Rembert Pitt, Judy's brother and a respected physician in Natchez, came up for a visit to congratulate his nephew. He tried to persuade young Hunter to come to Natchez and be his partner.

"I need a young doctor, Hunter, my practice is much too big for one man. Why stay here and starve for years when I've a booming business already established just waiting for the skilled hands of a surgeon?"

"You're very kind, Uncle Rembert, but I plan to stay here in Vicksburg. I know it will take a few years to build up my practice, but I don't mind. I'm more interested in research than in treating sore throats. Besides, I've been gone from home a long time. I'm looking forward to spending some time with Mom and Dad again.''

That very evening, William Alexander complained of a minor headache and excused himself from the party early. When the guests had all departed and Judy had kissed her son goodnight, she went up to her bedroom to see how her husband was feeling.

''Hunter, Hunter,'' she flew down the stairs moments later. ''Come quick, your father's very ill!''

Hunter laid aside the book he was reading and ran up the stairs two at a time and into his parents' big bedroom. William Alexander lay unconscious on the bed where he had collapsed, his clothes still on. Rembert heard the commotion and came also to William's bedroom. Hunter was bending over his father when his uncle pushed him aside and took his place. He knew immediately that it was yellow fever. He also knew there was little he could do to help. By morning William Alexander was dead and Judy Alexander's raspy voice, sitting red-eyed at her husband's bedside, told Hunter she too had contacted the fever.

Hunter carried her to another bedroom and kept a vigil over her for days. Sitting by her bedside, he refused to sleep, catching only brief naps throughout the long hours of her agony. She lingered for a week, delirious, her words rasping in her throat. Near the end, she quieted a little and reached out her hand to Hunter.

''Son, I haven't long, I know. And I know you're a grown man, a doctor and all. To me you're still my little boy, my beautiful blond child. Promise me you'll go to Natchez with your uncle. He needs you, Hunter, and you'll need him.''

''I promise, Mother,'' Hunter whispered and kissed her hand. She was gone. They were both gone. He was aware of his uncle in the room, standing quietly, shaking his head. They were both doctors and were powerless to do anything.

They'd rubbed her wracked body, applied hot water bottles, given her brews of camphor, calomet, and peppermint. None of it had helped. Hunter Alexander's first case as a medical doctor had ended in the death of his patients.

Hunter's parents were not the only ones to die in the yellow fever epidemic of June 1855. Half the slaves on the plantation fell victim and Hunter and his uncle stood helplessly by and watched as they slumped to the floors of their quarters, writhing in pain and fear. The death toll was heavy as entire families were wiped out. City officials burned tar in hopes of cleaning the air as carts and wagons made their way to the cemetery with the many corpses. Long trenches were dug and the bodies dumped in; there was no times for proper burials. Business came to a standstill as worried citizens refused to venture from their homes.

Two weeks after it was over, Rembert boarded a riverboat to go back to Natchez. "I wish you were coming with me today, Hunter. I hate to leave you here alone."

"Uncle Rembert, I'm very tired, as I'm sure you must be. I've spent the last several years studying furiously, taking very little time to relax. Then this tragedy happens upon my homecoming. I want to rest, to spend the summer just doing nothing and deciding what to do about the plantation. I think I'll probably sell it, but I must have some time to think about it. I will come to Natchez sometime in the fall and hopefully by that time I will be more ready to undertake my tasks with renewed strength."

"I understand, boy. You deserve a rest; I just wish you'd come to Natchez to do it. I shan't press you, but I'll be waiting to welcome you when you are ready. Goodbye, Hunter."

"I'll see you soon, Uncle. Thanks for everything."

Hunter pulled his collar up around his neck and started from the cemetery. He walked back to the house looking fondly at the place where he had grown up. No longer his home, he had sold it to a family from St. Louis. They would be moving in next week and he would be long gone. It didn't matter to Hunter, the place was not the same without the two people who'd made its walls ring with laughter and sunshine. It looked dark and cold now and he was anxious to leave. The carriage waited for him in front of the house, his trunks and suitcases already loaded. Hunter climbed in the back and settled himself for the ride to the river after a brief stop at the big home next door where Mrs. Rachel Bost would be waiting for him to say goodbye. The carriage moved down the drive and Hunter glanced briefly over his shoulder at the big empty house, its curtains drawn, the windows dark. Dry-eyed, Hunter turned around, his delicate features pensive and thoughtful. He looked to the long, slender fingers resting in his lap and hoped God would make them healing hands. Nothing else in life mattered to him, he wanted to be the best doctor he could possibly be. And he wanted to find a cure for yellow fever.

When Hunter swung down from the carriage in front of Mrs. Bost's big home, she came hurrying down the walk to meet him. A big, cheerful woman, she looked sad today, but she tried to smile at Hunter. "My goodness, Hunter, you sure look the part of the handsome young doctor. You're going to be the best one in this whole state."

"Thanks, Mrs. Bost, I'll try to be. I'm going to miss you," he smiled at her.

Her arms came around the slender young man standing on her front walk, a pan of freshly baked cookies still in her hand. "Oh, Hunter, I promised myself I wouldn't cry, but I'm not so sure I can keep the promise. I watched you grow up and I always told Judy if Mister Bost and I could have had a son, I would have wanted him to be just like you."

Hunter embraced the tall woman in his arms and patted her back soothingly. "You've been like a second Mom to me, Mrs. Bost, you know that. I shall miss you very much and you know I'll come back to visit you when I can." He gently pulled away.

Mrs. Bost tried her best to smile, tears on her lashes. She picked up the corner of her apron and wiped at her eyes. "I'm sorry. Here, I baked you your favorite cookies to take with you." She handed him the pan.

"Thank you," Hunter smiled broadly and took the present. "I have to go now. Take care of yourself." He kissed her cheek and went back to his carriage. She watched him drive away and felt lonely. The entire Alexander family was now gone and she would miss them all.

When Hunter stepped down from the carriage in front of his uncle's house in Natchez on December 23rd, Rembert ran down the long walk to meet him, laughing and waving. Hunter's own face broke into a grin at the sight of the wiry little man, so much like his own mother, the merry eyes the same deep blue. Hunter embraced his uncle and willingly let the older man lead him into the big house that was to be his new home. A roaring fire warmed him and a glass of brandy shared with his uncle made Hunter feel welcome and comfortable.

"As soon as the holidays are over, you can get right to work, Hunter. I know you must be eager to get started."

"Thanks, Uncle, I am. I've rested and read all summer and autumn. I enjoyed my solitude for a while, but now I'm ready for activity and work. I'll make you a good partner."

"That you will, son. Natchez is lucky to have you. And I suspect we'll be having more patients than ever once the fine ladies of Natchez have seen the handsome young doctor."

Hunter smiled, "I'll be much too busy to pay any attention to the young ladies."

Hunter was alone in the laboratory upstairs over the office. He had been working since the first light of dawn, studying, researching, hunting solutions from thick medical volumes scattered around the room. He rubbed his brown eyes and closed them for a minute. He got up and moved to the window, his hands in his pockets.

"Hunter," his uncle called to him.

"In here, Uncle Rembert," Hunter turned to the door.

"You never stop, do you, boy? It's Saturday, Hunter, you could ease off a little now and then."

"I enjoy my work, you know that. I will stop and have a cup of coffee with you, though."

"I've a better idea. I have a luncheon invitation and I'd like you to come along. They're very nice people, very prominent, you'll enjoy meeting them."

"I don't think so, Uncle Rembert, I'm not finished here and I . . ."

"I insist. A blind doctor will do no one any good. You're going to put your eyes out with all that reading night and day. Now get dressed. We're to be there in half an hour."

"I guess it wouldn't hurt to get away for a while."

"That's the spirit. Louis Beauregard and his wife are charming people. You'll enjoy yourself."

Hunter sat in the drawing room of San Souci making polite conversation with Louis and Abigail and his uncle. The room was warm and cheery against the January cold and his host and hostess were gracious people. Hunter was glad he had reluctantly agreed to come along. His eyes roamed around the high-ceilinged room as the four talked. His gaze kept coming back to rest on the portrait of a young girl hanging over the mantel. If she were half as beautiful in person as the artist had painted her to be, she must be a stunner. Her hair was one shade lighter than his own and her eyes were too blue to be real. The small, perfect mouth was turned up into a hint of a smile and she looked as though she might burst into laughter at any second. She looked no more than fourteen or fifteen in the portrait and Hunter wondered to himself who the lovely child belonged to. Uncle Rembert had made no mention of the Beauregards having a daughter. Hunter stole a glance at Abigail Beauregard sitting across the room from him. There was a resemblance, though her eyes were not nearly as blue as those of the girl over the fireplace. Perhaps it was a portrait of her as a child. She had certainly been a lovely one, still attractive now, but she hadn't lived up to the promise she held as a young girl. His eyes left Abigail and went back to the portrait. He was still looking at it when the servants announced that lunch was ready.

Hunter gallantly offered his arm to Abigail and they preceded Uncle Rembert and Louis into the big dining room. Four place settings were laid out and, as soon as Hunter had pulled out a chair for Abigail and seated himself, soup was served. Louis had turned the conversation to wines and Hunter only half listened as he spooned the creamy soup from the gold-rimmed china bowl. He heard a commotion in the foyer just outside the dining room and turned his eyes to the door as did his table companions.

"Oh, Father, I'm sorry I'm late. I do hope our guests won't think me too rude." Kathleen smiled at Hunter and Rembert.

Abigail's spoon dropped noisily beside her bowl. Hunter rose as did his uncle. Louis was speechless. He remained in his chair, looking at Kathleen, completely shocked by her unexpected entrance. He glanced at his surprised wife, then back to Kathleen.

"Father, aren't you going to introduce me?" She was smiling at the tall, blond youth standing across the table.

"Certainly, darling," Louis rose at last, smiling and confused. He put an arm around his daughter's slim waist and said, "Kathleen, you know Doctor Pitt."

"So nice to see you, Doctor Pitt," she said graciously.

"This is Dr. Pitt's nephew, Doctor Hunter Alexander. He's come to Natchez to join his uncle in his medical practice.''

Kathleen slipped from her father's arm and walked around the table to where Hunter stood. She reached out her hand to him and smiled warmly into his eyes. "I knew Doctor Pitt had a nephew, he's so proud of you, he's talked about you often. But I shall have to scold him, he never told me you were handsome as well as brilliant. Sit back down. I'll just sit right here beside you, if you are agreeable."

"I'm very pleased to meet you, Kathleen," Hunter pulled up a chair for her and she took her place beside him. With the snap of Louis's fingers, a place setting was quickly added for Kathleen and a steaming bowl of soup was placed in front of her. She daintily dipped her spoon in the soup and her eyes continued looking at Hunter. The young man found his appetite had mysteriously disappeared and he had difficulty eating enough to avoid being rude. The beautiful girl sitting on his right had completely unnerved him and the way she kept watching him and smiling whenever he looked up made him pleasantly uncomfortable.

"Kathleen, I'm so glad to see you're feeling better," her father said, then turned to Hunter. "Our daughter has been under the weather for a few weeks, Doctor Alexander. However, she seems much better today."

"I feel fine, Father, please don't bore Doctor Alexander with my unimportant ailments. I'm full, aren't you, Doctor Alexander? Why don't we go into the library to have our coffee." She took his hand and he rose to his feet, looking at the others. "I know you'll excuse us," Kathleen smiled and led him from the room.

Hunter was more than willing to be led into the library by the beautiful young girl whose likeness hung over the fireplace in the drawing room. The artist should have thrown away his paints and brushes. The smiling young girl holding to his hand was much lovelier than her portrait and the eyes looking up at him were so blue they took his breath away.

"Sit here, Doctor Alexander," Kathleen invited and extended her hand to the couch by the window. She sat down and Hunter joined her.

When he was settled, Kathleen moved closer to him as he turned to look at her. "Miss Beauregard, I hate to sound like a doctor all the time, but you do look a little pale and your father said you haven't been feeling well. Are you sure you're all right?"

"I have been feeling rather poorly, Doctor Alexander. Perhaps you should feel my brow to see if I've a fever." She leaned closer to the young physician.

"Please call me Hunter and, if I may, I'll call you Kathleen." He raised slender fingers up to her forehead and laid his palm against her cool skin.

"I insist on you calling me Kathleen. Do I have a fever, Hunter?" She looked up at him wide-eyed.

Slowly, Hunter removed his hand from her forehead, but she took the hand before he could move it away. "You have no temperature, Kathleen," Hunter said and cleared his throat nervously.

"You have the most interesting hands, Hunter." she took the hand in both of hers and spread it out on her knee. "Your fingers are so long and delicate, you must be a very skillful surgeon." She traced each of his fingers with her own while Hunter sat stiffly, embarrassed and not quite sure how to get his hand away from her. It lay precariously on her skirt, neither resting there nor moving away.

"I don't know about that, Miss Beauregard, I haven't had a whole lot of practice yet."

"You're too modest, Hunter, and please, you promised to call me Kathleen," She released his hand at last and he quickly moved it to his own knee.

"That's a lovely piano," Hunter tried to make small talk. "Do you play?"

"Heavens no, but I'll bet you do. Why with those hands you must be a pianist, too."

"Not really, I play a little but I . . ."

"Come now, I insist you play something for me." Kathleen was on her feet, begging him to come to the instrument.

"Kathleen, I really don't think . . ."

"Please, Hunter, I want you to. I'll sit beside you." She smiled down at him with the dazzling blue eyes.

Slowly, Hunter rose to his feet and followed her to the piano. As soon as he was seated on the bench, she was beside him, her body pressed close enough to him so that he could feel the softness of her breast against his arm. Her nearness was intoxicating to the young doctor and he found her an inspiration. He had never played better and when she told him how talented he was, he was flattered and offered to play anything she wanted to hear.

"Hunter, it's time to go." The two young people were interrupted by Doctor Pitt. Hunter stopped playing at once and rose, offering his hand to Kathleen. She took it and together they walked to the doorway where Rembert was standing with Kathleen's father.

"Doctor Pitt, I'm sorry you have to be going, but Hunter has agreed to stay and visit and have dinner with me tonight, haven't you, Hunter?" Kathleen smiled up at him and he could hardly refuse.

"If you don't think you'll be needing me this afternoon, Uncle Rembert."

"No, Hunter, stay if you like," Doctor Pitt said, looking puzzled.

"We want you to stay, Doctor Alexander. You and Kathleen can become better acquainted." Louis was beaming, happy his distraught daughter had forgotten Dawson Blakely and was obviously taken with the tall, blond doctor. "You stay, too, if you'd like, Rembert."

"No, thanks, Louis. Well, Hunter, I'll see you later this evening," Rembert said, but Hunter and Kathleen were already walking back into the library looking only at each other.

By the end of the evening, Hunter was infatuated with the

beautiful, talkative Kathleen Beauregard. ''Kathleen, I must be going, it's after nine o'clock. I've probably overstayed my welcome with your parents.'' He rose from the couch and helped her to her feet.

''They are happy to have you here, Hunter, you're being silly. But if you must go, I'll only let you if you promise to come back tomorrow.'' She smiled and slipped her hand into his.

They were to the front doors and Hunter said, ''I'd be honored to call on you tomorrow, Kathleen. Goodnight, it's been a lovely day.'' She stepped outside behind him and closed the door. ''Kathleen, you shouldn't be out here in the cold. You haven't been feeling well. Please go back inside and I'll see you tomorrow.''

Kathleen stepped closer to him and put her hands on his brown lapels, ''I'll go back in on one condition, Hunter Alexander,'' she said softly.

Slowly Hunter raised his hands to her shoulders. ''Name it,'' he said smiling, his eyes dreamy.

''Kiss me goodnight,'' she whispered and stood on tiptoe.

He grinned at her and bent and kissed her cheek, but before he could move away, she maneuvered her mouth to his. Surprised but pleased, Hunter's arms went around her small waist and pulled her closer. ''You're the most frightening girl I've ever met,'' he laughed, then turned serious, ''and also the most irresistible,'' and he kissed her lips tenderly. ''I can't wait until tomorrow,'' he whispered and quickly went down the steps.

Doctor Hunter Alexander's new practice suffered the following week. Every spare minute of his time was spent at Sans Souci with Kathleen. Completely enchanted by her, he thought of little else, rushed to meet her as soon as the last patient left his office. After six of the most glorious nights Hunter had ever experienced in his young life, a carriage ride through the cold January night was the best of all. When he got to Sans Souci to pick her up, his heart leapt in his chest when she came running down the stairs to meet him, her bell-like dress tipping up to show her dainty feet. "Don't take your coat off, Hunter," she came to meet him, "Let's leave right away."

He smiled happily and agreed, "I've got a blanket in the buggy. Here, I'll help you with your coat."

It was snowing lightly outside and Louis came into the foyer, saying, "Don't you think you two young people should stay in on a night like this? Where could you possibly be going?"

"We're going for a buggy ride, Father," Kathleen laughed while Hunter looked nervous and said, "I hope you don't mind, Mister Beauregard."

"He doesn't mind. Let's go, Hunter." Kathleen kissed her father's cheek and he smiled approvingly.

Hunter and Kathleen laughed as they went down the walk together and Hunter helped her up into the one horse carriage. They set out, Hunter driving the buggy himself. Kathleen spread the blanket over their knees and scooted close to her escort.

When Hunter stopped the carriage on the deserted bluffs of the river, Kathleen willingly came into his arms. Hunter's eager mouth covered hers and he pulled her closer. "Kathleen," he murmured between kisses, "I know it's too soon to tell you, but I'm falling in love with you."

"Oh, Hunter, it's not too soon. I love you, too."

Hunter pulled back a little and looked at her, "Do you mean it? You really love me?" His soft brown eyes studied her face.

"Hunter, Hunter," she sighed and pulled his mouth down to hers again. His lips trembled as he kissed her and whispered, "Darling, I love you, I love you."

"Then let's get married, Hunter, darling," Kathleen whispered in his ear.

"Yes, yes," he agreed.

"Soon, Hunter, I don't want to wait. Let's get married next week."

"Kathleen Beauregard," he was shocked, "you know we can't do that. I haven't been calling on you long enough. Maybe next June."

"Hunter," she whispered and slowly covered his face with kisses, "don't you want me? I want you, why should we wait?" Her mouth came to his and kissed him in a way that made him weak with longing. "Aren't you as anxious as I?" she breathed against his mouth.

"Oh, Kathleen, darling, next week, tomorrow, tonight!"

Ten

Becky Stewart Jackson put a hand to her back. Six months pregnant, she felt tired and listless, but refused to miss the wedding of her best friend. She whispered to Ben, then made her way through the crowd to the back of the church. She knocked softly at the door and Abigail Beauregard let her in.

"Oh, Becky dear, do come in, but let me find you a chair. You look tired."

"Thanks, Mrs. Beauregard, I'm all right. I just had to come back and see Kathleen before the wedding begins."

"Certainly. She's dressing now, but she should be ready any minute."

Becky had hardly settled herself into a chair before Kathleen came out of the other room where Hannah and Julie Horne had helped her into her antique satin wedding gown.

"Kathleen," Becky rose, "you look absolutely beautiful!"

"Becky, I'm so happy you came back for a few minutes," Kathleen smiled to her friend and came to her. "Please, sit back down," she took Becky's slim hand and eased her back into her chair.

"Hi, Becky," Julie Horne said from behind Kathleen, fussing with the long train on her friend's gown. Julie, small and pretty in her bridesmaid dress of rose satin, was as nervous as the bride. "Kathleen," she scolded, "you are going to muss your dress if you don't be still."

"Dear," Abigail interrupted, "it's almost time, we're all going out now and take our places." She put her arms around her daughter, "Darling, I love you and I hope you'll be as happy as your father and I have always been." She kissed Kathleen's cheek, her eyes swimming with tears.

"Thanks, Mother, I'm sure I will be. I love you, now go on," Kathleen smiled at her mother. Abigail dabbed at her eyes with a lace handkerchief and left the room along with several other ladies.

"Well, here we are," Kathleen looked at her two best friends, now alone in the room, except for Hannah.

"Kathleen, I have to get back out there and take my place beside Ben. I just had to come and say I hope you'll be happy. I'm sorry I couldn't be in the wedding, but I'm afraid it wouldn't look proper," she smiled and patted her large stomach. "Kathleen, marriage is so wonderful. The nine months Ben and I have been married have been the best of my life. I hope it's like that for you." She rose and hugged Kathleen.

"Thanks, Becky. It will be. See you in a while." Becky slipped out of the room and made her way back to her husband.

"Gosh, Kathleen, I envy you. I love Caleb so much, but you were right. His father insists he finish college before we get married and that will be years and years." Julie looked forlorn.

"I'm sorry, Julie," Kathleen touched her shoulder. "Maybe he'll change his mind."

"Kathleen," Julie said in a voice hardly above a whisper, "I think Doctor Alexander is so handsome and nice and you are really fortunate, but . . . now please, don't get mad at me for asking, but . . ." Julie looked away from Kathleen's face.

"What, Julie?" Kathleen said in a steady voice.

Julie looked up shyly and whispered, "What about Dawson Blakely? I've never understood what happened, I thought you were so much in love with him. After he left, I came to see you, but they always told me you were not feeling

109

well, so I never got to talk to you about it. Then when you told me you were marrying Hunter Alexander, I was so . . . shocked, I thought . . ." Julie hung her head and didn't finish.

"Julie, I never loved that man; I love Hunter Alexander. Please don't ever mention it again."

"I'm sorry, Kathleen, I shouldn't have said . . . I'm so sorry."

"Don't be, you're my best friend. I know you've both wondered. But, Julie, there is really nothing to tell. Dawson and I decided not to get married, that we weren't in love. And then he went away. It's that simple. Then I met Hunter and we fell in love."

"I'm glad you're happy, Kathleen," Julie leaned over and kissed Kathleen's cheek. "I hear the music starting, I'd better step outside and be ready. I love you." She hurried out the door.

Kathleen stood alone in front of the free standing mirror and studied her reflection. Hannah came up behind her and put her hands to Kathleen's slim shoulders. "Honey, you sho does look pretty," she smiled at Kathleen in the mirror. The touch of her mammy's hands broke the dam of tears behind Kathleen's sad eyes and she turned and flung herself into the woman's arms.

"Oh, Hannah, I can't do it! I *don't* love Hunter, I love Dawson, only Dawson." Sobs wracked her slim body and she clung to Hannah.

"Oh, my precious," Hannah stroked her hair, "I'se so sorry, I knows you loves Mistah Dawson. Honey, he done gone away and you knows you gots to be married. That baby gonna be here fo' we knows it. I'm sorry, chile, but Doctor Hunter, he be a good man, he be good to my lamb. Now, here, you gots to stop cryin, it's nearly time." She wiped tears from the sad blue eyes and patted at Kathleen's face with a large powder puff.

"You're right, I must do it. There is no way out. I will do

it. I'll get over Dawson someday, won't I, Hannah?"

"Yes, precious, you'll get over him. You learn to love Doctor Hunter in time. Lots of girls marries gentlemens they don't loves and it work out fine. You gonna be all right, honey."

Organ music was starting in the church and a soft knock came on the door. "Now that be Mistah Beauregard, Honey, I'm gonna have to let him in, it be time. Try to smile a little, baby girl." Hannah went to the door.

Kathleen took a deep breath and turned to face the door. "Oh, you look so beautiful, Kathleen," Louis beamed at his daughter. Hunter is a lucky man indeed," he came to his little girl and kissed her. Kathleen threw her arms around her father and held him tightly and Louis felt a lump forming in his throat. "I love you so much, Kathleen, I want you to be very, very happy."

"Oh Father," she said against his cheek, "I, I'm . . ."

"What, my darling?" He held his breath.

"Nothing, Father. I love you, Daddy."

His brown eyes stung with tears and he kissed her and said, "Oh, my darling. My precious, precious daughter, I love you, too. I hope you know that I would never do anything to hurt you, I want you always to be happy. You know that, don't you?"

"Yes, Daddy, I know. Is it time?"

"Yes, darling, it is." She took her father's arm and they made their way to the very back of the church.

Hannah closed the door behind them, leaned against it and cried softly. "My po' baby, my po' Kathleen," she moaned to herself. "It's all my fault. I shoulda tol' that chile. Oh, Lawd, forgive me."

When Kathleen Diana Beauregard floated down the aisle of St. Mary's Cathedral, she was as beautiful a bride as Natchez had ever seen and a soft buzz went through the church as every pair of eyes turned to look at her. Pale and delicate in her antique satin gown, her blond hair tumbling loose under the white veil, her face was calm and serene. If there were more tears shining in the blue eyes than should have been there, no one thought anything of it. She was an innocent seventeen-year-old girl and this was her wedding day. She was moved by the solemn, happy occasion, just as she should have been.

Doctor Hunter Alexander stood beside his Uncle Rembert at the front of the big church. He watched his lovely bride come down the aisle to him and his heart swelled with pride. He stared unbelieving, worshiping the vision in white who would soon be his wife.

Kathleen looked at Hunter and something about his blond, delicate face was strong and reassuring. She smiled to him and silently vowed to be a good wife to him and never let him know she couldn't love him.

"I'll just step down to the ship's tavern, give you a few minutes." Hunter said after they entered their stateroom. He kissed her cheek and smiled at her.

"Thank you, Hunter," Kathleen watched him leave. The two were on board the "Princess" riverboat, bound for a honeymoon trip to New Orleans. Hunter had wanted to take her there, said he couldn't wait to show her all the sights. She had visited many times since the Howards, her mother's family, lived there, but she had always stayed in their home and was told she was too young to get out and see the city. Now she didn't care whether she saw it or not. But she didn't say that to Hunter. She quickly agreed it would be the perfect place. Hunter was excited and the very next day had booked passage on the "Princess" and made reservations for a week at the St. Charles Hotel. Kathleen assured him she was as excited as he about the trip and could hardly wait to get away.

Kathleen heard the door close behind him and Hunter's

footsteps falling away. Relieved to be alone for a few minutes, she went to the tiny porthole and looked out. She closed her eyes and remembered the night on Dawson's boat. "I can't go through with this; I thought I could, but I can't. It's so wrong. Hunter's a kind man, but I don't love him. I don't even know him, he's a stranger." She sighed and turned away from the porthole and slowly her hands went to her neck of her traveling suit. She looked at the white lace nightgown all laid out and ready for her to don and she cringed. Like a sleepwalker, she undressed and slowly pulled the nightgown over her head. She slid her feet into the white satin slippers and reached for the white satin negligee, slipping her arms inside. She buttoned the three tiny buttons at the neckline, its thick white satin covering her modestly almost to her chin, the long satin sleeves reaching to her knuckles.

She sat at the small vanity and slowly began brushing her long hair. She was stroking it absently, trying not to think, when his soft knock came at the cabin door. She jumped as if the noise had been deafening. She laid the brush down, looked at herself in the mirror, and tried to smile. She rose and turned the lamp down until the room was dimly lit, almost dark. She stood facing the door and softly said, "Come in, Hunter."

Hunter entered and closed and locked the door behind him. At first, he didn't move or speak, just stood drinking in her beauty. She wanted to shout at him to do something, to speak, to grab her, to get it over with. Slowly, Hunter crossed the room to her and put his hands on her trembling shoulders. "Darling, you are so beautiful and I love you so very much," he whispered and kissed her.

"I love you, too, Hunter." She put her arms around his neck. He kept kissing her softly, murmuring his deep love for her. Finally, his hands went to the three tiny buttons at her throat and he deftly undid them and pulled the negligee away. Kathleen took her arms from his neck and he pulled

113

the negligee down over her hands and tossed it on the bed. She watched as fire leapt into his dreamy brown eyes as he looked at her in the revealing lace nightgown. He pulled her to him and was kissing her again, but the kisses had changed, they were more demanding, more passionate. He was pressing her to him and he could feel the trembling of her small body against his own.

"Darling," he put his lips to her ear, "darling, I know you are nervous and tired. I want you to know that I can wait. I can wait for as long as you need, my dearest love."

"No," Kathleen said against his shoulder and tightened her arms around his neck. "No, Hunter, you don't have to wait," she closed her eyes.

"Oh, my darling, thank you," Hunter said hoarsely and kissed her again. "I want you Kathleen, more than you can imagine." His mouth dropped to her neck and he pressed burning kisses against her soft flesh.

"I want you too, darling," Kathleen whispered.

Hunter kept kissing her, the fire inside him growing by the second. She responded to his kisses as best she could and, by the time he picked her up and carried her to the bed, her trembling had stopped and she was as ready to accept him as she would ever be. She lay with her eyes closed and when they fluttered open for a moment, she caught a glimpse of her husband quickly undressing before he got into bed. She closed her eyes tightly again and felt his weight as he got in beside her.

"Darling," he whispered and she opened her eyes to look at him, "you make me so happy." He covered her mouth with his own. His fevered mouth forced her lips apart and he was kissing her expertly, like he had never kissed her before. He was tender, loving, understanding, and took her finally after slowly, patiently arousing her. She lay in his arms and gave herself to her husband. She gave him her mouth which he took with his ardent kisses, willing her to respond. She gave him her body, which he accepted with reverence, taking

114

it with his own with all the gentleness he possessed. But, the heart inside her still belonged to the dark-haired lover across the ocean. As did the baby growing daily inside her.

Hunter lay on his back, sleeping peacefully. Kathleen turned and looked at him. Her husband. His fair, handsome face was in repose, a slim arm slung over his head. He was not unattractive; thick blond hair fell over his forehead, his strong chest was covered with silky blond hair, and his arms were long and delicately muscled. Hunter Alexander, her husband, was very handsome. Why couldn't she love him? He was a good man, intelligent, decent, congenial, kind, and he loved her.

Kathleen turned her eyes away and looked up at the ceiling. Tears were starting as the memory of another man, another night flooded over her. The dark, hooded eyes, the warm, sensual mouth on hers, the strong arms encircling her, holding her so close she could hardly breathe. The brown, lean body against her own, taking all the love in her so there was none left for anyone else in the world.

It was growing light outside before Kathleen Beauregard Alexander was finally lulled to sleep by the pitch and roll of the old riverboat steaming down the Mississippi on its way to New Orleans.

Kathleen Beauregard Alexander learned more about her husband in the week they spent in New Orleans on their honeymoon. Hunter was proud of his new bride and delighted in showing her the sights of one of his favorite cities, a place where he had been on numerous occasions with his parents and later with college friends. After checking into their opulent suite at the St. Charles Hotel, he took her to the famous Antoines Restaurant for some of the best Oysters Rockefeller she had ever eaten. After dinner, he escorted her to the famed Theatre d'Orleans, built in 1819. After the theater, he took her to a old fancy gambling house operated by John Davis, the man who owned the theater where they had spent their first evening. Kathleen played roulette for the first time in her life and laughed giddily when she placed money on number seventeen and and saw the little white ball fall into the very slot. Scooping up her chips, she smiled at Hunter and said, "This *is* fun, isn't it?"

Hunter tightened his grip on her waist and laughed, "It is when you win, darling," and stood watching happily as she won time after time.

Back in their suite, Hunter ordered a late night snack for his hungry wife and watched Kathleen's childish glee at being served tempting foods from solid gold tableware. She drank champagne for the first time in her life and after two glasses had the giggles. Her husband smiled and carried her to their bed. He made love to her; she was more relaxed than the previous night on the riverboat and Hunter made a mental note to have champagne sent up every night. And perhaps every afternoon, as well. She giggled and willingly came to his arms when he undressed her and laid her in their big, soft bed. Hunter Alexander had never known such happiness in his life.

The week was spent in nothing but the pursuit of pleasure and Hunter was a never-ending source of information about where to go and what to do in New Orleans. They toured the city in the afternoons and he pointed out the landmarks: St. Patrick's Church, the St. Louis cathedral completed in 1851, with its central spire, the spidery design of wood and iron; the First Presbyterian Church built just two years before, impressive with its lofty spire. He showed her other hotels in the city, though none could compare with the one in which they stayed. There was the Exchange St. Louis which had been built in 1853 after it burned in 1841, the Creoles Hotel, designed by the famous French architect, J. E. D. de Pouilly, built in 1840. He told her that both hotels had cost at least a million dollars each to build and laughed when she gasped at the thought of such large sums of money.

Hunter took her to the horse races. Her favorite was the Metairie Course founded in 1853, a mecca for horsemen from all over the United States. Kathleen boasted to Hunter that her cousin, P. G. T. Beauregard was a member of the Jockey Club and when they mentioned her cousin's name, they were seated right away and treated like royalty. He showed her the other three race courses, but agreed Metairie was his favorite, too, and if they wanted to see more races, they would return to the finest track.

He took her for carriage rides and pointed out the architecture in French, Spanish, and American styles. Many of the homes in the French Quarter and the Garden District were characteristically embellished with fine wrought ironworks so loved in the Creole city. She thought them lovely and suggested perhaps when they built their home in Natchez they should have wrought ironworks around their balconies. He agreed readily.

Hunter took her to Jackson Square and explained it was once used as a military parade ground. He showed her the newly unveiled statue of Andrew Jackson, the hero of the Battle of New Orleans. He took her to the United States Mint on Esplanade Avenue which had been started in 1838. He bought coins for her; a double eagle, an eagle, a half eagle, and a three cent silver piece. He suggested he could take them to a jeweler and have them put on a bracelet for her, if she would like. She loved the idea.

Hunter took her to Boudro's tavern on Lake Ponchartrain and told her the food was so good that Boudro's had been the caterer for the famous Jenny Lind when she visited New Orleans in 1850. Kathleen relished the fine food and drank so much Bordeaux that Hunter had to carry her through the lobby to their hotel room. She told him she really could walk, though her legs were a little wobbly. He laughed and told her he was more than happy to carry her. Laughing still, he helped her undress and found her a warm and willing lover as she kissed him wildly between giggles.

The week was over much too soon for the ardent, young Hunter Alexander and he was sure his lovely wife felt the same way. "I wish this never had to end," Hunter whispered as they lay in their big bed on their last night in the magic city. They had been to the St. Charles Theater where Kathleen had raved about its grand interior and seemed more fascinated with the building than the ballet they saw. After the ballet, they had gone to the Odd Fellow Hall on Lafayette Street to a glittering ball and danced until the wee hours of the morning. Tired and happy, they returned to their suite around 2 A.M. and, as if by magic, five minutes later a waiter rolled a white-clothed table into their room, iced shrimp and red sauce and a big bottle of champagne on its top. They ate and drank until their eyelids drooped and Kathleen was quite giddy. Hunter happily swung her onto the bed and she let him undress her without raising a finger to help. She was finding that Hunter was surprising in many ways. Not only was her husband a talented young doctor, he was well-read and informed on almost every subject, he was an excellent tour guide, and he was also a very passionate man. He seemed to want her endlessly and she felt, under the circumstances, there was little she could do but comply. She was glad she had the champagne always at her elbow; it helped her relax, helped her forget, helped her respond to his constant embraces and desires.

"Did you hear me?" Hunter raised himself on an elbow to look at Kathleen. "I said, I wish this would never end. I wish we could just stay right here for the rest of our lives, just you and me."

"I do, too, Hunter," Kathleen tried to sound convincing. "It's been lovely, but you do have a practice, remember."

"You're right, of course. But for tonight, let's forget about everything. You've made me so happy, Kathleen. I love you, darling," Hunter kissed her lips.

"I'm happy, too, Hunter," she said and let him slip his arms around her.

"Oh my darling," he whispered, slowly kissing her neck and throat. "I want you more all the time, I cannot get enough of you." His hands gently caressed her body as the champagne made it easier for Kathleen Alexander once again to make love to the husband she liked but did not love.

Eleven

When the carriage pulled up to the corner of Davis and Brook Streets in London, and Dawson Blakely stepped out into the rain, he was met immediately by a liveried footman rushing to hold a big black umbrella over the head of the arriving guest. "Welcome to Claridge's, Mister Blakely," he smiled, "you will enjoy your stay with us, I'm sure."

"Thanks, I know I will," Dawson answered in a flat voice.

Inside the inn, the manager of the hotel greeted Dawson warmly and told him the establishment was happy he had picked Claridge's for his home away from America. "You will find, Mister Blakely, that you have made a very wise choice. This is the home of noblemen and royalty and we will cater to your every whim without delay."

"All I want is to be left alone," Dawson glared at the man.

"Fine, fine. We are very discreet and your presence here will be kept secret if you so desire."

"I don't care who knows I'm here. I just want to get to my rooms and then I want some whiskey sent up."

The manager snapped his fingers and a bellman appeared and bowed to Dawson. "Welcome to Claridge's," he smiled and led his guest to his suite of rooms. Dawson found the apartment to his liking. An oversized bed had been moved into the spacious bedroom just as he'd requested. Dawson headed for the bed the minute his baggage was stacked in the room.

"Shall I unpack for you, sir?" the bellman asked, graciously.

"Later. Just leave it." Dawson tipped the man generously. "There is something you can do for me, however."

"Anything, sir."

"Send me a bottle of bourbon, make it two."

"Certainly," the bellman bowed and left.

Dawson took off his gray cashmere cloak and tossed it on a chair. He went to the tall windows and looked out at the city. It was dark and gray, the rain coming down in a slow winter drizzle. Dawson sighed and unbuttoned his white ruffled shirt. The whiskey arrived and Dawson poured himself a tall glass of the hot amber liquid. He raised it to his lips and swallowed all of it, made a face, set the glass aside. He slowly undressed, picked up the bottle, and went to the bed. He climbed in among the soft pillows, poured himself another drink, and drank more slowly. "I am going to stay right here for the rest of the winter," he said to himself and went about the task of drinking himself into a stupor. By nightfall, which was almost impossible to determine because of the gray sky, Dawson Blakely was sound asleep while the rain outside continued to fall.

Dawson awoke with a headache and a bad taste in his mouth. He made a face and got out of bed, walked to the windows and looked out. It was raining again. Or still. He had been at Claridge's for over two weeks and in that time it had rained every day. Dawson had not been outside his apartment, had taken all his meals there, and had spent his time suspended somewhere between drunkeness and semi-sobriety. He was sober this morning and felt terrible. The weather did nothing to lift his sagging spirits. He knew it was time he snapped out of it, but found it almost impossible.

A knock on the door made Dawson reach for a robe before saying, "Come in."

"Good morning, sir," the waiter smiled and rolled in the

121

breakfast table. Two bottles of whiskey sat on the tray along with the coffee and orange juice. He walked to Dawson and handed him a bundle of letters. "Sir, your mail has arrived by first post."

Dawson hurriedly rifled through his mail. Brody, his overseer back in Natchez, had promised to forward everything to him, no matter how insignificant it was. Dawson saw nothing that interested him enough to even open the envelopes and he tossed the letters on the table unread. The *Natchez Courier* was rolled up in brown paper. This Dawson stripped away before unfolding the newspaper. It was dated January 14. Dawson glanced at the front page while he sipped black coffee from a china cup. He skimmed the articles, bored, and turned the page. On page three, he saw bold type that immediately made him sit up straight and pay attention. It read:

Kathleen Diana Beauregard, daughter of Louis and Abigail Beauregard of Natchez, became the bride of Doctor Hunter Alexander of Vicksburg, Mississippi, in a double ring ceremony today in St. Mary's Cathedral. The bride, lovely in an antique white satin gown, was attended by . . .

Dawson lowered the paper with a shaking hand. He sat stunned, unbelieving, for several minutes. Then a wry smile came to his lips as he thought, "What a fool I am. I've been gone for two months and already she's married. And I thought she loved me. She forgot about me the moment I was out of her sight."

"Ah, Kathleen," he said aloud, "here I've been so worried about what I did to you and already you're in love with another. I've spent my nights in drunken agony trying to erase you from my brain while you've been in the arms of another man, your husband. Old Louis was right, he knew you better than I did. I meant nothing to you. Well, thanks, darling, for releasing me. I will see if I can't forget about you as you forgot about me." Sadly, he fingered the cameo hanging from a gold chain around his neck which she had left behind on the boat the last night he saw her. He had sentimentally had it put on a chain so it could always be near his heart. His fingers closed over the memento as he started to rip it from his neck. He couldn't do it; his fingers refused to move. Dawson sighed and rose from his chair. He rang the bell beside his bed and when the eager bellman appeared, Dawson said, "I want a hot tub of soapy water and all my clothes pressed. I've decided to see a bit of London. And take the whiskey away, please. Send up some food, real food, I'm famished."

"Yes, sir," the man smiled and went about carrying out Dawson's orders.

Dawson strolled through the lobby that night dressed in his evening clothes. Completely sober, he entered the dining room and glanced around. A lovely place of lights, flowers, and music, the aristocracy of Britain filled the spacious room. Noble lords and ladies from their big estates in Scotland, England, and Wales all made Claridge's their home while in London for business or pleasure. Dukes and duchesses, earls, counts and countesses, all were engaged in taking their meals in an atmosphere of regal comfort. Generals, financiers, and wealthy Americans on holiday mixed and mingled or remained discreetly aloof as was their pleasure. Dawson was led to one of the most coveted tables in the narrow passage near the entrance. Here he could see and be seen, which was exactly what he wanted on this rainy Saturday.

Dawson ordered Beef Wellington and a bottle of wine. He relaxed in his chair and let his dark eyes slide around the room. The crowd was a mixture of young and old. His eyes didn't travel far before they fell on a beautiful girl. She was small and blonde and she was lovely. She sat with a middle-aged couple Dawson took to be her parents. She looked up at the exact instant Dawson's eyes reached her. She smiled at him. He held her look for a moment, studying the delicate

123

features and the honey blond hair falling casually around her slender shoulders. He did not smile at her. She looked to be no more than eighteen or nineteen and Dawson dismissed her without a second look. He was in no mood for a sweet young thing, he had had enough of that. He continued to look around the room, leaning back in his chair, completely relaxed and only half-interested. A few tables away, another beautiful woman sat finishing her dinner. She was alone. She took a sip of wine and her eyes met Dawson's. Her hair was as dark as his own and her eyes were green and wide-set. She wore a black satin gown that dropped low over her bosom, exposing ample, creamy flesh. On her small hands diamonds flashed and around her neck a diamond choker an inch wide caressed her. Dawson sat up and nodded to her over his wine glass. She was perfect. She was dark and seductive and she looked to be at least thirty years old. She was just what he wanted. She was nothing at all like Kathleen Beauregard.

Dawson ate slowly, enjoying his meal, looking from time to time at the attractive brunette still sitting at her table, though she had finished her meal by the time he was seated. He knew she was watching him, waiting for him to finish. Finally, he laid his napkin on the table and stood up. She rose at the same time and he walked to her table. She smiled warmly as he approached and when he took her arm she went out of the dining room with him. He still hadn't said a word to her, but his eyes spoke for him and hers answered. They walked through the lobby of the hotel and Dawson asked the liveried doorman to summon a carriage for them.

"I don't have my wrap," she spoke at last and looked up at him.

"You won't need one," Dawson smiled and handed her into the carriage. He climbed in beside her and told the driver to take them to Crockford's. "I hope you like to gamble. I'm Dawson Blakely, an American. I've been here two weeks and I've wasted all that time because I didn't know you." He smiled his lazy smile and looked at her with his hooded dark eyes.

"I love to gamble, Mister Blakely. I'm Victoria Hastings; I'm here on holiday from Scotland and I love Yanks." Dawson laughed and put his arm around the creamy bare shoulder of this bewitching woman and pulled her against him.

They gambled and drank champagne at Crockford's while the rain outside continued to fall. Victoria sat on a velvet stool at the roulette wheel. Dawson stood behind her and supplied her with chips to place on the numbers. She laughed and squealed when her number came up and happily scooped up the brightly colored chips the croupier pushed in front of her.

"It's getting late, Victoria," Dawson leaned down to whisper in her ear.

"You're absolutely right, Dawson, cash me in." She rose from the stool.

She willingly raised her lips to his in the back of the carriage on the way to Claridge's and, when they arrived, she accompanied him to his rooms with no pretense of shock. Dawson ordered more champagne, poured them both a drink, and came to where she stood looking out at the rain. They touched glasses briefly, then set the champagne aside. Dawson took her in his arms and was delighted to find her as eager and willing as he. When he raised his fingers to the top of her dress in back and slowly unfastened it, she made no move to stop him. Within minutes, they were in his bed and he was kissing her with wild abandon. His kisses were met with respondant surrender from Victoria Hastings.

"Oh, Dawson," she sighed and put her fingers into his thick black hair.

"Yes, darling," he breathed against her mouth. She moved her hands to his back and pulled him down to her, his chest crushing against her.

"Ouch," she said, pushing him away. Her fingers went to the cameo he wore around his neck. She jerked on the gold chain and said, "Darling, you must take this off, it's hurting

125

me."

Dawson's sultry eyes turned cold and his hand grabbed her fingers. "I never take this off. Let go." He loosened her grip on the chain while the muscle in his hard jaw twitched.

"I don't understand," she said, looking up at him with questioning green eyes. Dawson moved away from her, laid back on his pillow, his arms folded behind his head, silent. "Dawson, what's happened? What did I do?" She raised up to look at him.

"Nothing's happened," he answered coldly, "it's getting late. Get dressed. I'll take you to your room."

"But, but," she stammered, clutching the sheet to her chin. "I thought you, I mean . . ."

Dawson was already off the bed, dressing, not looking at her. Slowly, she rose and dressed, completely bewildered by the dark, brooding man standing at the window staring out at the empty street.

Victoria Hastings ran into Dawson Blakely again in the dining room, but he looked right through her and she never had any idea what had gone wrong.

Two days later, Dawson was in the lobby buying cigars when a tall red-haired lady checked into the hotel with an entourage of maids, butlers, secretaries, and at least twenty-five pieces of luggage. Dawson stood and watched, amused, as the staff of the hotel dropped everything to make her welcome. She wore a traveling suit of beige cashmere, her deep auburn hair pulled up on her head under a matching beige hat. She was tall and slender and she was beautiful. Well-preserved, she could have been any age between thirty and fifty. Dawson didn't care which. He was attracted to her immediately and set out to find out who she was. It wasn't easy. The staff at Claridge's was discreet above all else and when he asked the room clerk who the red-headed lady was, the man looked distressed and said, "Oh, I'm sorry, Mister

Blakely, I cannot disclose that information."

"That's no problem, I'll find out," Dawson smiled and walked away. He watched the entourage move through the grand lobby and, just when the lady reached the door, she turned and smiled at Dawson Blakely.

Dawson knew she would be looking for him that night in the dining room. So he didn't go down for dinner, he ate in his room. After his meal, he sat smoking a thin, brown cigar. Then the knock came at the door. A uniformed hotel employee held out a small silver tray. On the tray, a lavender note read, "I missed you at dinner. Since there is no bar in this hotel, I hope you'll join me for a drink in my apartment." It was signed "The Baroness Le Poyferre. Suite 613."

Dawson smiled, refolded the note, and drew on his waistcoat. He strolled to her apartment in no particular hurry. He was met by the baroness' maid who bowed and smiled to him. "Come in, Mister Blakely," she invited.

From another room, the baroness swept in to greet him, wearing a long beige satin dressing gown. Her auburn hair was falling loose around her shoulders and her brown eyes were warm and inviting. Dawson smiled at her, "Baroness," he bowed and walked to her.

"How very sweet of you to come, Mister Blakely. I find it very depressing to be alone when it's raining, don't you?"

"I do indeed, Baroness," he agreed and took a seat on the couch when she invited him to sit beside her.

The baroness poured champagne for them and handed him a glass, "Now tell me about yourself, Mister Blakely."

"Call me Dawson. I'm from America; I'm spending the winter in London. And I'm going to enjoy my stay much more than I thought. And you?"

"Dawson, I'm delighted you are an American. To tell you the truth, I am, too. I married the Baron Le Poyferre seven years ago after meeting him in New York. I moved to Paris with him and have lived there ever since. The baron passed away last spring; he was quite old, so it wasn't tragic. I remained in Paris, though I do get frightfully homesick at times. Having you here is like having a little bit of home. Well, now that we're acquainted, what shall we do this evening?'' She smiled a dazzling smile.

"I'll be happy to take you anywhere you'd like to go, Baroness."

"Darling, call me Susan, that's really my name," she laughed, "and to tell you the truth, Dawson, if it suits you, I believe I'd rather just spend a cozy evening right here."

"I can think of nothing I'd like better."

The baroness rose moments later and held out her hand to Dawson. "Come," she said sweetly. Dawson rose and took her hand. She led him to her big bedroom. All the curtains in the room were open, the rain pelting against the panes. A roaring fire burned brightly in the fireplace, the only light in the room. The baroness closed the double doors behind them and looked at Dawson seductively, "Do you find me too forward, Dawson?"

"I find you utterly charming," he assured her, smiling.

"Good," she said and slipped out of the beige dressing gown and walked to the bed.

Dawson pulled off his jacket and followed her. She was between the satin sheets and looking lovely, the red hair falling about her on the pillow. Dawson came to the bed and sat on its edge looking at her. He unbuttoned his white ruffled shirt, took the studs from his cuffs, and took it off. He leaned close to the baroness and put his fingers to the cameo he wore around his neck. "You see this, Baroness?" he said evenly.

"Yes, darling, why?"

"I never take it off, never." He looked at her unsmiling.

She smiled and looked into his dark eyes, "Well, darling, I think you should leave something on."

Dawson smiled his lazy smile and pulled her into his arms. The cameo stayed around his neck all night and he got no complaints from the baroness.

"I'm sick and tired of this miserable rain," Dawson said two weeks later when he woke at 10 A.M. to find the baroness already drinking her morning coffee.

"Well, I like that," she pouted. "I thought we had been having a wonderful time, Dawson." She looked at him, hurt.

"Oh, my dear, I didn't mean it that way." Dawson took the coffee cup from her, took a drink, and set it aside. "Come here," he whispered and pulled her to him. She smiled and gladly laid her head on his chest. "We have had a lovely time, darling." He kissed the thick auburn hair. "It's just that I need to see the sun; the constant rain in London is beginning to get on my nerves."

"Dawson," she said, stroking the thick dark hair of his chest, "do you have to get back to America soon?"

"I don't ever have to get back."

"Then I've a marvelous idea." She sat up in bed. "I have a charming little villa in Monte Carlo, why don't we go down there for a few days?"

"You have a villa in Monte Carlo? What are we doing in dreary old London? Start packing, love." He smiled and kissed her.

A week later, Dawson felt his spirits lift when the two pulled up in front of a huge villa in the south of France. The sun was shining brightly and the palm trees swayed in the gentle breezes blowing in off the blue Mediterranean. House servants came to the carriage to greet the baroness and her new guest. Dawson smiled and said, "I may just spend the rest of my life right here," and followed his hostess up the steps to the villa.

The little villa was a thirty-two room mansion set high on a hill reached by a winding hairpin road from below. The view was breathtaking; the villa's white balconies overlooked a panoramic expanse of the principality of Monte Carlo with all its twinkling lights and the Mediterranean Sea beyond. The days were warm and lazy and Dawson's swarthy body grew darker still as he lay basking in the welcome sun day after glorious day while the baroness rubbed sweet scented oil on his long limbs and offered him sips of exotic drinks through colored straws.

Dawson was making her life very pleasant and it showed. She grew more lovely with each passing day, and though she never let him know, she was falling head over heels in love with her young, amorous lover. Dawson never thought of love; it was the last thing on his mind. He thought only of pleasure and that consisted of lying in the hot sun, drinking the cooling drinks she held out to him, gambling in the casino after the sun had gone down, and making love to the luscious redhead in the wee hours of the morning. He had no ambition to do anything else. He was as content as he could ever hope to be, never giving a thought to tomorrow.

Dawson lay on his back in the sun. It was almost three in the afternoon and he had been sunning himself since noon. A bottle of wine was cooling in a silver bucket within his reach. He was pleasantly tipsy and relaxed from the warmth on his body. The fair-skinned baroness wouldn't dream of laying out with him. She would have burned in just a few minutes. She was in and out of the villa to check on him, but knew better than to stay out for any length of time.

"Darling," she said softly and Dawson opened his eyes. "Why don't you come in for a while?" She grinned. She was standing over him in a white satin robe tied loosely at her waist.

"Why?" Dawson teased, "I like it out here."

"Darling, you know we have to go to a party tonight. It's a dinner party and I promised we would be there."

"Dear, the party doesn't start until 7:30. It's only three

o'clock, so what's the hurry?" He closed his eyes again.

The baroness dropped down beside Dawson on the beach blanket and put her hand on his muscled, brown chest, "I know, darling, but I would like to spend a little time with you before we go."

Dawson opened lazy, hooded eyes and smiled at her. Without a word, he reached up and put his hand to the nape of her neck and pulled her down to him. He kissed her and whispered, "Just what did you have in mind?"

"Oh, you," she said and tried to pull away, but he stopped her.

"I was joking, darling," and he pulled her down onto her back. He leaned up on an elbow and looked down at her. "Have you any idea how lovely you are in the sun?" He bent and kissed her again.

"Dawson, you're the most exciting man I've ever met," and her arms came around his neck. "We've been here for six months and it seems like only a few days."

"Yes, darling," he said and untied the sash at her waist.

"Dawson," she pleaded, but he covered her mouth with his, quieting her. She found it impossible to resist him and put up no struggle when he pulled the robe away from her creamy body. "Darling, darling," she sighed as he slowly caressed the satiny skin. "I love you," she murmured against his shoulder, but he only said, "Ummm," and stroked her again.

Two hours later they awoke and the baroness was already miserably sunburned. "Oh, Dawson, look at me," she cried.

"Oh, my sweet," he sympathized and, picking her up, he took her inside. He laid her on the big bed and her red skin against the white counterpane suddenly struck him as funny. He couldn't help himself; he started laughing.

"Dawson Blakely, this isn't a joke!" she shrieked at him.

He sat down beside her and pinned down the flailing arms that were trying to hit him. "I'm sorry, darling, it's just that

131

you look like a giant lobster and I find it irresistibly amusing."

"I'm glad you're amused," she sniffed, "but what about the party? Have you forgotten we are due at a dinner party at 7:30?"

"You'd best forget the party, love, you won't be able to wear any clothes."

"I'm well aware of that, thank you very much."

"Well, it isn't so tragic, we'll just stay right here and have dinner in our room. Then I'll try to rub some of the soreness from your lovely red body. How does that sound?"

"Dawson Blakely, the party is in our honor. We can't stay away!"

"You're being foolish. You can't go and you know it."

"Yes, I know, but you will have to go. You must go without me."

"I don't want to, I want to stay here with you." He grinned and kissed her red nose.

"Stop it, Dawson, you are going, do you hear me?"

"As you wish, madam!"

Twelve

When Doctor and Mrs. Hunter Alexander returned to Natchez after their week-long honeymoon in New Orleans, Louis and Abigail joyfully ran down the steps of Sans Souci to welcome the young couple home.

"Darling, darling," Louis called to his daughter. He swept her off her feet, turning round and round, laughing happily.

"Oh, Father, I'm so glad to be home," she said as she kissed his cheek.

Kathleen's new husband stood awkwardly watching this affectionate scene and smiled, but deep inside he realized that he was not to have his lovely bride all to himself anymore. A small twinge of jealousy lay just below the surface of his calm exterior. He knew she was just a young girl and loved her parents, was especially close to her father, but he secretly wished they were going to a home of their own where he could have her more to himself. For now, he would have to be contented with sharing her, but as soon as he could get her to agree, he wanted them to look for a place of their own.

"Hunter," Louis released his daughter at last and shook hands with the tall, blond doctor. "So glad to have you two back, we missed you terribly."

"Thanks, Mister Beauregard, it's nice to be home," Hunter smiled, while Kathleen walked up the steps with her arm around her mother.

"Come on in, son. I'll have Daniel unload the carriage.

How was New Orleans?''

"We had a wonderful time, Mister Beauregard, wonderful.''

"Ah, that's nice, but I'm glad you're here, safe and sound. Kathleen has never been away from home that long before, you know, and we have been lost without her.''

"I'm sure you have," Hunter followed his father-in-law into the big house.

At dinner that night, Kathleen was lively and entertained the family with her stories of all the things they did and the places they saw on their honeymoon. She seemed in high spirits and had her parents and her husband laughing through much of the meal. After coffee in the library, she asked Hunter to play the piano for them and he good naturedly complied. It all seemed the picture of contentment and happiness to young Doctor Alexander as he played soft, sentimental songs and looked across the room at his lovely young wife. It was still hard to believe she belonged to him, loved him.

When Louis began to yawn and nod in his chair, Hunter was secretly glad. "I'm afraid I must go to bed," Louis said and rose from his chair. "Dear," he extended his hand to his wife, "coming?"

"Yes, Louis," she took her husband's hand. "So glad you are home," she smiled to the two young people.

"Goodnight, Angel," Louis said, kissing Kathleen. "Night, Hunter. See you two in the morning.''

Hunter had risen from the piano and stood saying goodnight, smiling happily. After the Beauregards left the room, he smiled at Kathleen and said, "Darling, you must be tired from the trip. Shall we go up, too?"

"Oh, Hunter, why don't you play some more. It's so lovely, I like to sit and listen.''

Hunter once again played quietly, looking down at his hands. After several minutes, he looked back at his wife. She was asleep in her chair. Hunter grinned, rose, and walked to her.

"Darling," he whispered, "it's time to go up."

Her eyes fluttered open and she looked up at him, "I'm sorry, Hunter, I guess I was more tired than I thought."

"I know, darling, it's alright. Let me carry you." He bent and easily picked her up and carried her to their room.

When Kathleen came out of the dressing room in her nightgown, Hunter lay in their bed, the white sheet pulled up around his waist. She blew out the lamp and got in beside him. No sooner had she lay down than her husband leaned over her. "Darling," he whispered and kissed her, moving closer to her.

"Hunter, please," she said, "I'm so tired and sleepy, try to understand."

Hunter smiled at her and said, "I do understand, love. Go to sleep. I love you, Kathleen Alexander."

"I love you, too," she said and turned over on her side and shut her eyes.

Hunter laid back on his pillow, a slim arm slung up over his forehead. The beautiful girl sleeping beside him kept him awake. It was a long time before sleep came to her ardent lover, Hunter Alexander.

After a few hours of sleep, Hunter awoke at sunrise while Kathleen was still sound asleep. He looked down at her and felt his heart speed up. She was so very lovely, her face so angelic in sleep. Affection and passion mingled in him and he bent over her face and kissed her. She didn't waken so he continued to kiss her softly until she finally opened her eyes. "Good morning, sweetheart," he smiled down at her and caressed the silky blond hair falling around her face.

"Good morning, Hunter," she said. "What time is it?"

"It's early, darling."

"Then why are you awake?"

"I don't know, I guess sleeping with you is still so new to me it wakes me up." He brought his arm around her waist.

"Well, I'm getting up," she said and started to rise.

The arm around her waist tightened and he pleaded, "Kathleen, darling, I said it's early. We don't have to get out of bed yet. No one else is awake, I'm sure."

"But, Hunter, we're both wide awake now, so why lie in bed?"

"Kathleen, you were tired last night. You aren't tired now, are you?" he smiled at her.

"No, I'm not, but . . ."

"Good," he said and kissed her.

"But, Hunter, it's . . ."

"Please, darling," he whispered, "I want you so much. Love me, please."

"Well, really I don't think . . ."

"Don't think, darling. Forget everything but you and me," and he kissed her throat, then put his lips to her ear. "I love you so much, you're so lovely." Kathleen reluctantly gave in.

Doctor Hunter Alexander returned to his heavy practice of medicine and spent long hours away from Sans Souci tending his patients. When he was in his office at the home of his Uncle Rembert, he was able to forget about Kathleen completely, throwing himself into the work he loved so much, but when the day started drawing to a close, he found himself eagerly anticipating going home to his beautiful, new wife. He found it disconcerting that she was always in the drawing room or in the library with her parents when he arrived home after a long day at his office. He could never greet her the way he wanted to, had to content himself with the cold little kisses she placed on his cheek in front of her parents. He longed to come home and find her up in their room so he could rush up and greet her properly, in private. It never happened. She was always with them and they always ate dinner together at night. Hunter never had dinner alone with his wife, as he would have liked. He never complained and he was as gracious and charming as possible, but he would have preferred more time alone with Kathleen.

Kathleen sat at the vanity brushing her long blond hair. Hunter walked to her and kissed her on the top of her head, smiled at her in the mirror and said, "Come to bed, darling, your hair is pretty enough."

"Hunter, I, well . . ."

"What is it, Kathleen?" Hunter straightened and studied her face.

"Nothing, Hunter," she said and slowly rose from the dresser.

"Good," he smiled and slipped his arms around her. "I missed you today," he whispered, "I miss you everyday. I wish we could go away together again, don't you?"

"Sure," she answered and stepped out of his embrace. She walked to the bed and he followed eagerly. When she lay down, Hunter hurriedly undressed and blew out the lamp. He got into bed beside her and immediately put his arms around her and moved close to her.

"I love you, my darling," he said and bent to kiss her lips.

"Oh, Hunter, is that all you ever think about?" she said, irritated.

Stung by her harsh words, Hunter released her and said, "No, it isn't all I ever think about, but I love you, Kathleen, and I want you."

"Well, Hunter, I'm quite tired tonight. I just want to go to sleep."

"All right, Kathleen." He moved to his side of the bed. Hunter lay awake in the dark, longing to make love to his wife and confused by the coolness she'd shown him since they returned to Sans Souci. He wanted her to be like she had been on their honeymoon in New Orleans. She was so loving then; they had had such a good time, had laughed so much, and she had willingly come to his arms whenever he wanted her. She was different then and he had been so happy. Maybe it was all the champagne they had drunk. Perhaps it was because she was more relaxed when they were in a hotel alone. With his practice growing heavier by the day, there wasn't any hope of taking her on a trip, but he could have champagne on hand. Hunter fell asleep making a mental note to offer her a drink before bedtime tomorrow night to see if that would make things different. Hunter fell asleep smiling with anticipation.

When Hunter came home from his office the next evening, he had some news for Kathleen. Becky Stewart Jackson had given birth to a healthy baby boy.

Kathleen looked strange for a second, then smiled and said, "It's wonderful, but it came early, didn't it? What did she have, Hunter."

"A little boy, barely six pounds, but healthy and cute and Becky is doing fine."

"Good, I'll go see her tomorrow. Did your uncle deliver it?"

"Yes. I assisted him because he was worried about Becky. You know she isn't a strong girl, but luckily she came through it all right. And she's so happy, almost as happy as Ben."

Unexpectedly, Kathleen hugged Hunter and whispered, "Let's go upstairs. I've got a surprise for you."

"What, darling?" he put his arm around her waist as they walked up the steps.

"I'll tell you in bed," and she smiled up at him.

While Kathleen undressed for bed, her heart pounded in her chest. She dreaded telling Hunter she was pregnant, felt he would be able to look inside her and know her guilty secret. She closed her eyes tightly and shook her head. She had to convince Hunter she was pregnant with his child and was overjoyed to be. It was not an easy task and she wished there

138

was something she could do to make it less difficult. When she walked out of their dressing room, Hunter stood smiling near the bed. On the table by the bed sat a bucket with a bottle of champagne cooling in it. He held up two glasses and said, "Darling, may I pour you a glass of champagne?" It was just what she needed.

"Oh, Hunter, yes, I'd love a glass. How sweet of you to think of it."

Hunter poured for them and touched his glass to hers. She drank hers hastily and, when the glass was empty, she held it out for more. Delighted, Hunter smiled and poured her another glass and another. The bubbly wine worked and by the time her husband put his arms around her and said, "Let's go to bed," she was ready.

Kathleen laid back on the pillows. Hunter smiled and said, "I have a surprise for you too, darling. I had the coins we got at the mint made into a bracelet. I picked it up today. Would you like to see it now?"

"Hunter, you know I want to, where is it?"

Hunter went to his jacket, thrown over a chair, and took the bracelet out of his pocket. He returned to the bed, grinning like a little boy. He held it out to her and she took it eagerly from him. "It's lovely, thank you, darling, thank you," and put her arms around his neck.

"I'm glad you like it, sweetheart, now tell me your surprise."

"Put my beautiful bracelet on my wrist, then I will," she smiled at him.

Pleased with her obvious pleasure, Hunter beamed and fastened the bracelet around her slim wrist. She held up her hand and admired it, then put her hands on her husband's shoulders while he sat on the edge of the bed beside her. "Hunter," she looked into his dreamy brown eyes, "I think I'm going to have a baby."

Hunter pulled her to him and embraced her, saying, "Oh, darling, that's wonderful. I'm delighted. The thought of you

139

having my child makes me unbelievably happy." He pulled back to look at her face, "Do you want to go see Uncle Rembert tomorrow and find out for sure?"

"No," she almost shouted. "No, Hunter. Doctor Jennings has been my doctor since childhood; I want to go to him. You understand, don't you?" Her fingers caressed the curly blond hair at the back of his neck.

Hunter took her hand from his neck, kissed the soft palm, "Certainly, my love. You go see Doctor Jennings. Kathleen, I'm so happy!"

"I am too, Hunter. I'm so glad you are. I was afraid you might not, I mean I thought you would think, I . . ."

"I think it's wonderful and I think *you're* wonderful. I love you so very much, my darling," he said and kissed her. "Are you sure you wouldn't like another glass of champagne? You won't be able to have it very often now that you're pregnant."

"No more champagne, I just want you to hold me."

"Oh, honey," he sighed, undressed and got into bed, and kissed the wrist with the gold coin bracelet. "You want me to take this off?" he whispered.

"Never," she laughed and pulled him to her.

Thirteen

When Kathleen told her parents she was expecting a baby, they both hugged her happily and congratulated Hunter. Hunter smiled broadly and said he couldn't be happier. Dinner that night was a festive occasion and Louis made toasts to the young couple and talked of the happy day when his first grandchild would arrive. "I'm sure he'll be a doctor, just like you, Hunter," Louis smiled and lifted his glass.

"Only if he wants to be," Hunter said evenly.

"Kathleen, why are you so quiet?" her father asked her. "This is a celebration."

"I'm sorry, Father. I'm just a little tired, I guess." She tried to smile.

"Hunter, should she already be growing tired? Do you suppose everything is all right?" His father-in-law was concerned.

"I'm sure she's fine, Mister Beauregard. I'm taking her to Doctor Jennings in the morning. He will take good care of her."

"Louis, don't start worrying already," his wife scolded him.

"I can't help it. Hunter, you're a doctor. Can't you examine her, be sure she's . . ."

Suddenly, Kathleen pushed back from the table so rapidly her chair fell over. "You're all talking about me like I'm not here. I'm just going to have a baby. I'm not an invalid and I'm not deaf either! Quit making such a fuss over me! Can't you leave me alone!" and she ran out of the room in tears.

She ran up the stairs still screaming, "Leave me alone, leave me alone!"

The three looked at each other in silence for a moment. Hunter and Louis rose from the table at the same time.

"I'm going up to her," her father said.

Calmly, Hunter said, "No, Mister Beauregard. I'm her husband, I'll go to her," and he turned and left the room.

"But, I . . ." Louis slowly sank back into his chair, worrying about the strange behavior of his pregnant daughter.

"Kathleen, may I come in?" Hunter said softly through the door.

"Go away and let me rest!" she shouted, crying loudly.

Hunter sighed and pushed the door open. She was laying across the bed sobbing. He walked to her and sat down beside her. "Kathleen, it's all right. Cry all you want." He tentatively put a hand on her shaking shoulder. "You're just a little frightened, darling, and I understand. I'll take care of you, Kathleen. You're a strong, healthy girl and you'll get along fine." He began slowly stroking her back. "You're going to have a baby, darling, and that's the most wonderful thing in the world. I'll do everything I can to help you; you can count on me, Kathleen. I love you, I'll always be at your side. You are very precious to me and so is our baby."

Her sobs were subsiding and slowly she turned her face to look up at him. He smiled and wiped the tears from her eyes. She didn't struggle when he pulled her up into his arms. She rested her head on his chest and let him push her hair from her face and caress her while he whispered softly, "Everything's all right, sweetheart." When he calmly asked, "Do you feel better now?" she nodded her head yes, her eyelids drooping sleepily. Hunter smiled and kissed her forehead, "Good girl. Now I want you to get some rest. Do you think you can sleep?"

"Yes, Hunter, thank you."

"Shall I go downstairs?"

"No, stay with me please. I don't want to be alone."

"Then I'll get your nightgown, darling, and help you undress."

By the end of March, Kathleen's condition was apparent as her waist thickened and her cheeks grew fuller. Her mood swings upset everyone in the household, especially her young husband. One day she would be happy and sing loudly as she opened box after box of new baby clothes she'd bought. The next day she would be depressed and spend long hours in her room, staring out the window, refusing to talk to anyone.

It was evening and Kathleen had not come down for dinner. Hunter hurried through his meal so he could go up to his wife. When he walked into the bedroom, she stood at the window, pensive and uncommunicative. The tray Hannah had brought her sat untouched on a table. She didn't turn around when Hunter came in. Slowly, he walked to her and said, "Darling, are you all right?"

"I'm just fine," she answered without turning.

"Can't you eat some dinner?"

"I'm not hungry. Besides, I'm fat and ugly enough!"

"Oh, honey," he smiled and stepped up behind her, slipping his arms around her thickening waist. "I think you're lovely," he kissed her neck.

Kathleen brushed his hands away and whirled around, "Hunter, for heaven's sake, will you leave me alone! I'm sick and I don't want you pawing me all the time. You're driving me crazy. I want to be left alone, can't you understand that? Can't you please move to another room for a while? I'm not sleeping well, you know that. You're always hugging me in your sleep and I just can't stand it anymore! Do you want to hurt the baby? I need to sleep alone until the baby comes. You just don't know what it's like being pregnant." She was crying now and she stormed across the room

143

to the bed. She sat down and put her face in her hands.

Stunned and hurt, Hunter stood and watched her. Finally, he said, "Certainly, darling. I understand. I will move down the hall so you can sleep better. I haven't meant to upset you, Kathleen. I know you are going through a difficult time, even though it's impossible for me to know what it's like being pregnant. I don't want to make it harder. I'll leave now and you get some rest. I'll see you tomorrow," and he walked from the room and closed the door.

After he left, Kathleen threw herself across the bed and cried herself to sleep, longing for Dawson Blakely, her child's father, to hold her all through the night and every night. Hunter took an empty bedroom at the end of the hall and was not invited back into Kathleen's room. He was unhappy with the new arrangement, but his wife became more even-tempered and relaxed. She was kinder to him when he was in her presence because she knew at bedtime she could go to her room alone and not be bothered by her overly affectionate husband.

Hunter spent more and more time reading and studying. Each night he brought home more medical books and his room was slowly turning into his own personal library. He went there as soon as dinner was finished and worked far into the night. He missed the company of his wife, but told himself he must be patient, that she would surely be different after the baby arrived. In the meantime he busied himself with his research, desperately searching for the elusive cure for the yellow fever that had taken his beloved parents from him. Night after night, he worked in his room and, when finally he was so tired he could no longer hold his eyes open, he fell into bed alone and went quickly to sleep.

"I'm so miserable, Mother," Kathleen fanned herself and sighed.

"I know, dear, this heat is terrible. I think it's the hottest

144

August I ever remember and your condition makes it worse. I can't understand why you're so large. You can't be more than seven months, but you look like you are going to have the baby any day," Abigail said.

Kathleen coughed nervously and said, "Maybe it's twins, I don't know. But if you'll excuse me, I think I'll go up and lie down for a while before Hunter and Father come home for dinner."

"Yes, Kathleen, I think you should, you look so tired. Is there anything I can get you?"

"Thanks, no, Mother. I'm all right, I'll see you at dinner."

"Fine, dear."

"Hunter, why don't you go up and tell Kathleen it's time for dinner," Abigail said to him that evening. "She's been lying down all afternoon, she should be rested."

"That's good. I'll go get her." Hunter rose and went up the stairs. He knocked softly at her door and she immediately said, "Come in."

She was on the bed and her face looked white and drawn. Concern leapt into Hunter's eyes when he saw her and he rushed to the bed. "Kathleen, are you alright?"

"Hunter, I . . . oh, Hunter. I don't feel good, I'm having pains and I . . ." she clutched her stomach in obvious pain.

"Sweetheart, I'm going for Doctor Jennings right away. I'll send Hannah up to you and I'll be back with the doctor as soon as I can."

"No, Hunter, don't . . . I'm all right, really. I just don't feel like coming down for dinner. I'll probably feel better in the morning."

"Kathleen," he sat on the bed beside her, "how long have you been having these pains?"

"All afternoon," she admitted.

"Have they started coming regularly?"

145

"Yes, yes," she said and bit her lip.

"Darling, you're going into labor, I'm getting the doctor. I'll be back as quickly as possible."

Hunter hurried back down the stairs and summoned Hannah. Louis and Abigail heard the commotion and came into the hall. "What is it, Hunter? Is Kathleen ill?" Louis Beauregard asked him.

"No, she's fine, but she's going into labor. I'm going for the doctor."

"But, Hunter, she can't be. It's only been seven months. Oh, no," Abigail looked at him, frightened.

"Please don't worry, Mrs. Beauregard. She'll be fine. Now I must go," and Hunter left Sans Souci in a rush.

The worried parents hurried up the stairs to their daughter's room. "Oh, darling, how are you?" her father asked.

"I'm fine, please don't worry," she tried to smile at them.

"Now, Mistah Beauregard, you gots to get out of here," Hannah told them. "Doctor Hunter tol' me to get her ready, she gonna have this baby soon."

"No, she can't, it's too early, she . . . oh, Kathleen . . ." Abigail looked at her daughter.

"Come, dear," Louis led his wife from the room. "There, there, everything is going to be fine." He led her carefully back downstairs.

"Hannah, I'm so frightened," Kathleen started crying after they left. "And the whole world will know this baby came too soon. I just can't have it yet."

"Honey, babies comes early sometimes. Now don't you go thinkin' 'bout that now."

"I want Dawson. Oh, Dawson, Dawson." Kathleen buried her face in her hands and cried.

"Now Miz Kathleen, you stop that. You has a good husband and Doctor Hunter gonna be the father of this chile. Mister Dawson is gone, honey, and you gots to forget him."

146

"But, Hannah, it's Dawson's baby. It's Dawson's and no one else's."

"Honey, I know and I'm sorry. But nobody else gonna know. Now lift yo' arms and I'll get you undressed."

Hunter came back an hour later and he was alone. "I'm sorry," he said to Louis and Abigail, "Doctor Jennings is sick in bed, he can't come."

"No!" Louis shouted, "what shall we do?"

"I'll deliver the baby," Hunter said calmly and climbed the stairs to Kathleen's room.

"Where's Doctor Jennings?" Kathleen looked at Hunter, frightened.

"Darling, I'm sorry, he's sick."

"He can't be sick. Hunter, the pains are coming closer together," she shrieked, "You must do something!"

"I will, Kathleen, I'll deliver our baby myself."

"You will not," she shouted hysterically, "Get out of here, I want Doctor Jennings. I'm not having my baby without him."

Hunter calmly walked to the bed and sat down beside his crying wife. "Get away from me," she screamed and started pounding on his chest.

He pinned her arms to her sides and whispered softly, "Doctor Jennings is not coming. I am going to stay and I'm going to deliver our baby. Now I want you to calm down. You may not want me, but you need me and I need your help as well. Together we are going to have this baby and I want no further hysterics from you. I will not put up with it, do you understand?" He released her arms and laid her back on the bed. She lay completely still and looked up at him. "Now that's better," he smiled and started taking off his jacket and giving orders to Hannah. From then on, Kathleen did exactly as Hunter commanded and four hours later, when he held up the baby for her to see, saying, "Look, Kathleen,

147

our baby. A perfect little boy," she smiled through her tears and said meekly, "Thank you, Hunter."

A lump came to Hunter's throat and he said, "No, . . . thank you, darling." He then turned to hand the baby to Hannah, knowing that what he had suspected for several months was true. The eight-pound baby was much too large and healthy to have been fathered by him.

Fourteen

"I really don't want to go without you," Dawson said when he walked into the baroness' bedroom dressed in his evening clothes. He came to the bed and sat down beside her, taking her hand in his.

"I know, Dawson, but one of us has to show up. You're so sweet to go, I appreciate it. The Gaynors are such dear friends, I hate to disappoint them," Susan Le Poyferre smiled at him.

"Are you miserable, my poor darling?" Dawson said and raised her hand to his lips. "I feel so responsible, I'm sorry." He placed tender kisses in the softness of her palm.

"Don't blame yourself, Dawson. If I haven't the intelligence to get in out of the Mediterranean sun, I deserve this misery." Then she smiled at him and said, "Besides, I'm not so sure it wasn't worth it."

Dawson placed her hand back on the bed, leaned over and took her shoulders, barely touching them, and leaned down to kiss her on the forehead. "You're quite a lady, Susan Le Poyferre. I shall return as soon as I can graciously get away. When I get home, I'll rub a nice cooling cream into your tortured body. How does that sound?"

"Darling," she said, raising an index finger up to his full mouth, "It sounds so delicious that I insist you leave immediately so you can get back to me all the sooner."

The lips under her hand smiled and kissed her fingers as Dawson rose from the bed. "My dear, I shall be back very early, I promise. And when I return, I will make everything

149

up to you." He winked and left the room while the sun-burned baroness smiled at his disappearing back.

The ride down the cliffs to the Gaynors' villa took almost an hour. The mansion was situated north of the baroness' on one of the few expanses of beach in Monte Carlo. While the baroness had a breathtaking view of the little city and the sea, the Gaynors had an equally pleasing view of all the twinkling lights on the cliffs above them.

Jim Gaynor was a wealthy French banker, semi-retired, and he and his colorful wife, Jordan, spent as much time as possible at their seaside retreat. When Dawson's carriage pulled up in front of the big estate, every candle in the big house was ablaze and he could hear music floating out over the lawn. The sun was just setting behind the house and it turned the water below almost as pink as the pink stucco building he was headed for.

Dawson knocked and Jim Gaynor flung the door open wide, a broad smile lighting his granite-featured face, his thick gray hair glinting in the setting sun. "Dawson," he said in broken English, "so glad you finally arrived. Where is the baroness?" He looked all around like he thought she might be hiding behind Dawson's big frame.

"She sends her regrets," Dawson said, shaking hands with the shorter man. "The baroness is not feeling well. She said to tell you she's heartbroken she couldn't be here and hopes you'll forgive her."

"That is too bad. Nothing serious, I hope," he raised his silver eyebrows.

"No, an upset stomach. I'm sure she'll be fine by morning," Dawson smiled.

"Good, good, come on in and have a drink before dinner."

Jordan Gaynor joined the two men as soon as they entered the drawing room. "Dawson darling," she said and held out a bejeweled hand for him to kiss. Her dark hair was piled on top of her head and a band of diamonds holding it in place sparkled when she tossed her head. She wore a white gown that billowed out around her broadening hips and its daringly low neck dipped to a V in front, showing off her deep tan. She took Dawson's arm and said to her husband, "Do be a dear and get Dawson some champagne, I've so many people dying to meet him." She swept him around the room introducing him to their guests. "So sorry Susan couldn't make it, Dawson, but we will try to keep you from being lonely," she laughed gaily and squeezed his arm.

At dinner, Dawson was seated next to a house guest of the Gaynors. Gigi Lafitte was cheerful and attractive, but spoke not one word of English. Dawson spoke no French, so sign language and smiles were as close as they came to communicating. On Dawson's other side, a gregarious Englishman, down on holiday, told Dawson he owned and operated a large cotton agency in London. Dawson listened, interested, but made no mention of the fact that he was in the cotton business in Natchez. The Englishman, Richard Craddock, found the tall, dark American a pleasant table companion and hated to see the meal come to an end. Gigi Lafitte felt the same way and for the first time in her life wished she spoke English.

After dinner, the dancing began in the big ballroom at the back of the house. Wide, tall doors opening onto the veranda that spanned the length of the room drew in the welcome sea breezes from the beach just below the mansion. Dawson stood with a drink in his hand, watching the dancers with little interest, when Richard Craddock approached him.

"There you are, Dawson. I've been looking for you."

"You have found me," Dawson smiled and continued looking at the dancers.

"See here, old chap, Jim Gaynor just told me you're in the cotton business in America."

"Yes," Dawson said evenly, "I have a small plantation in

151

Mississippi.''

"Well, why didn't you tell me at dinner? I had no idea.''

Dawson shrugged his massive shoulders, "I don't know. I've been away for eight or nine months. I haven't really thought a great deal about cotton lately. I'm having too good a time, I suppose," he smiled warmly at the Englishman's intense face.

"Well, Dawson, it so happens you are just the man I've been looking for.''

"I don't understand.''

"As I told you, I'm a cotton agent. My business is good, but it could be even better. If you worked for me, or better still, if you became my partner, you could get some of those big accounts in the South, couldn't you?''

"Perhaps, but I . . .''

"I knew it, you would be invaluable to me, Dawson. Why not come back to London with me next week, we could talk . . .''

"Hold on, Mister Craddock. I'm flattered by your offer, but I have no interest in becoming a cotton agent.''

"But, son, think of the money we could make.''

"I don't want to think about money, Craddock.''

"Don't say no yet, think about it, I need you and I . . .''

"Mister Craddock, I appreciate your offer as I said, and I don't want to appear rude, but I'm really not interested. Now if you'll excuse me.''

"Just a minute.'' Craddock caught Dawson's arm. He reached inside his pocket and brought out a white card and presented it to Dawson. "Please take this card and if you should ever change your mind, contact me. It's a lucrative business, Dawson, and you'd be good at it.''

"Thanks, I'll do that,'' Dawson smiled and started to walk away.

"No, you put that in your wallet right now. I don't want you losing it. Here, I'll hold your drink.''

"Yes, I will,'' Dawson pulled out a thin, black leather wallet and tucked the card inside. "There. It's done. I'll keep the card."

"Good. I'll be hoping to hear from you." Richard Craddock handed Dawson his glass and patted him on the back.

"Now, excuse me," Dawson said and turned to leave. She was standing not ten feet away from him in a small circle of people. They were all talking and laughing, but she was paying no attention. She was looking directly at Dawson. She was very young and fair. Her long blond hair was flowing around her white shoulders. She was small and delicate and wore a light blue dress with ruffles. Her eyes were the color of the dress and they were enormous. She was beautiful and her perfect little mouth was smiling at Dawson Blakely.

Dawson realized he was staring and abruptly turned and went in the opposite direction without returning her smile. He set his empty glass down and hurried out the open doors onto the veranda. The cool breeze was welcome and he was glad the long porch was deserted. He walked to the pink wrought iron railing and gripped it firmly while the knees supporting him felt weak and wobbly. He looked down to the sea below and breathed deeply of the sweet salt air. When he felt a small hand on his shoulder, he knew without turning who it was.

"It's nicer out here, isn't it?" she said softly and he turned to look at her.

"Yes, it is," he answered, not smiling.

"I'm Amy Wentworth, Mister Blakely," she said in a familiar drawl. "I understand we're practically neighbors. Our hostess tells me you are from Natchez, Mississippi. I'm from Atlanta, Georgia. Isn't that a coincidence?"

"Yes, it is. What are you doing in Monte Carlo?"

"My parents own a villa here and we spend our summers in it. It's so dreadfully hot in Georgia at this time of year," she smiled. "You know what I'd like to do. I'd like to go down to the beach and take a nice walk in the moonlight. Doesn't that sound romantic?"

"Aren't you afraid you'll get sand in your dancing slippers?"

"That's no problem," she grinned and bent down in front of him, took off the silver slippers, raised them up and dangled them in front of his face. "There, it's taken care of."

Dawson smiled at last, took the slippers from her and slipped his hand over hers. "Let's go," he said and led her down the long, winding stone steps to the beach. They reached the warm sand and stood for a moment looking up at the villa high above them.

"The sand feels good to my feet," she giggled. "You should take your shoes off, Dawson," and she raised her skirts daintily and started down the beach. Dawson shook his head, laughing, and followed. Catching up to her, he put his arm around her small waist and slowed his pace to accommodate her small steps. She rested her head in the crook of his arm and her lovely blond head came barely to his shoulder. She looked up at him, smiling, the moonlight making a halo of her hair. And she asked him countless questions, rarely giving him time to answer. They walked for at least two hundred yards, the villa completely out of sight behind them.

Dawson stopped, dropped her shoes to the sand, and brought his other arm around her, saying, "You talk too much, Amy Wentworth," but he was chuckling. He held her close in front of him and together they stood looking out at the dark Mediterranean. Her small, delicate body felt good against his and the blond hair blowing softly just under his chin filled his senses with its sweet fragrance. His arms tightened around her waist and her tiny hands came up to his.

"I've got sand between my toes," she laughed and leaned her head back against his chest.

"I'll fix that," he said against her hair and slowly removed his arms from around her. He unbuttoned his black evening jacket, spread it out on the sand, and held out his hand to her, "Sit," he commanded and helped her down to the jacket.

154

"Dawson Blakely," she giggled, "your coat will get all sandy."

He dropped down beside her, smiling, and said, "Ah, but I can get a new jacket, while you, my dear, must make your pretty little feet last for a lifetime."

Amy Wentworth stretched her arms out beside her and watched him as he pulled her soft blue dress up over her ankles. He drew a clean white handkerchief from his trouser pocket, raised a small foot and meticulously dusted the sand from it, then placed it atop his jacket. He repeated the action with the other foot. Both feet were now free of any particle of sand. When he impulsively bent and kissed the instep of her right foot, Amy giggled nervously. Carefully, he pulled the blue skirt back over her feet and turned to look at her. "Is that better?" he asked and moved up to sit beside her, propping his arm behind them.

"It's perfect," she smiled at him, her blue eyes wide and shining, "You certainly know how to treat a lady, Mister Blakely. I'll bet you take good care of all your . . . your women, don't you. Are there many?"

"Hundreds," he teased, "but I told you, you ask too many questions, precious girl."

"I know, but can I ask just one more."

Dawson laughed louder than he'd laughed in months, his white teeth gleaming in the moonlight, his black eyes merry and dancing. "Yes, sweetheart, you may ask all the questions you please."

"Do you think you would like to kiss me?" she said and turned her face up to his.

"I think I'd like that very much," he answered and leaned down and kissed the corner of her mouth. He drew back instantly and the smile on his face faded slightly. The muscle in his firm jaw began to twitch and slowly he moved a hand up to her waist. "You are beautiful," he whispered, "so beautiful," and kissed her again. The fieriness of his kiss surprised Amy and, when he forced her lips apart, he pulled her to him

155

and held her so tightly she could hardly get her breath. She raised her hands to his chest and tried to push away, but he refused to loosen his grip. The experienced mouth probing her own ended her half-hearted attempts to draw away and she sighed and put her arms around his neck. Her surrender heightened his desire and the kisses became more forceful and demanding. The fierceness of his embrace pushed her backward and soon she was laying on the jacket. Dawson followed her to the ground, his lips never leaving hers. His kisses continued and became so intense she grew frightened. His hand went to the soft blue ruffles of her dress and he pulled them down from one shoulder. He moved his mouth to its bare loveliness. He was sighing softly and kissing her shoulder and she grew more alarmed by the heat of the mouth she felt covering her sensitive skin.

"Dawson," she said, "Dawson, I . . ."

He was mumbling now while the kisses continued and at last he moaned, "Oh, Kathleen, Kathleen, darling, please, I love you. . . ."

Amy's eyes flew open and she started pushing on him with all her strength. "Kathleen? I'm not Kathleen! I'm Amy Wentworth!"

Slowly, the mouth on her shoulder grew still and Dawson raised himself up. She looked up at him and said, "Who is she? You thought I was Kathleen," she said getting up.

"I'm sorry," he said without looking at her as he stood up. She got to her feet without his help. By then, he had walked to where her shoes lay in the sand. He came back slowly, bent down, and started putting the slippers back on her feet. She put her hands on his back for support and watched while he took the sole of her foot in his hand and slipped the shoe back on. He put the other one on in the same swift manner and rose in front of her.

"Dawson," she said, putting her hands up to his chest, "Look at me, please."

He looked down at her, but removed her hands from his

chest. "You'd better go," he said, tired.

"Aren't you coming, too? I don't want to go back without you."

"No, I'm not. I want to stay here for a while."

"Then I'm staying with you," she said, stepping close to him and putting her arms around him.

"No," he almost shouted as he took her arms away. "You're going back, it's getting late."

"Look, Dawson, it's all right. I'm not mad, honest. Let me stay," and she stood on tiptoe and put her arms around his neck.

He jerked her arms away and spun her around. Gripping her shoulders, he leaned down and said, "I'm not fit company for you or anyone else tonight. Now get out of here." He gave her a little shove. Confused and hurt by his complete change of mood, she did as he commanded. At first she walked fast, then she started running as tears stung her blue eyes. When she was a few yards away from him, she stopped and turned back to look at him. He hadn't moved, just stood there, looking at her coldly. Her pride and feelings hurt, she shouted at him, "I hate you, Dawson Blakely," and turned away, crying loudly.

"Good," Dawson said almost in a whisper and watched her full blue skirts billowing out behind her, the golden hair flying wildly around her head. Slowly, he dropped back to the ground, weary and alone. He sat for hours, his eyes cold and hard, staring out at the sea as it grew darker when the moon began to fade. His long legs bent at the knees, arms resting on them, he sat without moving, his body rigid, his mind aflame with the golden-haired love he had left in America. The fever in him soared until he felt his body would burst into flame from a desire that was impossible to sate.

Impulsively, he stood and stripped the clothes from his tortured body. He rushed headlong into the cold Mediterranean Sea. He splashed out into the water and felt its welcome coolness on his hot skin. He moved out to the deep water in

157

seconds and his body sliced through the waves as he swam further and further from shore. The lights grew smaller behind him and still he continued swimming. He swam and swam until he was exhausted from exertion and the muscles in his arms and legs ached. When he could go no further, he turned over onto his back and slowly floated in to land with the tide. Wondering at times if he would make it back, and considering if he really cared whether he did or not, Dawson floated slowly in, looking at the heavens overhead with tired, lifeless eyes.

In the shallow water at last, he got to his feet and walked to the deserted beach. The night air hit his wet body and he shivered from the cold and exhaustion. The long, tiring swim was like a healing potion. The agonizing heat was gone, washed away in the cold waters. He felt better, felt like he could get his breath, felt cleansed of his demons, felt like he would be able to sleep.

Dawson pulled his clothes back on his glistening body and slowly headed back up the hill to the villa. The sun was rising now, its first pink rays just visible on the horizon. All the guests had long since departed when he wound his way up the long steps from the beach, but, as if by magic, his driver and carriage stood ready in front of the mansion and without a word Dawson climbed in and was driven back up the hairpin curves to the baroness' villa.

He quietly let himself in and went up the stairs. When he passed the baroness' bedroom, the door was open and she called to him, "Dawson, darling." Dawson paused, turned, and walked in to face her. "Sweetheart," she said, "I was worried, it's, well, it's morning, and . . . Dawson, your hair's wet and so are your clothes."

"Susan, I'm very tired. I just want to go to sleep."

"Of course, darling," she said and pulled the covers back beside her, "Come to bed."

"I'm sorry, I'm going to bed in my room. I'll explain later."

"Why, Dawson, there's no need to explain anything to me. Get some rest, I'll see you this afternoon."

"Thanks," and he turned and left. The baroness watched him leave and a hint of a frown covered her lovely face. Without his saying it, she knew deep inside that the lovely affair with her handsome American, for reasons unknown to her, was coming to an end.

Dawson walked to the end of the hall and went into his room. He stripped off his clothes and let them fall to a wet heap on the floor. He stretched out atop the big bed and was asleep the minute his dark head hit the pillow, but Kathleen Diana Beauregard tiptoed into his dreams, her blue eyes looking into his, her soft blond hair framing her face. She was in his arms and she was whispering, "You do love me, Dawson, you do."

Scott Alexander was as beautiful a baby boy as his parents had ever seen and both worshipped him from the moment he took his first breath. Louis and Abigail Beauregard were delighted with their new grandson and Hannah was overjoyed to have an infant in the house to care for once again.

If Kathleen had been less than a perfect wife, she made up for it in motherhood. She adored her son and never tired of holding him and cooing to him, while Hunter sat beside her and looked at them both in awe and wonder. She was kinder to Hunter than she had been before the baby came and he was confident it was just a matter of time before they would once again be sharing the same room.

Hannah came into the baby's room and said, "Now it's time ya'll gits out o' here and let that little feller get some sleep. Miz Kathleen, you give that baby to me and I'se gonna put him right in his crib where he belongs. You'se tiring that po' little boy out." And she took the baby from Kathleen's arms, with Kathleen protesting, "Oh, Hannah, I just want to hold him for a while longer. He's so cute and cuddly, and it's only eight o'clock.''

"I don't care, you been holdin' that baby all the blessed day long. You is gonna have him so spoiled he is nevah gonna sleep in his bed.''

"Hannah, how can a six-week-old baby be spoiled? That's silly. Isn't it, Hunter? Tell her it's silly,'' Kathleen looked at her husband.

"Darling,'' he smiled at her and put a hand to her shoulder, "he really should be in his bed. You can hold him some more tomorrow. And, besides, it's really time you went to your room and got some rest. You look tired, darling.''

"Hunter, I'm fine, honest. I've felt really fine all this week. I'm perfectly all right. You sound too much like a doctor, Hunter. I felt badly last week because I hadn't been getting any sleep, but I'm fine now.''

"I'm glad, Kathleen, but promise me you'll go to bed soon. I realize I sound like a doctor, but that's what I am. I'm telling you you need to get all the rest you can. These two a.m. feedings are hard on you. You must keep up your strength, darling. Why don't you go on to your room and have your bath and I'll bring you some hot milk in an hour?''

"Yes, Dr. Alexander,'' she laughed.

An hour later, Hunter knocked on Kathleen's door and she quickly said, "Come in, Hunter.''

He entered, smiling, carrying a glass of warm milk on a silver tray. Kathleen laid her book aside and sat up in bed, propping the pillows behind her. "Thanks, Hunter,'' she said and took the milk from the tray.

"You're very welcome,'' he said and took a chair beside the bed. "What are you reading, dear?''

Kathleen blushed and admitted, "Hunter, you'll think me foolish. It's another of those Joseph Holt Ingraham serials. I can't help it, I just love them.''

"Don't be embarrassed about it, thousands of people are reading his novels, dear,'' he smiled. "Kathleen, is there

160

anything else I can get you?''

"No, as I told you, I'm feeling just fine. Don't I look all right?''

"You look lovely, dear." Hunter paused, then said, "Kathleen?''

"Yes, Hunter?'' she looked at him.

Without answering, Hunter got up from his chair and came to sit on the edge of her bed. He took her hand in his and kissed it, then whispered, "Darling, how are you really feeling?''

"For heaven's sake, Hunter, how many times do I have to say it? I'm fine, I feel great. Really!''

"Good. Darling, I've been thinking, now that the baby is here and you're feeling good, could we, I mean, will you let me . . .''

"What, Hunter?''

Hunter didn't answer. He looked at Kathleen with pleading brown eyes and bent to kiss her. Taken by surprise, he was kissing her before she knew what was happening and the kisses were passionate, demanding, his arms holding her tightly.

"Hunter, please, please,'' she struggled and pushed him away. "What's gotten into you?''

"Darling, I've missed you so much. I know you didn't want me in your room while you were pregnant and I understood. And then right after the baby came, you didn't feel like it, but darling, it's been six weeks and you said yourself you are feeling fine. Please, Kathleen, I want to share your room again, to make love to my wife. I've been so lonely without you and . . .'' he kissed her again.

"No,'' she pulled away, "Hunter, I'm tired, I . . .''

"I have just spent the last five minutes asking if you were tired and you said you felt fine.''

"Well, I am tired! Very! Can't you just be patient for a while? You don't know what it's like to be a new mother. I have to get up and feed him in the middle of the night and I don't sleep well and I . . ."

Slowly Hunter rose from the bed and said, "I'm sorry, Kathleen. I know it isn't easy. But I'll tell you something, this is not easy on me. I love you and I want to be with you. I know you have to get up every night. I wish I could do it for you. Look, I love Scott as much as you do, but is there never any time for me?"

"Well, yes, Hunter, of course there'll be time for you, for us. But give me a few more weeks, I . . ."

"Fine, Kathleen. I won't bother you again. Just let me know when I am allowed to come back into my own bedroom. But try to think about what it's like for me being shut out all the time," and he left the room.

Hunter lay awake in the big bed in his lonely bedroom at the end of the hall. One hand under his head, he smoked in the darkness, unable to sleep, though it was 2 A.M. He'd read and worked on his research until one, trying to tire himself purposely. He put his books aside finally, rubbing his eyes, hoping he was exhausted enough to fall asleep quickly. He blew out the lamp and closed his eyes. He lay as still as possible, sure this would do the trick. It didn't work; his eyes came open and his thoughts were once again crowded with his own personal problems. Kathleen had dashed his hopes of moving back into her bedroom when he'd been so hopeful. He was hurt and confused and now realized their relationship was to be no better now that the baby was here than it had been when she was pregnant. He had been so patient while she was carrying the child, understanding her need for privacy, knowing she was young and the experience was new and frightening to her. But he had dared to hope that once the baby came, she would be ready to be his wife again.

"She doesn't love me," Hunter thought sadly, "She never did, perhaps she never will. But I love her so much, so very much. Maybe in time she will accept me as her husband. I'll be patient, she's young, she'll grow to love me if I give her time. I must keep hoping."

Hunter sighed and rose from the bed. Putting the cigar out, he drew on his trousers. He quietly went down the hall toward the nursery. He wanted to look in on the baby, to check the covers, be sure he was still breathing. The tiny boy was still a miracle to him, so perfect and healthy, he loved him more than he ever dreamed possible and never tired of looking at him.

He neared the door making no sound, his feet bare, careful not to put his full weight down, so afraid was he of waking the baby. He promised himself he wouldn't touch the dear little bundle, he would just stand silently and look down on him, not even touching the crib. He was at door and a smile came to his face even before he looked inside. Hunter stepped in and what he saw was to him the most sacred, beautiful sight he had ever witnessed.

The room was dim with only a small lamp turned low, casting shadows on the tall ceiling. In a rocking chair near the crib, Kathleen sat, her head laid back against the chair, the silky blond hair falling loosely around her shoulders. She held the baby at her breast. The baby, now full, had fallen asleep, as had his mother. Hunter stood quietly looking at them both. The tiny baby, his dark head against the white of her skin, safe, secure. His beautiful wife, the alabaster breast exposed, sleeping, peaceful, serene. Hunter stood, looking at them both, love and pride swelling in his heart so he thought it might burst.

Kathleen had never allowed him to be in the room when she nursed their son, though he had told her he wanted to share the experience with them. She had told him that was the silliest thing she had ever heard of and she was nervous enough each time she fed him without having an audience. He had retorted that he was hardly an audience, he was the father and husband and also a doctor, he could be of help to them. But she was having none of it, refused to feed the baby even if he cried hungrily, as long as he was in the room. Hunter had given up and told her he understood how she felt and he would give her privacy, but he resented it and felt he was being left out.

Hunter leaned against the door frame and secretly enjoyed this beautiful scene for several minutes. It was the sweetest agony he'd ever known and he longed to rush to them and hug them both tightly, expressing just how much he loved them. Slowly, he tiptoed to the chair. He gently took the sleeping baby from Kathleen. He stood with the boy in his arms, feeling the warmth and the rapid infant breath of the tiny boy against his bare chest. He carried him to his crib and gingerly laid him down, pulled the covers up, and bent down and kissed the dark head. He turned back to Kathleen and studied her. Still sleeping peacefully, she hadn't stirred when he took the baby from her. He picked her up from the chair and she moaned a little, the thick eyelashes fluttering fleetingly. Sleepily, she laid her head against his chest and put her arms around his neck. "What is it? Scott, Scott?" she murmured, her eyes still closed.

"Scott's fine, darling," Hunter whispered and carried her across the hall to her room. She was fast asleep by the time he got to the bed. He gently laid her down, her limp arms falling away from his neck. Hunter knelt by the bed and looked at her. She was so young and beautiful. Hunter longed to kiss her, to get into bed beside her, and have her sleep in his arms all night long. That would be all he would ever ask for, it would be enough. Just to lie holding her sleeping body against his while he buried his face in her soft blond hair, to feel her soft skin against his body. But she did not want him there and would be upset if she woke and found him. He would not take advantage of her because she was asleep. With his surgeon's touch, Hunter reached down to the filmy white nightgown and slowly pulled it up over the full breast. His hands shaking now, he touched the long blond hair briefly, blew out the lamp beside her bed, and tiptoed from the room. When he got to the hall, he found he was weak, leaned against the door frame, whispering under his breath,

164

"Kathleen, darling, my darling." He straightened at last, walked back down the hall to his lonely room, and slipped into bed. It was a long time before sleep came to his tortured body.

Hunter threw himself into his work, turning his personal frustrations to constructive pursuits. He spent more hours at his office, his patient load growing daily. An understanding and caring man, word soon got around Natchez that young Doctor Hunter Alexander would render compassionate aid at any hour of the day or night, not as interested in the fees he collected as he was in caring for and curing his patients.

"Doctor Alexander," one patient would say, "I think maybe I'll be able to pay some of my bill next month. I just haven't the money right now."

"Now don't you worry about it, Mrs. Williams, you just take care of that arm. Getting you well is the only thing that counts," Hunter would answer.

"Doctor Alexander, Johnny fell and broke his leg. Could you come right over? I hate to ask you, I know it's past 10 P.M. but we didn't want to bother your uncle at this hour," another would say.

"That's just fine. I'm a doctor, it doesn't matter what time it is, if you need me, I'm available," Hunter would smile.

"Doctor Alexander," a slaveowner would catch Hunter as he left his office, "could you come over and take a look at a couple of my slaves? They're awfully sick. I don't know what it is, but I'm afraid it will spread to the others. Then where would I be?"

"Certainly, I'll come right now." Doctor Alexander would go to the large plantation, out to the slave quarters, and spend half the night at the bedside of a sick, grateful darkie.

* * *

Kathleen chided her husband about being constantly available to the entire population of Natchez. "Hunter, there are other doctors in this town. Surely you don't have to carry the weight of the entire city on your slim shoulders."

"Darling, if someone is sick and in need of a doctor, I can hardly refuse to help. I wouldn't be much of a healer if I failed to give aid."

"Hunter, you're too soft-hearted, I'm afraid. The Williams family would have the money to pay you if old man Williams didn't spend all his money at the joints of Natchez Under. He's a compulsive gambler and the whole town knows it."

"That may be true, dear, but it isn't his wife's fault, is it? If a woman has a broken arm, I don't ask her to tell her husband to quit gambling so he can pay me."

"You're right, Hunter. I'm sorry I said anything. I just hate to see people taking advantage of your good nature. You're a fine doctor, Hunter, but you should be paid for your services."

"Please don't worry about it, Kathleen. They'll all pay when they get the money."

Kathleen didn't spend too much time worrying about her husband overworking or the fact that he didn't always get paid for his efforts. She was a new mother and the baby occupied most of her time and thoughts. Scott Alexander was adorable and Kathleen worshiped him. She never tired of holding him, kissing him, looking down into the little olive face with its perfect features and dark hair. Each time she looked at the dear little face, she saw the face of the baby's father and recalled the tenderness and passion that had produced the beautiful baby. Kathleen knew it had been wrong and sinful, but when she looked at her son, she was glad it had happened. She still loved Dawson and, though he was gone and she would never see him again, a part of him would always belong to her, his son. She jealously watched over Scott, almost reluctant to let anyone share in her joy. When Hunter would sit holding the child, cooing to him, Kathleen felt the strong desire to rush to them and tear the baby from his arms and shout at him, "Let me have him. He's not yours. He'll never be yours. He's mine! Mine and Dawson's!"

Hunter loved the little boy just as much as his mother did. Shut out by his wife, he transfered his affections to the baby and as soon as he got home from his office, he bounded up the stairs to the nursery to grab the boy from his crib and hold him lovingly. An excellent father, Hunter could quiet Scott when no one else could. If Scott was fussy and refused to sleep, even Kathleen would call on Hunter. His very presence in the baby's room seemed to be sensed by the crying child. Hunter had only to stoop over his crib for the sobs to subside and when he picked Scott up and held him tenderly to his chest, the baby seemed to stretch happily and relax and was soon fast asleep, safe and happy in his father's arms.

"I don't understand it," Kathleen would look at the sleeping child, held in one arm against Hunter's chest. "I tried so hard to get him to calm down and you just have to pick him up and he falls asleep."

"Kathleen, it's because Scott knows you're nervous and upset, just as he knows I'm calm. A baby senses his parent's state of mind, darling."

"I suppose you're right, Hunter, but I can't help it. When he cries, I just can't stand it. I love him so much his tears just break my heart. I want to cry with him."

Hunter smiled and reasoned, "Dear, I understand, but you worry about him too much. He's a happy, healthy little boy. Now go to bed, Kathleen, he's fine now."

"Yes, Hunter," she said and kissed the boy's head while

Hunter held him in his arm. She turned and left the room with no kiss for the man holding the baby.

By Scott's first birthday, he was the apple of Hunter's eye. Beautiful and loving, the little boy was walking everywhere, his short legs churning, carrying him from one new adventure to another. He smiled and laughed endlessly and was a constant, unending source of joy to his parents, as well as the rest of the household. Kathleen had a birthday cake for Scott who promptly pulled the one large candle from the cake and tossed it to the floor, then laughed like he had performed an impossible trick. His mother and father sitting on each side of him laughed louder than the baby and thought his antics adorable. Kathleen kissed the little boy and said, "Happy first birthday, Scotty."

Scott Alexander grabbed a strand of her blond hair and said the only word he had thus far uttered, "Daddy!"

Fifteen

The tempo of the flamenco guitar sped up and the undulating hips of the dancing girl moved faster to stay in time with the music. She laughed, threw her head back defiantly, and raised her hands over her head. Her bare feet making no sound on the dirty floors, she spun round and round, her dark hair falling over her face, her peasant blouse dipping daringly low over one brown shoulder, her faded print skirt rising high around her long, tan legs with each spin. She was enjoying the dance and the appreciative whistles and cat calls from a table of four unkempt Spaniards, drunk from wine, laughing and shouting, watching her eagerly and clapping for more.

Maria looked at them, lowering her eyelids seductively, her mouth open in a provocative smile. She danced nearer and nearer to their table, while they grew louder and louder with their praise. One short, fat man rose from his seat to reach out to her. She laughed and whirled away at the last minute, dancing quickly away from them. She looked at the man alone at a table across the room. He had his head down, not even looking at her. She moved towards him as the guitar tempo slowed and the movements of her body worked to match it. The man raised his head, threw down a glass of Maderia, and poured another. He looked at her for an instant, but the expression on his face didn't change. His eyes were dark and brooding, his jaw set, his teeth clinched. His black hair fell over his forehead and he was in need of a shave. But he was handsome, very handsome.

Maria was intrigued by the dark stranger, she had never seen him at Manuel's Cantina before. His clothes looked expensive, though wrinkled. There was a look about him that told her he was no common *vaquero*. He must surely be some well-to-do Spaniard who for some unknown reason chose to drink the afternoon away at Manuel's. Maria, intent on making him notice her, moved closer and danced only for him. She turned, she whirled, she laughed, she swayed her hips. The stranger did not look up. Exasperated, she snapped her fingers for the guitar players to play faster once again. They obeyed and she danced wildly before his table, certain he had more money than the four men across the room had between them. And she was going to get some of it.

The man finally noticed her and she smiled at him. He didn't return the smile. He looked at her coldly and his dark eyes went back to the bottle in front of him. Maria sat down at his table, saying, "*Yo danza para usted!*"

The dark man looked up, studied her smiling young face, and said, "*No habla Español.*"

"Oh," she smiled, "you are English or American, *si?*"

"*Si,* American," he said flatly, "but you, are you American?"

"No, no," she laughed, "I am Spanish, can't you tell?"

"I thought you were, but you speak English. What did you say to me in Spanish?"

"I said, I dance only for you! Why don't you pay me any attention?"

"Haven't you enough of an audience? I think you're too young to be in here, much less dancing for a group of rowdy, drunken men."

"I love to dance and I am good at it."

"Yes, you are, too good, I'm afraid."

"Ah, you did like it! If so, will you give me *dinero?*"

"I certainly will not."

"Then buy me a drink," she smiled and leaned across the table, the white blouse slipping lower over her shoulder.

"Definitely not. Why don't you go home to your mother. I'm sure she must be worried and if she knew where you were and what you were doing, she'd paddle you."

"I'm a grown woman," she said haughtily, "she knows what I do."

"I doubt it," he said and poured another drink. "Now go away and leave me alone."

Maria rose from the table in a huff. "I don't like Americans," she snapped and flounced away. The music continued, grew louder, and Maria once again smiled and started dancing. She moved nearer to the table of Spaniards, casting a quick glance over her bare shoulder at the rude stranger, tossed her head, and put on a sensual show for the men, gaining their loud, drunken approval. When the music stopped, she stood directly in front of them, her hands raised high over her head. The short, fat man rose again and grabbed her waist. She laughingly let him pull her down onto his lap. He kissed her and dropped a *peseta* down her blouse while she smiled and said, "*Gracias, Señor, gracias,*" and asked for more money.

Dawson sighed and took another drink. He rose from the table and walked slowly across the room. He took the girl's elbow, "Get up," he said coldly, pulling her to her feet. The man whose lap she sat on rose immediately, his eyes flashing, protesting the intrusion. Dawson looked at the man and said, "*Mi hermana.*" The man quickly dropped back into his chair, throwing his hand up and repeating, "*Lo siento mucho! Mi dinero?*"

Dawson looked at Maria and asked, "What's he saying?"

"He say he is very sorry."

"That's not all he said. He wants his money. Give it back to him."

"No, is mine!" she tried to twist free of his grasp.

Dawson easily pulled her closer, reached down into the low-cut cotton blouse and drew out the *peseta* between two long fingers. He tossed it to the bewildered man who looked up at him and said, "*Gracias, Señor.*"

"You're welcome," Dawson said as he pulled Maria across the floor.

"Where are you taking me?" she demanded.

"Home, where you belong," Dawson tightened his grip on her arm.

"No, I do not want to leave." She struggled against him, trying to kick him.

"I don't care what you want, you're going home. So just behave yourself."

They were outside and Dawson lifted her onto the big black horse tied near the cantina. He climbed up behind her, pinning her in his arms as he took the reins and rode away. "Where do you live?" he questioned.

"Down the road about a mile," she answered, trying to act nonchalant, though she had never been on a horse and was frightened. "Turn in right there," she pointed. Dawson slowed the horse and turned into the narrow path. Maria's home sat at the end of a dusty trail, a tiny tin-roofed structure with no trees or shrubs around it. Half-naked children played in front of the house and came running to meet Maria and the tall stranger. Dawson dismounted and swung Maria to her feet. He started to climb back on his horse, but Maria smiled suddenly and said, "Come inside, please. Meet my mother."

"No, thanks, I . . ."

"Oh, *Señor,* please," she pleaded with big brown eyes.

"All right, but only for a minute." The young children were grabbing his hands, laughing and pulling him towards the door. Dawson looked down at the smiling brown little faces and grinned. They all chattered happily in rapid Spanish and he had no idea what they were saying. Inside the two room shack, more children of every age filled the room, some sitting on the dirt floor, others at the tiny eating table. Dawson was taken painfully back to his own childhood under the bluffs in Natchez. He himself had been raised in a home similar to this one, with one very large exception. He had been the only child in it, here he counted a dozen brown boys and girls. A tired, old-looking woman stood wearily bending over a cookstove. Her hair was still coal black, but her face was wrinkled and her eyes were dull and lifeless.

Maria went to the woman and kissed her cheek. "*Mi madre,*" she smiled to Dawson.

Dawson bowed to the woman and said, "Hello, *Señora.*" A slight smile came to the woman's lips as she nodded and offered him a chair at the table. "No," he turned to Maria, "tell her I can't stay." Dawson's eyes moved around the room, clean and neat, almost empty of furniture. Pallets lined the walls for sleeping, an eating table stood in the center of the room, very little else. Dawson felt depressed, sorry for the tired woman, sorry for the horde of happy children with little chance of bettering themselves, and sorry for the young girl who danced for money in a cantina of dirty, drunken men. "I have to go," Dawson said and took out his wallet. He took out all the bills he had and handed them to the woman. Her eyes widened and she looked up at Dawson with tears in her eyes. "*Gracias, Señor, Gracias.*" Dawson patted her hand and said, "*De nada.*" He turned and walked from the room, much more sober than he had been when he left the cantina.

Most of the children followed and Dawson gave them all the coins he carried in his pockets. They laughed and clapped their hands and ran back inside to show their mother. Only Maria continued walking with him to his horse.

"Goodbye," he said and started to mount.

"Goodbye, you are very generous. *Gracias,*" and she flounced away, but not in the direction of the house.

"Where are you going?" he caught up with her, leading his horse.

She put her hands on her hips and said, "Back to the cantina, where else?"

"No, you're not, you can't . . ."

173

"Yes, I can. You saw my home. How do you think we live? My mother knows what I do."

"But your father, what about him?"

"Ah, *Señor,* my father go away years ago. My mother find another husband, but he go away, too. He leave last year. So you see, I am the oldest, I must help feed us."

"Surely there's some other way. You don't want to go back to that bunch of drunks, do you?"

She shrugged her shoulders, "They are not so bad. They give me money and I . . ."

"Stop! Don't tell me anymore." Dawson lifted her from the ground to his horse, then again climbed up behind her.

"Where are we going?" Maria turned to look at him.

"Home. I'm taking you home with me," and the big horse bolted away and galloped down the dusty road with Maria holding tightly to the brown arms around her.

Dawson lived in a leased villa on the coast of Spain, about ten miles from Seville. The small four-bedroom house was situated on a deserted stretch of beach and the nearest neighbor was a good five miles away. It was just what Dawson was looking for when he came to Spain from Monte Carlo. He wanted only peace and quiet and to be left alone.

A kindly Spanish couple, Pedro and his wife Delores, were the only servants at the villa. Pedro diligently took care of the grounds and outside chores, while Delores cooked and kept the house spotless. Unobtrusive and energetic, they went about their work quietly, never imposing themselves on the tall, brooding American who seemed never to leave the house. The Spanish couple respected Dawson, but thought him moody and strange and they had never seen anyone drink so much. He had been at the villa for months and he never went anywhere. He read a lot, he lay on the beach alone in the hot sun, he rode his horse through the barren countryside, and he drank. He drank constantly and there were days at a time when he never bothered to eat. Delores would prepare the most tempting foods she could find at the market. She hummed happily in the kitchen while the delicious aromas filled the big cheery room. Pleased with the tempting feast she turned out, her happiness turned to frustration when she came back into the dining room an hour later to see Dawson hadn't touched his food, had not even come to the dining room. Delores would sigh and clasp her hands together and carry the untouched food away.

She wondered why a man so young and darkly handsome wanted to be alone all the time. He should be married to a lovely lady and have many beautiful children. He should have friends and entertain, the house should be filled with laughter and gaiety, but it never was. In all the time she had known him, she couldn't remember ever hearing him laugh. Dawson Blakely was the saddest man Delores had ever met.

"I don't know your name," Dawson said as he and the young girl rode home together.

"Maria," she said, "Maria Jones."

"Jones, you must be joking, that doesn't sound very Spanish."

"It's not. My father was American, just like you."

"That's why you speak English."

"Yes. What's your name? You look more Spanish than me."

"Dawson Blakely. I'm not Spanish, just dark."

"Pedro, Delores," Dawson called when they reached the villa. The two servants appeared immediately, bowing and eager to please. "This is Maria Jones. She is going to be staying with us for a while and I need your help. Pedro, I want you to go into the village and buy her some dresses. Let's see," he looked down at Maria, "I'd say size eight. Get several pretty ones and get her some shoes, probably size five. Get her some nightgowns, a brush and comb, and some perfume. That will do for now, I'll take her shopping later. Put it on my bill.''

''*Si, Señor,*'' the smiling Spaniard went to carry out his orders.

When Dawson took Maria into the house, she oohed and aahed in dazed wonder. She had never seen a home so large and beautiful and she roamed throughout the many rooms alone, touching priceless objects and heavy furniture, while Dawson stood in the kitchen speaking to Delores. ''And after you feed her, Delores, I want you to give her a bath. Make the water as hot as she can stand it and scrub her good. Wash her hair too, then clip her fingernails. The poor child looks like she has never had a bath in her life. By the time you've finished cleaning her up, Pedro should be back with the clothes. Take the ones she's wearing and burn them, I never want to see her in them again.'' He turned to leave. ''And Delores, fix up the bedroom across the hall from mine, it can be her room.''

''*Si Señor,*'' she smiled and started cooking.

''Aren't you going to eat?'' Maria sat at the big dining table greedily devouring the tasty fish Delores had prepared for her.

''I'm not hungry,'' Dawson said, raising a glass of whiskey to his lips. ''But I think you'll eat for both of us. When did you eat last?''

Maria rolled her eyes while she chewed a mouthful of food, ''Ummm, yesterday, I think. Yes, I'm pretty sure, yesterday.''

''From now on, eat as often as you like. Delores is a very good cook and it upsets her when I don't eat. She'll love cooking for you. Now, if you are full, I want you to go with Delores, she is going to help you with your bath.''

''*Si,*'' she smiled and rose from the table. Dawson picked up his whiskey bottle and headed for the back veranda. It was late evening and the sea breeze made the quiet, peaceful balcony an inviting place to watch the dazzling sunset. Dawson stretched out in a big padded chair and poured another drink.

In a room directly in back of the long porch where he sat, Maria stepped into a hot, soapy tub of water. She sighed with pleasure at the luxury of being allowed to bathe in the big brass tub, filled to its rim with hot sudsy water and some sweet-smelling oil Delores poured in. Her sighs turned to cries of indignation when Delores took a long handled brush and briskly scrubbed her body. Dawson could hear her protests through the open windows as she loudly berated the woman tending her.

"Ouch! That hurts! Do you have to scrub so hard?"

"I'm getting all the dirt off of you, *señorita*. *Señor* Dawson likes a clean household and if you are to be a part of it, you will be, too!"

"Delores, you're pulling my hair! Please, please stop for a minute."

"It is not my fault. Your hair is all tangled because it has not been brushed. We must wash and brush it nicely."

Dawson smiled to himself at the spirited exchange between the meticulous Delores and the dirty, unkempt little Maria.

"*Señor* Dawson," Delores came to the door, a worried expression on her face.

"Yes, Delores, what is it?" The woman let out an exasperated sigh, walked to him, and bent to whisper in his ear. Dawson listened intently, then threw back his head and laughed out loud. Delores straightened, shocked at his behavior. She had never heard him laugh before and here he was laughing loudly over something that was not at all funny.

Laughing still, he said, "Relax, Delores. Surely it won't scandalize the household if she has to spend one evening with no underclothes.''

"*Señor!*" Delores' hand flew to her mouth.

"I'm sorry, Delores. When I sent Pedro to town, I didn't think of underclothes and I never dreamed she had none of her own. We'll get her some tomorrow. It's almost bedtime, surely she can manage.''

"*Si, Señor,*" Delores left in a hurry.

A few minutes later, Dawson heard Maria's voice, "Where are you, Dawson?'' as she walked through the hall.

"Out here, Maria, come join me.''

She walked across the veranda to meet him and Dawson almost choked on his last big swallow of whiskey. She was wearing one of the new dresses Pedro brought from the village. It was a soft yellow muslin and it fit her perfectly. Dainty tiered ruffles went from the waist to her feet. The bodice was tight across her bosom and buttoned discreetly to her neck. Delicate sleeves just capped her brown smooth shoulders, on her feet yellow slippers fit snuggly. Her hair was glistening clean and brushed back off her face, held in place with a yellow hair ribbon. She was happy, smiling, and breathtakingly lovely.

"I can't believe this is the same *señorita* I met in the cantina today. You look beautiful, Maria. Absolutely perfect.''

"*Gracias,*" she said and came to join him.

Sixteen

At twenty-eight, Annabelle Thompson was at the height of her beauty and knew it. Her voluptous figure, never touched by the rigors and weight of childbirth, possessed an eighteen-inch waist, one of the smallest in all Natchez. Her breasts were firm and high and her hips were delicately rounded, her legs long and slender. Her thick, dark hair she wore pulled neatly atop her head, setting off her finely chiseled high cheekbones and perfect nose. Her sparkling gray eyes were rimmed with thick, dark lashes and her full rosebud mouth, when turned up in a small smile, displayed small, perfect teeth. She was a very stunning woman, worshiped and pampered by her loving husband until his untimely death from pneumonia.

Six months after his death, Annabelle was lonely and lost. Too much of a lady to seek or even accept the companionship of men, she spent her days and nights alone, rarely leaving her mansion except to attend church services or to see the doctor about the headaches and heart palpitations that had plagued her since her husband's unexpected death. Rembert Pitt had been her doctor since early childhood and she trusted and depended on the old physician.

Annabelle massaged her throbbing temples while her mammy dressed her to go into Natchez to see Doctor Pitt. She hadn't been sleeping well and felt that if she didn't get relief soon she would surely lose her mind. When Annabelle arrived at Doctor Pitt's office, she was surprised when he came out and took her hand and said in a soft, fatherly voice,

"Annabelle, dear, I do hope you'll forgive me. We've had such a busy morning and I'm not feeling too well myself. I need to go upstairs and lie down before I see any more patients. I don't believe you've met my nephew, Hunter Alexander, but I assure you he is a fine, dedicated doctor. Puts me to shame, as a matter of fact. I was wondering, if you wouldn't mind too much, you would see Doctor Alexander instead of me, just this one time. I know I'm presumptuous to ask this of you, but we've just been snowed under all morning, seems everyone in town is sick."

"But, Doctor Pitt, I've come all the way into town just to see you. I've a terrible headache and I . . ."

"Oh, I know, dear Annabelle, but Hunter can be as much help as I and, as I told you, it would just be this once. I'd never let anyone else have you as their patient, you know that, don't you?"

"Well, I guess if you . . ."

"Good, I knew you'd understand. Now, come with me. Hunter's in his office alone right now. I'll introduce you," and he led her down the hall.

Hunter looked up from his desk and smiled when his uncle led Annabelle Thompson into the room. He rose immediately and extended his hand when they were introduced. "Mrs. Thompson, so glad to meet you. My uncle tells me you haven't been well. I'm so sorry to hear it, I'll do my best to help you. Won't you have a chair."

Annabelle smiled at the tall, blond man and momentarily forgot why she had come to the doctor. She had heard that young Doctor Alexander was a handsome man, but she'd had no idea how handsome. She had never happened to run into him on her visits to Doctor Pitt; if she had, she would have remembered. The drowsy brown eyes looking directly at her made her feel embarrassed, flustered, in a pleasant, unfamiliar way. She looked into his face, then had to avert her eyes, and quickly drew her hand from his as though she had been burned. Her heart palpitations were stronger than usual and she felt quite faint. The good-looking doctor must have sensed it or else she looked very pale for he hurried around his desk to her, took her arm, and lowered her into a chair.

"You just sit here, Mrs. Thompson, you're going to be all right. Go on, Uncle Rembert, I'm sure Mrs. Thompson and I will get along fine." He smiled at Annabelle.

"Yes, Doctor Pitt, by all means, go lie down. And thank you for introducing me to Doctor Alexander. I have complete faith in him, just as I do in you." Annabelle managed a smile.

"Good, good," Doctor Pitt said and left the room.

Hunter went back around his desk and sat down, "Now, Mrs. Thompson, what seems to be your trouble? You're much too lovely and young to be ill."

Annabelle blushed and looked down at her hands. "Doctor Alexander, I've been having the most terrible headaches and my heart just pounds in my chest until I feel it may explode at any minute."

Hunter sat with his long fingers entwined on his desk top, looking at Annabelle and listening intently. It was impossible for him not to notice how lovely she was, but he put such thoughts from his mind and sympathized with her. "I'm so sorry to hear it, but perhaps it's nothing too serious. I don't mean to pry, Mrs. Thompson, but I understand you lost your dear husband several months ago."

"Yes, Doctor Alexander, I did, but . . ."

"Mrs. Thompson, sometimes extreme stress makes our bodies suffer physical ailments and this could be part of your problem. Certainly we want to check every possibility though and be sure there is nothing wrong with your heart." Hunter rose and walked to Annabelle. "Mrs. Thompson, if you'll just step inside the next room, I'll listen to your heart, make sure it's as it should be." He smiled and took her arm. Once inside the next room, he said, "Now if you'll just sit right up here on the edge of this table, we'll have a look."

"Yes, Doctor Alexander."

Hunter turned and picked up his uncle's chart on Annabelle, reading it hurriedly before placing it on the table beside her. He stepped closer to her and put a hand to her face. "I want to look into your eyes for a second," he said, leaning close, pulling each eyelid up and looking into the piercing gray eyes. He felt her head, apologizing for having to touch the carefully arranged coiffure, then moved his slender fingers to her neck, carefully examining the vertabrae, finding the muscles knotted and tense. Hunter removed his hands, wrote something on her chart, then smiled to her again. "Now, Mrs. Thompson, if you'll just unbutton the top three buttons of that lovely gray blouse, I'll listen to your heart."

"Yes, of course," Annabelle stammered and fumbled with the tiny buttons. Hunter stood patiently, the stethoscope in his hand.

"That's far enough," he said evenly and stepped closer to her. He raised the stethoscope to her throat and said, "Now take a deep breath, please." Annabelle gulped for air, so nervous her throat was alarmingly tight, making deep breaths next to impossible. Hunter seemed not to notice, simply said, "That's good. Now another," the stethoscope moving farther down. His face so close to hers was stifling to the young widow and she was afraid she might quit breathing completely if he didn't move away. Hunter didn't move back; he continued to ask her to take another deep breath and another, while the slender fingers holding the stethoscope moved the cold instrument farther and farther down inside her blouse until the soft skin under his fingers grew warm and tingling in spite of all Annabelle's efforts to remain calm. "That's good," he said at last and smiled at her. "You may button your blouse." He turned and wrote on her chart.

Back in his office, he sat behind his desk and extended his hand to the chair across from him. While he studied her chart thoughtfully for a few minutes, she sat nervously watching

182

him, unable to take her eyes off the handsome blond head bent over the desk. He looked up at her at last and Annabelle blushed instinctively. "Mrs. Thompson," he said, smiling, "I'm going to give you something for those terrible headaches. I want you to get plenty of rest. You must try to relax, though I realize that can be quite difficult at times. You have a strong heart, I assure you, and I really feel these palpitations are due to stress which is of course understandable after the tragedy you have gone through. I'm afraid there's not much I can do about them, only time will help. I'll be anxious to know if the medication I give you helps your head and I'll be checking with Uncle Rembert to see how you are getting along."

"Doctor Alexander," she said softly, "I want you to be my doctor from here on out."

"But, Mrs. Thompson, I . . ."

"Please call me Annabelle. We both know your uncle is growing old and will be thinking of retirement soon. I've heard he's already transferred many of his patients to you. I want you to be my doctor, Hunter."

"Very well, I'll speak to Uncle Rembert, Mrs. Thompson . . . sorry, Annabelle. If you should need either one of us, you know we're readily available. Now, good day."

"Good day, Hunter. And thanks."

Annabelle found it necessary to come in to see the young doctor at least once a week, much more often than she had been in the habit of seeing Rembert. Hunter was patient and understanding with her and treated all her complaints with the utmost interest and concern. He told her that physically she was very sound, but she refused to fully believe him. Or at least she said she didn't. She was not well, she said, he must do something to make her better. Each visit Annabelle made to his office lasted longer through no fault of Hunter's. The lovely young widow was obviously very attracted to him, though he did nothing to encourage her. No longer embarrassed in his presence, she flirted with Hunter and he could read in her flashing gray eyes a promise of further closeness if he would only say the word. He never did. He tried his best to remain only her doctor, nothing more, and found he was the one who was becoming nervous in her presence. When it was necessary to put the stethoscope to her bosom to listen to her heart, she willingly undid her blouse without his asking. Hunter's hand sometimes shook, embarrassing him greatly.

"I'm sorry," he said and looked at her sheepishly, "I suppose I haven't been getting enough rest. I seem to be shaky this morning."

Annabelle would smile into his eyes and say coyly, "Are you sure it's a lack of rest, Hunter?"

Clearing his throat needlessly, Hunter would look away and say, "That should do it for today, Annabelle. The palpitations are improving, perhaps it won't be necessary for you to come back for six months or so. Wouldn't that be nice?"

"Would it?" she smiled and touched his shoulder, the blouse still seductively open.

Hurrying from the room, Hunter said over his shoulder, "You may get dressed, Annabelle. If you'll excuse me, I'm quite busy."

Annabelle did quit coming to his office so often. A discreet lady, she was afraid Doctor Pitt and the other patients might notice her frequent visits. Rembert had already noticed and had cautioned Hunter. "Son, I know you would never take an undue interest in one of your patients, but I've noticed Annabelle Thompson is here to see you at least once a week. Hunter, there's nothing wrong with Annabelle but loneliness. You should try to persuade her to cut down on her visits, people might get the wrong idea, you know what I mean."

184

"I know exactly what you mean, Uncle Rembert, but you are worrying needlessly. Annabelle is a lonely, confused woman, but she thinks she is sick. I can hardly turn anyone away when they feel they need a doctor."

"That's true, of course, Hunter. All I'm saying is I'm afraid the beautiful young widow is attracted to you and it could be a real problem if not checked in time."

"I'll take care of it, Uncle, now I'm late for dinner, so goodnight."

A week later, Hunter sat in the library of Sans Souci after dinner. Kathleen and he had put Scott to bed and come down to read a while before retiring to their separate rooms. Hannah came lumbering into the room, a frown on her black face. "Doctor Alexander, that Mrs. Thompson' servant be at the back do'. He say Mrs. Thompson be sick and need a doctor. She got lots o' nerve if you ask me, bothering folks at this time of night!"

"Hannah, tell him I'll get my bag and be right over. Ask Daniel to saddle a horse and bring it around to the front." Hunter looked at Kathleen, "Sorry, dear. I'd better get out there and see her."

"Hunter," Kathleen looked up a him, "you are just too soft-hearted. Do you really think she would bother your uncle at this hour? Why didn't she call him?"

Hunter coughed nervously and told her, "Actually, she is no longer his patient. She switched to me a couple of months ago. Guess I forgot to mention it."

"You certainly did." She rose from her chair. "Hunter, do you think Annabelle Thompson is beautiful?"

"Why would you ask a question like that, for heaven's sake?"

Kathleen shrugged her shoulders, "No reason, but in case you haven't noticed, she is very lovely. And I'll bet she's more than a little lonely since her husband passed away, don't you?''

"I'm sure she is, dear. Now I must be going." He kissed her cheek and left.

"Good evenin', Doctor Alexander," a black servant threw the door open and invited Hunter into the Thompson mansion.

"Hello," Hunter nodded, "I'm sorry it took so long. It's a long ride over here from my home. I hope it's nothing serious with Mrs. Thompson."

"I don't know, Doctor. She be upstairs in her room. I understands why it take so long fo' you to gets here. I keep tellin Miz Annabelle she needs to sell this big ole place way off out here in the country miles from everybody, but she won't listen." The servant shook his head, then said, "You can go on up, she be in the last do' on the right, she be expectin you."

"Thanks," Hunter said and hurried up the stairs, carrying his black bag. When he reached her door at the end of the long hall, he knocked loudly and a soft feminine voice said, "Come in, please."

Hunter opened the door and stepped inside to see that Annabelle was alone in the room. She was reclining on a blue velvet chaise lounge, a small lamp on the table beside her was the only light in the big room. She was wearing a long gray satin dressing gown and her long dark hair was down, falling in soft curls around her shoulders. Hunter took one look at her, swallowed hard, and walked over.

"I'm sorry to hear you aren't feeling well, Annabelle."

She patted the velvet cushion beside her and said, "I hated to have to bother you, Hunter at this late hour, but my heart is threatening to jump out of my chest. I was terrified."

"I'm sure you were," Hunter smiled and sat down beside her. He took the stethoscope from his bag on the table and by the time he turned back to Annabelle, she had pulled the satin robe back, ready for him to listen to her heart. Under

186

the robe, she wore only a sheer gray lace nightgown and it barely covered the tops of her full breasts. Hunter felt his own heart speed up as he leaned over her to examine her. Trying to find someplace for his eyes to go other than the tempting flesh under his nervous hand, he looked at her face and she was smiling up at him in a teasing, inviting way. Without realizing it, Hunter was smiling back at her, mesmerized by her lovely gray eyes. When he started to moved the stethoscope away, her hand came up and covered his, "Hunter," she whispered.

Like a bolt of lightning, Hunter was on his feet. "Annabelle, your heart sounds fine to me, I must go."

She rose and put her hand to his shoulder, "Hunter, it's so lonely way out here, please stay for a few minutes. Have a glass of brandy with me, please."

"I can't, I have to go. I'm sorry," and the confused young doctor was down the stairs and out of her house as fast as his long legs would carry him.

Annabelle had seen the look in his soft brown eyes and smiled to herself after Hunter left. He was weakening, she was sure of it. The next time would be different. She climbed into bed and went to sleep, still smiling, planning for the next evening visit of the man she'd become infatuated with.

Hunter was again called to the Thompson mansion one evening three weeks later. Kathleen was already in bed asleep, completely unaware that he had left the house. When Hunter arrived at Annabelle's country home, he made no pretense of taking his black bag inside. Annabelle herself met him at the front door and without a word they strolled into the big library together. Not a servant was in sight. Hunter took a seat while she poured them both a glass of brandy, then she came to sit beside him. They sat holding hands, drinking brandy, and talking in a comfortable, relaxed way. When Hunter left, Annabelle stood close to him at the front door and raised her face up expectantly. Hunter smiled and kissed her forehead. "I enjoyed it, Annabelle. And if I've never told you before, I think you're incredibly lovely and if I were not a married man, I . . ." The muscle in Hunter's jaw twitched involuntarily and his eyes smouldered. He turned and went down the steps to his horse. Annabelle stood watching him gallop away, turned and went back inside, smiling broadly.

"Darling," Hunter said to Kathleen as she bent over Scott in the nursery. "I've some news for you."

"Really, Hunter?" She turned to look at him.

"As you know, I've been spending a lot of time on my research to find a cure for yellow fever."

"Yes, you've been on it for ever so long, are you making any progress?"

"Well, there's still no cure, but we are learning more each day and I'm hopeful it won't be too long before we find the cure. There's to be a seminar of many prominent physicians in New Orleans the last of this month. I'm very honored and flattered that they've ask me to read a study I've prepared at the meeting."

"Hunter, that's wonderful! I'm so proud of you. You're a fine doctor, Hunter Alexander."

Hunter smiled, pleased with her praise and said, "Well, darling, I've been thinking. Why don't you go with me to New Orleans? Many of the doctors will be bringing their wives along and it would do you good to get away from Sans Souci for a while. In fact, both of us could use the rest."

"Hunter," Kathleen said, frowning, "I can't leave Scott."

"Don't be ridiculous, darling, of course you can leave him. Kathleen, our son will be two years old next month. You haven't been away from him for a minute. You know he'll be well looked after while we're gone. Please say yes."

"No, Hunter. I just can't. I'd love to really, but . . ."

"Then do it," Hunter said and took her arm, "Please,

Kathleen, you'll never know how much it would mean to me, I want . . ."

"No. Absolutely not. I don't want to leave Scott! You go on and enjoy yourself."

"I will," Hunter answered coldly and left the room.

The next day after work, Hunter left his office, but he did not go home. He rode straight out into the country to Annabelle's estate. She saw him coming up the walk and rushed out to meet him.

"Hunter, Hunter," she smiled, "What a pleasant surprise."

"I can't stay," he said when he reached her. He raised his hands to her shoulders and said, "Annabelle, I've something to ask you."

"Anything, Hunter, you know that."

"Annabelle, I want you to meet me in New Orleans the last week of July. I'm going down for a seminar, but I'll have plenty of free time. I want to be with you, dear. I need to be with you."

"Oh, Hunter," she said and put her arms around his neck. "Yes, yes. You know I'll go. I can't wait. Please come on in and we'll talk about it. I'm so excited."

"I can't, I have to get home. But I want you to make all the arrangements and I'll take care of the expenses. I'm staying at the Creole Hotel, so book a room in some other nice place. We can't go down on the same boat, you understand, but I promise as soon as I get to New Orleans, I'll find you."

"I can't wait, darling. I'll get a suite at the St. Charles and I'll be waiting right there for you when you get to town. And, Hunter, it will be a wonderful week, I guarantee it. What day do you leave?"

"July 22nd."

"I'll leave the 21st."

"Good, until then," he said and turned to leave.

Annabelle refused to release him. "Hunter," she said and

stood on tiptoe, "don't you want to kiss me goodbye?"

"But the servants, it's broad daylight, I . . ." but he bent and kissed her tenderly, then whispered, "Just a preview of what it will be like in New Orleans."

"Hunter, darling, I'll make you happy."

"I know you will," he said and was gone.

Hunter had to go to dinner with the other physicians on his first night in New Orleans. Distracted and anxious for the evening to come to a close, he sat through innumerable boring speeches, knowing the beautiful Annabelle was awaiting his arrival at the St. Charles Hotel. Finally, at 11:30 P.M., he stood outside her fourth floor suite, his heart beating furiously in his chest. She answered the door herself, looking lovely. She giggled and drew him inside, locking the door behind her. They stood looking awkwardly at each other for several minutes, neither speaking. Slowly, he took off his jacket, walked to her, and took her in his arms. He kissed her tenderly at first, whispering, "You're so beautiful, Annabelle." She smiled and before she could answer, he was kissing her again, his hands moving lightly up to her hair. He undid her pins holding it in place and pulled back a little to watch it cascade down around her shoulders. He picked up a long dark curl and lifted it lovingly to his face. He breathed deeply and kissed the silky hair. Still holding the tendril, he kissed her again and felt her lips part under his. He pulled her closer as the fire in him grew and his kisses grew more intense, leaving her bright-eyed and breathless. When at last his lips left hers, he looked down into her smiling, beautiful face and whispered, "Annabelle, I've wanted you for so long . . . so long," and his mouth went to her neck. She stood against him, yielding gladly, wanting more and more of the handsome, lean body pressed to hers. Hunter could feel the rapidly beating pulse on her neck under his lips and her small hands clutching tightly to his back. He felt the hands leave his back and slip between them to his chest. He raised his head to look at her and saw she was slowly unbuttoning his white shirt. He stood completely still and watched her, enjoying every second as her tiny fingers deftly unbuttoned all the buttons. Without a word, he raised his wrist to her and she took out his shirt studs, tossing the onyx links on the table beside them. She pulled the shirt away from his body, then down over his shoulders while he stood watching her, smiling. Annabelle sighed and put her hands on his chest, gently caressing and stroking it. Hunter enjoyed it as long as he could, then once again pulled her against him and his fiery kisses were demanding. "Take off your dress, Annabelle," he murmured against her lips, and she said, "Yes, darling, Yes."

She pulled away a little, saying, "Darling, just let me go into the next room and put on something else. I'll be back in five minutes."

Hunter smiled and kissed her again, "I hope I can wait five minutes," he whispered hoarsely.

While Annabelle was in the bedroom changing, a knock came on the sitting room door and Hunter jumped nervously. Annabelle called to him through the open double doors, "Get that, will you, darling? It's a surprise for you. I've ordered a midnight supper for us. Champagne, oysters, everything."

"Good for you," he smiled and opened the door.

A white-jacketed man wheeled in a linen-covered table and placed it near the open windows. He was gone as soon as the table was in place. Hunter locked the door and turned back to the table. White roses were in its center, a candelabra on its edge, a magnum of champagne cooling in a silver bucket. Then Hunter looked at the beautiful place settings for two. His chest tightened and he felt a queasiness in the pit of his stomach. It was the solid gold service, a specialty of the hotel, used only on special occasions. It was the same tableware he and Kathleen had eaten from at their honeymoon supper. It brought back with distinct vividness the happiness and love of that memorable time together. Hunter sighed as all the passion of minutes ago drained away. He knew it was no use. He couldn't do it. He was in love with his wife. With Kathleen, now and forever. There could never be anyone else as long as she was in the same world with him.

Annabelle came to him wearing the most revealing gray negligee he had ever seen in his life. She was beautiful, alluring, eager, and ready. Hunter looked at her sadly and said, "Annabelle, I've done you a terrible injustice."

Seventeen

Dawson lay in bed, his arms behind his head. He had just put out the lamp to go to sleep. Bright moonlight streamed in the many windows of his big bedroom located at the back of the house. The sheer brown curtains blew gently in the ocean breezes and the sound of the breakers on the beach had a lulling effect on Dawson. He was tired; it had been a long, strange day. The lovely girl asleep in the room across the hall had sat on the veranda with him until very late. She asked few questions, but told him more than he wanted to know about her own life.

When he'd asked, "Maria, will your mother be worried? Don't you think we should tell her where you are, ask if it's all right for you to stay here?"

"She will not be worried, Dawson. I am gone many nights, she is used to it. I spend the night with . . ."

"Say no more, Maria, I understand. That's all going to change. I don't want you going to the cantina again and I . . ."

"Oh, you want me for yourself, Dawson? That's nice, you are so much more handsome than some of the men I . . ."

"No, Maria. I don't want you for myself."

"Why? Do you not think me pretty?"

"You're lovely, Maria, but . . ."

"Then I do not understnad. Why do you bring me here?"

"Dear, I brought you here because I want to help you, to make it possible for you to have a better life."

"But you buy me pretty dresses and perfume. Surely you

expect something in return," she looked at him questioningly.

"I do expect something. I expect you to let me teach you many things."

"Oh, Dawson, I know all about . . ."

"No," he shouted, "you don't understand! I'm going to teach you good manners, how to dress and act. I'll teach you about music, art, literature. I'll make a lady of you, Maria, if you'll let me and I'll help you to realize your dreams, to have a good, happy life."

She listened intently, her eyes wide, and she said, "Why are you so good to me, Dawson? You do not even know me, why should you help me?"

"Maria, I was raised in much the same way you were, but for a man it is easier to rise above it. My dear, sweet mother was a girl very much like you, young and beautiful, and a good woman, but she died in poverty because there was no one to help her. She deserved better, should have had an easier life."

"But your father, didn't he help?"

"My father died when she was eighteen years old, then she was alone with me to care for."

"I am eighteen, Dawson. Do you know by the time my *madre* was eighteen, she already had me and two others."

"How old is she now, Maria?"

"She is thirty-three or thirty-four, I think."

Dawson drew in his breath and shook his head, sadly. "I don't intend to let that happen to you. When you are her age, you will still be a beautiful woman and have a life of ease."

"But how, do you plan to marry me?"

"No, dear," he laughed, "but trust me. Now it's time you went to bed. I think I will, too. You know where your bedroom is. Delores is asleep, do you think you can undress yourself?"

Maria laughed and said, "I've been dressing and undressing myself since I was three. I believe I can manage."

Dawson lay awake now thinking about Maria and the hard life she had lived. And he promised himself he would help her and her brothers and sisters. He would not let Maria become an old woman at thirty-three. A soft knock on his bedroom door shook him from his thoughts.

"Yes," he called. The door opened and Maria came inside. She was wearing her new white nightgown, lace ruffles at its high neck and at her wrists, her feet were bare, and her dark hair was floating loosly around her shoulders and down her back. "Maria, what is it?" Dawson asked, raising himself up.

"Dawson," she walked to the bed, "I am lonely, can I sleep in here?"

"Good Lord, no, Maria!"

"But, Dawson," she said and came directly to him, "I was never in a bed alone, much less in a room."

Dawson took her hand and sat her on the edge of the bed. "Dear, young ladies are supposed to sleep alone. I thought you'd be pleased to have a room all to yourself."

"I am," she said, clutching his hand, "but I am afraid. I am with my brothers and sisters all my life and it is strange to sleep alone. I want to come into your bed, please."

"No! Maria, one of the first things you must learn is that you do not sleep with men!"

She dropped her head, hurt. "You do not like me, Dawson. If you did, you would want me in your bed, you would make love to me."

Dawson put a finger under her chin and raised her face to look at him, "Listen to me. I like you very much, but I do not love you. If I made love to you, it would mean nothing so it would be wrong. You are lovely, Maria and I could easily be persuaded to take you to my bed, but I'm not going to do it. I want to be your friend, dear. You need a good friend as you obviously have never had one. Now, I want you to go back to your room and I don't want you coming in here ever again. If you are frightened, you may leave my door open and yours. I'll be right here, so you needn't be afraid. All right?''

"I guess so," she looked at him, disappointed.

"Good! Now go back to bed and sleep well, my little Maria. I'll see you in the morning."

She rose and smiled, leaned down to kiss his cheek, "If you should change your mind . . ."

"Go!" he commanded and she left.

The months that followed were pleasant for Dawson as he watched the dirty, little urchin he'd brought home from the cantina turn into a well-mannered, polished young woman. She proved to be an apt pupil and spent long hours with Dawson, listening and learning. They were together constantly and Delores noticed that Maria was not the only one benefiting from the mentor-protegée relationship. Dawson became less moody, laughed more, and drank less. He started eating all the fine foods Delores prepared and complimented her on her cooking skills. He dressed for dinner each evening and insisted Maria do the same. The evening meal turned into a pleasant, formal affair and Delores was delighted. She placed silver candlelabra on the dinner table along with fresh cut flowers from the garden Pedro tended. She served the meals in courses in a grand manner and smiled to herself when Dawson escorted an immaculately groomed Maria into the dining room on his arm, pulled out her chair, then took his own place. Maria watched him intently and parroted his gestures, learning for the first time which fork to use. She sat in her chair with her back straight and rigid, no longer slumping or grabbing food off the platters as she had done when she first arrived.

After dinner, Maria would take Dawson's arm and go into the library with him for coffee and a glass of brandy. Dawson would light a cigar and sit talking to her about art and music, sometimes quizzing her on past conversations on the subjects. She would sit primly on the chair, a lace fan stirring the air, and sip her brandy slowly, listening with interest to what he was saying. Delores would come in to pour more coffee from a silver pot and was amazed by the intelligent conversation. Smiling, she would leave the room and go to bed thinking what a fine man Dawson Blakely had turned out to be.

After Pedro and Delores retired each night, the formal scene they witnessed in the library turned into one more warm and intimate. "Dawson, I can stand these corsets no longer," Maria would say, "I cannot breathe and I don't care if it does give me an eighteen-inch waist. I'm miserable! Sitting on these crinolines and hoops is not easy, either."

Dawson would laugh and say, "Dear, no more torture for today. Run put on your nightgown and we'll read some."

"Thanks, Dawson," and Maria disappeared to her room. Dawson would rise, take off his jacket, cast aside his cravat, and unbutton his white ruffled shirt. Then Maria would sit on a footstool at his feet, reading aloud, being corrected by him when she mispronounced a word, while he gingerly brushed her long, dark hair. Her beautiful hair fascinated Dawson and he never tired of brushing it, touching it, feeling its silky loveliness.

On nights that were especially warm, the two would stroll hand in hand down the beach, Maria's white nightgown whipping around her body, her feet bare, Dawson, shirtless, his lean brown chest gleaming in the moonlight, while he pointed out stars and their names to his wide-eyed little friend. Or they would sit in the sand, looking out at the endless ocean, Maria leaning her head on Dawson's shoulder while he smoked his cigar and told her about America and the rest of the world, making her geography lessons interesting and exciting.

Dawson bought Maria a gentle horse and she squealed

197

with delight when she saw the beautiful palomino, promptly naming it Golden Glitter. She wanted to ride it immediately and Dawson told her to go inside and put on the pretty new riding habit he'd bought her while he put the new silver-studded saddle on Golden Glitter's back. Maria was soon back, lovely in the black wool habit, the bolero jacket reaching just to her midriff, the ruffled white blouse buttoned to her chin, the red silk tie flying in the wind, the black felt hat set jauntily at an angle on her head, held in place with a red drawstring under her chin. Dawson lifted her astride the palomino, mounted his own black colt, and together they rode down the beach. Within weeks, Maria had learned to ride, spent every spare moment atop her beloved horse's back and challenged Dawson to races through the rocky countryside. He often let her win so he could hear her joyous laughter as she turned victoriously, her horse rearing up, waiting for him to catch up, her face a vision of happiness, health and youth.

She would jump down from her horse, breathless, and drop to the ground on her back, casting aside her hat, tears of laughter in her bright brown eyes. Dawson would drop down beside her, laughing too, while the horses grazed peacefully, glad to have the spirited riders off their backs. The sun warming their faces, Dawson and Maria would lazily lie on the grass, talking of the things she would learn tomorrow, and next week, and next year. Dawson would ask her what her dreams were.

Maria leaned up on an elbow to look at him, a long blade of grass in her fingers, tickling his face, "Well, I'll tell you my secret dream, Dawson." She laughed, looking at his closed eyes, "I want to marry a handsome matador!"

Dawson opened his eyes, "Sweetheart, matadors are not exactly the aristocracy of Spain. Most of them come from very humble beginnings, much like you and me."

"I do not care! They are brave and handsome and they are rich. They have very good lives. Besides, that's my second choice, really," she looked at him coyly.

"What's the first?" he said, smiling up at her.

"You."

"Now, Maria."

"I mean it. I would like to marry you, Dawson. Have I not learned to be a lady just as you wanted? Am I not beautiful and polished as you taught me to be?"

"Yes, dear, you are, but I cannot marry you."

"Why not? I will make you happy if you let me."

"Maria," he said and his eyes clouded, "I'm already in love with a woman."

"Then why are you not married to her?"

Dawson closed his eyes and said, "She is already married to another."

"She married another when she could have had you? She must not be very smart."

Dawson opened his eyes and reached up to touch a long, dark curl. "No, Maria, it is I who is not very smart. But, I'll tell you what, I am smart enough to see that you get to marry your handsome, brave matador."

"Really, Dawson?" She was excited, "How? How will you do it?"

"In two or three weeks, I'll take you to Madrid. We will go to the finest restaurants and you will wear beautiful new gowns. We will find out which places the matadors frequent and I'll take you to them. You're incredibly beautiful, Maria, and when they see you, I guarantee they will fall in love with you."

"Oh, thank you, Dawson," and she threw herself down on him, kissing his face happily.

At least once a week, Dawson took Maria home to visit her family. Delores would bake cakes and pies, hams and roast beef for Maria's many brothers and sisters. All the children would run happily to meet Dawson and their beautiful, well-dressed sister. Dawson enjoyed the visits and found the hugs and kisses from all the little brown children welcome and his affection for them grew with each visit.

He brought them clothes and books and toys and food. He held them on his lap and wrestled with them on the floor, laughing and frolicking as though he were their age. He scolded and spanked them when they were naughty, he praised and hugged them when they were deserving, he worried and walked the floor when they were sick. He was their playmate, teacher, father, brother and loved them as much as they loved him.

He gave their mother money. He hired the older boys to help Pedro tend the gardens at his own villa. He had Delores teach the older girls to cook and paid them each time they turned out another chocolate cake or apple pie which were his favorites. He told Pedro to start looking around in the village for a bigger, nicer home for the large family. Pedro wasn't long in finding the ideal place and Dawson, Maria, Pedro, and Delores helped the happy family move into their new home while Maria's mother wrung her hands and cried in happy gratitude.

Of all the children, three-year-old Arto was Dawson's favorite. A beautiful little boy, he smiled constantly, showing his perfect white teeth. When Dawson was around, Arto was never far away from him. If Dawson wasn't carrying him, which he usually was, Arto was by his side, following him, holding on to Dawson's trouser leg. He clearly worshiped the tall, dark man who gave him pretty presents. Dawson often looked down into the adorable brown face, the black eyes flashing, and silently wished the lad were his son. Or that he had a boy like Arto. Dawson looked at the trusting face and felt a sadness weighing down on his chest. He had no heir. He would never have a son of his own and that knowledge made him melancholy and lonely. It made him long for the life he could have had with his lost love, Kathleen Beauregard. As man and wife, they would have produced handsome, dark sons and lovely, blond daughters. But it was not to be.

Dawson found it impossible to sleep one night after a visit to Maria's family. He rose from his bed, pulled on a pair of trousers, and tiptoed past Maria's open bedroom door, down the hall, and outside. He walked the beach, dropped his trousers, and waded out into the ocean. The water was cold and chilling, its iciness invigorating. He swam easily through the pounding waves. Fifty yards from shore, he turned over on his back and saw her. Maria saw Dawson and waved happily, then unashamedly pulled her nightgown over her head and threw it to the ground. Dawson watched her splash naked into the water, her beautiful brown body gleaming in the bright moonlight. He decided not to scold her, but knew it was time to take her to Madrid and get her safely married to her handsome bullfighter. She was much too young and lovely, he was weakening. If he were to remain only her friend and teacher, the close relationship must end before he himself violated all his own moral teachings.

She was swimming to him, laughing, gliding through the water as easily as he had. "I didn't know you knew how to swim," he called to her.

"I decided that, although you've taught me everything else, you never intended to teach me to swim. So I teach myself. I come down here every night after you are asleep and I swim and swim." She reached him and threw her arms around his neck, "I love to swim, but it is more fun with you here."

Her bare body was close to his own and Dawson shuddered, pulled away, and said, "I'll race you to the pilings," swimming away. She took up his challenge and sliced through the waves beside him. Forgetting their nakedness, they were fish and mermaid and played freely in the water. She pushed his head under, laughing wildly, the smile disap-

201

pearing when he failed to surface. She looked around, shouting his name in fear, when he came up under her, tugged on a leg, pulling her down with him. Together they emerged, laughing and gasping for air, before continuing farther and farther from shore.

They clasped their tired arms around the splintery, white pilings, breathing heavily and pushing wet hair from their eyes. The full moon over them beamed down as bright as daylight on their bodies that were exactly the same color.

"I think I'll leave you here," Dawson teased and swam a few feet away.

"It's you who'll be left behind," she retorted and swam past him. He laughed and came after her, passing her easily. He turned to wait for her, grabbed her waist, held her high up over his head while she laughed and screamed, then tossed her backwards into the water. Dawson tread water and waited for her to emerge. She came up behind him and climbed onto his back, wrapping her legs around his waist. She laughed and pulled on his thick black hair until his head came back and they both fell over into the water.

When they came up again, Dawson said, "We're pretty far out, Maria, we'd better get back."

"Yes, Dawson," she laughed and together they headed for shore. Halfway there, Maria tired. She grew panicky, felt herself slipping under the current. She emerged briefly and cried, "Dawson, Dawson," and he turned and swam to her. He reached her just as she was slipping below the surface again, her eyes frightened, her mouth full of water. His arms came around her and easily pulled her up. She clung to him frightened and coughing. She gasped, "I'll drown, I. . ."

"No you won't, darling," he said and pushed the thick wet hair from her face.

"I can't make it back, I'm too tired, I'm afraid," and her arms tightened around his neck.

"I'll take you in, Maria. Now relax, lay on your back, you're safe with me."

She did as Dawson commanded, trusting him completely. Dawson put a long arm across her chest and easily swam back to shore as she lay against him.

"Thank you, Dawson," she said when they reached waist-deep water. They stood together and she put her hands to his shoulders.

"*De nada*," he said and dropped his arms away from her. "Now, Maria, I want you to get out of the water, put your nightgown back on, and go into the house and to bed."

"Aren't you coming?" she asked, puzzled.

"Maria, I'll come after you have gone in. Now, I shall turn my back and I want you to get out of the water."

"Yes, sir," she answered, stood on tiptoe and kissed his cheek, then started for the beach.

When Dawson felt Maria had had enough time to get covered, he turned back to look. She was walking across the beach at the water's edge. She carried in her hand the nightgown. Dawson shook his head, but found it impossible to take his eyes off her beautiful, bare body.

Later that night, Dawson slept soundly in his bed, tired from the long moonlight swim. He turned in his sleep and came in contact with another warm body against his own. She was laying close and, in the half sleep still possessing him, he did the only natural thing. Without even opening his sleepy eyes, his arm went around her and his lips sought out hers and covered them in a kiss. The mouth under his was fully awake and responded to him with alarming passion while her slender arms came around his neck and pulled him to her. Dawson's eyes flew open and he was instantly wide awake. He pulled back, shocked, while she moaned and murmured, "Dawson, oh, Dawson."

"My God, Maria, what are you doing in here?" He moved her arms from his neck and sat up in bed, clutching the sheet up to his chest.

"I couldn't sleep," she whispered, "Make me sleep, Dawson, please."

"Maria, I've told you it isn't right. And where on earth is your nightgown?"

"I didn't put it on after our swim, it's too hot."

"I don't care how warm it is, you are suppoosed to sleep in a nightgown!"

"Why, Dawson, you aren't wearing anything. Were you uncomfortable, too?"

Dawson reddened, flustered, and said, "Maria, here," and drew up the counterpane from the foot of the bed. "I want you to put this around you, go to your room, put on your nightgown and go to sleep . . . in your own room!"

"Don't be mad, Dawson. You didn't scold me when we swam without our clothes, so I didn't think you'd be upset if we slept together naked."

"Look, I should have warned you about the swimming. I made a mistake, it was wrong. I'm not mad, Maria, but I think it's time we go to Madrid. When you get up in the morning, tell Delores to help you pack. We aren't spending another night here."

"If you say so, Dawson."

"I do, now get out of here, please."

Maria rose and wrapped the bedspread around her while Dawson turned tortured eyes to the wall. He heard his door close, turned over on his back, and sighed. Maria went to her room and quickly fell asleep while Dawson lay in the moonlight, wide awake, cursing under his breath, knowing the special, happy relationship he'd shared with Maria Jones was coming to an end.

The next day, Dawson and Maria left for Madrid. Within a month, Maria had met several handsome matadors. Within three months, two of them were in love with her. Within six months, she had made her choice and, on Dawson's arm, walked down the aisle of an old Catholic church to become the bride of her handsome Spaniard.

At a large reception in the ballroom of a fancy hotel in the capital, Maria came to kiss Dawson's cheek and thank him for all he'd done for her. "I shall miss you terribly, Dawson," she smiled, tears shining in her eyes. "What will you do now that you no longer have to look after me?"

"My sweet little Maria, I've suddenly grown very homesick. I'm going back to America."

Eighteen

The morning of August 4, 1859, dawned blistering hot and humid in Natchez, Mississippi. The temperature had remained high throughout the night and, with the early rising of the summer sun, another still, sweltering day was assured for the southern river city. The dry spell had stretched for weeks and showed not a hint of abating. It was hell for the listless, lazy, and irritable inhabitants of Natchez Under, baking day after day in the airless little shanties with their tin roofs. The cotton barons' high-ceilinged mansions on the bluffs were only a few degrees more comfortable, but at least there were frosted goblets of cool drinks to quench endless thirsts and soothe the parched throats of the illustrious masters and mistresses. They sought the comfort of the shrubbery-filled gardens and welcome shade from the stately trees which bent their century-old branches almost to the ground in a seemingly conscious effort to protect the delicate white skin of the ladies and to offer a calming affect on the taut brown brows of the gentlemen.

At Sans Souci, Abigail spent most of her time in her large bedroom, the curtains drawn tight against the merciless sun, while Hannah pressed damp cooling cloths to her uncomfortably warm body and berated the damnable heat that was giving her mistress frequent headaches. Louis kept to himself, drinking more than usual, and shedding his white ruffled shirts when privacy permitted. Kathleen wore the coolest frocks in her closet, pulled her thick blond hair up off her neck, and was short-tempered when her three-year-old son insisted on running in and out of the big house, shouting and banging the doors. Hunter, usually placid and even-tempered, surprised the household by raising his voice on several occasions after a long hot day spent with cranky patients at his office. He had reached the boiling point, to his own dismay and that of the entire family, and found it increasingly hard to be pleasant as day after long day of the oppressive heat continued.

There was one member of the family who remained happily unfazed by the torturous weeks of humid heat. Scott never noticed the heat and was out in the sun as often as he was allowed to play outdoors. Going as near to naked as modesty and Hannah allowed, his young body grew even darker than his usual olive complexion until Hannah scolded him, saying he was going to be as black as she if he didn't get inside. He paid no attention to her warnings and his squeals of laughter pierced the quiet afternoons as he romped and played on the parched lawns of Sans Souci, crying in protest when he was dragged, kicking his bare feet, into the house by Hannah's strong, black hands.

Scott awoke early on the morning of August fourth. Excitement jangled the natural alarm in his tiny head for today was the day he was going on a new adventure and he had talked excitedly of it for weeks, questioning Hunter about the coming events until his easy-going father wished at times they hadn't told the child about the riverboat trip to New Orleans until the day of departure.

"Daddy," Scotty shouted, bursting into Hunter's bedroom. "Get up, Daddy, it's time to go." Scott ran to the bed, dragging a footstool up to use for a step ladder. He was bouncing on the soft bed while Hunter struggled to open his eyes. "Daddy, Daddy," Scotty was shouting as he climbed onto the chest of the sleepy man. Putting tiny hands into Hunter's thick blond hair, he was shaking Hunter's head when finally Hunter opened his eyes, no longer able to ignore the little intruder intent on getting him out of bed.

"Scotty, please quit yelling, I'm awake." he looked fondly up at the boy leaning over him.

"Daddy, it's time to go to New Orleans right now!" The excited, happy face of the youngster brought a lazy smile to Hunter's face as he looked at the little black eyes dancing with happiness. His arms came around the boy and he laughed and said, "I'll get up if you'll give me some sugar."

Scott gave his father a quick kiss on the lips, then made a face when Hunter's unshaven cheeks scratched his skin. "You stick me, Daddy." Scott pulled back.

"I do, huh?" Hunter tousled the black hair. "Well, let me show you what tickles," and he pulled the tiny body up to his face and blew on the naked brown stomach until Scotty was giggling hysterically and begging him to stop. Fully awake now, Hunter lifted his son off the bed and rose, the boy still laughing and begging, "Tickle me some more, Daddy."

"Why, Scott, if I do we'll miss the boat to New Orleans. Now run along so I can dress and I'll meet you downstairs for breakfast."

"Okay, Daddy," Scott looked up at him, then ran for the open door. "Hurry, Daddy," he said, running out the door, terrified they would miss the riverboat.

Hunter heard Scott's tiny footsteps flying back down the hall to his own room. He smiled and closed the door. He, too, was excited about the trip. The prospect of taking the loveable little boy on his first trip down the Mississippi filled him with pleasant anticipation. But there was another reason, another possibility of what could happen on this trip, that excited Hunter Alexander even more than the obvious pleasure Scott would derive from it.

Hunter smiled as he looked in the mirror to shave. He thought about the last time he had been in New Orleans with Kathleen. It had been their honeymoon trip, nearly four years ago. It had been the most wonderful week of Hunter's life and he was hopeful that perhaps he could recapture some of that happiness. Oh, not that there was a likely possibility the whole week could be that good. But, still, Kathleen had been unusually pleasant to him for the last several months, spending long hours with him in the library after the family had gone to bed. She had said it was because it was much too hot to sleep, and maybe it was, but it didn't matter. She seemed to enjoy his company and even when they both sat reading, not talking, there was a closeness, an unspoken comfortable feeling between them that had never been there before.

Kathleen was looking forward to this trip, as was the whole family. She hoped that getting out on the river would cool everyone off for at least one night. Hunter had agreed and then suggested they go out to the summer house and sit for a while; the moon was out and maybe there was a breeze stirring there. She had smiled, risen from her chair, and together they had walked out the door and across the lawn. They had sat for a while and when the next evening came and everyone had gone to bed, it was she who suggested they go outside for a while. He was delighted and quickly laid aside his book and followed her. So their long evenings in the library had turned into long evenings on the white settee in the summer house and, although Hunter's reading and research were suffering from the long summer evenings spent with Kathleen, it was worth it to him. He hadn't been so content in ages.

Many of those evenings after long stays in the garden, he would walk her to her bedroom door and when he kissed her cheek, she didn't pull away or seem surprised. There had even been a couple of times in the last two weeks when it had been she who had reached up and kissed his cheek and said lazily, "Night, Hunter, it was a nice evening." This encouragement gave him the courage to say, "You know, Kathleen, when we are in New Orleans, I know we will have to spend most of the time with the Howards. But wouldn't it be nice if you and I could slip off together for an evening or two on the town, maybe the ballet, go out to dinner, and even to a gambling house?''

"Oh, Hunter, that would be fun. Let's do it. I would just love to go to some of those fancy restaurants again. Do you know what I really want to do?'' she giggled.

"What, Kathleen?'' he laughed with her.

"I want to play roulette again. I just love that game and you remember I was lucky at it, too.''

"Yes, you were,'' he grinned. "We'll do it!''

"It's a date,'' she agreed and had no idea how delighted her husband was to hear her say it.

So Hunter smiled as he shaved and excitement filled his chest just as it did his three-year-old son. He intended to order gallons of the best champagne and pour it down her as fast as he could get her to empty her glass. He had visions of her giddy and carefree and willingly agreeing to go with him to the St. Charles Hotel for a late supper. When he got her there, he would convince her to spend the night, or a portion of it, with him in one of the luxurious suites in the grand hotel. She would laugh and agree and he would take her up and together they would recapture what they had experienced so long ago. She would finally be his wife again.

"Ouch,'' Hunter said aloud, then laughed at himself when he realized he had gotton so carried away with his secret fantasy that he had nicked himself with the sharp straight-edged razor. A tiny pinpoint of blood rose to his chin, but did not dampen the high, hopeful spirits of the very optimistic young man. Laughing still, he said to his reflection, "Some surgeon you are.''

The carriages were loaded with trunks and valises. The travelers were dressed and ready to go down to Natchez Under and board the stately old *Roxanne* riverboat. Louis, Abigail, and Daniel were to ride in one carriage, followed by Kathleen, Hunter, Scott, and Hannah in the second.

Louis was helping Abigail into the carriage, gingerly

lifting the long trailing skirts of her blue tulle dress, making sure it was safely inside the carriage. Scott, now dressed in a white summer suit with short trousers, his black hair neatly combed, white shoes and socks on his feet, was skipping happily down the walk in front of Kathleen and Hunter. Hannah lumbered along behind them, swatting at a droning bee threatening to attack the snow white bandana around her head. She was grumbling, "I hates summer, I always has. I hopes it gonna be cooler in New Orleans, but I doubts it."

A horse and rider approached and pulled up in the drive before Hunter and Kathleen reached their carriage. A tall black man was atop the big bay colt and he dismounted as soon as the horse stopped. Concern came over Hunter's face when he recognized Walt Samply, one of his Uncle Rembert's house servants.

"Good morning, Walt," Hunter called to the black man and walked to him.

"Doctor Hunter, I hates to bring you bad news, but your Uncle Rembert done took sick this mornin'. He be in his bed. He say not to bother you 'cause he knows you be goin' to New Orleans. He say you has been working real hard and you deserves a vacation. But, Doctor Hunter, I come anyhow."

"What is is, Walt, have you any idea?"

"No, suh, he jest look really bad and he be too weak to get up. He say not to worry none, but I can't help it. He be powerful mad at me when he find out I come for you, but Doctor Hunter, I jest . . ."

"You did the right thing, Walt, don't worry." Hunter looked at Kathleen, then at Scott, now inside the carriage, leaning over the back seat peering at him. "I'll be right along, Walt. You go on back and tell Uncle Rembert I'm on my way."

"Yes, suh, Doctor Hunter, I tell him you is comin'," the black man was back on his horse and galloping away.

"Hunter, is he that bad?" Kathleen walked to her husband.

"I don't know, dear, but I have to go."

"Certainly. Scott and I will stay here and I'll go over . . ."

"No. I won't hear of it, Kathleen. Scotty would be heartbroken, he's looked forward to this trip too long."

"Then we'll let him go on with Mother and Father. I'll stay here with you."

"No," Hunter said, taking her arm and leading her to the carriage. "You've looked forward to the trip, too, and you must be there to celebrate Scott's birthday."

"But, Hunter, I feel so bad about you, I really . . ."

"No arguments, Kathleen, you're going. I won't die of disappointment. I'm a doctor, you know it won't be the first time I've had to change my plans. Now, get in the carriage," he smiled and she obeyed.

"Daddy, get in," Scott was off the seat pulling on his father's hand.

"Scotty, Daddy's not going this time. I'm sorry, son, but it can't be helped."

"I want you to go with me." Scott threw his arms around Hunter's neck.

"I can't, Scotty. But you'll have a good time, so be Daddy's big boy and take good care of Mommy." He kissed the boy and handed him to Hannah. Hunter kissed Kathleen's cheek, "Take care, dear, and have a good time." He walked to the front carriage and explained to the Beauregards. Daniel hurriedly took Hunter's luggage from the carriage and Hunter waved goodbye until they pulled out of sight. Scott waved from Hannah's lap, tears streaming down his brown cheeks, clearly heartbroken that his father was not going with him.

Hunter sighed and said under his breath, "You think you're disappointed, Scott, I could cry louder than you," then he turned and dismissed it from his mind as the doctor in him took over and he hurried to his uncle's bedside.

Scott's disappointment soon vanished when he reached the riverfront and saw all the boats moored there. The *Roxanne* stood majestically at the pier and when Scott went aboard the white riverboat ready to take him magically down the Mississippi, his eyes grew big and round. He peered up at the tall twin smokestacks, then pointed to the giant paddle wheels. Holding his mother's hand, he wanted to explore every square inch of the big boat. When the whistles blew loudly and the bells clanged and the huge paddle wheels churned up lovely white foam, the little boy on his first riverboat trip was the happiest child in all Mississippi. He stood with Kathleen at the railing, talking excitedly of the many new wonders before his eyes. When time came for dinner, he said he was not going to eat, he was going to stay right there on deck all night, until finally the determined three-year-old had to be threatened with a spanking by his exasperated mother. Fed and in bed at last, Kathleen bent and kissed the dark little face and whispered, "Tomorrow you can stay on deck all the way to New Orleans, darling."

Scott's strong little arms came around his mother's neck and he kissed her happily, "I love you mommy. I'll be good from now on, just like Daddy told me."

"I know you will, sweetheart, now get some sleep."

"Goodnight, Mommy." He dropped his arms away, turned over onto his stomach, and promptly went to sleep.

The arrival at the big Howard estate in New Orleans was almost as joyous as the ride on the riverboat. Scotty had never seen so many cousins, aunts and uncles, and friends. He had never met them before that he could remember, but he was destined to have a good time for many of the cousins were near his age. He was not there fifteen minutes before he was merrily running around the big lawns, squealing and chasing his newfound playmates, delighting in their company.

Smiling, Kathleen looked after her happy son as he disappeared swiftly around the corner of the big house, three or four children with him. Scotty was going to have a very good time. The smile left her face momentarily as she thought about her husband, "Hunter, dear Hunter. How I wish he could have come."

Nineteen

The eleventh of August was Scott Alexander's third birth-day. It was also the last day of the pleasant visit in New Orleans with the Howard family. Kathleen decided that morning to make one last trip into town for shopping, she still had a few more items to buy for her son's birthday party. Scott begged to go along and Kathleen agreed.

Daniel drove Kathleen, Scott, and Hannah into town and Kathleen assured him it would take no longer than couple of hours to get the things she wanted. He was free to do as he pleased as long as he promised to have the carriage waiting at Lafayette Square at 2 P.M. to take the shoppers back to the Howard estate.

Scott loved the magical shops and when Kathleen took him inside Holmes department store on Chartres Street, with its tables filled with shiny new toys of every description, his eyes lit up and he happily pointed out a dozen things he would like to have. Kathleen made a mental note of the ones he lingered over the longest. When they left the store without her purchasing any of the wonderous treasures, Scott didn't cry, but was clearly disappointed and confused.

His mother merely smiled down at him and said, "Scotty, you will get lots of nice things tonight at your birthday party. Now I want you to go along with Hannah for a while and she will buy you some candy. I have some things I must do and I will meet you in an hour at the sidewalk café in front of the St. Charles Hotel." She winked at Hannah. The prospect of being allowed to eat candy at the lunch hour brought a smile back to Scott's face and he willingly took Hannah's hand. The two went off down the street and Kathleen hurried back inside the store and bought six or eight of the toys her son had expressed a desire to own. Happy with her selections, she told the pleasant, middle-aged clerk to wrap them in colorful packages and have them delivered to the Howard estate by the end of the afternoon.

Kathleen went on to the café to wait for Scott and Hannah. She ordered a cooling lemonade and sat contentedly sipping the drink and lazily watching the activity on the streets of the charming, colorful city. She sat with her back to the St. Charles Hotel, a large green and white table umbrella protecting her from the hot summer sun. Relaxed and radiant, Kathleen Alexander was pleasantly content, idly daydreaming, a pleased smile on her face.

"Kathleen," the warm, resonant voice came from behind her. She knew in an instant who was calling her name. No other voice on earth could caress her in quite the same way, make her heart leap to her throat, or send tingling messages through her entire body. Slowly, she turned around to face him.

Standing so close he filled the entire scope of her sight, she looked at him and opened her mouth to speak, but no words came. Taller even than she had remembered, she had to tilt her head back to look up at him. He was wearing a pearl gray broadcloth jacket and tight black trousers. His white ruffled shirt was set off handsomely with a gray silk cravat and in his hand was a wide-brimmed panama hat. His swarthy face was browner than ever, his flashing dark eyes as dark as midnight, and his thick hair so black it was nearly blue. One brief look at the handsome face brought back all the pain and longing she thought she had put behind her. She loved him still, loved him totally, unreasonably, foolishly, to the exclusion of every other human being on the earth.

Dawson Blakely had come down from his hotel suite and walked through the elegant lobby into the outdoor restaurant. He had seen only her back. The silky blond hair was neatly pulled into a chignon, but her slender white shoulders were exposed in the pink summer frock and the swan like neck and head were tilted at an angle too familiar to mistake. For a few minutes, Dawson had stood without moving, no more than ten feet behind her, his big hands trembling on the brim of his hat. Afraid she would flee, run away in anger if he approached her, he had considered hiding his presence. He could step back inside and content himself with looking at her back while she remained unaware of his eyes secretly feasting on her. He couldn't do it, it was not enough. He had to look at her face if only for a second before she fled from him in disgust. He had walked nearer and softly called her name. She hadn't turned immediately and Dawson's heart had begun to thump against his ribs. She had recognized his voice and was going to rush away without giving him even a glimpse of her lovely face.

But, then their eyes held, as both studied the pleasing countenance of the other. The face he'd carried with him across an ocean and which had haunted his tortured dreams night after night for years was smiling up at him. The lonely years he'd spent without her evaporated as he lost himself in the big blue eyes filled with an unmistakeable welcome. The open invitation in those dear eyes gave him the courage to speak.

"May I join you, Kathleen?" he said very softly.

"Yes, please sit down, Dawson," she answered without hesitation.

Dawson pulled a chair out across from her, ducked his head under the umbrella, and sat down. He laid his hat on the table and settled back in the chair while his dark eyes never left her. He wanted to touch her hand, but dared not risk so bold a move. He folded his big hands on the table in front of him and hoped she wouldn't notice that they were trembling. Kathleen looked at him and felt an overpowering urge to reach up and touch the beloved brown face, to feel its

217

strong jaw line under her fingers if only for a moment, but she sat with her hands clutched tightly in her lap. Her hands were turning white from the nervous pressure she applied, sending all the blood from the tips of her fingers.

After an awkward silence they began talking, Kathleen speaking first. "You're looking well, Dawson."

"Thank you, Kathleen, you are too. You're lovelier than ever, if that's possible."

Kathleen coughed nervously. "Do you live in New Orleans now? I thought you were still in Europe."

"I just got in last night from Spain. In fact, this is the first time I've been here in almost four years."

"Oh? What brings you here now? Do you have business or is this a pleasure trip?"

"I don't know why really," he answered as a hint of a smile came to his full mouth, "perhaps fate brought me. What about you, why are you here?"

"I . . . we're down visiting my mother's family. A vacation really, we're leaving in the morning."

"We?" Dawson said, interested, "Is your husband with you?"

"No. Unfortunately, Hunter had to remain in Natchez. His uncle fell ill at the last minute." Kathleen looked down at the table.

"That's too bad. Who did you come with, surely you aren't in this wicked old city alone?"

"Certainly not," she answered too quickly, "Mother and Father are with me and my . . ." Kathleen stopped talking because Dawson was no longer looking at her. He had turned his attention to something behind her and the smile had left his face. His black eyes widened and his expression was strange and puzzling. Kathleen turned to see what he was staring at.

Coming down the sidewalk toward their table, Hannah was being tugged along by an excited, laughing Scotty. "Mommy," he shouted, dropping Hannah's hand and running to Kathleen. "We had candy, Mommy. Chocolate."

"I see you did," she smiled, "and it looks like most of it missed your mouth, darling. Your face is all sticky."

Dawson's intent eyes were on the boy and when Scott turned to look at him, Dawson smiled down at the youngster. "Hello, son," he said quickly, then rose to speak to Hannah.

"Good Lawd, Mistah Dawson, if you ain't a sight fo' sore eyes! I can't believe it's really you," a big grin spread over her face and she looked up at him, happy to see him. Suddenly she glanced nervously down at Kathleen.

"It's good to see you, Hannah. It's been a long time, sit down, please."

"Naw, suh, Mistah Dawson, don't mind me none. I jest stands right here, I be fine."

Dawson sat back down and once again turned his full attention to Scott. "Will you sit on my knee for just a minute?" He held out his arms to the child.

"Oh, no," Kathleen said hurriedly, "he's dirty, Dawson, he'll get you . . ."

Scotty quickly went to Dawson's arms and was willingly lifted onto the stranger's lap. "How old are you, Scott?" Dawson asked, studying the flashing black eyes in the little olive face.

Scotty held up three fingers in front of Dawson's face. "It's my birthday," he announced proudly, "I'm getting all my presents tonight!"

Dawson laughed heartily and said, "That's wonderful! You know what? Today's my birthday, too."

Scotty looked at him and said innocently, "What did you get? Did you get any presents?"

"Yes, I did, son," Dawson looked over Scotty's head to Kathleen and smiled, "I got exactly what I wanted for my birthday."

Kathleen flushed and said, "Jump down, Scott, it's time for us to go home," and rose from her chair.

"Just a minute," Dawson said, still holding to the boy's

tiny middle. Dawson reached into his pocket and drew out a twenty-dollar gold piece and presented it to Scott. "I didn't know it was your birthday, so I didn't get you a present. Take this and buy yourself something."

Scotty grabbed the shiny gold piece and said, "Look, Mommy, can I keep it?"

Kathleen didn't answer, looked helplessly at Dawson. "Sure you can keep it, Scott," Dawson assured, "but only if you give me a good-bye kiss."

Scotty gladly threw his tiny arms around Dawson's neck and smacked him on the mouth, giving Dawson a sticky chocolate kiss before jumping down and running to Hannah to show her his gold piece. Dawson felt a lump in his throat; there was no mistaking his remarkable resemblance to the adorable little boy. He watched the child skip along beside Hannah, then turned back to look at Kathleen.

Ignoring his questioning eyes, she said, "It was nice to see you again, Dawson," and she held out her hand.

He took it in both of his, squeezed it gently, and said in a whisper, "I'm staying right here in this hotel. I'm alone, my room number is 412." She jerked her hand away as though it were burned, turned and left without saying a word.

Dawson slowly sank back into his chair and watched her walking away. She caught up with Scott and Hannah and took the boy's hand. He wished she would turn and look back. Dawson said to himself, "If she turns back to look at me, she'll come to me tonight," then held his breath, praying, willing her to turn around. She kept on walking, getting further and further away with each passing second. Hope slipped away and he knew he was never going to see her again. So far away now she would soon be completely out of sight, Dawson still watched, his eyes straining, every muscle in his body taut. he wanted to scream at her, beg her to look back. Just one glance! Please, dear God, turn around! His agony was reaching its painful climax and his lungs were exploding in his aching chest from lack of oxygen.

Kathleen turned and looked at him. And she was smiling. Dawson exhaled and felt his aching lungs filling up with sweet, rarefied air. His long, tense body relaxed and a grateful smile lifted the corners of his full mouth as his black eyes danced with happiness. She turned the corner and went out of sight.

The sticky traces of a chocolate kiss from the son he'd never known remained in the left corner of Dawson's mouth. Almost reluctantly, he took a clean white handkerchief from his pocket and wiped off the chocolate. The kiss could not be wiped away.

Scott's birthday party was held on the back lawn of the big Howard estate. A picnic supper was spread out on a long table under the magnolia trees and family and friends gathered at sundown. A huge birthday cake with three blue candles was placed before the birthday boy after the meal was finished. When Scott blew out the candles, Kathleen stood behind him and said, "Scotty, make a wish."

He leaned his head back against her waist and looked up at her, "I wish my daddy was here."

"I do too, darling, I really do."

A mountain of gifts brought squeals of happiness from the delighted child and when Hannah carried him upstairs three hours later, he was still begging to stay outside and play with his many new toys. More exhausted than he knew, he was nodding sleepily by the time she undressed him and tucked him in his bed. Kathleen came in and kissed him goodnight, whispering, "Happy Birthday, sweetheart," but the black lashes were already closed over the dark eyes and he was fast asleep.

Kathleen went to her own bedroom and Hannah gathered up the dirty clothes she had taken off of Scotty. She picked up the little shirt and trousers. Something fell from the pocket of the short pants and Hannah bent to pick it up. It was the twenty-dollar gold piece Dawson had given him. Scott had forgotten about the coin and about the dark stranger who had given it to him. Hannah held the gold piece in her hand and thought about Dawson. She looked down at the tiny boy sleeping peacefully and shook her head. She wondered for the thousandth time if she had been wrong in not telling Kathleen about the overheard conversation that had so painfully altered her life. Hannah sighed heavily, "It's too late now, much too late." With the gold piece in her hand, she left Scott's room and went to Kathleen.

Kathleen stood at the open windows in her dressing gown, her mood pensive, the blue eyes wistful. She was looking out, seeing nothing. Hannah entered the room and without a word she walked to Kathleen and handed her the gold coin. Kathleen looked at it, then her fingers closed around it as her hand went to her breast and her eyes closed. Hannah understood and turned and went to the closet. She returned with a blue muslin gown over her arm and said to Kathleen, "Honey, it sho hot tonight, ain't it?"

Kathleen's eyes opened and she said, "What? Oh, yes, yes it is Hannah. Very hot . . ."

"I thinks maybe you needs to take a little carriage ride, cool off a bit fo' you tries to sleep."

Kathleen turned to look at Hannah. The big black face was full of concern and affection. Kathleen knew Hannah was reading her thoughts, "Oh, Hannah," she flung her arms around her mammy's neck, "you're the only one who understands."

"There, there, chile," Hannah said and hugged her, "I know how my baby's suffered. I don't see no harm in you jest seein' him for a few minutes. Now come on, I'll help you dress. I done tol' Daniel to bring the carriage to the side entrance in half an hour. Nobody gonna know you gone. Daniel, he won't say nothin'."

Kathleen smiled, saying, "I love you, Hannah," and let Hannah help her into the soft blue dress. A lovely dress she'd never worn before, Hannah assured her the high ruffled neck set off her delicate features "jest right." Kathleen swept her long blond hair up onto her head and was slipping down the stairs twenty minutes later with Hannah leading the way to make sure no one saw her leaving. Safely inside the carriage, Kathleen sunk back in the seat and giggled, feeling like a guilty schoolgirl while her mammy stood watching her leave, tears swimming in her eyes.

Kathleen was shaking when she knocked softly on the door of room 412 at the St. Charles Hotel. He didn't come to let her in, he called in an even voice, "It's open, Kathleen." She went inside, closing the door behind her. He stood across the room looking at her, his face solemn. He was wearing different clothes from this afternoon, tight tan trousers with pencil sharp creases, a clean white shirt open to his waist. he was freshly bathed and shaved as though he had been expecting her. At last, he smiled the lazy, sensual smile she remembered so well and all at once her heart was beating wildly with pleasure. His dark eyes were glowing with a hot light and she felt herself growing weak. Neither spoke. Without a word they rushed to each other and fell into each other's arms. They were greedily kissing, holding tightly to each other, stroking each other. They kissed, they trembled, they laughed, they cried. They could not get enough of each other. Like two wild animals finally let out of their cages, they moaned and growled, they sighed and gasped. They pawed each other, they explored each other. Eager hands roamed wildly up and down over faces and bodies. Bodies strained to get ever closer to each other. Burning mouths moved from lips to eyes to ears to hair and back again, each taking and giving in a frenzy of unbridled emotions.

Finally, calming a little after the first electric shock of being together again, Kathleen, still clutching tightly to a hand full of Dawson's black hair, gasped, "Oh, Dawson, do you think we'll go to hell for this?" Her blue eyes were serious.

Dawson looked down at her and his eyes turned serious too. "Darling, I've been in hell for the last four years," and he pulled her to him and kissed her again, his lips moving against her mouth, "Surely even sinners deserve one night in paradise." He was kissing her again, tenderly now, taking his time, slowly and expertly arousing her again. He raised his head and looked at her. The concern had left the blue eyes and the answer he wanted was shining in them. He took her hand and started leading her into the bedroom adjoining the big sitting room where they stood. She stopped and he looked down at her, puzzled.

"Dawson," she whispered, then moved her eyes down to his shirtfront, "before you take me to your bed, will you do something for me, please?"

"Anything, love, anything," and he meant it.

She looked up at him shyly and said, "Will you hold me on your knee for just a minute, the way you did on the *Diana Mine?*"

Dawson threw back his head and laughed heartily and pulled her to him. "Yes, darling, I will." Still laughing wildly, he looked down at her and teased, "Do you want to strip for me, too, just like you did before?" She gave no answer, but she smiled up at him.

Still chuckling happily, Dawson led her to a chair at the desk, pulled it out and sat down, pulling her down on his knee. "I love you, Kathleen Diana Beauregard," he smiled and pulled her mouth to his. She pushed back a little and said, "Dawson, my name is Kathleen Alexander."

The laughter died on Dawson's lips, the muscle twitched in his hard jaw, and he said very softly, "My love, tonight your name is only Diana mine." Very slowly, he raised his hand to pull back the blue ruffles around her neck. He leaned down to kiss the soft hollow of her throat. Kathleen sighed with pleasure and kissed the dark head bending over her and arched her back up to him. While his hot mouth slid further down into the softness of her bosom with each fiery kiss, he murmured against her tingling skin, "I still worship you, Diana mine."

All Kathleen's pain and longing of the past four years were gone. No one and nothing existed but Dawson Blakely. She was his, she had always been his, she always would be his, and she was ready for him to claim what belonged only to him.

Dawson raised his head and smiled lazily at her. Rising, he easily lifted her in his arms, holding her firmly against his hard chest. With long, determined strides he moved across the drawing room and into the dimness of the bedroom. Kathleen, with her arms looped around his neck, laughed and kicked her shoes from her feet, all the while kissing the warmth of his throat, his lean jaw, his temples. A small hand slipped from behind his head and moved timidly down into the open shirtfront, the fingers spreading over the muscled wall of his chest. Dawson's rapidly beating heart was under her palm, reassuring her that he was truly there; that he was real, and home, and hers.

Raising his lips to hers, he kissed her again when they reached their destination. Slowly, he let her slide down from his arms while his mouth remained on hers, kissing her long and lovingly. Her stockinged feet now touching the floor, she stood on tiptoe and clung to him, never wanting to let him go. Finally, Dawson's mouth left hers and he said through fevered lips, "God, you're so little. I'd almost forgotten how small you are."

Her head tipped back to look up at him, she smiled, "It's just that I'm not wearing my shoes." When she leaned to him, her mouth was on the level of his dark chest and she put her lips where her hand had rested. Dawson trembled. While she sprinkled soft little kisses over the expanse of his chest, her hands pulling the white shirt apart, Dawson raised a hand to her hair.

"Kathleen," he murmured throatily, "I must take your beautiful hair down. Do you mind?"

225

"My love," she said, her mouth on his warm skin, "You may do anything you like to me."

The thought of doing anything he wanted with her was so temptingly exciting to Dawson that his big hands shook uncontrollably as he pulled the pins from her golden hair. Free of its restraints, the long hair cascaded down around her shoulders and Dawson bit his bottom lip and let his long fingers run through its shiny length.

Kathleen kidded him, saying, "Dawson, is this all you want to do to me? Just run your fingers through my hair?" Her small hands went to his wrists and she slowly pulled his hands from her hair and down to her shoulders. "Please," she whispered, "help me with my dress."

Smiling down at her in the familiar way she loved so much, Dawson's dark eyes flashed with desire and his hand went to the back of her dress.

"Do you want me to turn around?" she offered.

"No," he said emphatically, "I want to look at you while I undress you."

Too much in love with him to be hesitant about disrobing in his presence, she laughed and said, "Good. I want to look at you, too."

The blue dress was quickly unfastened and Dawson eased it over her head and tossed it to a chair. The petticoats followed quickly and Kathleen was standing before him in a lacy white camisole and her pantalets.

"What, no corsets?" he kidded as he unhooked the camisole.

"Not tonight," she admitted, "not with you."

"I'm glad," he said as the last hook was opened and he slowly pulled the delicate camisole apart and down her arms. His eyes burning her with an intense gaze, Kathleen winced when he raised his hands to her bare, full breasts. Shudders of longing filled her as she looked down to see the large brown hands filled with the pale flesh of her swelling breasts.

"Dawson," she breathed and swayed to him.

"Yes, my darling," he whispered hoarsely while his hands gently caressed and aroused.

"Please," she said and raised her fingers to his lips, "take off your clothes, darling."

Kissing her fingers, he said softly, "Kathleen, I thought perhaps you'd rather I wait until you . . ."

"No, Dawson. I want you to undress right now." She brushed his hands from her breasts and started tugging on his white shirt. Dawson laughed and pulled off the shirt, tossing it aside.

In seconds, they stood naked facing each other and both let their searching eyes roam freely over the beloved body of the other. Not touching, they examined each other while love and lust filled them to overflowing. It was Dawson who could bear it no longer; slowly, he reached out and ran his hand over her gently rounded belly. His touch brought a happy sigh of pleasure and he smiled and lifted her roughly up into his arms. Her naked breasts were crushed against his bare, heaving chest and her hip and thigh pressed against his hard flat abdomen. His hands were almost cutting into the bare skin of her ribcage and thigh.

Dizzy with desire, Kathleen felt herself being placed on the softness of the bed and Dawson's heavy weight as he stretched out by her. Then his mouth was descending to hers again and she closed her eyes as her lips parted in welcome. His mouth, hot and moist, was on hers while his hand swept over her body, caressing, arousing, exploring.

The long, deep kisses continued until Kathleen was flushed and breathless, her hands clutching at him, slipping along his smooth brown back up to his wide shoulders. His lips moved from hers to the softness under her ear. "Kathleen," he murmured, his breath ragged in her ear, "I love you, I never stopped loving you. Oh, God, I'm so sorry for everything." He pulled her against him and his big body was shaking with emotion. It was more than the distinctive trembling of rising passion, it was more like . . . Alarmed, Kathleen pushed on his chest and pulled back to look at him. His swarthy face was contorted and his eyes were tightly shut. The thick dark lashes were wet and matted. Protective pain stabbed through Kathleen's bare breasts. Dawson was weeping. This big, powerful man had tears in his eyes. The father of her only child was sobbing and she felt tears stinging her own eyes as she realized her only love had suffered just as she had. He'd missed her too; he was sorry he had left her; he loved her just as she loved him.

"Darling," she murmured, kissing his wet cheeks. "It doesn't matter, Dawson. None of it matters. I love you, I'm here, naked in your arms. Kiss me as though it never happened. I'm still yours. Love me, make me whole again."

"Kathleen," he moaned and kissed her wildly. Salt from his tears clung to his full lower lip and Kathleen kissed it away while the heart inside her swelled with the fullness of her love for him. When his lips left hers, they slid down her cheek to her neck, then to the hollow of her throat. "My precious love," he breathed as his lips grew more demanding and slipped down over the curve of her breasts. Kathleen held her breath and waited anxiously for his mouth to close over a hardened nipple. When at last she felt the welcome warmth enveloping it, she sighed and put her hand into his hair, pulling his head closer while she whispered, "Yes, Dawson, oh yes, please."

For a long, glorious time Dawson kissed her breasts while she lay, an arm thrown over her head, enjoying the sweet tugging of his mouth, her eyes opening and closing in happy, relaxed contentment. But soon it was no longer enough and Kathleen was clutching his shoulders, her hands roaming restlessly down the rippling muscles. "Dawson, Dawson," she pleaded and Dawson, his dark eyes glazed with passion, raised his head and looked at her. "Please," she whispered and Dawson moaned and began greedily to kiss her stomach, searing her with molten kisses. His knee was between her thighs, his hands on her rounded hips. He shifted until he was over her, his face inches from her own.

He kissed her softly and whispered, "Now, darling?"

"Yes, yes," she breathed and lifted her hips to him.

His penetration was swift and deep and both gasped with the pleasure it brought. They began to move rhythmically as though they were one body while declarations of undying love spilled from their heated lips and the world around them ceased to exist. The only truth, the only love, the only joy, was in this room, this bed, as the two sweat-dampened bodies, one big, brown, and powerful, one small, white, and slender, moved sensuously in the age-old act of mating, moving closer and closer to the pinnacle of passion, unthinking and uncaring of anything, save the deep fulfillment only their lovemaking could bring. No other man on earth could make Kathleen Alexander shatter into a million pieces while she cried out in ecstasy. She clung to Dawson as wave after wave of frighteningly sweet explosions claimed her. No other woman in the world could bring to Dawson Blakely the blessed release that cleansed his soul and satisfied his raging passions. Only the small blond beauty under him had the power to take him to dizzying, undreamed-of heights, to lift him sweetly and completely to the supreme apex and then hold tightly and tenderly to him while he slowly descended with her wrapped in his happy arms.

Kathleen dozed for a few minutes. She awoke with a lazy, satisfied feeling and turned her head slowly to look at Dawson. He lay on his back, fast asleep, a brown hand on the pillow near his head. The steady rise and fall of his chest was a safe, reassuring sight to her. Kathleen turned on her side and raised up on an elbow to look at him. Content to lay and watch him, she was completely still, carefully studying the sleeping face. His thick black lashes rested on the brown cheeks, the jaw and mouth were relaxed, the whole face in repose. A knife-sharp pain sliced through her chest as she quietly adored the face, so innocent-looking in sleep, so hauntingly the same as the face of his beautiful son. Raising herself up for a better look, she was jerked back sharply. She looked around to see what was holding her. Dawson had insisted she take her long hair down to fall around her shoulders. Now she saw the brown hand flung up on the pillow was entangled in her curls. She lay back smiling and slowly loosened the long fingers, one by one, that were gripping a long strand of her hair. She freed herself without waking him, though he moaned slightly and turned his head in his sleep. She leaned over him, noticing for the first time a gold chain around his neck. She leaned closer and in the dim light saw what was on the chain. The tiny cameo was resting on his chest, nestled in the thick black hair. The cameo she was wearing that night they were together on the *Diana Mine,* the last night she had seen him. She stared at the little cameo resting on the body she loved so dearly and tears filled her eyes. She knew she had to leave, had to leave now before he woke up, for if she waited . . . if he woke . . . if those strong arms came around her again. . . .

Kathleen slipped from the bed, dressed quickly, and tiptoed into the sitting room. She went directly to the desk and took out a piece of blue note paper and pen and ink. With shaking fingers, she wrote a brief message, folded it, and went back into the bedroom. She placed the note on the pillow beside him and started from the room. Nearly to the door, she stopped and walked back to his side of the bed. Leaning over him, she kissed her own fingers and slowly lowered them to his lips. The fingers stopped an inch from his mouth. She drew her hand away, covered her mouth to stop the sobs that were welling up inside her. She ran from the bed, out of the room, and out of his life.

At 2 A.M. Dawson woke. With eyes still closed and yawning sleepily, he put his hand over to feel for her. There was only the softness of the empty bed. His eyes flew open and he jumped with a start. He called to her hoping she was still in the room somewhere. Or maybe in the sitting room. But knew she wasn't, knew she was gone. Gone without saying goodbye, without telling him if he would see her again, without telling him about their son, without a final kiss.

He saw the small blue piece of paper, grabbed it eagerly, and sat up in bed. His fingers shook as he unfolded it to read what she had written.

My Love,

You made it a night of paradise and I shall carefully tuck it away in my memory to be taken out in private, over and over again, to relive and cherish, to sustain me for a lifetime. But, darling, it changes nothing, it can't. If it meant anything to you, please don't try to see me again.

Your Diana

Dawson read and re-read the note, folded it, and held it tightly in his hand. Slowly he laid back down, his eyes turned up to the ceiling, sightless. In a fit of agony, he rolled over onto his stomach. Moving to her side of the bed, he buried his face in the pillow where the golden head of his beloved had lain. Only her sweet fragrance remained.

Twenty

Doctor Rembert Pitt's illness proved to be nothing more than exhaustion and within two or three days he was feeling much better. Hunter willingly nursed him back to health and was greatly relieved that his uncle's chest pains were not caused by his heart as both had feared.

"Hunter, I feel just terrible for keeping you from your long-planned trip to New Orleans with your family. Can you ever forgive me?"

"Don't talk foolishly, Uncle Rembert. I was glad to come over and I'm just relieved you are all right. There will be other trips, so don't worry about it." Hunter smiled at his uncle.

Uncle Rembert raised himself up in his bed and propped two pillows behind his back. "You're a good man, Hunter." Rembert was silent for a minute, then said, "Hunter, I've been wanting to have a talk with you for some time," and his face grew serious.

Hunter leaned back in his chair beside his uncle's bed and replied, "Now you have the perfect opportunity, Uncle. What's on your mind?"

"You are, son. You and Kathleen." He looked at Hunter's face. "Hunter, I've heard some news I think you should know."

"Then tell me," Hunter said and set his glass of wine on the night table.

Rembert looked up at the ceiling briefly, then at his nephew. "Son, I heard in town that Dawson Blakely may be coming back to Natchez.''

"Should that mean anything to me, Uncle?" Hunter said, the expression on his face never changing.

"Don't pretend with me, Hunter. I'm your uncle, I love you."

"Uncle Rembert, I'm not hiding anything. Dawson Blakely is free to come and go as he pleases, I don't see that it's any concern of mine or yours for that matter."

"Dammit, Hunter! I've told you before, Blakely and Kathleen were inseparable for an entire year before you came to Natchez. There was talk they would be married and no one ever knew what happened between them. Aren't you worried? Don't you believe in honor?" Rembert was very agitated, his face now turning red. "If that man comes back here, I think you should challenge him to a duel! Get this whole matter settled once and for all!"

"Uncle, I appreciate your concern, I know it's because you love me. But I'm telling you as I've told you before, I do not care what happened between my wife and Dawson Blakely before I met her. It has nothing to do with me and, as for Dawson coming back, if he tries to see Kathleen, no one could keep him from that but her. You are worrying needlessly; the man's no fool, Uncle. He knows she's married and, for your information, in the last few months Kathleen and I have drawn closer together. I love her, Uncle, I've always loved her. I can't kill a man because he once loved her, too. I don't blame him for that."

"Hunter, you are much too kind," Rembert's face contorted and he continued, "If you won't challenge him to a duel, by heaven, I'll will myself," and his chubby hand hit the bed beside him.

"You'll do nothing of the kind," Hunter got up from his chair. "Kathleen is my wife, if there's anything to be decided or taken care of, it's my place and mine alone to handle it. I've told you I intend to do absolutely nothing about it. Their relationship happened before she became my wife, so I want to hear nothing further on the subject. If you feel it is some-how hurting your honor, I'm sorry, but I forbid you to do or say anything to anyone about it, do you understand?'' His soft brown eyes narrowed.

"Yes, Hunter, but . . ."

"The subject is closed, Uncle, don't ever mention it to me again."

"Very well, son," Uncle Rembert lay back on his pillows, shaking his head.

"Thank you, Uncle. Now it's getting late, I want you to get some rest. Quit worrying about unimportant things," and he rose and left the room.

Kathleen stood at the railing of the *Roxanne* in the warm summer evening, the breeze from the river cooling her face and soothing her confused brain. After boarding the river-boat at 8 P.M. for the trip to Natchez, the family had dinner together in the ship's big dining room. By the end of the meal, Scott was yawning and gave her no trouble when she told Hannah to get him to bed. Kathleen shared one last cup of coffee with her parents, then Abigail said she too was tired and Louis accompanied her to their cabin on the bow. Kath-leen presumed they were both sound asleep by now. The deck was practically deserted at this late hour and Kathleen was glad. She stood alone, looking out at the murky waters while the riverboat churned slowly north, taking them home to Natchez. Taking her away from Dawson. Kathleen closed her eyes and felt again the full mouth on hers, the strong brown arms holding her tightly, the hard, lean body next to hers. Once again she could see the dark, hooded eyes looking into hers, hear the deep, resonant voice murmuring her name. Without realizing it, Kathleen was smiling to herself, so lost in her own thoughts that she didn't hear her father ap-proaching.

"Kathleen," Louis said softly and touched her arm.

234

Kathleen jumped instinctively and turned, "Oh, Father," she smiled at him, "I thought you and Mother were in bed."

"Your mother is brushing her hair, preparing to retire. I decided I would come up on top for one final cigar before turning in. Would you like company or did you want to be alone?"

"Oh, Father," she smiled and slipped her arm through his, "I'm always happy to have your company, you know that."

Louis Beaurgard patted her hand lovingly and said, "You were smiling when I walked up, darling. Did you have a nice time in New Orleans?"

She looked up at him and without hesitating, said, "Yes, I did, Father. It was wonderful, just perfect."

"I'm so glad," he said, "I think the trip was good for you, Kathleen. There's a look about you, darling. All day long I've noticed that you look . . . well, I don't know, peaceful somehow, and lovelier than ever."

Kathleen flushed in the darkness and said, "I do? I didn't realize. I suppose gettting away for a while was good for me, for all of us."

"Yes, darling, it was. I'm just sorry Hunter couldn't come with us. He's been working so hard and he looks so tired."

Kathleen removed her hand from her father's arm and once again looked out at the peaceful river. "Yes, it is too bad he couldn't be with us."

"Well, perhaps next time. I know he's anxious to have his wife and son back, I'm sure he's missed you terribly."

"Yes, I know he has. Scotty . . . we have missed him, too. I'm glad we'll be home tomorrow."

"I am too, dear. I guess I'd better get back to your mother. Goodnight, darling," he said and kissed her cheek.

"Night, Father," she smiled and looked at him.

Louis Beauregard made no effort to move, but stood looking down at his daughter. He cleared his throat needlessly then said, almost in a whisper, "Kathleen?"

"Yes, Father?"

"You are happy, aren't you, darling? I mean, well, it seems I never get the chance to talk to you the way I used to do and I worry sometimes. You know I always want you to be content, don't you?"

"Father," she smiled and patted his hand, "I am. I have a good, caring husband and a beautiful son. And the best two parents in the whole wide world, I'm very happy."

"I'm glad," he beamed and kissed her again, "I love you so much, my precious girl. Now promise me you'll go to bed soon," and he went to his cabin.

After he left, Kathleen sighed to herself and, feeling tired from the sleepless night she'd spent, went to her own cabin, next to Scotty and Hannah. Hannah appeared through the connecting door and undressed her for bed. Wordlessly, the old black woman unhooked her summer dress and helped her into the long white nightgown. Kathleen took a seat at the small vanity and Hannah took down the thick blond hair and stood gingerly brushing it until it crackled and snapped with electricity.

"Hannah," Kathleen said softly to her mammy's reflection in the mirror, "Do you think God will punish me for being with Dawson last night?"

The hairbrush stopped in midair and Hannah leaned down and took her shoulders, softly saying into the mirror, "Honey, God don't work lak that. You jest stop yo' frettin'. De good Lord understands a powerful lot more than folks gives him credit fo'. He be forgivin' you ifin you had done anything wrong. Now you put that notion rat out of you mind. You needed to see Mister Dawson and he needed to be with you and that's all there is to it. Ain't nobody gonna know. Go to bed, chile, you is tired and you upsetting yo'self fo' no reason."

"Thank you, Hannah. You get some rest, too, I'll see you in the morning," and she smiled at her mammy.

"Night, honey," Hannah kissed her cheek and went into the next cabin where Scotty slept peacefully.

At just after 4 A.M. the next morning, while the illustrious passengers onboard the *Roxanne* were sound asleep in their cabins and the old riverboat slid quietly through the waters just north of Baton Rouge, Louisana, the most dreaded fear of all riverboat travelers happened. A boiler exploded. The powerful blast hurled sleeping passengers on the hurricane deck high into the air and bodies fell back onto the boat and into the river, many in pieces. A giant smokestack collapsed into the hull, pinning screaming men in the wreckage. Within minutes, the boat was ablaze from stem to stern and screams of men and woman filled the still night air as they were scalded to death in their frantic efforts to crawl over each other and get out of the inferno. People trampled each other to death as the flames rushed through the cabins and terrified passengers in the center of the burning boat pushed and crowded those on the outer edges over the side and into the river. Confused victims, most of them in nightclothes, rushed to the bow and stern, jumping overboard onto each other, many going down into the deep never to emerge again. Many who could swim were pulled under and lost by hysterical flounderers.

The bow section of the boat went first, roasting its sleeping passengers in their beds, leaving the sickening stench of burning flesh to spread through the air. Barrels of whiskey exploded with deafening sounds, spewing their flaming liquids over helpless passengers, burning them to death in minutes. The remaining boilers all exploded and the brave pilot, staying at the wheel while the cabin around him burst into flames, steered for the bank. The tiller ropes burned completely through and the flaming vessel was unmanageble. The captain died at the wheel.

Louis and Abigail, asleep in their cabin near the bow,

were among the first to die. With him arms around his wife, Louis threw open their cabin door and was met by heat so terrific that the oxygen was quickly sucked from the small cabin. They were dead within seconds, clinging together, Louis powerless to protect his beloved wife for the first time in their lives. They never felt the scorching flames licking their bodies and burning their nightclothes away. They were smothered to death before the horror of the flames could do their work.

With the first explosion, a section of the deck where Kathleen, Scotty, Hannah, and Daniel slept was blown into the water. The four, stunned, clung to their raft as it floated away from the burning boat. Kathleen held tightly to her crying son and watched in horror as burning bodies flew through the water around them. In a nightmare worse than anything she could ever have dreamed, she lay atop the life-saving wreckage, her nightgown soaked to the skin, while Hannah moaned loudly and her big body shook with terrified sobs. Daniel stared, speechless and afraid. For what seemed an eternity, they clung to their raft and watched helplessly as a scene from hell on earth took place within sight of their frightened, unbelieving eyes. With a sickening certainty, the horrible truth began to dawn on Kathleen. Her mother and father were still on the boat, captive in the roaring flames. A blood-curdling scream mixed with the cries of the dying still trapped on the boat. Kathleen never knew it had come from her.

At Rembert's home, Hunter sat in the large dining room having his morning coffee with his fully recovered uncle. It was almost 8 A.M. when an excited Walt, Rembert's oldest house servant, ran into the dining room waving his arms, his big eyes terrified. "Oh, Doctor Hunter. Sompin awful's happened. I jest got back from town. Oh, Lawd have mercy. The *Roxanne* done gone down outside Baton Rouge."

238

Hunter and Uncle Rembert looked at each other in horror. They rose at the same time and Hunter said, "Walt, do they know . . . are there many dead? Are they all right?"

"Oh, Doctor Hunter, I'se afraid there be lots dead. I don't knows 'bout Miz Kathleen and the boy!"

"I must go at once," Hunter said and started for the front door.

"Hunter, what are you going to do?" his excited uncle followed him.

"I'm going to charter a boat and go to Baton Rouge immediately. Walt, drive me to the river please, I must go." His soft brown eyes were filled with fear.

Dawson lay asleep in his big suite at the St. Charles Hotel. A knock on the door roused him from a deep slumber. "Just a minute," he called and pulled on a pair of black trousers. A nervous bellman stood at the door and said, "Sorry to disturb you, Mister Blakely, but there's a big black man downstairs who says he must see you right away. He says it's an emergency, sir, and . . ." Dawson ran back into the bedroom, jerked on a shirt and jacket, slipped on his shoes, and ran down the stairs. Sam was waiting for him, his big eyes wide with fear. "Oh, Cap'n Dawson, the *Roxanne* has gone down just north of Baton Rouge."

"Oh, God, no," Dawson said, "are they . . . is she all right?"

"Cap'n, I don't know. There's folks dead, lots of em, I . . ."

"Come on, Sam, we're going to Baton Rouge right now." Dawson ran into the street, hair uncombed, in need of a shave, not stopping to go back for anything. He waved down a carriage and Sam followed him shaking his big head. "Is the *Diana Mine* ready to leave?" Dawson asked the frightened black man.

"Yes, Cap'n, we can be underway in half an hour."

* * *

Hunter stood alone on the bow of a chartered riverboat speeding for Baton Rouge. He stood completely rigid, his brown eyes narrowed. He had been standing in the exact same position since leaving the pier four hours earlier. Fighting the fear welling up in his slim frame, he silently prayed for the safety of the wife and son he adored.

Dawson paced the hurricane deck of the *Diana Mine*. He had been pacing back and forth since the boat left the pier in New Orleans some four hours before. He smoked endlessly and muttered to himself as he walked up and down the bow, his black eyes flashing with fear. A sick feeling gripped his taut middle as he said aloud to himself, "They can't be dead, they can't be. I love them too much!"

Hunter arrived in Baton Rouge first. Making inquiries on the busy riverfront, he learned the survivors had been taken to St. Mary's Catholic Church and he hurried there with his heart loudly pounding in his chest. At the entrance to the church, he paused, took a deep breath, and made his way inside. A mass of humanity greeted the frightened doctor as he made his way amid the injured and dazed lining the walls. Cries of pain filled the air and sobs from friends and family who could not find their loved ones brought a shudder from Hunter. Working his way through the crowd, he carefully peered into every face, searching frantically for his own loved ones. With sheer panic just below the surface of his calm exterior, he felt his hopes running out when suddenly he heard a childish voice call to him. Hunter looked in the direction of the sound and saw them. Huddled together on the floor at the rear of the church, Kathleen sat, blankets pulled tightly around her, her hair a tangled mass around her tired face. Scotty was standing in the circle of her arm and he was smiling. A terrified Hannah sat beside her, crying softly to herself while Daniel patted her back.

Pushing through the crowd, tears of happiness and relief

stinging his eyes, Hunter dropped to his knees in front of them. Grabbing his son, he crushed him to his chest saying, "Oh thank God, thank God." The chubby arms of the small boy were around his neck and Scotty was crying now. Hunter drew back slightly, still holding to the boy's waist, and leaned down to Kathleen, whispering, "My darling." As he embraced her trembling form, her arms came around his neck as loud sobs escaped her cold lips. "Oh, Hunter, they're gone. Mother and Daddy. They're dead. Hunter, help me." Hunter released his frightened son and pulled her into his arms, "Darling, darling," he murmured and caressed her. She collapsed in his arms and the hands on his neck tightened to a viselike grip as she pressed against her strong, understanding husband and transferred part of her grief to him.

When Dawson and Sam arrived in Baton Rouge, the first thing they did was to try to find out if Kathleen and Scott were alive. Almost hysterical, Dawson started asking anyone he saw on the riverfront about their safety.

"Cap'n, come with me," Sam said and took his arm. "I knows a stoker on the *Natchez*. If he be here, he know everything that's happening." Dawson followed Sam to a small shack on the pier. Inside, several black men from various boats were talking of the tragedy. Sam knocked on the door and shouted loudly, "Amos, is you in there?"

A short, stocky black man came to the door and opened it. "'Sam," he called a greeting and came outside.

"Amos," Sam shook his hand, "the cap'n here had some friends on the *Roxanne*. Does you know where they might be?"

"Sho, Sam, they take 'em all to St. Mary's Catholic Church in town. Who is you wantin' to know 'bout? I bet I can tell you if they made it or not."

"Kathleen Alexander," Dawson quickly answered, "and

241

her son, Scotty. Are they alive?'' He reached out and took the short man's arm.

Loosening himself from Dawson's grip, the short black man said, ''Relax, Cap'n, they is all right. They got blowed away from the boat and they floated into sho'. I was there when they was taken out of the water. They's alive.''

A broad smile came to Dawson's strained face and he said happily, ''Oh, thank God,'' and pulled his wallet out of his trouser pocket. Taking all the greenbacks he had out, he thrust them at the short man and said, ''Thank you, thank you.'' In Dawson's haste to give the man all his money, he didn't notice a small white card fall from his wallet to the ground. Sam stopped and picked it up, holding it in his hand while he watched the short black stoker refuse to take Dawson's money.

''No, suh, I don't want no money. I's jest glad I could give you good news, Cap'n.''

''I insist,'' Dawson said happily, thrust the money into the man's shirt pocket, and turned to leave. ''Come on, Sam, we've got to get to the church, she will need me.'' Sam smiled at his black friend when the man handed him Dawson's money. Sam said, ''Thanks, Amos, I'll give it to the cap'n,'' exchanged a few more words with the stoker, and put the money and the white card into his own pocket.

Dawson and Sam were nearing the church, both eagerly walking fast. Sam stopped and grabbed Dawson's arm, restraining him.

''What are you doing, Sam?'' Dawson protested. ''We're nearly there. Let go of me!''

''Cap'n, look over there.'' Dawson's eyes followed his friend's finger. At the door of the church, Hunter stepped outside, his arm protectively around his wife's shoulder. His other arm was wrapped around Scotty Alexander who sat atop his father's slim hip, his little arms tightly clinging to Hunter's neck. Hannah, wrapped in a blanket, a dazed expression on her sad face, was supported by Daniel. Kath-

242

leen's head was on her husband's chest and her hands were clutching his shirtfront.

"I guess she doesn't need me, Sam," Dawson said tiredly and the two men turned and walked back to the riverfront. They walked in silence for a few yards, tears of relief and frustration stinging Dawson's eyes. Finally he spoke. "Thanks for your help, Sam. They're safe, they're alive, that's all that matters to me," and he shrugged his massive shoulders and sighed.

Sam smiled at his friend, "You is right, Cap'n, long as she still be alive, you haven't lost her fo' good," and he patted Dawson's tired back. They walked a few paces farther and Dawson said, "Sam, what about the Beauregards? Did Amos say they made it?"

Sam shook his head, "I'm sorry, Cap'n, they didn't. They both got killed in the explosion."

Dawson said softly, "Poor Abigail, God rest her soul, she was a sweet lady."

"What 'bout Mistah Beauregard, Cap'n?"

Dawson's black eyes narrowed into slits and he said evenly, "Sam, may Louis Beauregard find his rightful home for all eternity," and he spat on the ground.

Back onboard the *Diana Mine,* Dawson stood alone on the bow, returning to New Orleans.

"Cap'n," Sam came to join him for a minute, "Here be yo' money back. Amos, he didn't want to take it."

"I hate that he wouldn't accept it, I wanted him to."

"And here be a card you dropped on the ground. It might be important," Sam handed the white card to Dawson.

Dawson held it up and read: Craddock Cotton Agency, Talifar Square, London, England, Richard Craddock, President. Dawson had forgotten the man who had given it to him so long ago in Monte Carlo. Richard Craddock had said, "If you should ever change your mind . . ."

"Sam," Dawson put the card in his wallet and looked at his friend, "I'm going back to Europe."

"But, Cap'n, you jest got home. I thought you was gonna go to Natchez for a while."

"I have changed my mind. I'm going to London to become a cotton agent. There is nothing here for me. It belongs to someone else," and he smiled at his concerned friend.

Twenty-one

Hunter Alexander got his stunned family safely back to Sans Souci the next day. Two days later at the memorial services for Louis and Abigail, St. Mary's Cathedral was overflowing with broken-hearted friends and family, as the shocked city turned out to pay their last respects to one of the most prominent, well-liked couples in Natchez. Kathleen stood like a statue, dry-eyed, in a state of shock, her black dress covering her from head to toe, the veil of her black hat covering her face. Barely able to stand, she was supported by Hunter who stood with his arm around her waist, concern and love written plainly on his delicate features. The heat inside the church was oppressive, adding to the misery of the mourners. Kathleen felt her knees buckling under her and had no strength to fight it. The movement of her small body was felt by her husband and he picked her up and carried her from the church while their confused son followed him down the long aisle.

The carriage, with Daniel in the driver's seat, waited just outside the church and Hunter hurriedly lifted his wife and son inside and told Daniel to take them home. Hannah came waddling out behind them, sobbing as though her heart would break, and Hunter turned to help her up into the carriage. The fresh air did not revive Kathleen and when Hunter pulled her close, her cheek felt cold against his. At Sans Souci, Hunter picked Kathleen up and carried her up the long walk into the house. Without stopping, he started up the stairs and to her bedroom. Hannah followed them, wringing her hands and crying. When Hunter got to Kathleen's door, he turned, still holding her in his arms, and said to Hannah, "I want you to go to your room and lie down, I'll come in a little later and see how you are."

"But, Doctor Hunter, I's got to get Miz Kathleen undressed, she need to be in the bed and I . . ."

"Hannah, please do as I say. I'll see that she's comfortable," and he carried his wife into her room and closed the door. When Hunter placed her in a chair, she sat just as he placed her, not moving, giving no indication that she even knew where she was. Hunter took off his coat and tossed it to the foot of the bed. He went to his wife's bureau and took out a clean white nightgown and came back to her.

"Kathleen," he whispered, "I want you to get undressed and get into bed. You're tired, I want you to rest."

Her eyes never changed, she looked right through him. Hunter laid the nightgown across her knees and tried again, "Sweetheart, I've brought you your nightgown. You must undress and get into bed." Still the glazed eyes stared into space and her hands made no move for her clothing. Worried, Hunter felt perspiration soaking his shirt. Whether it was the August heat or his frayed nerves, he had no idea. He took off his cravat, then unbuttoned the damp white shirt and cast it aside. His bare chest glistened, but when he bent down to his wife and took her hand, it was ice cold and the heavy black dress she wore was completely dry. More frightened than ever, he dropped to his knees in front of her. "Darling," he whispered, "I'm going to undress you and put you to bed. Is that all right?"

The blue eyes looked at him when he spoke, but she didn't nod her head. She was as she had been for the last two horrible days, completely silent, seemingly unaware of what was going on around her. Hunter finally managed to undress his wife and modestly pull the gown down over her hips. He whispered, leaning over her, "I'm going now, Kathleen. I want you to sleep. Do you think you can?" Her eyes stared at him and Hunter sighed and rose. He picked up his shirt and started for the door when the dam within Kathleen burst at last and she was sobbing loudly, "No, don't leave me! Please don't leave me!" Hunter dropped the shirt where he stood and hurried back to the bed. He lifted her quickly from the mattress and stood holding her in his arms while she clung to him, her arms holding tightly to his neck, repeating, "Don't leave me. It's all my fault. *I* killed them!"

"Shhh," he whispered, "I'm here, darling, with you. Nothing's your fault. It's certainly not, Angel," and he walked the floor, holding his wife in his arms as though she were a baby. She continued to sob and bury her face in his chest saying, "Hunter, forgive me, please, please, forgive me."

His lips in her hair, Hunter kissed her lovingly over and over while he soothed her. "I'm here, lean on me. Let me help you. I've got you, my darling, I'll take care of you forever. Nothing is your fault. Cry it out, my love, there, there."

Kathleen continued to sob, her tears wetting her husband's chest. He could feel the dear head burying trustingly closer to him and relief flooded his body because the wet cheeks of his sobbing wife were no longer cold, they were flushed and warm. In fact, her body was hot and the clean white nightgown he had put on her was soaking with perspiration. She was going to be all right. Hunter continued to walk the floor, holding her close, whispering to her until at last the sobs subsided and she grew tired and calmer. Only then did Hunter walk to the bed and lay her gently down. He smiled at her and she tried to smile back. He sat beside her on the bed and leaned close, "Darling, I'm going to get you another nightgown."

"Yes, Hunter," she said, "I've ruined this one, I'm afraid."

"Don't worry, darling," he said and brought her another. She dutifully lifted her arms and he pulled the nightgown

247

over her head. With no embarrassment on either part, Kathleen let her husband slip a clean nightgown over her naked body and she lay back on the bed to let him button it up and pull it down over her hips. "Thank you," she whispered and Hunter trembled slightly and said, "You're welcome, Kathleen" as he moved from the bed to the chair.

"Promise me you'll stay," she said and took his hand.

Both his hands covered hers and he whispered, "My darling, I will stay with you forever."

"Hunter?" she said softly.

"Yes, Angel," he said and leaned close to her face.

"I'm tired, I'm so tired," she said and her eyes closed.

"I know, my darling, sleep. I'll be right here beside you."

As the last rays of an August sun streamed through the windows, Hunter sat by his wife's bed in the semi-darkness, still holding to the tiny hand resting in his.

Without Kathleen asking him, Hunter came to her room every night. He sat beside her bed while she drifted off to sleep, promising to stay there should she awaken and need him. His presence helped her to sleep and when, on more than one occasion, she awoke with a start in the middle of the night, screaming in terror from the horrible nightmares she had started experiencing, Hunter was there in a chair by the bed, ready to reach out to her, to sit her on his lap, to hold her and rock her and pet her until she once again could go back to sleep. Then he would gently place her back in her bed and drop back into his chair to doze for the rest of the night. But one evening, her arms stayed around his neck and she murmured, "No, Hunter, don't leave me, don't."

"I won't, Darlng, I'll be right here in the chair beside you," he assured her.

"No," she said sleepily, "I need you to hold me while I sleep."

"All right," he whispered and laid down on the bed beside

248

her. She snuggled close to him and immediately went peacefully to sleep. Hunter laid with his arm under her head, her face resting in the crook of his shoulder, so close he could feel her warm breath. He carefully put an arm around her waist and she moved closer to him, molding her small frame to his. With his tight trousers still on, his chest and feet bare, Hunter lay with his wife in his arms for the first time in years. Hunter didn't go to sleep as quickly as Kathleen. Although the bed he now lay on was much more comfortable than the chair he'd been sleeping in, he found that the nearness of the woman he loved so much awakened all the love and passion he'd tried to put behind him. He felt almost guilty as he lay with her in his arms and let his hands run over the dear body while she trustingly slept pressed close to him. He sometimes wondered to himself if he were out of his mind because, as hard as he tried, he could not suppress the happy smile that came to his lips in the darkness as he kissed the silky blond hair falling carelessly into his face.

His sleeping in her bed quickly became a routine and he gladly lay down beside her each night without asking if he could. She seemed grateful to have him there and willingly put her arms around him as though they had always slept together. Hunter awoke one night after sleeping fitfully for an hour or so. Smiling as he always did when he awoke to find her in his arms, he bent down to kiss her forehead. It was hot, much too warm. He lifted his hand from her waist and put it to her cheek. She was burning up with fever. Hunter hurriedly slipped out of bed and leaned over her, ''Darling,'' he whispered, ''Kathleen.''

Her eyes fluttered open and she licked her dry lips, ''Hunter, I don't feel well.''

''Oh, darling,'' he said, ''I know, I know.''

For the next three days, Kathleen was completely out of her head. Her fever raged in spite of anything her husband did for her. Not sleeping at all, Hunter stayed by her bedside night and day and refused to let anyone else take over for him no matter how exhausted he was. On the third day, when her fever still had not subsided, Hannah stood beside him, wringing her hands and saying, "Oh, that po' baby gonna die. What we gonna do, Doctor Hunter, what we gonna do?"

"Hannah, she isn't going to die, I will make her well. Now I want you to get a pan of cold water with ice in it and some alcohol. Bring it to me right away. The medication I've given her isn't working, we must try something else right now."

"Yes, suh," Hannah sobbed and hurried from the room.

"Darling, darling," Hunter whispered, "I love you, please don't leave me, don't." Kathleen didn't understand what he was saying. She was delirious and violent chills wracked her thin body. Her sick blue eyes looked at him, but she made not a sound. Hannah returned with the ice water and alcohol.

"Doctor Hunter, I take care of her, I bathe her and make her better."

"No, Hannah, I want to do it. You go back and look after Scott."

Hunter built a roaring fire in the already stifling room. He pulled all the curtains tightly closed and took off his shirt. He pulled the covers from her bed and removed the nightgown from Kathleen. Lovingly, he dipped clean cloths into the icy water and bathed every inch of her sick, hot body. He opened the alcohol and repeated his actions with it. All the time he bathed the burning skin, he begged in a soft voice, "Please, my darling, you must get well. I cannot live without you," and the slender fingers continued to bathe and massage the fevered body, carefully sponging every precious part of her.

The bath completed, Hunter pulled the covers back over her. Then he stripped his own clothes off and got into bed with her. He held her chilled body to his and in a matter of minutes, due to the overheated room and exhaustion,

Hunter fell asleep. He awoke as the sun was setting, his own body dripping with perspiration. Hunter put his lips to Kathleen's cheek and felt a welcome coolness. He pulled back the covers. The body lying next to his was glistening wet. She was perspiring, the fever had broken. Elated, Hunter cried, "Darling!" He laughed when she opened her eyes to look at him. "You're better," he whispered, "Sweetheart, you're going to be all right!"

Hunter pushed the covers to the foot of the bed as she whispered, "I'm hot, Hunter, very hot."

"Yes, darling," he laughed and hugged the slim, glistening body to his.

"I'm thirsty, Hunter," she whispered against his chest.

"I'll get you something nice and cold, darling," he said and slipped out of the bed. He pulled on his trousers and turned back to Kathleen. He dropped on his knees and took her hand in his, "Stay just as you are, I'll be right back," and his happy hand went to her hip and slid completely down the white, shining thigh to her knee. He rose and hurriedly left the room while she smiled.

Kathleen improved daily and Hunter was by her bedside constantly. Jealously, he guarded his most precious patient and refused to let anyone do anything for her but him. Hannah was incensed and mumbled when she brought a tray of food up, "I could feed that chile myself. I always takes care of the sick folks in this house and I . . ."

"Hannah, there's no need for that. I will feed Kathleen," and Hunter would take the tray, set is across Kathleen's lap, take his place on the bed, and patiently ladle every mouthful to her.

"I can feed myself, Hunter," Kathleen said when she started feeling better.

"I know you can, darling, but I don't want you overtiring yourself. I'm happy to do it for you," and he meant it.

She was completely well within days and, although Hunter went back to his practice, he still spent each night in her room. Some nights he sat beside her bed, others he climbed in beside her and she put up no arguments. Hunter felt needed and wanted and he soon became hopeful that it was only a matter of time before they would be man and wife again, lovers.

Night after night passed and he slept in her room, her body curled to his. It began to be less pleasant and soon Hunter was not satisfied with the arrangement. She was well, he wanted her, could no longer stand to be so close and not possess her. One bedtime, he rose from his chair and, instead of lying down on her bed, he started for the door.

Surprised, Kathleen said, "Hunter, are you leaving? Aren't you going to stay with me tonight?"

Hunter turned back to look at her and said in an even voice, "Kathleen, I would love to stay with you tonight and every night. But, darling, if I do, I am going to be more than just a comfort to you." He stood completely still, barely daring to breathe, waiting for her answer, hope surging in his chest.

She looked at him for several minutes and softly said, "Hunter, I'm sorry, but I . . ."

Hunter turned, determined to hide the hurt in his eyes, and left the room.

Twenty-two

The deaths of Louis and Abigail brought about a great change in Kathleen's life and in the whole Alexander household. But, theirs was not the only one in the south changing at this period in time. On a nippy October evening in 1859, a small band of men stormed the U.S. Arsenal at Harper's Ferry, Virginia, intent upon inciting the slaves to rise up against their southern masters. Tensions that had been mounting between the north and the south grew more intense after the incident. Everywhere she went, Kathleen heard talk of war. At a time when the slaves at Sans Souci needed the strong, firm hand of her father, her placid husband was now in charge of the plantation and would never raise his voice to anyone, including the slaves who he had always thought should be free men and women.

Hunter was a brilliant doctor, but he was no businessman and in a matter of months Kathleen could see a change already taking place on the big estate. Hunter was not really interested in running the plantation and left most of the decision-making in the hands of the overseer. The overseer, who had always respected and been half afraid of her father, grew lazy and lost interest himself. Hunter hurried to discharge any duties concerning the running of the cotton plantation as quickly as possible so he could get down to what really interested him, learning more about medicine, specifically his neverending search for a yellow fever cure. His patient load continued to grow and his kindness brought more and more overdue bills, as profits on other plantations fell and the people who were now late or did not pay him for his services were not just the poor people of Natchez, but some of the pillars of the community. Hunter could not bear the thought of asking them for the money and refused to turn away anyone in need of medical attention, even if they had not paid their bills in the past.

Kathleen understood her husband's nature and no longer scolded him for being less than a shrewd businessman. She grew to admire her husband more with each passing day and no one understood his kindness better than she. The way he had babied and consoled her after the death of her parents was something she would never forget. She could not have made it if it had not been for Hunter. And what Hunter did not know was that, if she had not felt so terribly guilty over the night she spent with Dawson, she might have been ready to accept him as her lover. Sleeping with her husband through the long tortured nights after the accident had saved her sanity as well as her health and there had been a time or two when she had wanted to turn to him in the darkness and whisper, "Make love to me, Hunter," but the horror of the tragedy for which she felt responsible was still too fresh in her mind, as was the fateful rendezvous with Dawson that pre-ceded it. So she had sent Hunter away and he had never come back to her room. She missed him more than he would ever know and it seemed as time passed she missed him more not less.

Kathleen was not sure how Hunter felt. He was always kind and talkative when they were together and at dinner every night she enjoyed the company of her husband and her son. After dinner, they would often sit in the library together while Hunter read from his medical books, choosing to stay with her instead of going up to his room to study. They would share a glass of brandy, Hunter would have a cigar, and tell her of the amusing things that often happened at his office during the day. They rarely went out in the evenings, being content with their own company. They often shared the reading of a bedtime story to their son, taking turns reading his favorite ones over and over. Both loved little Scotty and he was a strong, common bond between them. After he was asleep, they would once again sit comfortably in the library or on the veranda on warm evenings and Kathleen felt content. If Hunter were not content, he never showed it.

So the days and months slipped pleasantly by and Kathleen grew happier, thought less about the tragic accident that took her parents, and less about Dawson. And she thought more and more about Hunter. She found herself watching him and she was often amazed at how incredibly good-looking her blond husband really was. She found herself daydreaming about her own husband! And she couldn't believe it. What was happening? She would think about Hunter and find herself smiling like a lovesick schoolgirl. Something was changing and she didn't know exactly what. Or why. All she knew was that she wanted to be with her husband more all the time and anxiously looked forward to the end of the day when he would return home to her and Scotty. Kathleen got in the habit of bathing and putting on one of her prettiest frocks when it was nearly time for Hunter to come home for the evening. She would have Hannah help her dress her hair and spend an inordinate amount of time studying herself in the mirror.

"Looks lak to me somebody tryin' to look extra pretty tonight," Hannah would grin at her.

"Don't be silly, Hannah. I'm merely dressing for dinner as I have always done."

"Um hmmm," Hannah would nod, "maybe so, but I suspects there's somebody else round here falling in love with Doctor Hunter jest lak I'se done."

"Hannah, that's foolish. He's my husband," but Kathleen would smile and realize she was indeed finally falling in love with her husband.

Winter turned to spring and summer and winter again and by the new year of 1861, Kathleen admitted to herself that

255

she had, at long last, fallen completely in love with her kind, strong, good-looking husband. Now the only problem was how to make him come around. Although he was attentive and good company and seemed more than content to be with her and nobody else, he never made any move to be more than friends. He kissed her on the cheek when he came home, but at no other time did he even try to touch her. Not since he had wanted to stay with her after the shipwreck had he ever tried to persuade her to let him back into her room. If the thought ever crossed his mind, he hid it well and Kathleen doubted that it did. The tables had turned, now it was she who wanted him. Now she knew how he must have felt all those times when she turned him down, for she longed to go to him, but she was afraid. What if he rejected her? She certainly couldn't blame him if he did. But the thought was so horrible she couldn't bear to think about it, so she did not go to him, though not a day went by when she didn't consider it.

On a chilly evening in February, Kathleen was alone in her room reading. She and Hunter had stayed up quite late and she had been reading for over an hour when finally her eyelids began to droop. The book was interesting and she hated to put it down, but she couldn't stay awake, it was impossible. She yawned and reluctantly laid the book aside and stretched. Good heavens, no wonder she was sleepy, it was after one o'clock. Kathleen turned back the covers on her bed and went to her dressing room. Completely stripped, she came back into the room and went to the bureau and took out her nightgown. Deciding she would check on Scotty before she retired, she tossed the nightgown across the bed and slipped on a robe, tied it loosely at the waist, and went across the hall.

She tiptoed into his room, using the dim gas light coming from the hall. Barefoot, she made no sound on the thick carpet and when she leaned over his bed, Scott didn't move. All the covers were kicked to the foot of his bed. His little brown arms were flung up over his head and a leg hung over the edge of the bed. Kathleen smiled at the sleeping form, gingerly lifted the leg back onto the bed, and pulled the covers up to his chest. Still smiling, she quietly closed his door.

Her hand still on the knob, she heard light footsteps in the hall and turned. Hunter was coming up the stairs toward her, smiling. He wore no shoes, his white shirt was open with the long tail outside his trousers. His blond hair was touseled and falling onto his forehead. Kathleen's heart speeded at the sight of him looking so casual and she smiled back at him.

"What are you doing up so late?" he whispered.

"I thought I was tired when I came up, but I couldn't sleep so I started reading a Dickens novel and I got so interested I had no idea it was so late," she laughed. "What about you? you should have been in bed hours ago. You have to go over to see the Hamilton sisters in the morning, remember?"

"I know," Hunter grinned sheepishly, "I promised Lena Hamilton I would be there by seven sharp to check on her sister. To tell you the truth, I think Lana Hamilton is as healthy as you or me, but you know how they are."

"Yes, I do, one or the other imagines herself sick constantly. You are really patient with them, Hunter."

"I feel sorry for the poor eccentric ladies, just as you do. How's Scotty?"

"Sleeping soundly." Kathleen started laughing, putting her hand over her mouth to quieten her giggles.

"What?" he laughed with her, "what is it?"

"I was just thinking how he was trying to copy you at dinner, using his left hand. Bless his heart, he just can't understand why it is so easy for you to eat with your left hand. He tries and can't get the food to his mouth."

Hunter shook his head, laughing, "I know. I keep trying to explain to him that you are born right- or left-handed and it's very difficult to switch, but he can't seem to understand." He took his hands from his pockets and stretched a long arm to the wall, resting a hand above her head.

"Well, it's almost sad, he wants to do everything you do and he can't manage. It's so frustrating for him. But it is funny to watch," she giggled again.

"Yeah, he's quite a boy," Hunter laughed, then yawned sleepily. "Pardon me. Guess I better be getting to bed," but he didn't move.

"Me, too," Kathleen agreed. "Goodnight, Hunter," she looked up at him, smiling.

"Night," he whispered. Slowly, he leaned down and kissed the corner of her mouth impulsively. "Night," he sighed again and straightened. He was still looking at her, hadn't moved, his hand still rested on the wall near her head. To Kathleen, he looked like a young boy, so handsome, his thick blond hair falling casually over his high forehead, his brown eyes drowsy, the hint of a smile still on his full mouth. Without raising her arms from her sides, Kathleen stood on tiptoe and kissed him lightly, barely touching her lips to his. She immediately leaned back against the wall and looked down, embarrassed by her actions.

"Thanks," Hunter said and put his fingers under her chin, raising her face to his. The smile was no longer on his handsome face and his drowsy eyes were keenly alert. He was looking at her intently and his strong jaw was set. The way she looked back at him changed the expression on his face and she watched as a slow, sensual smile spread across his delicate features. He stepped closer and kissed her, lightly at first, then more fiercely. All at once, his mouth was moving on hers, commanding her to respond. And she did. Before she knew it, she was matching his warmth with a fire burning in her that grew even greater than his. She molded her body to his and her arms were around his neck, caressing the thick blond hair at the back of his head. Her response ignited Hunter anew and the arm resting above her head moved down to pull her closer. His mouth never left hers and he kissed her with such intensity that she felt he was drawing the very life and breath from her body. Her brain was spinning and for the first time the hot, moving mouth of her husband completely drove away the face that had never left her before. The handsome, swarthy face of Dawson Blakely faded and there was only the boyish face of Hunter Alexander.

The intensity of his kisses graduated swiftly and his hand went to her robe. The satin lapel between his fingers slid away as he jerked it free of their bodies pressed tightly together and Kathleen felt her passion heighten as his hard, lean chest was against her bare breast, his curly thick hair tickling her, exciting her. She felt the other lapel being pulled and she moved back a little to help free it. She pressed herself closer to him as nothing remained between them. Her fevered body was screaming for him and her brain was spinning while an inner voice was saying, "Hunter you must stop or I shall faint." But a stronger voice said, "Oh, darling, don't stop, please don't ever stop!"

His lips were on her throat now and he was moaning softly and whispering her name. She arched her back to give him better access to her as shivers went up her spine and she felt she might cry out. Her eyes fluttered open and she watched the downward movement of the handsome blond head and he opened his mouth against her skin and let her feel the fiery wetness of his kisses. "I want you," he breathed against her tingling skin, "I must have you tonight, darling."

"But, Hunter, we can't . . ." she gasped.

She felt him stiffen at once. His lips left hers and he straightened and was once again looking down at her. He raised both hands to her robe and quickly covered her, then his hands fell from her. "I'm sorry," he said in a cold, tired voice and he turned and started down the hall.

Kathleen stood watching him walk away, her breath coming fast, her brain confused. She wanted to scream at him, "Darling, I meant we can't make love here in the hall. Hunter, Hunter, please, darling. Come with me to my room! I want you, too, my darling, I want you. Come back. I love you, Hunter, you've misunderstood! I want you, I want you," but Hunter had reached his own room and he was quickly inside and closing the door behind him.

Dazed and frustrated, Kathleen stood pressed against the wall for support. Hot tears stung her eyes as the full weight of their misunderstanding bore down on her. She had hurt him again, turned him away though she never meant to do it. If only she'd remained silent. If only she'd said yes. Yes, yes! But she hadn't, she'd driven him away when both their lives could have begun again tonight. She'd killed his passion thoughtlessly and totally. She cried inside, "What a bumbling fool I am. He thinks I don't want him and will never believe differently. If he only knew how much I do want him. It's all my fault. I've made him suffer from the start and now I've hurt him again. Oh, my darling, Hunter."

Slowly, she crossed the hall to her room, walked directly to the bed, pulled off her robe, and slipped under the covers. She buried her face in her pillow and cried bitterly. She sobbed with longing and desire for the man she had never really longed for before.

Hunter paced the floor in his room and tried to clear his head of her. Once again he'd been a hopeless fool, begging her for love, repulsing her with his desires. He hated himself for his foolishness. How could he be so stupid? Had she ever really wanted him? Had his passion ever been returned by her? No! Not even when he'd first married her. She had given herself to him then, but now he knew why. Then he'd thought she was an innocent, inexperienced young girl he would have to awaken and teach. "What a laugh on me."

Calm returned to Hunter, but he vowed silently to himself, "Never again. She will never get the chance to humiliate me again. It's all my fault, I keep trying to press myself on her and she doesn't want me. It's that simple, my wife does not want me, she does not love me, she never has and she never will. And I will keep my hands off of her from now on. *Never again!*"

Twenty-three

Kathleen stood in her big bedroom, holding tightly to the bedpost of her fourposter. Hannah stood behind her, puffing and blowing, lacing up Kathleen's tight corset. Kathleen held her breath and admonished Hannah, "You must pull it tighter, Hannah. I want my waist to be as small as possible."

"Honey, it won't get no tighter, yo' waist is plenty small. You ain't no sixteen-year-old girl anymo'. Havin' Scott put 'bout an inch or so on you that you ain't never gonna get rid of."

Kathleen smiled, "I know, Hannah, but at least he was worth it. Measure my waist."

Hannah obeyed and held the tape measure out for Kathleen to see, "It say twenty inches, honey. That be pretty small if you ask me."

"Yes, that's good enough," Kathleen put her hands to her hips and turned round and round. "It's just that I want to look special for the party."

"Why sho, honey. But you always looks special, I thinks. Don't you think it's a mite early to be havin' yo' party outdoors? Why, the flowers ain't even bloomin' yet."

"I know, Hannah, but unfortunately Hunter was born on March 30th, not later in the spring. Flowers or no flowers, I want to have it outside. And it is very warm today, thank goodness. I'm so excited, it's got to be a splendid party, Hannah. I want Hunter to have a wonderful time."

"He will. Now let me get this dress on you, I gots to get on downstairs and help out in the kitchen." Kathleen smiled and raised her arms. Hannah slipped a new yellow and white flowered muslin dress over her head. "I tol' you it be too early to wear this dress, honey. Couldn't you find sompin else?"

"Absolutely not! I want to look as pretty as possible and this dress is what I want to wear. As I said, it's warm today so this will be just fine."

"Well you's the boss, but I think this dress is a little daring to be wearing in the middle of the day. Yo' bosom's is practically showin', honey."

"Yes," Kathleen smiled impishly, "I hope Hunter notices."

"He will, but I's afraid everybody else will, too."

"Don't be a nag, Hannah. Oh, I hope today goes just like I've planned. I've invited at least a hundred people. I've tried to think of the ones Hunter likes best. And I've planned for all his favorite foods and I got a minstrel group and I've . . ."

"Honey, I ain't never seen you carry on over Doctor Hunter's birthday lak this befo'," Hannah smiled, "You got sompin on yo' mind?"

"Why, Hannah, it's a very special birthday. Hunter is thirty years old today." Then she turned and looked at her mammy. "Oh, Hannah, you know exactly what I'm doing. I've got to win Hunter, I love him. At long last I'm in love with my own dear husband and I must make him fall in love with me."

"Shoot, Doctor Hunter always loved you, you knows that."

Kathleen's face clouded slightly, "I know he used to love me, but I'm no longer certain." Then she smiled again and said, "But tonight I intend to make him love me. Hannah, from this day forward I intend to be a wife to Hunter. So I want this historic day to be perfect in every way . . . then when all the guests have gone home and Hunter and I are alone . . . oh, I can't wait."

Hannah smiled and said, "Honey, it's 'bout time. Ain't nothin' make old Hannah happier than to move all Doctor Hunter's things in yo' room. Yes, suh, that would sho be wonderful."

Kathleen hugged her mammy and laughed, "Well, dear Hannah, after tonight, you may start moving his clothes. Now run on downstairs, I'll be down in a minute."

"Okay, honey. Sho is quiet round here without Master Scott, ain't it?"

"Yes, it is. He was so excited about spending the night with Johnny Jackson last night. When Becky and Ben came by to pick him up yesterday, he couldn't wait to get away. But I'll bet he's more than ready to get home today."

"Wall, I think he be too young to be stayin over at somebody's house. He might a got homesick, I'm thinkin'."

"Don't be silly, Hannah. Johnny Jackson is Scott's best friend, they love being together. Johnny has certainly stayed over here enough."

"That be different, I don't mind that, but I don't like for Scott to be away from home."

"Go, dear Hannah go."

"I'se goin."

Downstairs, the big mansion was a bustle with people preparing for Hunter's birthday party. Sweet-smelling aromas escaped the big kitchen; the cooks at Sans Souci had been busy since dawn turning out tempting foods to feed the expected guests. Roasts of beef, huge and rare, were pink and succulent. Virginia hams, fried chicken, crisp and brown, leg of lamb, fresh catfish, and shrimp, were among the many meats to be served. Pies and pastries of every description were being baked, including pecan which was Hunter's favorite.

Outside white-clothed tables lined the big veranda and overflowed onto the freshly manicured lawn. Huge white and green umbrellas covered the round tables, ready to shade the delicate white skin of the ladies who would be present. A long white table spanned almost the length of the big yard, fresh cut flowers dotting its top. The table would soon groan under the weight of all the foods being prepared inside. At the opposite side of the yard, another table already held hundreds of clean sparkling glasses and enough liquor to make the entire population of Natchez pleasantly tipsy. Kentucky bourbon, wines, and champagne were at the ready, while cooling lemonade and fruit punches were being prepared for the children. Daniel, splendid in a crisp white jacket, stood behind the table, giving orders to the three black servants with him. A stack of silver trays, all freshly polished, stood in a row, ready to be loaded with various drinks for the guests and passed among the crowd by the white-coated helpers Daniel was in charge of.

When Hunter came home from his office at four o'clock, everything was ready, the food on the big table, a group of Negro musicians from New Orleans were in their place near the summer house, fresh cut flowers stood on every table, and in the kitchen a giant white cake was hidden from him. Hunter smiled as he hurried up the walk and rushed into the house.

Kathleen came to meet him, saying, "Hunter, dear, you must hurry. The guests will be here any minute."

"Give me fifteen minutes," he smiled. "Sorry I'm late, but my office was so full of people I had trouble getting away," and he bounded up the stairs to dress for his party.

Half an hour later, when the first of the guests pulled up the drive at Sans Souci, a clean, handsome Hunter Alexander stood beside his wife at the front of the long walk wearing tan cashmere trousers with razor sharp creases, a snow white shirt buttoned to his throat, set off with a brown silk cravat, his dark brown waistcoat draped perfectly over his slim shoulders, his thick blond hair freshly washed and combed. Kathleen in her white and yellow muslin, her blond hair pulled atop her head, her happy blue eyes shining, looked up at him and said, "You look magnificent, Doctor Alexander."

Hunter smiled down at her and said, "Thank you, Mrs. Alexander. You are lovely, as always," and they turned to greet their guests.

"Mister Craddock, so glad you could come. I want you to meet the lady who sent you the invitation. Kathleen, dear, this is Richard Craddock from London. He's our new cotton agent."

"Mister Craddock," Kathleen held out her hand, "so happy to meet you. Thank you for coming."

Craddock kissed her outstretched hand and said, "Ma'am, it's my pleasure, I assure you." Then he turned to Hunter. "Hunter, old chap, you have the loveliest little wife in all Mississippi."

"I certainly do, Richard. Have a drink."

Lena and Lana Hamilton, wearing identical dresses bought a decade ago, were smiling and twirling their parasols over their heads. The two sisters, one fifty-five, the other past sixty, held out their hands for Hunter to kiss and hugged Kathleen.

"It's so wonderful to be here," they said in unison. Then Lana, the older sister spoke for both of them, "We do just love parties, you know. Why, when we were younger Papa said we were the belles of Natchez, as never an evening went by when we weren't attending a gala party. Those were more elegant times, I tell you."

"I'm sure they were," Hunter smiled, "How are you two feeling today?"

"Oh, Sister felt terrible this morning, Doctor, but I really think it was just a case of the vapors, what with the excitement of the party and all. Don't you think that's what it was, Lena?"

265

"Yes, I'm much better now," Lena smiled.

"Well, we're glad you're well," Kathleen smiled at her, "and we're so happy you were both able to come to the party."

"Oh, Sister, look there's punch, let's go have some." Lana took Lena's arm and they moved across the lawn to the liquor table.

"Happy Birthday, Hunter my boy." It was Crawford Ashworth, smiling and patting Hunter on the back. The state senator, now Hunter's friend and attorney, said, "Do you know Mrs. Annabelle Thompson, Hunter?"

Annabelle, lovely in a daring gown of the palest gun metal muslin, looked up at Hunter and smiled, offering him her hand. Hunter cleared his throat and said, "Yes, she was once a patient of mine," and he took her white hand and kissed it. "So nice to see you again, Annabelle. I trust you are feeling well."

"Thanks for your concern, Doctor Alexander, I couldn't be better. How are you, Mrs. Alexander?"

Kathleen smiled and said, "Just fine, thank you. So glad Crawford brought you today."

Annabelle, reluctant to leave, had to be led away by the Senator.

"My, my, Hunter, you certainly must be an excellent doctor," Kathleen smiled up at him.

"What do you mean?"

"Mrs. Thompson looks the picture of health and beauty. Is she finally well enough so she doesn't need to come to see you every week?"

"Kathleen, she is no longer my patient. She sees Uncle Rembert, I suppose. I don't keep up with his patients."

"He sure doesn't," Uncle Rembert stood before them. "Kathleen," he smiled and kissed her cheek. "But I agree that he must have cured Mrs. Thompson. I don't see her very often myself, she seems to be in better health these days."

Hunter coughed nervously and said, "Uncle, go have a drink and mingle with our guests."

"Daddy, Daddy," Scott Alexander was calling to his father before he got out of the carriage with Becky and Ben Jackson and their young son, Johnny.

"Scotty," Hunter beamed and the boy ran to him. Hunter lifted him up and set him on a slim hip while Scotty hugged him happily, waving a flag around his head. Kathleen leaned up and kissed the brown face and said, "Darling, I've missed you."

"Me too, Mommy," Scott said and hugged her neck.

"Becky," Kathleen hugged her, "were the boys a lot of trouble?"

"Don't be silly, I just let them do as they please, so they're no bother," she smiled. "Ben was good enough to take them off my hands this morning and it's a good thing, I was sick all morning," she patted her thick waist.

"Hunter," Ben smiled, holding to Johnny's hand. "Good to see you. Can't you do something about Becky being sick every morning?"

Hunter shook his head, still holding Scotty on his hip, "Wish I could, Ben, but I'm afraid 'til she gets through her third month, there's not much we can do. She's doing fine, though, Ben, so don't worry. I think she will have a much easier time of it than when Johnny came." He ruffled the boy's hair.

"Daddy," Scott interrupted, turning his father's face back to look at him, "see what I've got!"

"Say, what is this?" Hunter took the flag from his son's hand.

"Come on, Becky, you need to sit down," Kathleen said and slipped her arm around her friend's waist and led her to a chair.

Scott showed his father his flag, the new official one of the state of Mississippi: a magnolia tree in its center and the bonnie blue flag in the upper left hand corner. "It's beautiful, son. Now jump down, I have to greet our guests."

"Okay, Daddy, but guess where I went this morning?" Scott's dark eyes flashed with excitement.

"Tell me quick," Hunter said and set the boy on his feet.

"Johnny and me went to the slave block," Scott announced proudly, then took Johnny's arm and pulled him across the yard, running and yelling, holding his new flag over his head. Ben Jackson followed the boys, walking to his wife to see if she were feeling all right while Hunter turned back to the arriving guests.

People were coming in a steady stream and soon Kathleen was back by Hunter's side, welcoming them to Sans Souci. The party was in full swing as the crowd milled about happily, eating and drinking, gossiping and laughing. Happy children romped on the lawn, squealing and chasing each other. Lovely ladies in new spring dresses promenaded under the trees and the men stood in twos and threes talking quietly and drinking champagne. Soft music from the imported orchestra drifted across the lawn.

A twitter went through the crowd as most of the guests turned to look at a late arriving couple alighting from their carriage in the driveway. Kathleen and Becky, sitting at one of the tables on the lawn, turned, shading their eyes in the brilliant afternoon sun, "Oh, my Lord, it's Julie and Caleb," Kathleen laughed. "I can't believe it, I didn't know they were back from Europe," and she ran across the lawn to meet her girlfriend. "Julie, Julie," she called and hugged her tightly. "Darling, you look wonderful, when did you get back?"

Julie, laughing too, said, "Dear, I hope you don't mind us crashing your party, Mother told us about it and we . . ."

"Don't be a goose, I'm thrilled to death you came." She turned to Caleb Bates, nervously twisting his hat brim and beaming down at the two women. "Caleb, dear Caleb. How wonderful to see you!"

"Thank you, ma'am," he grinned and blushed when she

kissed his cheek.

Kathleen stepped in between the two honeymooners and took their arms. "I had no idea you were back or I would have invited you. Oh, I'm so glad to see you both, this makes the party perfect." She led them into the crowd and the two young people smiled happily, accepting congratulations from their friends and telling everyone that married life was absolutely wonderful.

Negro minstrels sang songs and, as their sweet voices filled the late afternoon air, most of the guests filled gold-rimmed china plates from the big table of food and scattered out around the veranda and the big yard to eat heartily and wash it all down with champagne.

Hunter stood in a small circle of men, Ben Jackson, Crawford Ashworth, and Uncle Rembert, as Becky and Kathleen joined them. The talk was of the tensions between the north and the south, as it had been at every social function during the last year.

Ben Jackson was speaking, "Hunter, we could whip them easily and we are going to have to do it sooner or later."

"Ben," Hunter smoked a long brown cigar, "I'm afraid that's your southern pride talking for you. The north has an availability of combat manpower that's at least double that of the south and they're self-sufficient. We would be penniless without the foreign market and you know it. A blockade would mean we wouldn't have a chance in a war."

"But, Hunter," Crawford Ashworth said, "England couldn't survive without our cotton. Don't you think economic pressure would force Britain to ensure the flow of it?"

"He's right," Ben agreed, "and they wouldn't stop at economic support, they'd take military intervention. They'd have to, it means as much to them as it does to us."

"I don't agree with either of you. I think that our only hope in a war is that the north will grow tired of the expense and duration of it. Maybe they'll give up and let us have our own government."

269

"Wrong, absolutely wrong. They'll never give up, they don't want us to have our way of life, they're dead set on taking our slaves from us and seeing the south down on its knees. But, Hunter, it won't be a long war, anyhow. We're united and we have brilliant military men. If war breaks out, you know the best officers in the army will resign and come home to fight for the Confederacy. We'll be victorious, I'm sure of it."

"Ben, you're still forgetting they have all the resources. We don't have enough food, clothing, and weapons to fight a war and win. And you're forgetting something else. This squabble is not over slavery. I myself do not believe in slavery, I've never tried to hide that fact from anyone. I have Crawford working right now on the special legislation to free the slaves at Sans Souci."

"That's right," Crawford said, "it's just a matter of time before all these darkies you see here will be free."

"Well, you better take a good look at them then," Ben laughed and took a drink of whiskey, " 'cause everyone of them will hightail it out of here the minute they are free."

"I don't believe that, Ben." Hunter said.

"I swear, Hunter, sometimes you sound like a Yankee yourself!"

"Ben, please," Becky tugged on his arm. "Here Kathleen invites us over for Hunter's birthday and you stand here insulting him."

Ben removed her hand from his arm and turned to her, "Becky, go sit down, you look tired."

"But, Ben . . ." she pleaded.

Hunter smiled and said, "Don't worry, Becky. I'm not upset, but perhaps you and Kathleen should go sit down for a while."

"Yes, come Becky, you shouldn't be standing," Kathleen said and drew her away from the circle of men.

With the women gone, the men once again turned back to the subject of slaves. Hunter turned to Ben and said, "I didn't want to say this in front of the ladies, but I don't want you taking Scotty to the slave block anymore."

"Why, Hunter, the boys enjoyed it, I don't see any harm in it."

"Ben, we've been good friends for five years, you know how I feel about slavery."

"Hunter," Ben said, smiling, "slavery is a fact of life in the south. There is nothing wrong with it and someday your son will own slaves just like you and me. Are you telling me I'm wrong to own slaves?"

"Ben, that's not what I said. I don't know if it's right or wrong. I just said I don't want my son at the auction. I intend to teach him it's wrong. You may teach your son whatever you like."

"Well, thank you very much, Doctor Alexander. I'll do just that. I never knew you felt this strongly about it, are you sure you're a southerner? I'll tell you, you're being foolish. You free the slaves on this plantation and Sans Souci will cease operating!"

"Ben, I love the south as much as any of my neighbors and I would fight to the death to defend it. But I'm telling you the issue is not slavery and, as for all these people working the plantation, I still think they would stay and work here if they were free. It has been done before you know. Crawford tells me Dawson Blakely freed all his slaves years ago and the Negro servants and workers on his plantation didn't leave. In fact, they have been loyal to him, wouldn't think of leaving him."

"He's right, Ben," Crawford Ashworth nodded his head. "It might not work in every case, but it has certainly worked for Blakely."

"Dawson Blakely probably pays them all twice what they're worth," Uncle Rembert snapped and took a drink of whiskey.

* * *

Kathleen and Becky sat at a table a few yards away watching the men, overhearing bits and pieces of their conversation. "Kathleen, I'm a nervous wreck. Ben's been talking louder than anyone and I'm afraid he is insulting Hunter."

Kathleen smiled and said, "Relax, Becky. Ben may get angry, but I assure you Hunter won't. I've never seen him get mad. He's an easy-going man, he's never been really upset."

"Well, I would hate to see him if he ever did lose his temper. I'm sure his wrath would be a great deal more frightening than my hot-headed Ben when he gets mad."

"Don't worry, Becky, Hunter won't even raise his voice," Kathleen reassured her girlfriend. "Look, Becky, there go Caleb and Julie slipping off to be by themselves. Have you ever seen such a lovesick couple in all your life? They've hardly had anything to do with any of the other guests they are so wrapped up in each other."

"Yes, it's wonderful," Becky smiled, but immediately turned back to look at the small circle of men where her husband was now waving his arms and talking loudly.

Kathleen turned back to look at them, too, and she looked only at Hunter. The expression on his delicate features had not changed at all. He was talking, but the smile never left his handsome face as he logically discussed the South and all its problems with the excited Ben and the other gentlemen. The two women fell silent and looked at their husbands. As Kathleen watched Hunter, a delicious grin of anticipation spread over her face.

"Becky," she said lazily, "don't you think Hunter is handsome on his thirtieth birthday?"

Becky turned and looked at Kathleen as though she had lost her mind, "Kathleen Alexander, I have always thought Hunter is the best-looking man I've ever seen in my life. Good Lord, are you just now noticing it?" She shook her head.

"Perhaps I am," Kathleen smiled and rose. "Excuse me,

Becky, I think I'll ask that very handsome man if he will take a walk with me," and she went to the circle of men. "I hate to interrupt you all when you're quite obviously solving all our problems," she smiled and slipped her arm through her husband's, "but if you don't mind, I'd like to steal the birthday boy for a few minutes."

The men laughed and Crawford Ashworth said, "Just in time, I would say."

"Excuse me, gentlemen," Hunter smiled and left with his wife.

The sun was starting to set in the west, casting long shadows over the lawn. The relaxed, happy crowd milled around the big yard. Kathleen and Hunter walked in silence down the long path toward the white summer house. When they neared the small family cemetery, the slim forms of Lena and Lana Hamilton could be seen, bent over the graves of Louis and Abigail. Kathleen and Hunter walked to meet them.

"Miz Kathleen, we just wanted to put our new Mississippi flag on the grave of your dear father, we hope you don't mind."

"Not at all, ladies, that's very sweet of you. I'm sure Father would be more than pleased."

The sisters rose and Lana said, "I hope so. Oh, Kathleen, your father was such a fine man, we thought him one of the nicest gentlemen ever to live in Natchez. We will never forget when Lafayette came to Natchez in '25, your father entertained him grandly in this very house and he invited us to join in the celebrations. Oh, there were gun salutes echoing off the river banks, parades and picnics and balls . . . it was just wonderful." She clasped her hands together, remembering. "Those were the days, I tell you, no one knew how to entertain better than your dear father. He was the epitome of class and good taste. Wasn't he, Sister?"

"Oh, yes indeed, Mister Beauregard was a man among men, no doubt about it."

"Thank you, ladies, you're very kind," Kathleen smiled

273

at both of them and the sisters went off together, talking about the old days.

"They're really charming, aren't they, Hunter?" Kathleen looked up at her husband.

"Yes, they are," Hunter smiled, watching the two slim figures carefully pick their way back through the gardens and into the yard. "Kathleen, it's so sad. I've never mentioned it before, but you should see their home. It is literally falling down around them. Nearly all the furniture has been sold and the wallpaper is hanging in loose shreds, there are huge holes in the floors, and their doors are boarded up against the weather." Hunter shook his head, "You just wouldn't believe it, it's terrible. I've asked them more than once if I couldn't have some of our men come over and do a little repairing for them, but they won't hear of it. They say everything is just fine and for me not to worry about them, they will take care of it."

"I had no idea it was that bad. Bless their hearts, why won't they let you help them? I don't understand it."

"I guess, dear, all they have left is their pride. I wouldn't want to take that from them."

"No, of course not. What are we worrying for, they're happy in their own way, I suppose."

"Sure they are, let's forget it. Thank you for my party, it was very sweet of you and I appreciate it. Shall we go back to our guests now?"

"No, Hunter, not just yet. Come, let's sit in the summer house for just a few minutes and watch the sun set."

"I really think we should get back."

"Please, Hunter, just for a while." She smiled seductively and took his arm.

They went inside the white-latticed gazebo and Kathleen sat down and patted the long white settee. Hunter took a seat beside her and, when he was settled, she moved over closer to him. They sat silently in the twilight as the last rays of the sun disappeared below the horizon.

Kathleen smiled and said, "Hunter, do you think I look pretty today?"

Hunter looked down at her and said, "You always look beautiful, Kathleen."

"No, Hunter, I mean I wanted to look especially pretty for your birthday party, for you, dear."

"Well then, you look especially pretty today. Satisfied?"

"Hunter, put your arm around me, please."

"Kathleen."

"Please, Hunter, put your arm around me."

Slowly, Hunter raised his arm and put it around his wife's shoulder, letting it drape over the back of the settee.

"That's better," she smiled and looked up at him lovingly. "Hunter, if I've never told you, I think you're a very handsome man."

Hunter cleared his throat and said, "Kathleen, you're embarrassing me."

"Don't be, darling," she whispered and put her hand to his cheek. She saw the strained look on his handsome face, but smiled and raised her face and kissed his cheek. He sat stiffly not moving while her mouth went to his lips. She kissed him lightly and pulled back a little to read his expression. She saw confusion written plainly on the delicate features and the muscle in his jaw began to twitch. She smiled and kissed him again and her arm went around his neck, her fingers caressing the curly blond hair at the back of his head. "Kiss me," she whispered and moved closer. Hunter sighed and bent to kiss her lips. The mouth on hers was warm, responsive and Kathleen kissed him with wild abandon. She felt his hand come to her shoulders and she was sure he was about to wrap her in a powerful embrace. Instead he pulled her away and said evenly, "No. Stop."

"But, Hunter, darling . . ."

Hunter rose and said, "Kathleen, this is a party, we have guests."

"You're right, darling," she smiled and rose, too. "Later

tonight?''

"No," he said and moved away, "No. I have no desire for anymore teasing from you," and he stepped out of the summer house.

"No, darling, I mean, I want you to . . ." Kathleen said softly, but Hunter's long legs had already carried him away. Kathleen bit her lip and sat back down. "What have I done wrong? What do I do now? I must convince him I want to be his wife. Perhaps it's too late, maybe he no longer wants me. That can't be true, it can't be. His kisses told me that. He still wants me, I will try again after the guests have gone." Kathleen rose and went back to join the party.

The celebration continued until late that night and, when at midnight some of the men still remained to play poker in the library, Kathleen sighed and went up to her room. Hunter was not playing, but he stood watching, a drink in his hand.

"I think I'll go on up, dear, you coming?" Kathleen put her hand on his shoulder.

"In a while," Hunter said evenly.

"Go on, Hunter," the men laughed, "we might be here all night. You don't mind, do you?"

"Certainly not," Hunter laughed and turned back to Kathleen, "Go on now. I'll be up later."

Kathleen sighed and climbed the stairs alone. Hannah was waiting in her room to undress her for bed. "Honey, how was the party? Did everything go like you wanted it to?"

"Not exactly, Hannah, Hunter is still downstairs. That's not the way I planned it."

"Never you mind, chile. He probably jest wants to give you time to undress. He be up soon."

"You're right," Kathleen smiled. "Get me undressed, I want to be ready when he does come up."

Hannah lifted the dress over Kathleen's head. She laid out a new gold satin nightgown for Kathleen to slip into. "Honey, if this gown don't do it, nothin' will," Hannah

276

laughed as she pulled it over Kathleen's head. The gown came high up to her neck and tied in back, but it dipped to her waist in the back and on each side it was slit past her thighs. So daring, even Kathleen blushed and giggled, "Hannah, I'm not sure I have the courage to wear this."

"Sho you does, honey, Doctor Hunter won't be able to resist you when he see you, now sit and I take yo' hair down fo' you." Hannah's work was finished, she left the room, saying, "Good luck, honey. I spects he be up real soon."

Kathleen waited nervously in her room, sitting awkwardly in the revealing satin gown, praying Hunter would soon come upstairs and be pleased with her daring. She rose and paced nervously, finally walking to the door to crack it just a bit so she would know when he came up. She didn't have to wait long. She heard him saying goodnight to the poker players as he stepped onto the bottom step, "Stay as long as you like, there's plenty of food and liquor. I really have to get to sleep. Night all." He started up the stairs.

Kathleen opened her bedroom door a little more and stood waiting for Hunter. Hopeful he would stop of his own accord, her breath caught in her throat as he neared her room. Hunter walked past the door without looking.

"Hunter," she whispered and he stopped and turned. Slowly, he walked the few paces back to her and said, "What is it?"

"Hunter, will you come in for a minute? We can't talk with you in the hall, our guests will hear us."

"I'm sorry, Kathleen, I can't. I'm going to talk to Scotty."

"Scotty?" she smiled, "Darling, he's sound asleep."

"Then I shall wake him up," he said evenly.

"But, why, I don't understand . . ."

"I need to have a talk with him, that's why. What did you want?"

"Tell you what, you go on in and see him a minute, then come back."

Hunter looked at his lovely wife in the skimpy gold satin nightgown. The sight of her immediately brought erotic thoughts to him, but he fought it and said, "No, Kathleen, I'm not coming back. I'm going to bed and to sleep. Goodnight," and he turned and left.

"But, Hunter . . ." Kathleen watched him go. She closed the bedroom door and leaned against it. Tears of hurt and frustration filled her eyes. He had turned her down. Turned her down cold when there was no doubt at all what she wanted. Humiliated, Kathleen walked tiredly to the bed and picked up the slim, gold-wrapped box from the pillow. Hunter's birthday present. She had planned to give it to him when they were alone. She clutched the new gold pocket watch to her breast. She laid back on the bed and cried, spoiling the gaily-wrapped package.

Hunter tiptoed into Scott's room. The boy was sound asleep, one leg hanging over the edge of his bed, arms over his head, one hand clutching the new flag. Hunter smiled and pulled up a chair.

"Scott," he whispered, "Scotty."

"Ummmm," Scotty murmured sleepily.

Hunter took the flag, laid it aside, and said, "Scott, it's Daddy. Wake up, son."

"Daddy," Scott opened his eyes and sat up in bed. "What is it?"

"Nothing important, darling. I just didn't get the chance to say goodnight," Hunter smiled at the sleepy dark face.

Scott put his arms around his father's neck and said, "Goodnight, Daddy, I love you," and laid back down.

"I love you too, Scott. Honey, there's something I want to talk to you about, all right?"

"Sure, Daddy."

"Do you remember saying you went down to the slave block this morning?"

"Yes, Daddy, Mister Jackson took Johnny and me."

"Darling, what did you see there?"

"They sold niggers there."

Hunter sighed, but smiled at his son. "Darling, those men are Negroes. Never call them niggers. And you are right, they were selling them. Scotty, what they were doing is wrong. I want you to remember that. I don't ever want you to go down there again, promise me."

Puzzled, Scott looked at his father, "I promise, Daddy."

"Good. Scott, one man should never own another. Can you understand that? You wouldn't want anyone owning you or me, would you?"

"No, Daddy, that would be awful."

Hunter smiled and said, "Yes, it would, son. And I promise you, no one will ever own either of us. Now go back to sleep. I love you," and he kissed the dark, sweet face of his son.

"Daddy," Scott said, "I want to be just like you," and he turned over and went back to sleep.

Twenty-four

Reluctant to go to bed, Hunter stood at the cold fireplace in his bedroom. He had removed his shirt and the tight black boots and put out all the lights in the room except the one on the night table by his bed. He turned down the covers on the soft feather bed and raised his hands to his belt buckle. His hands dropped to his sides and he sighed. There was no use going to bed, he knew he would not be able to sleep. He picked up a long brown cigar from the table and lit it, blowing the smoke out slowly. He paced the room aimlessly, running a hand through his thick blond hair. It was warm and stuffy in the room and he strolled to the open doors leading onto the balcony. He stepped out and breathed deeply of the sweet, humid air. The night was thick and heavy, no stars visible, hardly a breath stirring, and still uncomfortably warm though it was well past midnight.

Hunter saw the light coming from Kathleen's room, casting irregular patterns on the gardens below. He stood watching the flickering flame, transfixed, wondering what she was doing up so late. Her room went dark as she put out the last light. The house was now completely dark except for the lamp by his bed. Everyone was asleep. Everyone but him. He sighed, tossed away the half-smoked cigar, and went back inside. He walked to the fireplace and stood there, a knee bent, a foot on the hearth, a long arm resting on the mantel, the other hand placed loosely on his hip.

A soft knock came at his door. Hunter looked up and said, "Come in," without moving. Kathleen stepped inside and closed the door behind her. Hunter's eyes widened when he saw her and, as he watched her cross the room to him, the hand resting on the mantel tightened its grip. She was in her nightgown and the sight she presented made his heart start beating faster in his chest. The gown was some soft, filmy material and so transparent that he could see her body as plainly as if she wore nothing at all. Its color was the palest ice blue, it had long, full sleeves and soft lace ruffles covered her hands, reaching to her knuckles. The bodice was the same blue lace as the ruffles covering her hands, barely concealing the top of her breasts, and the blue ribbon tied tightly underneath pushed up the bosom to strain against the lace in a provocative, tantalizing way. From under her breast, the gown fell in soft, full layers that gave revealing glimpses of the satin smooth skin underneath.

Hunter drew in his breath at the sight of her. Then he quickly averted his eyes as he said, "What is it, Kathleen? What do you want?"

She had reached him and stood before him, the light from the single lamp by the bed silhouetting her, the golden hair flowing loose around the white shoulders, catching the softly flickering light, making her hair appear to be on fire. "Hunter," she said softly, "I want to talk to you."

"All right, Kathleen," he answered, his eyes still turned away, seemingly studying his own slender hand gripping the mantel.

"Hunter," she whispered and reached up to his face, "please look at me. I can't talk to you this way." She slowly pressed his cheek and he turned to face her.

Still not moving, he looked briefly at her face and she watched as his dreamy brown eyes slid slowly from her face and down over her body. The softness left his eyes and was replaced with a tormented look, as the muscle in his jaw began to twitch involuntarily. At last, his eyes returned to her face and he said in a hoarse voice, "Kathleen, don't you think you need a robe?"

Her fingers never leaving his tense cheek, she smiled at him and said, "Hunter, it's very warm tonight. And you are my husband. Is it necessary for me to wear a robe in your presence?"

He looked at her coldly and said, "It may be warm, Kathleen, but in the future, if you need to discuss something with me, for modesty's sake, I prefer you cover yourself." He paused, then spoke of what was really on his mind. "Or do you take pleasure in torturning me, my dear? I've respected your wishes and left you alone, but you are being cruel. If you don't want me to touch you, I'd advise you to get out of here and put some clothes on." He raised the hand resting on his hip and closed it over her fingers caressing his cheek. He moved her hand away, pushing it firmly to her side. "Now, if you'll say what you've come here to say, I'm really quite sleepy, it's getting late."

"Hunter," she said undeterred, "I don't want to torture you, really I don't," and she stepped closer.

"Well, then why in heaven's name do you . . ."

She covered his lips with her fingers, silencing him in mid-sentence. "Shhh, I've come here to say something important, Hunter, and you are going to listen." She lowered her head for a second, nervousness rising, her throat tightening, then raised it again and looked into his eyes. "Darling," she began, "I've been a blind fool and I'm sorry. I've made you suffer for years, but I want to make it up to you if you'll let me. I've suffered too, darling. I've been falling more in love with you with each passing day." Hunter's eyes widened in disbelief, but he remained silent, staring at her. "I've been trying to get up the courage to come to you for a long time. I have started down that hall a dozen times in the last few months, stopped before I reached your door, and fled back to my room, fearing you might turn me away. I couldn't blame you if you did. I finally decided it was a chance I would have to take and if I shamed myself before you, so be it, it would be worth the risk. I know you loved and wanted me once, I'm praying you still do, darling.''

Hunter's eyes had changed again and she read the confusion plainly as he looked at her, speechless. He opened his mouth at last, but before any words formed on his lips, she stopped him, saying, "Please, Hunter, let me finish, then if you want to send me away I'll go and not bother you again.'' Growing more and more nervous, Kathleen took a deep breath and Hunter watched the ample white bosom strain against the tight blue lace of her gown. He grew weak and beads of perspiration were starting in his hairline. She continued, "Darling, do you remember that night in the hall a couple of months ago? I wanted you that night more than you'll ever know. It was a misunderstanding, I swear it. I wanted you to come to my room or take me to your room, but you left thinking I was rejecting you. It's not true, I wanted you desperately. I just meant we had to stop, not go any further there in the hall. I should have followed you that night, made you understand, but I didn't and I've regretted it ever since. Hunter, I want to be a real wife to you. I want to share your bed. Darling, I love you, I want you.''

She looked at his face, trying to read his expression. Pain was still written on the delicate, even features, but she could see the bare chest heaving with his labored breathing. "Darling," she smiled, taking his hand in both of hers, "my heart is beating fast, too. Feel it,'' and she took his hand and gently placed it directly under her left breast, over her heart. She dropped her own hands away and watched his face. Silently, Hunter commanded his trembling hand to move, to drop away from her, but it refused to obey him, instead tightened its grip gently on the soft white flesh, caressing it lovingly. Hunter felt a groan starting deep in his throat and the hand still resting on the mantel moved to her back. His eyes began to close helplessly as the hand he'd moved to her back went up to the soft blond hair of her head. Kathleen smiled and put her hands on her husband's shoulders and raised herself on tiptoes, saying, "Darling, I've been such a fool. I love

283

you, dearest, very, very much," and she began kissing him softly on his lean, bare chest. His eyes flew open and the groan escaped his lips as he looked down to see the golden head bent over him sprinkling soft, sweet kisses over his heaving torso. He stood, not daring to move, enjoying the sweet agony as she pressed closer to him and sighed, "Darling, please love me. Oh, Hunter," between the continuing kisses until he could stand it no longer. His hand tightened slightly on her golden hair and he gently pulled her head away from his chest. She looked up at him, her eyes full of love, smiling at him. Her small hands moved up from his shoulders and went around his neck as he bent and covered her mouth with his. He kissed her over and over as the hand underneath her breast reluctantly moved and went around her waist to pull her closer. She molded her body to his and when his lips dropped to her throat, she murmured, "Darling, I've been so wrong."

Her sincere, tender declarations of love made all doubt leave him and he once again raised his lips to her mouth. Kissing her wildly, he said with his lips still on hers, "Oh, my God, I love you too, Kathleen, I want you so much, I must have you or die," and he carried his wife to his bed as the hot, sticky air outside turned into a violent spring storm, blowing the blue curtains wildly in the blinding rain, while the thunder boomed and lightning cracked and skittered across the night sky.

Hunter stood her beside his bed. While he looked into her eyes, his long fingers went to the blue ribbon tied underneath her full breasts. Gently he tugged until it came untied. He raised his hands to the gathered bodice of the gown and slowly pulled it down to her waist. Clutching her shoulders tightly, he pulled her up on her toes and leaned down to kiss the gentle slope of her breasts. Her arms pinioned in the long sleeves of the gown, she was held a willing prisoner to her passionate husband's caresses.

"You are mine, darling, and I'm going to possess you at

last," he leaned to her and his mouth claimed hers in a hot, demanding kiss. He ravaged her mouth, searching out the sweet recesses so long denied him. She responded to his blazing kiss with all the love in her and whimpered softly, longing for her arms to be freed so that she might embrace him.

Hunter raised his head and pulled the long sleeves of the gown down her slender arms and over her hands, dropping it then, letting it ride casually around her hips and stomach. Pulling her immediately back into his arms, he sighed with happiness when he felt her soft, slim arms come around his bare back.

"Hunter, Hunter," she sighed, her lips against his throat. "I love you, my darling. Teach me to please you, I'll do anything you want."

Trembling, he crushed her closer and began kissing her lips once again. In a violent rush, the blood surged through his veins as her full, high breasts were pressed temptingly against his bare chest. His breath grew labored as he buried his face in her neck and murmured, "Just let me love you until I get my fill."

"Yes, love," she whispered and sought his lips with her own. She unconsciously pressed her swelling breasts deeper into his chest while his fiery lips made her weak and faint and his delicate hands roamed up and down over her sensitive back.

His lips were taken from hers and her eyes came open as he kissed her cheeks, her neck, her ear before his mouth slid slowly, seductively down the cord in her neck. With his hands firmly gripping her waist, Hunter slowly eased down, his lips trailing fire from the hollow of her throat over the swell of her bosom. He was on one knee in front of her, pulling her closer, while his heated mouth closed over her breasts. He kissed them greedily, his breath hot on her skin. Kathleen's hands came up to the golden head moving so provocatively on her and she clutched at his hair as she moaned her approval.

Hunter raised his head just as the most violent lightning of the worsening spring storm gave the room the brightness of day. He looked up and saw the angelic face of the woman he loved, the blue eyes shining with love and passion, the bare, lovely breasts rising and falling with her excited breathing, her long golden hair disheveled and shimmering, falling down around her white shoulders. She was the most beautiful creature Hunter had ever seen.

In a wave of uncontrolled passion, Hunter jerked the gown to her feet as the loud, ear-splitting thunder followed the lightning.

"Hunter," she half-screamed and swayed to him, naked and vulnerable.

Clasping her gleaming body, he filled his hands with her rounded bottom, pulling her to him. While the blood pounded hotly in his throbbing temples, he hungrily kissed her silky smooth stomach, his open mouth drinking in the sweetness of her flesh. Her hands twisted and pulled at his hair while she threw back her head, shaking the long hair down her back, lost in her mounting passion and the frightening sensations his mouth was bringing her. "Hunter, Hunter," she gasped from dry, fevered lips while his demanding mouth moved to her thighs and his hands slid slowly down her legs to her knees. When he'd kissed her until she thought she would surely ignite and burn, Hunter rose in front of her.

Her eyes flew open to see his hands go to the waistband of his tan trousers and with the speed of the lightning still dancing across the night sky, he was standing naked in front of her. She was allowed only the briefest glimpse of his slender, lightly muscled body before he roughly grabbed her and pulled her against him. His hand went to her hair and he cradled her head while he kissed her, his other arm wrapped tightly around her, molding her quivering, excited body close to the aroused hardness of his. The powerful closeness of his embrace, combined with the pressure of his burning lips on hers, made Kathleen momentarily fearful for her life when she couldn't get her breath. Pushing on his chest, she whimpered until Hunter's lips left her mouth and moved to her throat. "What, sweet?" he said and nipped at the soft skin with his teeth.

Her legs trembling beneath her, Kathleen again clasped his back and whispered, "Darling, I feel so weak."

Scooping her up in his arms, he placed her in the middle of his bed, fluffing a pillow under her head. For a minute, he stood looking down at her. Her eyes traveled unabashedly over him and she smiled up at him and said softly, "This is much better, darling. Won't you join me?" She raised her arms to him as he bent over the bed. Clasping her hands behind his head, she pulled him down to her. He stretched out on his side, resting his weight on an elbow. Kathleen let her hand run caressingly over the blond mat of hair on his chest while his hand went to the curve of her breast. Letting its soft weight fill his hand, he rubbed lightly with his thumb and bent to kiss her lips. Her tongue met his in sweet surrender and Hunter withdrew and allowed her to dart her sweet tongue into his mouth. Burning from his caresses, she raised herself up, twisting her mouth, pulling him closer, her body straining to his. Hunter took his mouth from hers and she looked at him with pleading blue eyes, "Darling, please, please . . ."

"Kathleen," Hunter rasped as his mouth sought the soft, warm flesh of her throat. While he nuzzled there, Kathleen placed nervous kisses on his cheek and his hand slid from her breast down past her waist. He lightly caressed the silky stomach he'd kissed earlier and then his fingers strayed out to a rounded hip, finally to a warm thigh. Lightly stroking, Hunter moved his hand to the sweet inside while Kathleen willingly moved her legs apart.

His lips went back to hers to drink of her sweetness and Kathleen moaned and reeled under the heavenly pleasure his mouth and hands were bringing her. She looped her arms around his neck and began to move her heated body in slow, provocative circles against him. She could feel her husband's aroused body pressing against her thighs and all at once the agony became too sweet, she could no longer bear not having him completely. Her small hand slowly slid down his chest, over his flat abdomen to the hardness against her stomach. Hunter moaned and bit his lip when her hand gently clutched him, stroking him tenderly.

Lifting his mouth from hers, he looked into her eyes and his hand covered hers as together they guided him into her waiting warmth. Feeling a blessed sweetness he never dreamed existed, Hunter knew that for the first time ever, he was home. He was finally a husband whose loving wife wanted him. He was the lucky man to whom the beautiful naked woman in his bed belonged. The warm, silky body moving under him was his own beloved Kathleen and she was willingly giving herself to him.

"Kathleen," he whispered, "how long I've wanted you, how much I've dreamed of this night."

"It's here at last, my darling. Make love to me, Hunter."

She raised her lips to his and her kiss was hot and flaming. She abandoned herself completely to desire and began moving wildly against him, thrusting her aching breasts into the curly blond hair of his chest, raising her hips tantilizingly. Trembling, Hunter began to move above her, slowly at first, then more desperately as the fire inside burned out of control and her erotic movements brought him dangerously close to fulfillment. Carefully guarding against such an occurance, he held himself in painful check until Kathleen was writhing uncontrollably beneath him, the first, full violence consuming her. Only then did Hunter join her, casting aside all restraint, glorying in the full mindlessness of mutual rapture.

"Hunter!", Kathleen's eyes flew open and his name escaped her lips as the fury of her attainment rocked her with sudden, alarming completeness and she was buffeted by the depths of the tides washing over her with such ferocity that she was afraid of losing consciousness. She clung to her loving husband as tears of happiness and fright filled her big eyes and the only thing that saved her was his handsome face just above hers, whispering softly, soothingly, "Yes, my baby, yes. You're safe here in my arms. I love you, Kathleen. You're fine, darling. Cry if you want to."

Feeling blessedly satisfied and extremely powerful, Hunter soothed her with soft, sweet kisses on her temple, her damp hair, her flushed cheeks, as she clasped him tightly to her, small tremors still shaking her. For the first time ever, he had brought his wife to the full and unmistakeable pinnacle of passion and he was extraordinarily elated. He wanted to fling himself from the bed and rush to the balcony naked, shouting for the world to hear that he had made love to his wife and that she had been passionate and wild and that he had successfully and soundly satiated her, making her cry out in ecstacy. Instead, he moved to her side, gathered her now limp body into his long arms and softly murmured his love for her while he tenderly kissed the tears of happiness from her damp eyelids.

"Kathleen," he mused quietly, his lips hovering close to her face, "never in all my life have I been so happy. If it were all to end tomorrow, there'd be no regrets. You have given me all I've ever wanted, darling, and the reality is even better than the dream."

Calming now, Kathleen raised a hand to his temple, smoothing the thick blond hair with her fingers, "Hunter Alexander, I hope you will believe me when I tell you that it was just as wonderful for me. I love you more than you'll ever know and, darling, it won't end tomorrow. It will last for as long as you want me." She raised her lips to his, kissing him lightly before lowering her head back to the pillow.

Unable to speak, Hunter, his chest aching with sweet pleasure, held her to him and together they lay in silent happiness while the spring storm continued, the rain growing heavier, pelting loudly on the roof above them. They lay completely still, secure in the knowledge of each other's love, their minds and bodies finally in harmony. When a particularly bright bolt of lightning would bathe the room or a loud clap of thunder would break over the old house, Kathleen would bury her head closer into the warmth of her husband's chest, but neither ever considered pulling the covers up over their bare bodies. Still unaccustomed to the beauty and touch of each other, they lay naked together, each lazily beholding the strange, dear unfamiliarity of the other.

Kathleen slowly raised her head and looked at this spectacular man. His soft brown eyes were on her and in them was a look of love and possession that thrilled her. She shivered when his hand went to her breast while he smiled at her with an easy, boyish grin.

Brushing his hand away, she bent over him and started kissing his lean chest. She felt his heart speed under her lips and she whispered against the curly blond hair, ''Hunter, my husband, my lover.''

He moaned softly and put his hands behind his head while she rose on all fours, kissed him lightly on the mouth, then sat back on her heels and once again dropped her lips to his chest. Slowly, sensually she began kissing every inch of his chest until his breath was becoming rapid and his skin was growing warm.

''Kathleen . . .'' he began.

''Shhh,'' she whispered, ''let me please you, Hunter.''

Her sweet, searching mouth moved to the line of thick blond hair going down his middle. She could feel the muscles in her husband's flat abdomen tightening under her probing, moving tongue. She kept kissing him tenderly while her small hands caressed him gently, timidly. He was moaning now and still she kept kissing, touching, loving as the fire began inside her and her own skin was growing heated once again. She feathered kisses over his stomach and let her mouth glance out to a prominent hipbone, then glide down to a bronzed leg. She softly kissed it and when she began to move her hot, wet lips to the warm inside of his sinewy thigh, Hunter groaned and reached for her.

Grabbing her under her arms, he quickly pulled her up over him, bringing her sweet, roaming mouth up to his. His lips were hot and hungry and he kissed her with urgency, plunging his tongue deep inside her mouth. His hands clasps her waist and, locked tightly in his embrace, his mouth never leaving hers, Kathleen was turned over in one fluid movement and Hunter was atop her. He lifted his head and looked down at her.

"Never begin something you do not intend to complete," he grinned, passion clouding his eyes.

"I won't," she assured him. "Take me, Hunter. I want you again."

"Oh, sweetheart," he moaned and bent to kiss her waiting lips as his hands slid to her hips and once again they became two burning, starving lovers, determined to taste all the carnal pleasures of the flesh. Mounting desire quickly consumed them and they gave themselves up wholly to the storm violently raging within.

The fury of the sudden raging storm was no match for the long pent-up, now unbridled emotions of the two lovers occupying the big feather bed. When a strong gust of wind blew out the lamp beside the bed and the rain pelted in the open doors, it was noticed by neither.

Hunter lay wide awake the next morning, a pleased, contented smile covering his face. Kathleen lay asleep beside him, his arm underneath her, her head resting on his chest, the soft blond hair falling around her delicate face, touching his skin. Careful not to move and waken her, he lay and watched her, love filling his chest, his happiness complete. The thunder and lightning of the night before had ceased and it was now raining steadily, a slow, soft spring rain, the sky

291

still dark and gray. The smell of the fresh, welcome rain filled the big room and cooled the humid air. Hunter closed his eyes tightly and sighed, feeling the irresistible urge to laugh out loud. Suppressing the delicous urge, he bent and kissed the silky head resting trustingly on his happy chest, breathing in sweet fragrance, pressing his lips to its golden beauty.

A loud rap on the door startled him from the tenderness of the moment and before he could speak, Hannah's enormous frame waddled in carrying a breakfast tray. Hunter quickly reached for the sheet, pulling it rapidly over Kathleen and him. The quick, jerky movement roused Kathleen from her slumber and she opened her eyes sleepily and smiled at Hunter.

"Hannah, just put that tray on the table, please and leave," Hunter said, color rising in his face.

"Yes, suh, Doctor Hunter," Hannah was smiling broadly as she continued to come closer to the bed.

Pushing her hair from her face and clutching the sheet, Kathleen said, irritated, "Hannah, when you knock on a door, you are supposed to wait until you are given permission to enter."

"Shoot, Miz Kathleen, you forgettin', honey, I diapered you when you was a baby, you don't need to mind 'bout ole Hannah," and she walked directly to the night table by the bed, where she placed the breakfast tray.

Kathleen saw her husband's embarrassment, his hands clutching the sheet tightly up to his chin as though he were afraid it would be jerked away at any minute. She laughed softly and touched his cheek and once again scolded Hannah. "That may well be true, Hannah, but this is Hunter's room and, although you never pay any attention to me, I expect you to respect his privacy from here on out. Do I make myself clear?"

"Why, sho, honey. Doctor Hunter, you jest relax, I jest be a minute," and the big grin never left her face as she looked around the room and gingerly stooped over to pick up Hunter's trousers from the floor and the blue nightgown a few feet away where it lay in a colorful heap. She clicked her tongue and giggled, further mortifying the already uncomfortable young man. She made a big show of neatly folding the trousers and draping them over the back of a chair. The nightgown she arranged with great care, then went to Hunter's bureau and pulled out the middle drawer, placing the gown in with the stockings and handkerchiefs belonging to Hunter.

"Hannah, will you please get out of here," Kathleen said to the bent-over back.

"Yes, I'se goin'," but Hannah walked to the tall double doors and shook out the wet curtains, spreading them over the backs of chairs to dry out. "Sho is a pretty day, ain't it?"

"Hannah, it's raining and the sky is as black as midnight. Have you taken leave of your senses?" Kathleen shook her head.

Hannah turned back from the double doors and lumbered across the room, grinning and bobbing her head, "I think it's a lovely day, don't you, Doctor Hunter?"

Relaxing at last, Hunter had to smile, "Yes, Hannah, it's as wonderful a day as I've ever seen," and he winked at her. She ducked her head then and hurried to the door. She put her hand on the doorknob and turned back to look at them, "Now ya'll eat yo' breakfast fo' it gets cold. Doctor Hunter be needin' to keep up his strengh, I'm thinkin." Then the biggest grin of all split her face, the white teeth showing from ear to ear as she said, "I spects we be havin' some more babies in this ole house fo' long, yes suh, we be havin us a little sister for Master Scott. Uh huh!"

"Get out," Kathleen shouted and threw a pillow at the disappearing back of the big black woman. She turned to Hunter and said, "I'm sorry, darling. I'll have a talk with her, I promise."

"Maybe you'd better, sweetheart. I didn't even think to lock that door last night." Pushing the sheet away, he crossed the room hurriedly and latched the door. He came back to the table beside the bed and picked up the silver coffee pot.

"Hunter, dear, what are you doing?" Kathleen got up on her knees and reached up to stop the hand before he could pour.

He looked at her and smiled, "I was going to bring you your breakfast."

"Darling," she said softly as her hand moved up his arm, "I'm really not very hungry, are you?" The hand dropped from his arm and she sank back to the bed, putting her arms up under her head and smiling.

He stood for a moment, the coffee pot poised over the cup. A slow, wicked smile started at the corners of his mouth. Slowly, he set the pot back down on the tray and said, "I'm not either and you know what else? Old Hannah is right, it is really a beautiful day." he slipped back into bed, moved close to his wife, and pressed his mouth to the soft flesh of her warm throat while she sighed lazily and her arms came around his back.

The breakfast tray sat untouched on the table, growing cold in the damp, sweet air.

Twenty-five

Young Scott pounded on the locked door, "Daddy, are you in there? Daddy, where are you?"

Hunter, half dozing with Kathleen asleep in his arms, opened his drowsy brown eyes when he heard his son's voice. "Yes, Scott, just a minute, I'll be right out."

Kathleen moaned and opened her eyes, "What is it, Hunter?"

Hunter smiled at her and whispered, "It's our son, I'm afraid we almost forgot we had one and he doesn't like it."

"Oh, Hunter, that's right, it must be mid-morning by now. I'm sure he's confused and doesn't know what to think. Any day you stay home from the office he thinks belongs to him. You've spoiled him, Hunter," but she smiled and touched his lips.

"I know," he said, grinning, "just as I intend to spoil you from now on."

"Darling," Kathleen whispered and leaned up to kiss the lips she fingered.

"Sweetheart," Hunter breathed against her mouth, "Scott's right outside the door."

"He will just have to wait his turn," she laughed and kissed him again.

"That's it!" Hunter laughed, "I either leave now or I won't be able to," and he bounded off the bed and pulled on his trousers. Kathleen watched her husband from the bed. He was lean and hard, his body delicately muscled, his back smooth and beautiful. The thick blond hair was disheveled, there was a smile on his full, perfect mouth, and the dreamy brown eyes held a happy, satisfied look she'd never seen there before. "Hunter, have I ever told you I think you're a beautiful man from head to toe?"

"Honey," he said smiling as he walked to the bed, "men aren't supposed to be beautiful. Couldn't I just be nice-looking?" and he sat on the edge of the bed to put on his shoes.

Kathleen moved up beside him and gently caressed his bare back. Her hands went to his shoulders and softly worked their way down to his trim waist. "You're more than that, my love, you are beautiful in a manly, Adonislike way," and her lips went to the smooth skin and moved sensuously down the cleft of his back.

Hunter jumped off the bed laughing, "I love our son, but right now I'd like to wring his demanding little neck," then he bent over the bed, put his hand to her hair, and said, "Darling, you stay in bed a while. Get some sleep while I play with Scotty. I'll come back in an hour and wake you, we're having luncheon guests, I'm afraid, so you'll need some time to get ready." He kissed her quickly and turned to get a shirt, slipped it hastily on, and went to the door to greet his son. "Hi, Scott, what are you up to?" he said, lifting the tiny dark child up into his arms.

Kathleen stayed in Hunter's bed, yawning and stretching. The sun was beginning to come from under the clouds and stream into the big room. Kathleen smiled with pleasure and snuggled back down into the softness of the pillows. The wild, passion-filled night had been exciting, almost scary. But the sweet, love-filled morning had been even better as her husband proved to be an expert, caring lover, concerned and delighted with her pleasure, brining her to ecstacy with his tenderness and patience. Kathleen closed her eyes tightly, "Hunter, Hunter," she said his name, rememberbing. Happy and content, she curled up, her knees to her chin and went back to sleep, still feeling her husband's gentle caresses on her glowing skin.

"Daddy, I couldn't find you and I was scared," Scotty said as Hunter carried him through the long hall and down the stairs.

"Scott, I've been right there in my room all morning." He kissed the boy's cheek.

"I looked for you all over, but Hannah wouldn't let me come upstairs. Don't you think she's mean?"

"No, I think she is very nice and you shouldn't say things like that, Scotty. Hannah loves you and takes good care of you and Mommy, you know that."

"Daddy, is Mommy in your room, too?"

"Yes, she is, darling," Hunter smiled happily.

"Why? She's supposed to be in her room, but I looked and she wasn't there."

"Scott, from now on your mother and I will be in the same room every night."

"Why, Daddy?"

"Because, darling, we want to be together."

"Daddy," the child said and took Hunter's face in his hands, "You wouldn't ever leave me, would you?"

"Sweetheart," Hunter looked down at the tiny face, the penetrating brown eyes, "Why on earth would you ask me a question like that? You know I would never, ever leave you or your mommy."

"Good, Daddy," the child smiled and hugged him tightly, "I was just scared when I couldn't find you."

Hunter kissed the brown forehead and said, "Scott, I love you so much and I promise I will always be here. Now, why don't we go out back and throw the ball around for a while?"

"Oh, goody," Scott said as Hunter set him on his feet. Together they walked out the back door and into the big yard. Scott ran immediately to hunt for the elusive ball.

Finding it at last in a flower bed of early blooming roses, he shouted happily, "Here it is, I remember that's where I put it last time."

"Sure you do," his father laughed and raised his hands saying, "Put 'er here!"

Scott tossed the ball to Hunter, but by the time it reached him it was down around his knees. He stooped in time and scooped it off the ground. "Scott, I've told you, you will never throw better if you don't quit trying to use your left hand," and he easily threw the ball back to the boy.

"Daddy, I want to throw it the way you do. You use your left hand, I want to throw with mine," and he tossed another with the same results.

This one missed Hunter and instead of going to retrieve the badly-thrown ball, he walked to his son and got on his knees beside him. "Scott, he said, bringing a hand up to rest on the boy's middle, "we have been over this so many times. I am left-handed, you are right-handed. Now you're being obstinate when you keep trying to change, it just won't work and you must face it."

Clearly disappointed, Scott turned hurt eyes up to his father and said, "Daddy, it's just that I want to be like you."

Hunter ruffled Scott's thick dark hair and smiled, "I know, Scotty, and that pleases me more than you'll ever know, but darling, you must be like yourself, no one else. When I get the ball, I want you to throw with your right hand and see how it works out, all right?"

"Yes, Daddy, but what it obstinate?"

Hunter laughed and rose to his feet, "Stubborn," he said laughing, "just like me," and went to get the ball.

Scott threw the ball with his right hand and found it was much easier to hit the spot he was aiming for. "Hey, this is better," he laughed happily and his father said, "It's great, son, better than I can do."

* * *

Hunter came back to his room after an hour spent with his energetic son. He opened the door quietly and looked at Kathleen. She was sleeping soundly, a slim arm tossed up over her head. Hunter smiled and tiptoed to the bed. He carefully sat on its edge and leaned over her. His heart raced at the sight of his beautiful wife sleeping in his bed. Her hair lay fanned out on the pillow, one long strand across her pale cheek. The sheet just covered the bottoms of her full breast and one slim leg was outside the sheet, exposing the satiny smoothness of her thigh. She was absolutely breathtaking and she was his. His face flushed with the recollection of the stormy night together. He had no idea his wife was capable of such wanton passion and it had excited him beyond all reason. And then this morning, that had been sweeter still, as she lay in his arms and let him caress and worship her until he got his fill. Hating to wake her, but knowing he must, he slowly bent and kissed her lips.

Kathleen's eyes came open lazily and she put her arms around her husband's neck and smiled, "Could you arrange to wake me up that way every day for the rest of our lives?"

"I can think of nothing I'd like better." He kissed her again. Her lips parted under his and she responded, his mouth eagerly probing hers. His arms went around her and he pulled her up to him until they were both in a sitting position on the big feather bed. When she pulled away at last, she put her lips to his ear and whispered, "I love you, Hunter Alexander. Do you love me?"

"Oh, darling," he said and his lips moved to her shoulder, "you will never know how much I love you."

"Show me," she teased, looking down at the blond head covering her bare shoulder with fiery kisses.

Hunter straightened reluctantly, "Darling, I can't. There isn't time, but I brought you a surprise," and he rose and walked across the room to where he'd left the long-stemmed red rose from the garden. Putting it behind his back, he came to the bed grinning, sat down, and held it out to her.

299

"Oh, Hunter, it's beautiful. Thank you, darling," she smiled and took the rose and smelled it.

"Now, my beautiful love, you must get up and go to your own room. I told you we are having guests for lunch, remember?"

"Hunter, I wish they weren't coming," she said, fingering the long stem of the rose. "Who is it anyway?"

"Our English cotton agent, Richard Craddock, is coming to collect. It's that time, I'm afraid." Hunter paused, looked at Kathleen still smelling the rose and smiling. He took a deep breath and continued, "He's bringing his partner with him, dear. Dawson Blakely."

Without looking at Hunter, the smile left Kathleen's face and the fingers holding the stem of the rose tightened automatically. She made a face as the thorny stem pricked her finger, drawing blood.

Never taking his eyes from hers, Hunter reached out and took the rose from her. He threw it to the floor, lifted her finger to his mouth, and gently, lovingly sucked the bright red blood from it. He lowered the finger at last and still holding her hand said softly, "I love you, Kathleen Alexander, very, very much. I know you love me and nothing else matters, nothing and no one," and he put his arms around her.

"Hunter, Hunter," she said and threw her arms around him, holding as tightly as she could, "I do love you, my darling, I do."

"I know," he said and they sat quietly in an embrace while he stroked her hair and her back and whispered, "There's only you and me, Kathleen, just us." When Hunter knew his wife was completely calm and over her fear, he pulled back and said, smiling, "Now, I suggest you go wash that finger and put some alcohol on it. And please, don't ever tell anyone how I treated it. They would take my license away."

"I loved the way you treated it, darling," she laughed and rose from the bed. "Hunter, I just thought of something terrible."

"What?" Hunter said, alarmed, and put his hands around her waist.

"I don't have any clothes in here. How am I going to get to my room?"

Hunter laughed and pulled her to him, "I wish we never had anything more troublesome than that to worry about."

"That may well be true, but it is a problem to me. What shall I do?"

Hunter released her and walked to his closet, taking down his black silk robe, "Madam, I will loan this to you if you promise to return it," he held it out to her.

Kathleen turned, slipped her arms inside, and tied it tightly at her waist, "Never, I like it, I intend to keep it," and she turned back to face him.

Hunter smiled and pulled the lapels together up to her chin, "You know what? You look so cute in it I've decided to let you have it. Now, go, darling, it's time to get dressed."

The black silk robe reaching almost to the floor, the sleeves hanging down over her hands, Kathleen put her arms around his neck and said, "I'm going, just one last kiss and I'm off. Tonight, Doctor Hunter Alexander, you may have the pleasure of seeing me in your robe again. It's comfortable, I may never wear anything else."

Hunter laughed and watched her slip out the door, then turned and started dressing for their guests.

When Kathleen came down the stairs, the guests had already arrived. Hunter sat in the drawing room with Craddock and Dawson. She heard their voices and stopped on the stairs for a moment before coming in to join them. She heard Dawson's deep voice, "I agree with you, Doctor Alexander, a lot of the land in Mississippi is wearing out, many plantations are already only half as productive as they once were, mine included. But I'm sorry to hear that Sans Souci is ex-

301

periencing problems. The flush times are coming to an end, I'm afraid.''

"Thanks for your concern, Mister Blakely, but to tell the truth, I'm not all that worried. It was inevitable, I saw it coming, and besides I've been trying to have legislation passed to free all the slaves here. I believe you did the same thing years ago.''

"Yes, I did, but they all stayed with me as paid employees. Richard, you see, I'm not the only one in the south who doesn't believe in slavery.'' He looked at Craddock and smiled, then turned back to Hunter. His eyes moved suddenly to the doorway.

Hunter followed Dawson's gaze. Kathleen stood in the door, looking lovely and fresh in a spring dress of the palest pink. She was smiling and Hunter rose when he saw her and walked to her, "How lovely you look, dear. Come in and say hello to our guests,'' he put his arm around her waist and led her into the room.

"Dear, this is Richard Craddock, you met him at my birthday party, remember?''

"Yes, of course. So nice to see you again, Mister Craddock. Please, sit back down.''

"A pleasure to see you again, Mrs. Alexander,'' and he bowed slightly.

They turned to Dawson, "I think you're acquainted with this gentleman.''

"How are you, Mister Blakely?'' she smiled and extended her hand.

"I couldn't be better, my dear,'' he bent and kissed her hand. "So nice to see you again.''

"Thank you,'' she said and moved to the couch with Hunter where they both sat down.

At lunch, the conversation once again turned to slavery and the turmoil between the north and the south. Kathleen

302

was glad no one seemed to expect her to say very much. And she was more than grateful to Dawson for considerately not staring at her all the time as she had been afraid he would. He looked her way hardly at all, seemed not to notice she was there and Kathleen began to relax, deciding Dawson had finally gotten over her. She was happy he had. She loved Hunter and wanted no trouble and she didn't want Dawson hurt and still caring for her. It had all worked out at last. She looked at the two men engaged in spirited conversation. Dawson, so dark and big, handsome as ever, self-assured, his resonant voice lifted as he made his point. Hunter, slim and blond, placid and understanding, his long delicate fingers curled around his wine glass, his brown eyes intent as he listened with interest to what Dawson was saying.

"I've tried to tell everyone that myself," Hunter answered, "but it falls on deaf ears. We haven't a chance if the war, or should I say, when the war breaks out."

"It's suicide, Hunter, and we both know it. We have no resources down here and we can hardly shoot cotton balls at the Yankees and expect them to fall."

"Ah, I know," Hunter shook his head. "I love the south as much as any man, as I'm sure you do, Dawson, but our hardheaded pride is going to do us all in, I'm afraid."

"You're right, and I'll tell you, if we think the north is going to let up keep our pleasant way of life, we're fooling ourselves. They resent it bitterly and are determined to put an end to it."

Richard Craddock looked from one man to the other, not understanding exactly what the problem was, but fascinated by the exchange between the two southern gentlemen.

"I agree and it makes me furious," Hunter declared. "The north cares no more about the slaves than the man in the moon. They just resent us having them because they were not productive for them. If they had been, they'd own slaves and we both know it."

"Exactly. This fuss is over states' rights, not the slaves,

303

and I expect it is going to blow sky high any minute."

"You're right, Dawson, you're right."

After lunch, the four sat in the drawing room having coffee when Craddock said politely, "Dawson, pleasant as this visit is, we really have to be going before too long."

"I'm sorry, Mister Craddock," Hunter smiled, "we got so carried away over our regional problems, we haven't really discussed what you came here to talk about. Forgive me. Kathleen dear, if you would like to be excused now, we will . . ."

"I've a better idea," Dawson said. "Why doesn't Kathleen show me the garden, I see it's already starting to bloom, while you and Richard take care of the necessary negotiations."

Kathleen stiffened slightly, but she smiled and Hunter turned to her, "Yes, darling, do that. We won't be long, I promise."

"Certainly," she smiled. Kathleen rose and Hunter kissed her cheek, rising too, as did Richard Craddock. "Go along, darling," and he squeezed her hand.

"Right this way, Mister Blakely," and she started from the room while Dawson fell into step beside her. "The back gardens are the prettiest, do you want to see them?" She turned to look at him.

"That would be very nice," he answered politely and followed her down the long hall to the back of the house. They strolled into the yard in silence and down the path to the gardens, the sun now brilliant over the heads, the sky a bright blue. "Are you sure you won't blister?" Dawson looked down at her.

"It's nice of you to worry about me, but I'm fine, really," she said without looking at him.

"Some of the roses are blooming," she pointed to thick vines filled with huge red blossoms.

304

"They're lovely," he continued to look down at her, paying no attention to the flowers. They walked under a huge magnolia tree, its branches bending low to the ground.

"Watch your head," she said and before the last word was out of her mouth, Dawson had pulled her into his arms.

"My darling," he whispered and immediately kissed her lips.

Shocked and alarmed, Kathleen pulled away and pushed him, "No, Dawson, no. We can't, it's all changed."

"What is wrong? You're still mine and I want to hold you." He pulled her closer. "No one can see us."

"No!" she shouted, "Please let me go."

Dawson released her, totally confused. "What happened? Darling, the last time I saw you we . . ."

"Don't. That was two years ago, Dawson. It's different now, you have to understand. I love Hunter, I love my husband. I didn't the last time I saw you, but I do now. I'm sorry, Dawson. I never wanted to hurt you, you know that. It's over between us. All over. Please don't make it any harder than it is."

"I'm sorry, Kathleen, I didn't know. I want you to be happy, dear. I always want that."

"Thank you, Dawson, I'm sorry, I . . ."

"Don't be sorry, darling, you haven't done anything to be sorry for. Now, come, we'll go back inside. It is I who am sorry, I was out of line, forgive me."

"Thank you, Dawson. You don't have to be forgiven, you didn't know. Now, let's do go back in."

"I'll just go up to my office and get a bankdraft," Hunter said when his wife led Dawson away. "I'll be back in five minutes. Pour yourself another drink." Hunter took the stairs two at a time and flung open the door to his room. He walked directly to the big desk in front of the windows facing the back gardens. He pulled out the middle drawer and lifted

305

out a ledger. Glancing out the window, he saw Kathleen pointing out the early blooms to Dawson. Hunter smiled, she looked so little and pretty, walking along beside Dawson in her new spring dress. He stood for a second watching them and he stared, unbelieving, as Dawson Blakely pulled Kathleen into his arms and kissed her.

Hunter whirled around immediately, clutching the desk, shock and hurt making him weak and dizzy. He stood leaning against his desk for support. He couldn't believe it. How could she? Hunter shook his head while bitter tears of hurt stung his eyes. Then it all came clear. Once again, she had made a fool of him. She didn't love him at all. Once again, he was merely a substitute for Dawson Blakely. She didn't know he was back in town. She would never have given herself to him if she had known her lover was in Natchez. What an idiot he'd been to believe she really loved him. A substitute husband and a substitute father, that's all he'd ever been, all he'd ever be. His son and his wife both belonged to Dawson Blakely. And why shouldn't she love him. I'm no man at all. I've no business sense, the plantation is going down daily, I'm no provider, she hasn't half the things she had when her father was taking care of her. I'm no lover, she must have closed her eyes and pretended I was Dawson Blakely. I'm no hero, I've put up with her all these years, stayed with her when I knew she didn't love me. How could she possibly care for me? I'm nothing at all like Dawson Blakely.

Hunter was shaken from his tortured thoughts by a commotion downstairs. He steadied himself, wiped the tears from his eyes, sighed heavily, picked up the bankdraft and started down the stairs. He could hear Daniel's excited shout in the hall, "Our cousin, General P. T. Beauregard, done fired on Fort Sumpter! We's at war, we's at war!"

Kathleen and Dawson were back inside the house when Hunter came down the stairs. They were in the hall with Richard Craddock and Daniel, all talking excitedly about the news.

"Looks like it's started, Hunter," Dawson turned to him.

"Yes, I heard," Hunter said evenly. "Here's the bank-draft, Mister Craddock."

As soon as Dawson and Richard Craddock were out the door, Hunter turned to go up the stairs. "Where are you going?" Kathleen asked.

"To pack," he continued slowly on.

Hurrying after him, Kathleen grabbed his arm, "Hunter, what are saying?"

"I'm going to Virginia to join the Confederate Army."

Twenty-six

Private Hunter Alexander sat on the ground smoking a cigar under the shade of a giant oak tree. Legs bent in front of him, long arms resting on his knees, he blew out the smoke and looked around with drowsy brown eyes. Hunter was more bored than usual on this hot August day in 1862. Eight months of sitting in reserve in Richmond, Virginia, under General Robert E. Lee had held little action and had given Hunter too much time to think. Time to think of Kathleen and Scott back in Natchez. Time to think of the sight of Kathleen in Dawson Blakely's arms in the garden at Sans Souci. Faint nausea rose in his stomach as it always did when he vividly recalled that day.

The overly cautious Union general McClellan made fighting slow and sporadic for Hunter and the men in his Confederate troop. Hunter wished the slow-moving general would charge, put an end to the painful waiting which gave him too much time to remember. Hunter lay back on the ground, a long arm slung up supporting his head, and shut his eyes. Still the picture of his wife in another man's arms remained.

"Hi, sir, what are you doing?" Hunter opened his eyes and saw Jason Mills standing over him. The ten-year-old drummer boy from Charleston, South Carolina, spent a lot of time around Hunter. As fair and blond as his idol, he was a small, beautiful child with eyes brown and dreamy, very much like Hunter's. The first day Hunter had seen the lad, he was shocked to see a boy so young in the army.

"What in the name of God is that child doing here?" he

asked Captain Cort Mitchell, the troop's fiery, high-spirited leader.

"Why, good Lord, Hunter, he's practically a grown man," Captain Mitchell winked at the approaching boy. "Aren't you, son?"

"Yes, sir, Captain Mitchell. I'm ten years old and I'm ready for those Yankees."

Captain Mitchell laughed loudly, patted the boy's back, and teased, "You sure you're not from Texas, kid? I thought we were the only ones who bragged like that!" The captain strolled away, still chuckling to himself.

"What's your name, son?" Hunter asked the youth.

"Sir, I'm Jason Mills from Charleston, South Carolina, and I'm pleased and proud to be serving in the Confederacy."

"Well, Jason, I'm Hunter Alexander and you needn't call me sir. I'm a private, just like you are."

After that day, Jason Mills spent a lot of time in Hunter's placid company. Hunter told him about his own son back in Natchez and told the boy he would have to come for a visit after the war ended. Jason told Hunter he was an only child, too, and that he wished he had brothers and sisters, but his mother and father were old and had told him there would be no more children. He told Hunter that his father was disabled and couldn't join the Grand Cause, so he was honored to serve in his father's place and he hoped to make them proud of him.

"I'm certain your folks are very proud of you, but I'm just as certain they miss you and worry about you, Jason," Hunter said kindly.

"Oh, they needn't worry about me, I can take care of myself."

"I know you can, Jason," Hunter laughed and patted the small boy's back.

Today Jason dropped down beside Hunter and, parroting

the gestures of the older man, slung a slim arm up under his head and laid down.

"I'm just resting, Jason, what are you up to?" Hunter turned to look at him.

"Not much, sir. I'm bored, aren't you? I wish we could see a little action!"

Hunter reached out to the unruly blond hair, touseled it playfully, and said, "Jason, to tell you the truth, I hope you get to stay bored for the next ten or fifteen years."

"Oh, don't say that, Mister Alexander. I'm almost a man," the soft brown eyes were quite serious. "Sir, could I have a cigar?"

"Jason, I hate to sound like your father, but you're much too young to smoke," then Hunter laughed at the irony of a boy too young to smoke but old enough to go to war. "Son, why don't we close our eyes and take a nap?" He tossed his cigar away.

"All right," Jason agreed.

"On your feet, men," It was Captain Cort Mitchell's voice booming down to them. Hunter and Jason opened their eyes and looked up at the tall, imposing figure. A stir went through the resting men and they crowded around, moving closer to their leader to hear what he had to say.

The tall, prematurely gray-haired Texan was smiling and he raised his voice so all could hear, "Men, we're finally going to move." A cheer went up from the bored, restless soldiers under his command. Captain Mitchell grinned and waved his long arms, signaling for quiet. "We are going to Gordonsville, Virginia, to re-enforce General Thomas J. "Stonewall" Jackson. Mount up, men, it's a forty-mile ride and I'm itching to get there." Tall, long-legged Captain Mitchell dismissed the men and strode to his coal black horse, his gray hair flying around his head, the pink mouth under his gray mustache grinning as though he had been invited to a party.

The chance for some action and the high spirits of their captain were infectious as the Confederate troops scurried to break camp and mount up for the long ride to Gordonsville.

"We're going to help out old Stonewall," grinned a dark-haired man standing next to Hunter. "Maybe at last I'll have something to write home about."

"I hope so," Hunter agreed and mounted up for the ride.

Captain Mitchell and his men had no sooner arrived at Gordonsville than they were ordered north as part of an advance guard to stop Pope's army from advancing south. At high noon on August 9, 1862, Captain Mitchell led his men north across the Rapidan River. The hot sun beat down mercilessly on the tired heads of the men crossing the river. It was quiet and still in the beautiful Virginia countryside as the men, many now dismounted, crossed the river just west of Cedar Mountain. With part of the Confederate troops still in the river, Captain Mitchell encountered an advance Federal cavalry. The slow-moving Confederates were taken completely unawares. The ensuing skirmish quickly led to pitched battle as the Union cavalry charged, the hot desire for revenge coursing through their veins. Longing to reek deadly punishment on Jackson and his men, they descended on the Confederates ready and thirsty for bloodshed and fought like men possessed of demons. No match for the steely Union troops, Captain Mitchell's untried Confederate left flank caved in and took flight.

Hunter had spent too many months safely behind the lines, sitting back in reserve at the static battle of Richmond. He was in no way prepared for the hellish realities of war. He was marching peacefully along, leading his horse in the scorching August sun, thinking of his wife and son back in Natchez, Mississippi. The serene Virginia countryside's stillness was shattered by a rifle shot. Sounds of gunfire,

311

screams of the wounded, and frightened horses snorting and whinnying filled the air around Hunter. Loud rebel yells escaped the lips of the Confederates as they tried to mount up in the volley of bullets flying around them.

Hunter's mind was foggy and he didn't fully realize what had happened. His hand went up to his right shoulder and, when he drew it away, he looked with shock at the red of his own blood in his hand. Dazed, he looked down at his shoulder and saw his tunic turning a bright crimson before his frightened eyes. He wondered, "But why isn't there any pain? What am I to do? Someone tell me what to do."

Hunter started running. Bleeding, in pain and shock, he panicked in the face of danger, threw down his long rifle, and ran as fast as he could. Completely mindless of the battle taking place around him, he didn't see or hear the men, horses, shots, and shells all about him. He just wanted to get to safety. His brown eyes wild with fright and confusion, he fled on long legs, running madly through the thicket, away from the ambush. Away from the dreaded Union troops pursuing him. Away from the sure death that lay behind him. Blinding pain helped to bring back logical thought and he took his bearings. South! I must go south. I have to get to the safety of the Rapidan river. He was running, running, growing closer and closer to the river.

Suddenly, Hunter stopped dead in his tracks. The momentum of his fast-moving body pitched him forward onto his stomach and he fell to the ground short of the river. Hunter's months of soldiering did not discipline him to stand his ground like a man, but his years as a physician and the Hippocratic oath turned him back in the face of death. Ten-year-old Jason Mills, the blond drummer boy from Charleston, lay unmoving on the ground. Blood was rushing from his head and chest and his little face was ashen.

Hunter forgot his own pain and fear. He crawled back to the still lifeless form of the boy. While Confederate troops swiftly retreated past Hunter and the injured child, and

Union rifleballs hissed past his ears, Hunter calmly went about his lifesaving task as though he were in a quiet operating room. No longer afraid of dying, no longer feeling the searing pain of his own wounded shoulder, he raised slender fingers to the blond hair falling on the boy's forehead. He gently pushed the child's hair out of his face and looked down at the small mouth, as blood trickled from the tiny purple lips. Hunter knew he was gravely wounded, knew the injured boy could not hear him, but he put his own mouth close to the child's face and whispered, "Don't worry, Jason. I will take care of you, I won't let you be hurt anymore."

Hunter swung into action, reached into his kit bag, and took out a small bottle of whiskey and some clean rags. His long, slender hands did what they were meant to do as he gently, meticulously cleaned the wounds of the still, small body. Deftly, he tied off a vein and, reached to a hastily discarded rifle at his feet, made a splint of the bayonet and wrapped it around Jason's little chest. Hunter felt a slight pulse and knew there was hope. There had to be hope.

"Dear God," Hunter whispered, "please don't let this child die here in the hot sun on a battlefield he is too young to be on. Take my life if you must, but spare this dear, sweet little boy and let him grow up to be a man. Let him live, please, let him go home to his mother and father who love him. Help me, God."

Yankee bullets now stirred the dust beside the two, but Hunter was obsessed with saving the life of the young drummer boy. Calmly, he rubbed the small cold arms briskly as Union troops advanced on horseback not two hundred yards from where Hunter and the child lay. The Yankees moved closer and closer and more shots hit near them. Hunter moved his long, slender body over the young boy, sheltering him from further harm. He was strangely calm as he supported his weight on his right arm, that he realized was no longer hurting. If they were to kill Jason Mills, they would first have to kill Doctor Hunter Alexander.

"Hunter," he heard a low familiar voice. He looked up and Captain Cort Mitchell, astride his big black horse, was looking down at him. He was smiling, his gray hair flying wildly under his campaign hat as his horse reared up. In the captain's left hand was a yellow rose and in his right a long-barreled Navy Colt 44 revolver. In the midst of shells flying around him, the fearless captain winked at Hunter and shouted, "Take care of the boy, Private Alexander, I'll get these Yankee bastards off your back." He spurred the big black beast and moved off to the left. He let out a bloodcurdling rebel yell and rode directly into the oncoming blue horde.

Fleeing Confederates saw him and took heart, returning with their gallant captain into battle. Rebel yells now filled the air as the gray tide stopped and turned to face their enemy like the proud southern men they were.

Hunter stood and lifted Jason into his arms. He took the helpless child across the river to safety. Under the shade of a tree, with sounds of the battle in the distance just across the river, he mended the boy's still form. He then covered the small boy with his bloody tunic and, with his left hand, cleaned his own wounds. His shoulder bandaged and throbbing, Hunter sat down beside the boy and put a hand to the faintly beating pulse in his neck. He began the long vigil of waiting to see if the boy would live.

The battle was over at last. The Union troops were routed and the Confederates returned, forming up a line. Hunter still sat by the boy's side, slender fingers still on his pulse, looking for any change, when the hot sun of August finally set on the longest day he had ever lived in his life.

"Hunter," he heard his captain's voice over him.

"Yes, sir," Hunter wearily looked up at him.

The gray-haired man, looking fresh as if he had been out on a Sunday stroll, sat down beside Hunter and put a hand to his good shoulder. "Hunter, the boy will make it. Why don't you get some rest? I know that shoulder's hurting, drink some whiskey and take a nap."

"Thanks, Captain, but I really want to stay with the boy a while longer. He might need me."

Captain Mitchell smiled and said, "Private Alexander, I'm putting you in for a promotion. I think it's time you were breveted Lieutenant."

Hunter looked down at the ground, embarrassed, ashamed. "Captain, I don't even deserve to be a private under you. I'm a coward, I ran away. I was scared to death. All I wanted to do was flee. I'm no soldier and I certainly don't deserve to be an officer. Lieutenants should be brave like you, sir."

"Hunter, you're a hero. I saw you shielding the lad with your own body in the middle of the battlefield. That's hardly cowardly. You're a doctor, aren't you, Hunter?"

"Yes, sir."

"Why didn't you tell them that when you enlisted?"

"I wanted no special duties or favors, sir, and I still don't."

Captain Mitchell smiled, his gray eyes dancing, "You'll not get any from me, kid, so don't worry. Now goodnight."

Jason Mills lived through the night. Hunter took no credit for it. He thanked his God for answering his prayers. Jason was awake when they took him to the field hospital at dawn. Before he was carried away, Hunter kissed the boy's pale cheek and a slight smile came to Jason's face. "I'll see you soon, son, take care of yourself." Hunter squeezed his hand.

"Thanks for saving my life, sir," Jason said, "When I get well, I'll come right back and make you proud of me."

Tears came to Hunter's dreamy brown eyes and he whispered, "I'm very proud of you now, Jason. You're quite a man."

Twenty-seven

Totally confused and hurt by Hunter's sudden departure, Kathleen cried herself to sleep after her husband left without so much as kissing her goodbye. He'd avoided her questions and refused to give her a reason for his abrupt change in behavior. On a day that had started out as one of the happiest in her whole life, she was in utter despair by nightfall and found it almost impossible to keep from Scotty how badly she suffered.

"Mommy, will Daddy be gone very long?' the dark eyed boy asked as he watched his father gallop down the estate road.

"I hope not, sweetheart. I'm sure he'll return to us as soon as he can."

"I don't want him to go," Scott started to cry, his small chin quivering.

"Darling, your father feels it's his duty to go. The army needs all the men they can get. You know he didn't want to leave us, but he has to defend our homeland. Don't worry, Scotty, he will write to us and maybe it won't be too long before he can be home for a visit."

Kathleen mouthed the words and hugged her crying son, but deep inside she knew it was not true.

After Scotty was asleep, Kathleen went to her own room, flung herself across her bed, and cried helplessly. What could it be? Why on earth would he leave me this way? "Oh, darling Hunter, why, why? Just last night we lay in your bed and made love and it was wonderful. Over and over we declared our love for each other and there was no doubt in my mind that you meant every word you said. Or did you? Were you pretending to love me so you could inflict this grief on me today? Have you waited all this time to get even with me for making you suffer? Is the man I thought the kindest man on earth actually the cruelest? Hunter, how could you? Oh, Hunter, I love you, I love you. Why did you leave me?''

As the months passed, Scotty received sweet, loving letters from his father. Kathleen never heard a word from her husband. She hid her anguish from her son and happily read the letters aloud to the little boy.

Dearest Scott,

I am in Virginia and the countryside here is breathtakingly lovely. I miss Natchez very much and, most of all, I miss you. I think of you each night when I retire and if I close my eyes real hard, I can see your face, smiling and happy. Son, you'll never know how much I love you. No matter what happens, I want you always to remember that. You have brought me some of the happiest moments of my life and I will never forget them.

I wish I were there right now so we could go out into the back yard and throw the ball around. Perhaps you can persuade Daniel to take my place in the department and, remember, throw with your right hand.

Darling, it's late and I must go to sleep. Be a good boy and mind your Mommy.

Your loving father

''Mother, do you think Daddy will be home for my birthday?'' Scotty said when she finished reading the letter to him.

''No, darling, not this year. But don't worry, we'll have a nice party and you can invite Johnny Jackson and all . . .''

"I don't want a party if my daddy isn't coming," he said and went outside with his bottom lip protruding.

Summer came and with it oppressive, humid heat. Listless and unhappy, Kathleen tried to carry on a normal life, though she missed Hunter terribly and the pain of his unexplained departure still hurt her as though a knife had pierced deep into her heart.

The war had begun to change everyone's life as, one by one, the young men of Natchez joined the Confederacy and left home. Becky Jackson's husband, Ben, had joined a week after Hunter left and was somewhere in North Carolina. Caleb Bates had soon joined, leaving his lovesick bride, Julie, behind to weep and lament over the fact that West Virginia was too far away for a husband to be from his wife. Becky and Julie came to visit Kathleen as they had done years before in happier, more peaceful times. Together they passed the hot quiet afternoons sitting in the summer house at Sans Souci, watching Scotty and Johnny romp on the lawn, squealing and happy. The mercury climbed with each passing day and Julie and Becky, both pregnant, took turns sighing and saying how much they missed their husbands.

"Kathleen, don't you think you'll just die of loneliness?" Julie asked. "I miss Caleb so much and to think when I found I was pregnant he was already gone and I didn't get to share the happy news with him."

"Certainly I miss Hunter, Julie, I miss him terribly," Kathleen smiled at her friend. "I'm sure you've written Caleb that he's to be a father and we both know he was thrilled to death to hear it."

"Julie, you're luckier than I am," Becky complained. "Sure, Ben knew I was pregnant, but did that stop him? No, sir, he left me just the same and here I am big, fat, and alone. In October, I'll be having this baby by myself!"

"Becky, you'll have us, it won't be so bad," Kathleen assured her.

Julie laughed and said, "Kathleen, how come you're the only one of us who didn't get pregnant before the men left?"

Kathleen's eyes clouded, "I wish I had. If I were carrying Hunter's baby right now, maybe I wouldn't feel so alone."

"That's nonsense," Becky pointed to the lawn, "Hunter's son is playing right before your eyes. Good Lord, be grateful you're not going to be having a baby with him away. You can get pregnant when he gets home."

"You're right, Becky. When he gets home, I'll give him a daughter," but Kathleen knew she and Hunter would never have a daughter or a son.

Kathleen was at Becky's side when she gave birth to Ben's daughter in the middle of October. A cute, cuddly little girl, Kathleen held her and felt a great sadness that she didn't belong to her. The healthy, red-headed little girl grew quickly and her big brother and Scotty loved her and played with her by the hour.

On Christmas, the three friends gathered at Sans Souci to make the best of the lonely holiday without their husbands. Unlike Christmases of past years, the tree in the big drawing room didn't reach to the ceiling and there were not as many gifts wrapped in bright-colored paper. Hunter sent his son several little presents, nothing to his wife.

"Kathleen, where's your present from Hunter?" Julie, now uncomfortably pregnant, asked innocently. "I don't see it under the tree."

"Oh, Julie, I couldn't wait, I've already opened it," Kathleen lied.

"What was it? Let me see."

"It's a lovely shawl, but its upstairs, I'll show you later. Come on, let's have a glass of egg nog. I've a great idea, why don't you and Becky spend the night with us."

"We can't," Becky said, holding her baby daughter in her

lap. "We have to go to Grandma Jackson's house. We sure enjoyed it, though, Kathleen. Johnny," she called, "come along, it's time we were going."

"I can't stay, either, Kathleen. Mother Bates has made me promise to come over there. 'Bye, dear," she kissed her friend's cheek.

The big house was quiet after they left and Scotty sensed his mother was blue and lonely. He came to her chair and kissed her, "Mother, thank you for all my nice presents. And Mother, don't worry, I'm sure Daddy is lonely for us, too. Maybe next Christmas he'll be back with us."

"I hope so, darling, now it's time for you to go to bed. I love you, Scott."

After the little boy retired, Kathleen sat alone in front of the dying fire. She had never felt so lonely and she wondered if ever again her life would be whole. "Merry Christmas, Hunter," she whispered, put her face in her hands, and cried.

By the time summer rolled around again, there were no white and pink cotton blossoms rising majestically to meet the warm sun. Almost all the slaves had left the plantation and Kathleen was powerless to stop them. Stealing off one by one in the night, they left her alone to face an uncertain future and as her money ran lower and lower, her life began to change rapidly. She could no longer go into Natchez and buy half a dozen dresses at the best shops. The huge dining table at Sans Souci was no longer loaded down with an abundance of fine foods. There were no more fancy balls and fish fries and wine suppers. The flush times were fading quickly for Kathleen Alexander and the rest of the South.

Hunter continued to write to Scotty regularly and Kathleen was grateful. It was enough. At least she knew he was well. She also read glowing reports about her husband in the *Natchez Courier* and townspeople congratulated her on the gallantry of her husband. She gracefully accepted their praise and assured them she was very proud.

There had been so much sadness in the past few months; Kathleen no longer selfishly wished Hunter would write, she was just happy he was alive and unharmed. Her friend, Julie Bates, was not so lucky. In February, dear, frail Julie had given birth to a stillborn child and wept heartbrokenly after the tragedy. Hardly had she gained her strength back and begun to feel she could live through the despair than her husband, Caleb, fighting in the bloody March battle of Shiloh, Tennessee, was wounded and almost killed. In a battle where ten thousand southerners gave up there lives, Caleb's life was spared, but at a great price. He lost both arms at the shoulder and came home in April a broken, pitiful man. Julie cried, but thanked God he was alive and ran to meet him when he came dejectedly up the front walk.

"Oh, my darling," she said, tears streaming down her pale cheeks. "Caleb, it's so good to have you back." She threw her arms around his neck and covered his tired, sick cheeks with kisses. Caleb Bates stood against his wife while tears ran down his face. He wanted more than anything in the world to embrace her.

Caleb's misfortune made fear grow inside Kathleen and night after night she prayed that Hunter would be spared. "Even if he never speaks to me again, it doesn't matter. Just let him live, please God, keep him safe. In September of 1862, General Robert E. Lee crossed the Potomac into Maryland and the south was confident that at long last the war would be won. Lee had the Yankees on the run after trouncing Pope's Union army in August at the second battle of Bull Run and throughout Natchez and the rest of the Confederacy, hope ran high. Doctor Hunter Alexander once again was written up grandly in the *Natchez Courier*. Breveted a second time, he was now Colonel Hunter Alexander and

Kathleen was proud of him, cutting out the article to press and preserve among her souvenirs.

Victory was still elusive for the south as Lee was forced to retreat across the Potomac and back into Virginia. Lee had a victory in Fredericksburg where five thousand Union soldiers lost their lives charging up the steep slopes of Marye's Heights. southerners again took heart and Kathleen, like the rest of the ladies in Natchez, assured each other that maybe soon their men would be coming home again.

Life had been made even harder to endure during the last year as the Union army occupied Natchez without a shot being fired. There was no one there to defend the jewel of the south. All the able men were off fighting, leaving only the old men and young boys to look after their womenfolk. Kathleen would never forget the day six Yankee gunboats steamed up the Mississippi and took the city. On that fateful day, she fully realized for the first time that life would never be the same.

Now Union officers had headquarters in some of the finest mansions of Natchez, a fact that brought fear and dread to Kathleen. What if they should decide to take over her beloved Sans Souci. What could she do but step aside and let them have it. Who was there to stop them? This new fear kept her awake at night and she slept with a pistol under her pillow, though she had never fired a gun in her life and wasn't sure she would be able to pull the trigger no matter how great the danger threatening her.

Kathleen had not seen or heard from Dawson since the day Hunter left for the war. But she did hear about him from her friends. Dawson hadn't joined the cause. He had become a blockade runner and in his own way did as much for the south as the men fighting on the battlefield. He also became very, very rich. If Kathleen would have let him, he would willingly have helped her. He heard about her through his friend and attorney, Crawford Ashworth.

"How are they, Crawford, I'm worried about them," Dawson asked his friend as they dined together on one of Dawson's infrequent visits to Natchez.

"If you had listened to me years ago, you wouldn't have to be worrying about Kathleen Alexander now," Crawford looked at him.

"I didn't heed you and I've never regretted it. Now tell me how she is. What about the boy?"

"They're doing as well as any of the aristocratic families who have lost all their slaves and money. They manage, Dawson. Kathleen's turned out to be a pretty spirited, tough young lady. I see her at church now and then and, though she is not turned out in the latest fashion anymore, she isn't starving and she's still as pretty as ever. The boy's growing like a weed and he's a handsome and bright child."

Dawson's dark eyes clouded, "Look here, Crawford, isn't there some way I could give them some money, help them out? I can't stand to think about them having to do without the things they're used to. I've got more money than I've ever had in my life, you know I'm making around 90,000 pounds British sterling with each trip I make through the blockade. I want them to have some of my money."

"Forget it, son, she's much too proud. She wouldn't dream of taking money from you and you know it. Dawson, I do wish you'd find some lady and get married. It's time you quit carrying a torch for a married woman. It's hopeless and it's time for you to have a son of your own." He raised his eyebrows.

"Scott's my son and you know it," Dawson answered.

Twenty-Eight

In early May, 1863, Colonel Hunter Alexander, twice breveted for "gallant and meritorious conduct," was with General Joseph Johnston outside Jackson, Mississippi. Hunter had heard rumors that General John C. Pemberton had refused to leave Vicksburg, Mississippi, in spite of orders from Johnston to desert the city. They had to maneuver to avoid General Grant's Union troops until the Confederate troops could be concentrated and beat Grant. Colonel Alexander, knowing the Union army would soon be moving in on Vicksburg, sought permission from General Johnston to go to the beseiged city.

At twilight on May 14, Hunter approached the fifty-six year old General Johnston in his headquarters just outside the captured city of Jackson. The small, well-built general looked up at Hunter and rose. A dandy in his dress, he was immaculate, his coat ablaze with every star and embellishment, a bright new sash, big gauntlets, and gleaming silver spurs. His hat lay on the table, decorated with a star and feather. He was every inch the southern general.

"Yes, Colonel?" General Johnston looked at Hunter with steely eyes.

"By your leave, sir, may I request to be allowed to take a volunteer brigade and work my way around the enemy lines to Vicksburg? You see, Vicksburg is my home and I know this part of the country like the back of my hand. I'm sure I could make it and I would be more than honored to take any personal message you might wish to convey to General

Pemberton.''

"You're a fool, son. The entire countryside is crawling with Union troops from here to Vicksburg. Sherman and Grant are surrounding the city. Their objective will be accomplished any day now. It's suicide, I'm afraid, Colonel.''

"It's a chance I'm willing to take, sir.''

"Then I won't stop you. And if you make it, tell General Pemberton it's too late now for our armies to combine, but I'll do my best to come to his aid as soon as I'm sent reinforcements.''

"Yes, sir, General Johnston. And thanks.''

"Good luck, son.''

On Sunday, May 17, Colonel Alexander and his brigade of native Mississippians successfully made it through the enemy lines just before the menacing blue ring sealed the city off from the rest of the Confederacy. Hunter's heart saddened as he and his men rode past wan, hollow-cheeked, dirty, tired, footsore men limping back into the city, defeat plainly written in their eyes. The pitiful state of his countrymen shocked Hunter, though he tried to hide it from the weary men.

At sundown, as Colonel Alexander and his men rode past Courthouse Hill, a band played "Dixie" and "Bonnie Blue Flag" and pride in his homeland swelled painfully in Hunter's chest. He knew he had done the right thing by coming home. If he were to die in this senseless, cruel war, what better place to die than his own beloved hometown of Vicksburg.

At dark, fresh Confederate troops from Warrenton joined Hunter's brigade while the ladies of the town waved and cheered them. The lively, fresh troops doffed their hats and promised to die gladly for the ladies, laughing in the face of danger and swearing never to run from the enemy. The contrast between them and the poor, dejected souls resting on the ground, looking on in silence, ashamed of their defeats, was heartbreaking. Pemberton's tired troops continued to stream back into Vicksburg and tumble into the trenches and breastworks, beaten back by the advancing blue tide.

While most of the ladies smiled and called to the joking, happy, fresh troops marching by, Hunter noticed one kindly lady passing among the tired, weary soldiers, offering them cooling drinks and stopping to pat their hands or give a word of encouragement. Her kindness brought a hint of a smile to the sad faces and murmured words of thanks. Hunter pulled his horse up at the sight of the familiar back stooping over a young shoeless soldier. A smile came to Hunter's lips as he dismounted and happily called her name.

"Mrs. Bost," he called and walked to her.

She rose and looked at him and happiness flooded over her broad, mobile features. "My stars above," she shouted and ran to him, still carrying the jug of water. "Hunter, darlin'." She dropped the jug to the ground with a thud and threw her arms around the slender, blond man. "I can't believe it, it's really you," she laughed and tightened her arms around him, crushing him to her heavy frame.

"It's me, Mrs. Bost," Hunter grinned, "and I'm delighted to see you."

"Hunter, Hunter," she said over and over, pounding him on the back, laughing and crying at the same time. Hunter let himself be embraced, gladly clinging to the woman he had loved since childhood.

At last, she pulled back a little, saying, "Let me look at you, Hunter," and she took his face in her hands and patted the dear cheeks. "Oh, son, you are the handsomest man I've ever seen. How are you? You're so thin, Hunter. Have you been eating right? What are you doing in Vicksburg? Why, honey, it's not safe here, you shouldn't have come. The Yankees are on the way, don't you know that?"

Hunter laughed and kissed her hand. "Yes, I know. It's you who shouldn't be here. Why didn't you leave, Mrs. Bost? Now it's too late, you should have gone while there was still time.''

''Shoot, Hunter, you think I'm going to let a few Yankees drive me out of my own home?'' she smiled, wiping tears from her eyes with the corner of her apron. ''No, sir. They aren't getting my home. I've lived in that house all my married life and no bluecoat's going to sleep in my feather bed! Honey, why don't you come home with me, I'll fix you something to eat. I'll bet you're starving.

''I wish I could, but I must report to General Pemberton. Mrs. Bost, what about my home, is it . . .''

''Oh, darling, it's all boarded up. The family who bought it left the city months ago. But, don't worry, I take care of your parents' graves myself. I won't let their resting place grow up in weeds, so just don't you be troubling yourself about that.''

''Thank you, ma'am. That's so kind of you. I wish I could visit the graves, maybe I'll get the time while I'm here. Now, I must go. God bless you.''

Mrs. Bost grabbed him again and hugged him tightly, ''Honey, you take care of yourself, don't go getting shot! You come see me if you get a chance, promise.''

''I will,'' he smiled and kissed her cheek. Hunter mounted and waved goodbye and Rachel Bost stood watching until he was out of sight.

Hunter reported to General John C. Pemberton at 8:30 P.M. on that warm Sunday evening. General Pemberton, forty-eight years old, a northerner who had chosen the southern side, an Eastern aristocrat, tall and slim, had dark brown eyes, hair, and beard. He, too, wore a crisp, tailored uniform. He looked up at Colonel Alexander standing at attention before him and the expression in his tired brown eyes never changed.

''Colonel?''

''Sir, I'm Colonel Hunter Alexander, newly arrived from

General Joe Johnston's battalion outside Jackson.''

"I see. Well, what is it, Colonel?''

"Sir, General Johnston asked me to give you a message.''

"If he wants me to rendezvous with him he's insane. As you can see, I've got my hands full here. Or didn't you know we are being surrounded by enemy forces?''

"Yes, sir, I know. General Johnston wants you to know he will come to your aid as soon as his army is reinforced. I have come in with a brigade and we are here to offer you our services.''

"Colonel, I can use all the men I can get. You will take command of the 3rd Mississippi. The first thing I want you to do is get a detail of men together and burn houses along the lines.''

"Sir?'' Hunter was horrified.

"Colonel, our line of fire on the enemy cannot be obscured by anything. I want the houses razed immediately.''

"Yes, sir, General Pemberton.''

Hunter and his men set mansions afire all along the lines, lighting the night sky with the awful spectacle. A great sadness filled their hearts as they obediently destroyed the handsome country residences, many of which had been built in the last few years. Such were the horrors of war.

On May 18, the circle had completely closed around Vicksburg, Mississippi. The little city was successfully cut off from the rest of the world, the siege had begun. Dawn broke with pandemonium as huge Union ironclads approached on the Mississippi river from below the town and immediately commenced bombardment of the city. The heavy batteries on the bluffs guarding the little community quickly responded. The still May morning air was filled with the sharp report of the rifled artillery and the scream of a variety of deadly weapons. Minie balls whizzed, cannons boomed from the rear, mortars replied in rapid succession from the front.

The terrible battle had begun and how long it would last was anyone's guess.

On May 22, Hunter could see the Federals massing their forces, preparing for a charge. The line of bluecoats extended as far as the eye could see and at 11:00 A.M. the signal went up and the entire Union line charged. The blue masses rolled forward in a gallant manner, coming in two lines. Hunter gave the order for his Confederate artillery to fire as the charging Federals approached the breastworks. The infantry, their rifles raised and ready, began firing as soon as the enemy was in range.

The firing was deafening and Hunter watched in horror as the bluecoats dropped like flies in the bloody, desperate fighting. They made their attack on Hunter's right, but suffered terrible injuries. Undaunted, they still advanced. Hunter and his men of the 3rd Mississippi watched with admiration and wonder as just to the right of their position, the brave, noble regiment of the 2nd Texas Infantry repulsed and slaughtered the advancing Union soldiers streaming in untold numbers in their assault.

Union gunboats steamed up the river, but were quickly fired on and turned back, badly damaged. Finally, the beaten Federals were commanded to fall back under a hail of lead from the Confederates. The bloody fight ended with the northern soldiers unable to penetrate the breastworks. Hunter joined his Mississipians and the men of the Texas regiment in cheering and congratulating each other in turning back the mighty Union army.

On May 25, the rotting bodies of the Union soldiers who had died in the attack were still lying where they fell just outside the breastworks. The putrifying smell was horrible and the decomposing remains were dangerous to the health of the Confederates so near to them. General Pemberton sent out a flag of truce and offered the Union army the chance to bury their dead or even to have his own men do it.

Cheers went up from the men on both sides as a three-hour truce took place and the cannons and muskets were stilled. Confederates and Federals alike hoisted flags and rose to crowd the breastworks, cheerfully chatting with each other.

Hunter stood atop the breastworks and gladly accepted an invitation from a Union officer to come over for a talk. Men streamed over the works to visit the Union lines, where they were welcomed and entertained. Hunter walked across the ground where the horrible massacre had taken place three days earlier.

"Colonel Hunter Alexander, 3rd Mississippi," he extended his hand to the dark Union officer.

"Captain Alex Ward, 113th Illinois Volunteer Infantry," the man shook his hand warmly.

Captain Ward offered Hunter a drink and the two sat on the ground in the warm May sun, drinking whiskey and smoking their cigars, discussing tactics and the possibilities of the war's end. They laughed and chatted in easy camaraderie, both gentle and intelligent young men. Under different circumstances, they could have been friends.

Two young men, not ten yards away from Colonel Alexander and Captain Ward, were embracing and laughing loudly. Tim and Jim Manning, eighteen-year-old twin brothers, natives of Missouri, were delighted to see each other again. Confederate soldier Tim said, "How's your wife?"

Federal soldier Jim replied, "Guess what, you're gonna be an uncle, she's having a baby in August!"

"That's great, hope it's a boy."

"How's your girl? You two married yet?"

"No, not yet. Kate's fine, she's in New Orleans with her folks. How's Mom, you heard from her lately?"

"I had a letter about two weeks ago, she's fine, did you get a letter from her?"

"Nope, not for a month or so."

When the welcome truce drew to a close, Colonel Alexander rose to his feet and shook hands with Captain Ward. "Let's hope we meet under better circumstances someday, Captain," Hunter smiled.

The friendly man from Illinois returned his smile and said, "May this horror end soon, Colonel Alexander."

Tim and Jim Manning hugged each other goodbye and as Confederate Tim turned to leave, he said, "Jim, you know I'll be trying to blow your head off tomorrow, don't you?"

"Sure, Tim, no hard feelings. I love you."

By May 26, the hardships of the siege began to be felt and the Confederate soldiers had to remain behind the breastworks and in the rifle pits, unable to raise a hand or a head as the Union parrot guns shot all day. Colonel Alexander worried about his men as day in and day out they remained in the pits, never leaving even to bathe, change clothes, or eat their meals. Food was prepared by details of men and brought to them. Through heat and drenching rains they remained, as their clothes rotted on their tired bodies and still not a word of complaint was heard from them. Hunter remained with his men and, although he did not become ill as so many did, he grew slimmer each day and the once crisp grays he wore hung on his slender body in dirty tatters. The most disheartening of all the hardships he and his men were forced to endure was the lack of ammunition to fire back. It had to be saved for repelling assaults. Hunter, like so many of the men, felt helpless and discouraged.

On May 27, their spirits picked up considerably when the ironclad *Cinncinnati*, one of the fiercest of the Union fleet, was penetrated by a Confederate ball. The gunboats were to engage and silence the upper batteries, while General Sherman assaulted the works on the extreme left. The plan failed and the sinking of the *Cinncinnati* brought out the ladies of Vicksburg to wave handkerchiefs and cheer as the ship went down. The despondent soldiers in the trenches saw the ladies cheering and gained renewed hope from them.

On that night, Hunter felt he could no longer stand being in the pits for another minute. He strolled through the dark night to the top of the breastworks. His head visible over the top, a bullet from a Union rifle whizzed past him, barely missing its target.

The report of a rifle not six feet from him answered the Union sniper, quickly quieting him. A young sharpshooter from his perch atop the works shouted at Hunter, "If you want to keep your head, soldier, you'd better keep it down." The sharpshooter looked down at Hunter then and said, "Sorry, Colonel, I didn't see the insignia in the dark."

"That's all right, soldier, thanks for the advice," Hunter smiled to the young man. "I'm Colonel Hunter Alexander, 3rd Mississippi."

The young man lowered his rifle, "Pleased to meet you, Colonel. I'm Private William Henderson, 62nd Tennessee Mounted Infantry."

"Private Henderson, let me take this opportunity to commend you on your sharpshooting. I'm told we have some of the best in either army."

The slim young man from Tennessee grinned and said, "Aw, it's nothing, Colonel."

"I think it's something, Henderson. Get down for a second and let me shake your hand. Thing's are pretty quiet right now."

Obeying his superior, the tall guard lowered his rifle and climbed down to shake hands with the tall colonel. The two southerners fell into easy conversation and Henderson told the colonel his home was Sweetwater, Tennessee, "the prettiest part of the beautiful state." Hunter smiled and said, "I've always heard that is lovely country. Perhaps when this is all over, I'll have the oportunity to visit."

"If you do, sir, look me up, Mama's the best cook in the county. Where's your home?"

"We're standing in it, Private. I was born and raised right here in Vicksburg, Mississippi."

"Well, sir, I know it must be sad to see your home being surrounded by the Yankees. Maybe we can hold them off long enough for reinforcements to come and help us out. I'd hate to see what the Union soldiers might do to Vicksburg if they get in."

"Henderson, what do you think? Is there a chance we can continue to hold them off?"

"Sir, I can't say it'll be easy. We're already on half rations and the ammunition is getting pretty low. But as the 3rd Louisiana likes to say, 'it's pretty tough, but we can take it' ", he smiled at Hunter.

"You're right," Hunter returned his smile. "I must get back, keep up the good work, Henderson."

"Yes, sir, Colonel," Private Henderson shook his hand and added, "We won't let 'em take your hometown. As far as I'm concerned, we'll hold 'em off until kingdom come!"

Twenty-nine

By early June the beleaguered city of Vicksburg was a shadow of its former splendor. The women and children still in the city had moved from their homes to live in hastily-dug caves in the soft earth, taking with them furniture, rugs, and bedding. The houses they left were delapidated, torn up by the constant shot and shell penetrating their walls. Streets were barricaded and defended by the artillery. They were deserted except for starving and wounded soldiers. Palatial mansions were standing in ruins, walks torn up by shells and the gardens trodden down by hundreds of marching feet. Fences were dismantled to use for firewood.

The spectacle of the lovely residences now falling down once would had brought wails of despair from the lovely ladies who had dwelled inside. But there were no tears for their lost homes, the caring gentle women of Vicksburg shed tears only for the brave, starving men who fought against all odds and daily gave up their lives amid the deep-toned thunder of mortars and the whistle of the never-ending rifleshot and shells. Many a gaunt, sick soldier breathed his last while holding to the hand of a fearless Vicksburg lady bending over him, heedless of the danger of whizzing minie balls. A delicate hand on a clammy brow, soothing words whispered low, and tender glances escorted many a dying Confederate soldier to the other side.

Hunter's slim frame was growing gaunt and the high cheekbones sunk further in with each passing day. The soldiers were now on rations so drastically cut that each man received only a mixture of ground cow peas and meal and four ounces of bacon. Exposure to the merciless Mississippi summer sun bronzed Hunter's delicate features and bleached his blond hair almost white. In spite of the changes in his appearance, he remained a handsome man, though all the hardships and hell of real war turned the drowsy brown eyes to alert, knowing eyes of a man who had seen the cruelest realities of life and refused to break under the strain.

Hunter shook his head, sadly thinking of the men, so young and brave, who were in his command. Night and day, they remained in the trenches through scorching heat and drenching rains, while their bodies grew filthy and weak and many were infested with vermin. Malaria and dysentary claimed many a starving soul and through it all they fought gallantly on, determined to hold their ground until the Angel of Death, constantly sitting on their shoulder, tapped them lightly and told them it was their turn to go. With unbelievable courage, these brave, uncomplaining men held their positions, danger no longer causing any fear. Exploding shells and whistling bullets were commonplace and even the death of a comrade brought little more than indifference. Death became so familiar the daily occurrence of bloodshed hardly changed the expressions in the tired, sick eyes of the duty-bound men.

Some things in life never changed. The high-spirited and loveliest of Vicksburg's young ladies looked on the young officers as heros. Hunter, one of the handsomest of the officers, found it embarrassing, yet amusing, to be catered to by the lovely young women, some of whom were children of six or seven when he left Vicksburg to go to college, now quite grown up and ready for adventure. Their unceasing attentions were enjoyed by most of the officers and having their socks knitted and their handkerchiefs hemmed by delicate hands was appreciated almost as much as the blossoms placed in their buttonholes when they started for the batteries. Smiling young faces were there to welcome the men back in the evenings and, in the cave dwellings after dark, the handsome young officers, brave and godlike to the girls, forgot the war momentarily while eating homemade candy and singing songs amid freshly-cut flowers and candlelight. The happy festivities of the gay evenings replaced the harsh realities of the gloom-filled days.

Hunter never went to the caves, though he was invited often. When it was impossible for the officers to leave their posts, the daring young ladies, brave as they were beautiful, made up riding parties and carelessly rode through the setting sun amid the falling shells to the eager young officers in the trenches.

Hunter, though known to all as a married man, was irresistible to several of the girls. More than one eager young face turned up to the charming, blond Vicksburg native's in the moonlight to smile and flirt and remind him that "there's a siege going on, Colonel. We're cut off from the rest of the world and a stolen kiss or two would never be missed by me or your wife back in Natchez." Hunter, flattered by their attention, grinned sheepishly when presented with a new pair of socks by a fair, flirtatious young lady and stood rigidly while a soft pair of hands thrust a blossom into his tunic while the sparkling eyes of the flower's presenter looked up into his, a hint of promise shining brazenly behind thick lashes.

Not once did Hunter seek out the promise held in those eyes or give any of the girls reason to hope for more than a smile of appreciation for their giggly attentions, a fact that proved to make the tall, blond officer more attractive than ever because he remained so maddeningly unattainable. The heart inside his chest sometimes beat faster at the sight of a fair young face openly admiring him, but never rapid enough to make him forget the beautiful wife in Natchez he loved still, though she'd betrayed him with another.

In an upside down world, romance flourished and conquered the gloom. Lasting relationships were formed between single officers from Tennessee, Missouri, Louisiana,

Mississippi, Georgia, and Texas and the fair, fearless young girls who worshiped them for holding off the despised Yankee battalions who threatened to occupy their homes and take away their gracious life.

Colonel Alexander enjoyed seeing and talking to the young girls, for their loveliness and laughter helped him to recall all the precious things he was fighting for, but he felt guilty to receive so much of their attention when the poor souls under him received no such pleasant respite from the rigors of war. Even with a sweetly-scented, silky-haired young belle sitting close to him, raising her voice in melodious songs, Hunter found himself worrying about the brave young men in the trenches who had no such compensations. Youths who were sunburned and blistered, sick with malaria for which there was no cure, half-starving, afflicted with fevers and dysentary, lonely and afraid. Boys whose homes and families were far away, longing for the sweethearts and wives they'd left behind, not knowing if they would ever see them again. Desperately lonely, red-blooded young men who craved and needed attention from pretty-faced young ladies, but received only aid from the kind women of Vicksburg, women old enough to be their mothers and intent only on healing their physical pain and nursing their shrapnel-torn bodies back to health. One smile from a pretty girl could have eased their loneliness, banished their nightmares, and soothed the lonely ache in their homesick hearts. If Hunter Alexander could have transferred all the attention he reluctantly received from the girls to the affection-starved men under him, he would willingly have done so.

By June 15, the already desperate situation in Vicksburg had worsened. Though rumors had been rampant in the past few days that General Johnston, fortified by 22,000 troops, would soon come to the aid of the gallant defenders of Vicksburg, the rumors could not be verified and the long, hot summer days dragged on with no help from the outside. Ammunition grew scarcer as fewer couriers were able to break through the formidable line of Union troops surrounding the city. If ammo was scarce, food was even scarcer and the starving Confederates were reduced to eating mule meat until that commodity, too, ran out.

At twilight, Hunter, now painfully thin and wan, dined with his adjutant while minie balls whizzed over their weary heads and fierce cannonading continued unabated.

"Captain," Hunter said, as he chewed a mouthful of the stringy, undercooked mule meat, "this tastes as good to me as the finest roast beef I've ever eaten."

"Colonel," the man grinned and licked his lips, "I guess if we'd known how good it was, we'd have considered it a delicacy long before now."

"I agree, but I will admit that I must draw the line at dog or cat meat. I don't think I could ever get that hungry."

"Me neither, there are some things I just refuse to eat."

All too soon, they ate their words as mule meat ran out and there was nothing left to fill their bellies. Within a week of their dinner conversation ruling out dog and cat meat, the two men had not only eaten both, but had added rats to their menu as well. Neither batted an eye, as they, like the rest of the poor souls in the starving battalions, worried about only one thing, what would they eat when there were no more rats.

Back home in Natchez, Kathleen was aware her husband was in Vicksburg, not eighty miles away from her. Scotty received a letter from his father dated May 14, 1863, and Kathleen held her son on her lap and read it to him.

Dearest Son,

I am nearer to you now than I have been since I saw you two years ago. I am in Jackson, Mississippi, and I am leaving this night to go to Vicksburg, my home. Although I cannot see you, it helps to know you are so close to me. Perhaps the time is drawing nearer when once again I can hold you in my arms, tuck you in your bed at night, and be a father to you again.

I am in good health, high spirits, and hopeful that this long separation will be over soon. I'm sure you have grown so much I will hardly recognize you, but think of the fun we will have getting to know each other again.

I love you, my precious son, and I pray before the year is over that I can once again look on your dark, handsome face.

Your loving Father

Kathleen folded the letter after reading it to Scotty and smiled at her son. "Darling, I will put this letter with the others you are saving from your daddy. Now, why don't you go outdoors and play for a while."

"Okay, Mother," he smiled. "Boy, my daddy is going to come home soon."

"I hope so, darling," Kathleen answered.

In the weeks that followed, Kathleen unfolded the letter and reread each line, her hands shaking as she thought about how near her husband was. He was in Vicksburg, not eighty miles away. If only he could slip away for a few days, come to Natchez to see Scotty. Maybe then she could make him tell her what had happened. If only he would come. Just eighty miles.

"Hannah," Kathleen rose and went to look for her mammy, the letter still in her hand. "Hannah, where are you?"

"In here, Miz Kathleen, I's in the kitchen."

Kathleen hurried through the double doors of the dining room and Hannah looked up from the dough she was rolling out on the cabinet. "Hannah, you know Hunter's in Vicksburg now."

"Well, honey, he might as well be in New York City, you knows that they's cut off and under siege."

"Hannah, my husband is in just eighty miles away and I'm going to see him."

339

Hannah dropped the dough and raised her floured hands, "Is you crazy? He can't come home and you know it. There's Yankees 'tween here and Vicksburg. 'Sides, you said yo'self, Doctor Hunter done left without no explanations. You sure he wants to see you? Course, I knows he be dying to see Scotty, but . . ."

"Hannah," Kathleen paid her no mind, "what's today?"

"Why, honey, it's the twenty-first of June. Why?"

"Because I'm going to Hunter tomorrow."

"You ain't doing no such of a thing. You done lost yo' mind, I tol' you there's Yankees all over the roads and the river, ain't no way you gonna be able to get to Vicksburg!"

"I am going, Hannah, I've made up my mind. I want you to tell Daniel to have fresh horses ready at daybreak and tell him he is going with me."

"You jest quit that silly talk. You ain't going nowhere, you is staying right here where you belongs! Why, you'll be kilt if you tries to get to that city, you got a son to raise. You ain't goin' nowhere."

"Hannah, I am going and nothing you can say will change my mind. I must see Hunter if only for an hour!"

Hannah wiped her hands on her apron and her black eyes flashed. "Well, ifin you insist on bein' a fool, I's goin with you."

"No," Kathleen put her hands on her mammy's shoulders, "you can't. You must stay here and take care of Scotty. Trying to make it through the lines could be dangerous, just as you say. If anything should happen to me, you have to be here with Scotty."

"Oh, honey," Hannah begged, tears stinging her eyes, "please, please don't do this. I worry myself sick 'bout you if you tries to do this foolish thing."

"Darling Hannah. I don't want you to worry, but you don't understand. I have to see my husband, he means more to me than life."

Kathleen left her worried mammy looking after her and

raised her skirts and ran up to her room. She hurried to her closet and took out a box. She threw it on the bed, opened it, and took out the bright yellow sash. A sash for Hunter, she had spent several evenings embroidering his initials in navy blue. She smoothed the long ribbon out and admired its beauty. She'd felt closer to her husband as her nimble finger lovingly stitched the letters on the new yellow material. She smiled to herself as she looked at the lovely gift. If fate were kind, within two or three days her hands would tie the sash around the middle of her dear husband. Kathleen stretched out beside the sash and let her hand run up and down its length, dreaming of the hour when she would also be touching the man for whom it was made.

Hannah left the kitchen and tearfully went to Daniel. "She done made up her mind, Daniel, ain't nothin' we can do. She says you is goin' with her at daybreak."

"Yes'm, Hannah, if that chile says we is going, then we is going."

"Daniel," Hannah called him back. "You is not to tell Miz Kathleen, but I wants you to get word to Big Sam, Mistah Dawson's boat captain, that Miz Kathleen is goin to Vicksburg."

On the night of June 24, Hunter, bone-tired, dirty and ragged, hunger knawing at his insides, walked along the breastworks alone. Unafraid of death which was now so commonplace, he strolled leisurely along the parapet, unfazed by the whizzing of the minie balls and reports of Union rifles. Constant danger from exploding parrot shells no longer made him flinch.

"Colonel, I told you before, you're going to be hit if you are not more careful." It was the voice of Private William Henderson, manning his post, successfully sniping at any Yankee foolish enough to give the dead-aim sharpshooter a chance to fire.

"Hello, Henderson, how's it going tonight?" Hunter smiled to the young man from Tennessee.

"I think something must be up, Colonel. They're too quiet to suit me." He, too, had grown so used to the cannon's boom and the whizzing minie balls, he hardly heard them anymore.

"Come on down and let's visit for a while, there'll always be more Yankees to shoot at."

Henderson lowered his rifle and agreed, "Colonel, sometimes I think they're over there multiplying like a bunch of rabbits," he laughed and sat down beside Hunter.

Hunter was shocked at the change of appearance in the young man he'd met not a month before. Henderson's slim frame was now gaunt and the tattered gray tunic he wore hung from protruding shoulder blades. The long fingers holding the rifle looked like the hands of a skeleton. The veins of the young boy's forehead stood out prominently and his face had the pinched look of a starving man. Hunter realized he was looking at the mirror image of himself.

"Are you all right, Henderson?" Hunter asked softly.

"Well, sir, I'm awful hungry, I keep daydreaming about homemade biscuits."

"I know what you mean, I think I'd gladly die tomorrow if I could just have one more good meal before I went," he smiled sadly.

"Colonel, I don't see why you didn't have them send you to the field hospital. I've heard you're a doctor, you could have had it easy. I've even heard they've got brandy up there and they eat good."

"You're wrong, son. Sometimes I think I'm the cowardly one for not being up there with them. I went the other day and you can't imagine how rough they are having it. I visited a brigade hospital and the scenes I saw were a nightmare. The tents are filled with the wounded and dying and the surgeons are unbelievably brave. They operate day and night while bullets whiz past their heads and they pay no attention.

342

The ground was filled with arms, legs, and hands that had been amputated and discarded. Men who once possessed great manly beauty are no longer recognizable, made hideous by the loss of noses and eyes or part of their faces. It was horrible, Henderson, worse than anything you could ever imagine."

"Sorry, sir, guess I hadn't given it a lot of thought. But I still say you're more valuable where you are. You're an inspiration to your men, your unfailing fearlessness and determination have kept them going through this."

"Thanks for those kind words. Now, I guess you'd better get back to your post. By the way, Henderson, do you smell that terrible odor? Do you think it's me or you?"

Private Henderson rose, laughing, "Sir, it's both of us. I can't remember the last time I had a bath, can you?"

"No, I can't, Henderson, I really can't."

Thirty

Kathleen rose before sunup on June 22 and Hannah helped her dress, begging her to change her mind about going to Vicksburg. Kathleen was adamant; she was going and nothing or no one was going to stop her. While Hannah wrung her hands and cried, Kathleen went about preparing for her departure, strangely calm and hopeful.

She took little with her, but the one important thing she was intent on packing was the new bright yellow sash she had made for her husband. She also took a new box of cigars along. Ready at last, she tiptoed into her son's room to kiss him goodbye. She considered waking him, thought better of it, leaned over and kissed him, whispering, "My darling son, I love you more than you'll ever know and if it be God's will I will return safely to you." She turned and hurried from the room and down the stairs.

Daniel stood at the front gate with the horses, obedient, ready to see his mistress safely through the dangers that lay ahead. He helped her mount her horse and climbed on his. The two rode off together with Sans Souci still wrapped in darkness behind them. Hannah stood and watched them leave and said aloud, "Oh, dear Lawd in heaven, protect that chile. Send her safely back to watch that baby upstairs grow up."

For the next two days, Daniel and Kathleen made their way north to Vicksburg, skirting details of Union soldiers, at times dismounting and hiding in the trees until they could once again mount and cover more ground. Every mile they

344

rode brought Kathleen nearer to Hunter and with hope and determination she galloped mile after mile, never feeling the tiredness of her slim body, never considering the dangers that could lay just beyond the next bend in the road. Daniel was just as determined to see her safely to her destination and when they stopped to sleep, he laid down beside her, his old fingers curved around the trigger of his pistol, ready to shoot down anyone who might try to harm her.

With numerous odds against them, Daniel and Kathleen entered the outskirts of Vicksburg at 2 A.M. on June 25. They made their way cautiously into town and were met by gallant Confederate soldiers, telling them it was not safe for them to be there. They should go at once to the caves under the bluffs. Kathleen explained that she had come from Natchez to see her husband and would much appreciate it if any of them could tell her where she might find him.

The daring Colonel Alexander was known to many of the men in the various regiments and she was graciously led to his tent by three helpful men from Texas. Nearing his quarters, she spoke to the young private stationed outside.

"Soldier, I'm looking for my husband, Colonel Hunter Alexander."

"Ma'am, he's inside his tent alone, I'll be happy to get him for you," Private Bell assured her.

"No," she said, taking his arm, "Please, I want to see him alone."

"Ma'am," Private Bell smiled, "I'll stand guard, you will not be disturbed."

"Kathleen!" Hunter looked up from the table, shock and disbelief written on his gaunt features. He rose and stared at her as though she were unreal, a ghost.

"Oh, Hunter," she cried and started towards him. Something in his tired brown eyes stopped her midway across the small tent and she stood still, clutching her hands together in front of her.

"How did you get here? Why . . . is . . . oh, my God, is

345

it Scott? Has something happened to Scotty?'' His eyes filled with fear.

"No, Hunter, he's just fine, dear, he's back home with Hannah, he's safe.''

"Then, what is it? How did you get here? What do you want? Kathleen, it's not safe, why did you come?''

"Hunter, I came because I had to. I . . . we . . . Daniel and I made it through the lines. Oh, please don't scold me, I had to see you, I had to.''

"Why?'' he said coldly, "what have we to say to each other?''

"How can you say that to me, you're my husband! I've been worried sick about you.'' Tears were streaming from her eyes, running down her cheeks. "I pray for you each night and you're on my mind constantly. Hunter, I love you and I've never understood how you could leave me the way you did. You must tell me, I've come all this way to see you, to make you tell me why you left me, why you never write to me. You owe me that much at least.''

"Kathleen, please, I'm tired and I really don't have time to play games with you. I have no idea why you are here, but I want you to leave. It isn't safe for you to be here, you were quite foolish to come.'' Kathleen took a step closer to him and threw up his hands and said coldly, "Stay where you are. There is nothing left for us to say to each other. Nothing.''

"What do you mean? I risked my life to find you! My Lord, do you hate me so much, I . . .''

"I don't hate you, Kathleen. I feel nothing for you, I have finally gotten over you, given up hope. I'm sure you thought I would never tire of having you make a fool of me, but I have. So, please, play your little games with someone else and leave me alone. I've work to do.''

"Hunter Alexander, I will not go until you tell me what you are talking about. Darling, I know I hurt you for years and I shall regret it forever, but I am in love with you now. I thought everything was wonderful between us. You loved me, I know you did, then you just left without a word, as though I didn't exsist. What happened? Please, please tell me."

"Kathleen, how can you stand there and lie to me? You see, I was looking out the window when you escorted Dawson Blakely into the garden that day I left. I saw you in his arms. You never loved me, it was him from the start. I thought at first I could make you feel something for me. I spent all those years trying and I loved his son as though he were my own."

Kathleen looked at Hunter, a cold sense of bewilderment spreading through her body, "Hunter, you mean you always knew Scotty was . . ."

Hunter smiled wryly, "How can you be so shocked? You must think I am the densest man you've ever met. I knew from the start, I knew before he was born, and I knew why you married me. You were pregnant with Blakely's child and you had to have a husband. But you know what, Kathleen? I loved you so much then, I wouldn't have cared if you'd had a dozen children by other men. I want you so much it just didn't matter. But it does matter that you continue to lie to me now. I'm sick of it, fed up, worn out. I can't take it anymore, I . . ."

"Hunter," Kathleen was sobbing loudly, "Please, please listen to me. It's true I married you because I needed a father for Scotty. I was in love with Dawson Blakely, I won't deny it. But, darling, I swear on my dear parents' grave that I fell in love with you, totally, completely. The day you saw me in the garden with Dawson, I was innocent. He embraced me and I pulled away as quickly as possible. If only you'd watched a little longer you would know I speak the truth. I told him I loved you and only you. Told him it was completely over with him and that he must leave me alone. That's the truth, Hunter! You must believe me. I haven't seen him since that day, I swear it. He's left me alone because he knows I want only you. I do, darling, please, please believe me!''

Hunter stared at her, studying her face, looking at the sad blue eyes, listening to her pleading. He wanted to go to her, he still adored her, would always want her. ''Kathleen, how can I know it's true? All I know is you were kissing him, you were kissing the father of your child, the man you loved when you married me, the man who kept me out of your bedroom for five years.''

''You must listen. You must! What can I do to prove my love for you? I'll get down on my kness, I'll write it in blood. I've ridden through the enemy to see you, I'd risk it every day if I had to. Hunter, you can personally kill me with your own saber if you find I'm lying.''

''Oh, Kathleen,'' his voice was shaky, ''don't you know I want to believe you, I just . . .''

''Darling, you have to believe me, it's our lives we're talking about. Hunter, I'm telling the truth. Dear God, please!''

The pain-filled brown eyes welled with tears and he said softly, ''Kathleen, my darling, I do believe you.''

''Hunter,'' she cried and started to him.

''Stop,'' he shouted, ''don't come near me!''

Pulling back abruptly, she questioned, ''But why, if you believe me?''

''Because,'' he said in a commanding voice, ''I'm . . . I'm too dirty to touch you. Stay right where you are, I'll come right back.''

''Hunter,'' she was laughing and crying at the same time, ''I don't care how filthy you are. It doesn't matter to me, I love you.''

''It matters to me.'' He picked up a sliver of soap and headed for the tent opening. He turned, pausing with his hand on the flap, ''Promise me you won't run away. I'll be back in just a few minutes,'' and he hurried from the tent while she stood watching him, relief and happiness flooding over her.

Hunter ran to the breastworks, climbed to the top, and shouted to the tall guard standing with his rifle raised, his grayish-green eyes alertly scanning the enemy lines for any sign of movement. "Henderson," Hunter called, smiling broadly, "Henderson, I need you. You must leave your post for a few minutes."

"Gladly, sir," William Henderson turned to him, "is it something important? I could use some action, things have been too quiet all night."

"Private Henderson, it's of the utmost importance! I'm going to take a bath and I want you to guard me while I do it." He threw back his head and laughed, a happy man.

Henderson laughed with him, "Sir, I can't think of anything more important than that, let's go," and he lowered his rifle and followed the laughing, blond man down to the Mississippi river.

The young soldier stood on the muddy banks of the river, his rifle poised in his hand, his eyes keenly alert, looking for any sign of danger. Hunter stripped off his tattered uniform and splashed into the water. He lathered his body, face, and hair, and scrubbed himself until the thin frame was clean and his thick blond hair was shining. His thin, bronzed face was almost pink from the vigorous scrubbing. "You see," he said from the water, "the reason this is so important is that my wife, who I've not seen for over two years, has bravely broken through the enemy lines to see me. Can you believe it, she came all the way from Natchez to find me."

"Well, sir, if she's anything like these fine fearless ladies of Vicksburg, it doesn't surprise me. But I'll say this, she must love you a lot to have risked her life to get to you."

"You really think so, Henderson?"

"I know it. Now you better get out of there and go greet her properly."

Hunter smiled and walked out of the water. "I was so excited, I forgot to bring anything to dry off on," he looked at Henderson, sheepishly.

"Sir, if you'll hold my rifle for a minute, I'll take off my tunic and you can use that. I wouldn't want you going back to her all wet."

"No, I'll use mine, I . . ."

Handing his gun to Hunter, William Henderson quickly stripped the tunic from his thin frame, "You'll use this, you're having a visit with a lady, I want you to look nice, and besides, a wet tunic will be mighty comfortable for me in this heat."

"Thanks, Henderson," Hunter took the offered tunic and dried himself. Once again dressed in his own tattered but dry tunic, he headed back up the river bank, as eager as a young boy on his first date. The young guard followed him, glad to see a man as nice as his colonel happy in the midst of utter chaos.

"Night, Colonel," Henderson smiled and returned to his post.

"Thanks, Henderson," Hunter called after him. "May God watch over you," and he turned and hurried to Kathleen.

Hunter stepped just inside the tent opening and looked at his wife. Bowing grandly from the waist, he smiled and said, "Ma'am, may I welcome you to my hometown, Vicksburg, Mississippi."

Kathleen, her tears now dried, smiled sweetly and curtsied, "Colonel I find your home a charming, beautiful place."

Slowly, Hunter walked to her and whispered, "I'm clean now, so Kathleen, darling, please, please touch me just for a minute," and he kissed the corner of her mouth. Kathleen looked up at the handsome, bronzed face and touched the wet hair, plastered to the dear head.

"My darling," she said and put her hands to his tattered tunic. Hunter watched her, holding his breath, while she carefully unbuttoned the faded gray blouse. The tunic now open to his waist, she slipped her fingers inside and heard

Hunter release his breath while she softly caressed the thick blond hair on his chest. The sensation of the soft, tiny fingers stroking his skin in tender circular motions made his pulse quicken and the heart under her hands speeded noticeably. The magic fingers continued their tender stroking and moved further down his chest, slowly exploring his taut, flat abdomen. Kathleen could see the reaction on her husband's face and it heightened her own excitement and made her bolder. While one hand moved back up to rest over his rapidly beating heart, the other slowly traced the narrowing line of thick blond hair that went down his stomach and disappeared into his trousers. Her hand stopped at his buckle, but the fingers gripped the belt and slowly pulled him closer.

"Thank you, darling," he whispered and covered her lips with his own. His shaky arms came around her and crushed her to his bare chest and she could feel the violent trembling of his slim body against hers. She responded to his warm kisses, her mouth moving hungrily on his. Her total surrender matched that of her husband and they embraced wildly until it was painful for them both. Hunter's lips left hers and moved to her ear while he continued to hold her tightly, wanting more. He whispered, "Oh, Kathleen, I . . ."

"Make love to me, darling," she whispered against his shoulder.

"But darling," he murmured, his eyes closed, "Think where we are, there's a siege going on, this is no dime Joseph Engram novel, it's real, we can't . . ."

"Hunter," she whispered, "there will be no fighting until you make love to your wife!" and she pulled away and started unbuttoning her dress.

Hunter made love to his wife in the middle of the hot June night and the Confederate gray blanket on the small cot supporting their eager bodies felt as glorious to them as the silky satin sheets of their honeymoon suite at the St. Charles Hotel in New Orleans. For an hour, there was no war for Hunter and Kathleen Alexander. There was no hunger, fear, grief,

351

disappointment, or care of any kind. There was only the two of them, man and wife, amorous lovers, lost in each other. There was total understanding, physical gratification, spiritual beauty, an end to their longing, a hunger sated, a kaleidoscope of emotions, passion, lust, friendship, love displayed in the strongest bond known to human beings on the earth.

Amid the roar of Confederate cannons still protecting the bluffs and the sporadic cannonading from the powerful Union army moving ever closer, while the whiz of the minie balls filled the hot, still air, while shot and shell continued to terrify the trapped soldiers and the townspeople of Vicksburg, Mississippi, Hunter Alexander made love again to his wife and they both forgot completely where they were, what was happening around them, and what might befall them on the morrow. An hour of total, absolute happiness existed inside the tiny tent and if the world had ended at that period in time, neither would have cared.

Hunter rose to his elbow at last, "Darling," he bent to kiss her brow, "I wish you could stay with me forever, but you must go. I want you out of here, out of the city before dawn. You must leave under the cloak of darkness, for I could not live if anything should happen to you."

"Yes, sir, Colonel," she threw her arms around his neck.

"I mean it, Kathleen, you must hurry," and together they rose and dressed.

Ready to depart, Kathleen turned to the small bag she had brought with her. She took out the yellow sash and held it out to him, proudly showing him the blue embroidered initials, *H.S.A.*, she had labored so long to make. "Sweetheart, I wanted to bring you something. A memento you could keep to remind you of me."

"Kathleen, it's beautiful," Hunter took it from her, smiling. "Darling, I shall wear it until I come home to you," and he carefully tied the new yellow sash around his slim waist. He looked up and saw the tears shining in her eyes and pulled her to him, "Darling, darling, don't cry. I will return to you. To my wife and our son. Nothing is going to happen to me, I promise.''

She clung to him and fought back the tears, cold fear now descending upon her, not for herself but for the tall blond man she held. ''I know you'll come home, Hunter,'' she bravely released him. Hunter took her hand and led her out of the tent.

''Private Bell,'' he called to his orderly, ''Accompany my wife to the outskirts of town, take four men with you.''

''Yes, sir, Colonel,'' and the young soldier went to where Daniel waited with the horses, calling to four men lounging nearby. In a matter of minutes, he returned, Daniel following, leading their horses. Hunter shook the black man's hand, ''Daniel, I appreciate what you've done. I'm depending on you to take care of her.''

''Yes, suh, Doctor Hunter, I protect that chile with my life.''

''I know you will, Daniel,'' Hunter smiled and turned to his wife.

''We're ready to go, Colonel,'' Private Bell and the others were mounted.

''Well done,'' Hunter said to him and looked down at Kathleen. ''Kiss our son for me, darling.'' He squeezed her hand and lifted her onto her horse. He stood beside her and she leaned down to kiss him goodbye.

''I love you,'' she whispered.

''May God take you safely home, my love,'' he smiled and nodded to the orderly to leave. The horses trotted away and Hunter stood watching until they were out of sight. He smiled to himself, sighed, and returned to his tent.

Hunter's men escorted Kathleen and Daniel to the southern edge of the besieged city and bade them farwell. Wishing them good luck and a safe journey home, the men left to return to their posts. Kathleen and Daniel rode on alone

353

through the darkness and Kathleen, filled with the glow of love and happiness, felt no fear. Through the moss-covered trees they galloped and had traveled less than five miles when a shot pierced the night air and Daniel slumped forward and fell from his horse.

Thirty-one

Kathleen screamed in horror, jumped down from her horse, and ran to the fallen Daniel. Before she could reach him, a pair of strong hands jerked her back. She looked up into the meanest face she had ever seen. A gigantic Union soldier was holding her and he was grinning a sadistic smile as he looked down at Kathleen's body wriggling against him. He licked his lips. A new, unspeakable fear gripped Kathleen and in that instant she knew her fate was to be worse than Daniel's merciful, swift death. She would suffer first. A revulsion started deep in her stomach, mingling with the fright, and she fleetingly prayed to God to let her die.

The strong fingers were holding her arms tightly and pulling her closer. She writhed and jerked against the big, solid body and was pulled back with such force it momentarily knocked the breath from her. Kathleen felt strong blows falling on her back and looked up at her captor. He laughed and said, "Don't want you passing out, that wouldn't be no fun for me!" She gasped as her lungs filled up again and with the first breath she was begging.

"Please, please, let me go. Or kill me, just kill me. Get it over with."

The big, dirty hand that had slapped the breath back into her clutched a portion of Kathleen's hair. He jerked her up to him, "Oh, no girlie," he leered, his hot liquor breath inches from her face, "I ain't about to kill you. A pretty little thing like you was meant for pleasure," and he crushed his cruel mouth down over her trembling lips. Kathleen's attempt at a loud, chilling scream was no more than a stifled whimper as the salivating mouth of her tormentor covered her lips with a force so powerful her mouth was bruised and crushed against her teeth. She could taste her own blood as the soft flesh of her lips tore under his brutal assault. She fought against him, pounding on him with an arm she wrenched free for a moment. The other arm was still in his viselike grip, his fingers holding it so tightly she couldn't budge it.

Kathleen's furious struggling made him chuckle and her terror fanned the flame of the base passion stirring in his loins. "Look, boys," he laughed and shouted to the others, "we got us one of them lil ole southern belles that likes it wild." He looked back down at Kathleen, raised a dirty hand and wiped the blood from her mouth, saying, "Bet you're one of them gals that like a little scratchin' and bitin' to spice it up a bit." He moved a big hand over her back and let it slide slowly down her hip and leg. "That's fine, honey, 'cause you got the right man here. I love it fiery. Yes, sir, little darlin', we're going to have a good time," and he licked his lips again.

Kathleen shuddered, her body trembling violently with fear and disgust. Her frightened eyes were vaguely aware of three or four blue-coated soldiers moving towards them. A new horror registered in her muddled brain as the animal holding her said in a hoarse, guttural voice, "Look, boys, this little thing is trembling all over, guess she's as stirred up as I am. There's enough in this little package for all of us. She's probably been frustrated by the soft, lazy gentlemen they produce down here that never knew how to give her what she really needs." He looked back down into her face and grinned, "Don't worry, honey, we'll take care of you. I'll show you what it's like to be taken by a real man."

"Dear God, please, please," Kathleen looked helplessly at the other men now encircling them. "Help me, help me," she begged, but the others were grinning at her and each pair of eyes held the same dirty gleam of determination as those of the giant holding her.

"I'm first, boys," the hot whiskey breath said into her face, then turned to the others, "when I'm finished, you can have what's left." Loud, throaty laughter rose from the others and they crowded up closer. Agreeing that since he had found her, he should have the first go, a tall, slender man with a patch over one eye said very softly, "Save some for me," and reached out and stroked the shiny blond hair, smiling wickedly.

Kathleen felt her head spinning and her stomach churning with nausea. She prayed she would vomit, that she would wretch and repulse them. A lightheaded blackness of fear spread over her and a small hope of relief surfaced as she felt herself starting to faint. The next movement of her captor stole the last hope of unconsciousness as he roughly shoved her away, snapping her head back, bringing her to full awareness. He leered at her, his mouth watering, and Kathleen watched in suspended horror as his huge, hairy hand came up to the front of her dress. With one quick jerk, she heard the material tearing and closed her eyes as the entire front of her dress and underclothes were stripped away. She heard lewd whistles and felt cool air on her exposed body. Her eyes fluttered open in time to see the hand coming at her again. Her flesh crawled as the hand came in contact with her bare skin and he pushed her to the ground. She was lying on her back, trying to struggle to her feet, when the hand pushed her back with a force so powerful she couldn't move.

Kathleen raised tired, shaking arms across her breasts, trying to cover her nakedness, when the big man stepped over her, stood directly above her, his legs apart, a foot on each side of her body. His hands went to his belt buckle. A resigned whimper of terror escaped her lips as her hands went up to cover her face and brace herself for the horror that was inevitable.

The cold barrel of a Colt .44 came swiftly to the temple of the man standing over Kathleen and an even colder voice said, "Do you enjoy raping helpless women as much as robbing the graves of babies, you lowdown Yankee bastard?" The hammer of the gun clicked and the shocked eyes of the man with his hands still on his belt buckle widened, though he made not a sound. Through splayed fingers, Kathleen watched as a brown hand pulled the trigger of the gun and in unreal slow motion saw the big man's head explode and a fine pink mist of brains and blood float through the still night air.

She was jerked from the ground by a strong hand and in a half-crazed daze she looked up into the face of her savior. Relief flooded her and her shaky, weak body swayed against him as he quickly removed the long black cloak from his body and she felt it come around her trembling shoulders. The same hands pulled the cloak together, shutting out the cold and the fear. The face above looked strangely familiar and the body she leaned against was lean, hard, and reassuring.

"You're safe now," Dawson said and pushed her behind him as he turned to face the other Yankees. Kathleen clung to the tall back and could see nothing as she huddled close to him.

She heard several more shots and heard Dawson shouting, "Behind you, Sam," and more shots were fired. Kathleen peeked and saw the tall man with the patch falling in the death throes.

Kathleen realized then her vision was unobstructed and she saw Big Sam, a revolver in each hand, his huge eyes blazing as he whirled around, checking to make certain that all the Union soldiers were dead or dying. At last, his eyes turned on Kathleen, but left her in an instant. They went to the ground in front of her and, with a sickening agony, it dawned on Kathleen why she could now see all around her. Dawson was on the ground at her feet. She screamed and fell to her knees beside him as Sam reached them. She was leaning over Dawson, watching in horror as a tiny circle of blood on his white shirt grew bigger. Sam roughly pushed her away, bent over Dawson, and with one quick motion lifted his lifeless form and slung him over his shoulder like a sack of flour. Kathleen was still on her knees, frozen with fear. Sam bent again and jerked her to her feet. He then stooped and she felt a powerful arm come around her thighs as he lifted her against his body, her feet dangling helplessly. He was running, breathing heavily, supporting the weight of both their bodies. "Sam, Sam," Kathleen shouted, clutching his broad neck, Daniel, he's still . . ."

"He's dead, we can't take him, there's no time. Those shots will draw more Union soldiers," and the big black man continued to run with Dawson draped over his shoulder and Kathleen in his arm. Kathleen cast one fleeting glance at the still form of her murdered friend. The tall Union soldier with the patch lay close to Daniel and Kathleen saw him move and heard his groans as he lay dying on the ground. Dawson was losing blood rapidly, dark red saturating his white shirt and soaking the blue cotton shirt of the man carrying him. Kathleen clung to Sam, her arms around his neck, her eyes on the still, helpless body slung over Sam's shoulder.

"Sam, I can walk," Kathleen was afraid his strength would give way.

"No," he shouted and continued running, "There's no time, they'll be coming." He tore through the thick undergrowth and headed for the river.

The *Diana Mine* was moored at a hidden nook in the river, all its lights darkened. Kathleen could barely make out its smokestack sticking up through the trees in the darkness, but Sam was already shouting from fifty yards away, "Stoke the boilers, get her ready," and the skeleton crew on board swung into action.

Sam's big feet had hardly touched the deck when he released Kathleen. She lost her balance and fell on her hands and knees. Sam went directly to the captain's cabin while Kathleen scrambled to her feet and followed. Sam gently laid Dawson atop his big bed and turned and ran out of the cabin, brushing past Kathleen. "Sam, Sam," she shouted, running after him, "don't leave him," and grabbed his arm to stop him.

With one hand he moved her aside and hurried out, shouting behind him, "Watch him, I've got to get this boat going or we'll all be dead."

He was gone and Kathleen turned and ran back to the bed. She bent to Dawson and called his name, but the dark eyes were closed and the brown face was ashen. She gasped when she looked down at his chest and saw the circle of blood on his shirt getting larger with each passing second.

Her fingers flew to the shirt buttons as she opened it to pull it away from his body. She jerked at the shirt and it wouldn't come. She unbuckled the belt at his waist, then unbuttoned the trousers to free the long shirttail. She pulled the shirt out of the trousers and away from his body and her hand flew to her mouth when she looked at the bullet-torn chest. The blood was coming fast and, frantic, she looked around, snatched a pillow from the bed and stripped away its white case. She folded it into a thick square and pressed it to the oozing wound while tears streamed from her eyes and she begged the lifeless form to live. Within minutes, new panic rose in her while she watched helplessly as the thick folds of the pillowcase turned red under her fingers. "Oh, my God, Dawson, please, you cannot die!" She applied more pressure to the quickly reddening makeshift bandage. Having no idea what she should do, she threw herself cross him, pressing her body to his, willing her own trembling body to put life back into his. She held her chest tightly to his and murmured against his neck, "I won't let you die, Dawson, I won't. Take my life, take mine." The heart in the chest under her own was barely beating and she could feel blood from that chest wetting the black cape she still wore and her naked flesh underneath. She was still laying atop him when finally Sam returned and pulled her away.

"Get down to the crew's mess hall and get all the tablecloths you can find," Sam commanded her. "First, get a bottle of whiskey out of Dawson's desk and hand it to me. The bottom drawer." She flew to the desk and handed the whiskey to Sam and ran up the steps to carry out his orders. When she returned, she carried four white tablecloths. She went to the bed. Sam had cut the shirt from Dawson's body and it lay in a bloody heap on the floor. He was bathing the wound with whiskey and looked up at her. "Hand me one of those cloths and start tearing another into long strips." She did as she was told, but when she tried to tear the cloth, it would not rip. "Here, hold this against him and I'll tear the strips." She traded places with Sam, holding the thick white cloth to the wound and looking at the gray, still face. Sam quickly tore long white strips and was at her side again. "Now, I'm going to lift him up easy," Sam looked at her, "and I want you to try to support as much of his weight as possible while I tie these strips around the bandage, do you think you can manage?"

"But, Sam, I've got blood all over me, I'll get it on Dawson," she looked at him.

"It doesn't matter, we'll be changing this bandage again in a little while. Right now we've got to stop his bleeding or he's not going to live." Sam went to the top of the bed and carefully lifted Dawson's limp body into a sitting position. Kathleen sat behind him and let his weight drape against her, using all her strength to avoid toppling over. He was dead weight and she was terrified she wouldn't be able to support him. Sam saw her struggling and, while he swiftly wrapped the long strips of cloth around Dawson's body, he sat down on the bed in back of Dawson and pulled him against his own chest. With the bandages tight in place, Sam got up and gently laid Dawson back on the bed. "You better get out of here now, I'm going to undress him and get him under the cover," Sam looked at her.

"I'm not leaving, Sam, I'll help you." Kathleen was adamant.

Sam walked to the end of the bed and pulled the long black wellingtons from Dawson's feet. Together, Sam and Kathleen removed his trousers and pulled the covers up to his waist.

"I've got to get back to the wheelhouse. Watch him and if you need me, I'll come." He was hurrying from the cabin. "Miz Kathleen, there's some of Dawson's clean shirts in the closet, why don't you wash up and put one on," and he was gone.

Kathleen leaned back over Dawson to make sure he was still breathing. Satisfied that he was, she slowly untied the bloodied black cape from around her neck and let it fall from her shoulders. The torn dress was hanging loose and her bosom was red with Dawson's blood. She looked down at herself, touched the now-drying blood, and cried, "It's my fault, oh, Dawson, I've killed you." and sobs wracked her bloodied body.

Calm returning at last, Kathleen walked to the bureau beside the bed, picked up the pitcher of water on its top, and poured the cold water into the large china bowl beside it. She stripped the torn clothes off and picked up a clean washcloth and began dipping it into the water. She stood bathing the blood from her body, turning the water in the basin a bright pink. She picked up a bar of soap and lathered her skin, trying to wash away the horror of the entire nightmare. Rinsing away the soap, she dried herself and went to Dawson's closet. A half dozen clean white ruffled shirts hung there; she took one down and slipped her arms into it. So long it reached to her knees, she buttoned it up to her throat and rolled up the sleeves over her hands. Turning back to the bed, she pulled up a chair and sat down to watch Dawson. His face was still gray and a shudder of fear once again claimed her weary body. She pulled the cover up over him and tucked it under his chin. Her hand went to the black hair and gently she smoothed it from his forehead, then sat back to wait. There was nothing else she could do. How long would it be before she knew? Would he live long enough to get to a doctor? She sat helplessly by while the man willing to give up his life for her lay dying before her.

"How is he?" Sam was back in the room. She had no idea when he had returned.

"There's no change, Sam. What are we going to do? Is he going to live?"

Sam looked at Dawson's ashen face then at her, "I don't know if he will or not. That bullet has to come out, but I have no idea how close it is to his heart. There is only one good sign; he didn't bleed from the mouth, so maybe the lungs weren't punctured. If they aren't, he may have a chance. There's nothing else we can do for him. We have to get him to a doctor."

"When will that be, Sam? He needs one now."

"I know, but we can't risk it. All these shores are full of Yankee soldiers. It would be suicide to try to get him through the lines. Our only hope is to stay on the river and hope we aren't stopped by a Yankee gunboat before we get him to Natchez."

Sam bent over Dawson and put a hand to his throat. The pulse was weak, but had a steady beat. Sam then moved his hand to Dawson's face and felt the cold lips. He pulled back the covers and looked at the bandage. "The bleeding has just about stopped, I think, but I'm worried, his body is so cold."

Kathleen leaned over the bed and felt his forehead, "Oh, Sam, he's freezing. Can't you make him warmer? He must be kept warm."

"There's not much I can do about it." He walked to the closet, got another blanket, and spread it over the bed. "I have to go back up now, I'll look in on him when I get the chance," then Sam paused at the door and looked at Kathleen. "If you can think of anything to make him warmer, do it."

Kathleen turned back to the bed. She bent and pressed her fingers to the pale lips of the man on the bed. They were cold and lifeless and Kathleen winced and straightened. She continued to look down at him and her heart filled with affection and concern for the man she had once loved so much. She stepped closer and slowly pulled back the covers. Kicking her shoes from her feet, she crawled into bed beside him. He didn't move, had no idea she was there. Kathleen pulled the covers over both of them and moved closer to him. She curled her body to his lifeless form and gently put an arm around his waist. Her hand went up to the thick black hair, lingered for a second, and moved to his cold cheek. Then she carefully slipped the hand under his neck and around his shoulder, laying as close to him as she possibly could.

"You will not die," she whispered, "I will make you live, Dawson, I will breathe life back into you," and her warm mouth covered his icy lips. The lips under hers moved not at all, but she continued covering them with life-giving kisses, willing him to survive. She kissed the cold brown cheek and his neck and vowed to his still body that she would not let him leave her. Finally, the kisses stopped and she lay with her cheek to his. Her hand moved from his waist slowly up his body to the cameo he wore around his neck. She lightly fingered the cameo and the gold chain supporting it as her eyes closed.

Hunter's handsome face came before her and she cried. She wept for the cold body laying against hers, for the man who had been her first dear and special love, the man who'd fathered her only child. She cried for Hunter under siege in Vicksburg, the man who was her husband, whom she had fallen in love with after all the patient years he had spent at her side, the man whose arms she had lain in earlier this very night and vowed to love until death. And she cried for herself, whose life had been torn between Dawson and Hunter for so long she was not certain she could ever be whole again. She belonged to both of them, would never be free of either, and neither would ever be satisfied to share her. Tears streamed down her cheeks as once again she turned to Dawson and said with her eyes still closed, her fingers still caressing the cameo around his neck, "Forgive me, Dawson. Forgive me, Hunter. Forgive me, God."

Thirty-two

After Kathleen's departure, Hunter lay down on his cot, his hands behind his head. He closed his eyes and recalled the silky blond hair falling into his face, the luminous blue eyes looking into his with love and trust, and the baby softness of her skin touching his own. Tired and happy, Hunter fell asleep with a smile on his gaunt, bronzed face.

Two hours later, he awoke feeling rested and refreshed. He summoned his orderly into the tent. "Private Bell, I want you to go below the cliffs where the townspeople's caves are located. Make the necessary inquiries until you find a Mrs. Rachel Bost. You should have no problems, everyone in Vicksburg knows her. When you find her, ask her to accompany you back here to me."

"Yes, sir. Rachel Bost. I'll be back as soon as I find her."

"Thanks, Bell."

"Hunter, darling," Rachel Bost smiled and hugged him.

"Mrs. Bost, it's good to see you again. Are you making it all right? How is your health?"

"Honey, look at me, I'm as strong as an ox. But what about you, why, you're little more than a scarecrow." She shook her head and frowned. "Breaks my heart to see my boy so thin."

Hunter smiled, "You're not to worry, I've never felt better in my life. I've a favor I must ask you, that's why I've called you here this morning."

"Hunter, I'll do anything for you, you've only to ask."

"I'd hope you'd say that. Mrs. Bost, there's a drummer boy in our regiment, he's no more than ten years old, just a baby. I've reason to believe this day is going to be a violent one and I'd like you to take the boy with you. Keep him in the cave where he'll be safe."

"Is that all? Of course I'll take him. Where is the lad?"

"I'll get him," Hunter smiled and went out to speak to Private Bell. Shortly, ten-year-old Joey Jonas entered the tent and stood at rigid attention before Hunter. A beautiful child with dark eyes and hair, small for his age, he reminded Hunter of Scotty.

"Drummer Jonas, at ease," Hunter said to the boy.

"Yes, sir, Colonel Alexander."

"Joey, I want you to do something very important," Hunter put his hands on the child's shoulders.

"Yes, sir, Colonel."

"This kind lady here is Mrs. Rachel Bost. I'm asking you to accompany her home and stay with her, she needs your protection."

"Colonel, I can't do that!"

"Drummer Jonas, I'm ordering you to go with Mrs. Bost."

Suddenly, the young soldier standing before Hunter turned into the little boy he was. The frown on his olive face showed his displeasure and soon tears filled his disappointed dark eyes as he shouted, "I'm not going! I'm staying here where I belong."

Undaunted, Mrs. Bost took the little boy's arm and smiled, "You're going with me, Joey, so just dry those tears. Time's wasting. You've got your orders, let's go."

"No, no," the boy screamed and kicked.

"Goodbye, Hunter, I'll take good care of him. I'll keep him with me until this latest battle is over. There's lots of children down at the caves. Why, by noon he'll be having a good time."

"Thanks, Mrs. Bost. Have Private Bell get Joey's drum, I'm sure he'll want to take it with him."

She winked at Hunter and dragged the rebellious, unhappy young soldier from the tent.

Hunter sighed after they left and said aloud, "Son, I don't care how angry you are, if it saves your life, it's worth all your wrath."

For weeks, the Federals had been boring a mine in front of the Confederate fort on the north side of Jackson Road. Although every endeavor had been made by the Rebs to foil their attempts, under the cover of darkness, the Union soldiers had succeeded in making an excavation large enough to protect them from hand grenades thrown by the Confederates. Powerless to stop the enemy from completing their mine, the Confederates set to work on a new line, built in the rear of the fort.

On this morning of June 25, the work was completed. The Confederates moved from the mined fort and took up their positions in the new line. Hunter and his brigade, along with the 3rd Louisiana, were stationed there. Hunter, dressed in his tattered gray tunic, the new yellow sash tied proudly around his waist, his saber strapped to his side, took up his post. He stepped into place and a chill ran up his spine, as though someone were walking over his grave. For the first time since that day in Gordonsville, Virginia, so long ago, Colonel Hunter Alexander was afraid. Kathleen's visit had given him so much to live for, cold fingers of fear tickled his frail back.

Standing rigidly in line with his men, Hunter waited nervously for the battle he knew was going to take place. Just after noon, the Federals sprung the mine beneath the fort. A terrible explosion shook the ground under Hunter's feet and large chunks of earth flew high into the air. The melee had begun.

"Men of the 3rd Mississippi, fix bayonets, fall into line, prepare to meet the enemy and die!" shouted their now-calm colonel. Heavy columns of Union soldiers rushed the gap blown in the works, determined to gain possession of the ruins. "North ramparts at one hundred yards, commence firing!" Hunter shouted. "Fire," he commanded as the loudly cheering Federals stormed towards the ruptured fort. A hail of bullets greeted the advancing Union soldiers. "Independently fire at will," Hunter shouted his last order, took aim, and began firing himself. A desperate, bloody battle ensued and the Confederates, woefully outnumbered, fought manfully, repelling the onslaught of the rushing blue tide. Close columns of Federals stormed over the parapets to be met by the defending Confederates.

The bloody battle was a severe test for the half-starved Confederates, but their courage never wavered as they met the enemy with valor and determination. While musketry and rifle fire filled the air in the raging encounter, Federal batteries in front and rear continued their cannonading. Hunter and the men under him bravely fought alongside the tough 3rd Louisiana, one of the best fighting regiments in the entire Confederacy. Calm and detached, Hunter fired his rifle at close range, mowing down the shouting Federals near enough to him that he could have whispered to them and they would have heard every word he said.

Fighting valiantly against the terrific odds, help arrived for the beleaguered, outnumbered southerners. Suddenly the 6th Missouri reinforced the regiments. Gladly, the men from Missouri rushed into the deafening melee. Hunter smiled as he watched them pouring in to help. A fresh young soldier stood next to Hunter, their slender shoulders touching. They exchanged glances briefly and, in the next instant, the young Missourian, hit by a Federal grenade, dropped to the ground. Wounded above the left elbow, the lower part of the young blond man's arm lay limply at his side, almost severed. Hunter quickly dropped beside the fallen soldier, stripped off his new yellow sash and tied it tightly around the injured man's upper arm, making a tourniquet.

"Thanks," the still-conscious boy smiled.

"You're welcome," Hunter said and rose to fight again. Before he could get to his feet, the terrible sound of the whizzing minie ball greeted his ears. The unquestionable, close-at-hand sound of 'bzzzzip' was the last thing Colonel Hunter Alexander heard. He fell across the dying Missourian as the battle around them raged on.

Unmoved and unconquerable, the combined regiments of Mississippi, Louisiana, and Missouri turned back the defeated Federals. The Union suffered heavy losses in the desperate, hard-fought battle and, when the sun went down, large numbers of wounded and dying Union soldiers lay before the damaged works.

"Hunter," Rachel Bost leaned close, pushing a lock of bloody blond hair from his forehead. Hunter lay on a cot in one of the field hospital tents, barely alive. Shrapnel from the exploding minie ball had pierced his forehead, cheek, left arm, and legs. White gauze, saturated with his blood, covered his left cheek and a similar bandage was wound around his head. His tunic had been cut away, his skinny chest was bandaged, and his injured left arm lay lifeless by his side. His face was gray, his brown eyes glazed. But he was conscious. "Hunter, darling," Mrs. Bost tried again. He looked at her, but his eyes held only a dazed, questioning look. Rachel felt tears stinging her eyes and a black fear clutching her heart. "Darling, it's me," she whispered, trembling, "Rachel Bost, Hunter." She took his right hand and pressed it to her cheek. "Oh, Hunter, are you all right, son?"

His lips began to move and she leaned closer, "I . . . I'm sorry," he murmured, "I'm afraid you have the advantage, ma'am, I don't know you."

"Hunter, Hunter, Rachel Bost! Your dear mother's

friend. Your friend since you were a babe in arms.''

Hunter's eyes peered into the kindly face of the woman bending over him, frustration and a sense of bewilderment written plainly on his damaged delicate features. ''Hunter?'' he whispered softly, ''Hunter?''

''Oh, dear Lord,'' Rachel clasped her hand over her mouth while the tears streamed from her worried eyes. Tenderly, she placed Hunter's hand beside him and turned to a pan of clean water nearby. Wiping the tears from her eyes on the back of her hand, she dipped a cloth into the water. Turning back to Hunter, she pressed the cloth to his confused face and smiled into his eyes. Lovingly washing the blood stained-face and shell-torn body, she said, ''Now don't you worry, Hunter, darling. I'm going to take good care of you. Yes, I will, you'll be fine, son.'' Then she cast her eyes heavenward for a second and looked back down at him. The familiar brown eyes stared at her in confusion as she whispered, ''I'll take care of your body, we'll leave it up to our Heavenly Father to take care of your mind.''

''Yes, ma'am,'' Hunter answered meekly and passed out.

The siege continued and once again the Federals mined and blew up the damaged fort. On June 29, at four in the afternoon, the explosion could be heard throughout the lines. The Federals succeeded in breeching the ramparts, but they did not storm the works. The 3rd Louisiana, occupying the line throughout, suffered great losses, but willingly held their line, refusing to give up their position against every effort by the Federals to force them back. When the siege had begun, 450 men made up the regiment of the 3rd Louisiana. Only 250 were left when the day came to an end.

By July 2, 1863, rumors of Grant's intention to storm and take Vicksburg, at long last, began circulating among the soldiers and townspeople alike. Starving and badly beaten, the Confederates knew there was little hope of holding out much longer without outside help. To a man they remained determined to fight on to the end, the thought of surrender repugnant to the proud southerners.

The Vicksburg newspaper, *The Daily Citizen*, now being published on wallpaper, expressed their opinion thus:

> *The great Ulysses—the Yankee Generalissimo, surnamed Grant—has expressed his intention of dining in Vicksburg on Sunday next and celebrating the 4th of July by a grand dinner and so forth. When asked if he would invite General Joe Johnston to join him, he said, 'No! for fear there will be a row at the table!' Ulysses must get into the city before he dines in it. The way to cook a rabbit is 'first to catch the rabbit.'*

Mrs. Bost returned to Hunter's bedside every day, but he lay unconscious, never knowing she was there. She sat beside him, patting his hand and talking in soothing tones, and her heart broke as she looked at the lifeless form of the gentle young man who no longer knew her or himself.

On July 3, General John C. Pemberton, knowing all hope was gone, surrendered the city of Vicksburg to Union General Ulysses Grant.

"Kingdom came" on July 4, 1863. The siege was over. The Confederate general had surrendered. Hunter was spared the sight of the tragic fall of his beloved hometown. He was spared the tears streaming down the pale cheeks of the brave women of Vicksburg as they shook hands with the gaunt, defeated Confederate soldiers, their eyes downcast, shame and frustration written on their hollow-cheeked faces, tears shining in their eyes, forlorn, their uniforms tattered, their brave, proud hearts broken.

Hunter was spared the spectacle of all Confederate arms stacked in the center of the streets while a look to the north of the fallen city brought the sight of shining bayonets and sabers of the mighty Union army. Splendid in their clean blue uniforms, the Federals were led by General Grant himself over the Glass Bayou bridge while the river front presented a view of Union transports, gunboats, and broadsides, their flags flying grandly, saluting a victory dearly won.

Hunter was spared the sound of the might Union soldiers marching into the city, their field bands playing "The Star Spangled Banner". They streamed over the stacked guns of the Confederacy, over the breastworks, through the dazed, defeated Rebs, right down Jackson Road. He was spared the agonizing sight of the Stars and Stripes flying high from the cupola of the courthouse, where once the flag of the Confederacy had proudly flown. He was spared the shouts and cheers of the mighty hosts moving in to claim his hometown for their own. He was spared the shame of the white flags of surrender flying high over the works and he shed no bitter tears for a battle gallantly fought and lost through starvation. Hunter was spared this last crushing humiliation. He was unconscious on this hot, muggy 4th of July, mercifully unaware that the "cause" was lost and life in his beloved hometown would never again be the same.

July 4, 1863

The Daily Citizen

Two days bring about great changes. The banner of the Union floats over Vicksburg. General Grant has 'caught the rabbit'; he has dined in Vicksburg, and he did bring his dinner with him. The Citizen lives to see it. For the last time it appears on 'wallpaper.' No more will it eulogize the luxury of mule meat and fricasseed kitten—urge southern Warriors to such diet nevermore. This is the last edition, and is, excepting this note, from types as we found them. It will be valuable hereafter as a curiosity.

At the end of the long, hot, heartbreaking day, Mrs. Bost went to visit Hunter. A dark young man occupied the bed now and Rachel grabbed a young surgeon by the arm, demanding to know where the blond young man who had occupied the bed had been taken.

"Ma'am, I have no idea. I would presume, if he is no longer in his bed, he has passed away. Now, please excuse me, I'm very busy."

Rachel stumbled from the tent, shocked and heartbroken. Just outside the tent opening, a barrel containing discarded bandages and refuse blocked her path. Atop the heap, a blood-stained yellow sash lay amid the other trash, its discolored tail blowing gently in the summer breeze. The initials, *H. S. A.*, were neatly embroidered on it, the navy blue letters showing plainly through the caked blood. Rachel vividly remembered seeing it on Hunter's slim middle the morning he had called her to his tent. Her blunt-fingered hand slowly pulled the sash from its resting place, as she whispered, "My poor Hunter. Probably buried in one of the mass graves, no stone marking where he lies. Lord have mercy on his soul."

The blood-stained sash held tightly in her hand, Rachel Bost walked wearily home. She was met with more heartbreak when she arrived. Blue-coated soldiers were swarming all over the yard and in her house. She walked past them without a word and into the large drawing room. She dropped into her favorite rocker and slowly rocked back and forth, the sash across her lap, dry-eyed, while the despised Yankees roamed through every room of the big mansion where she had lived since her husband brought her there as a bride when she was a girl of seventeen.

"The Gilbraltar of the West" had fallen!

Thirty-three

Dodging Yankee gunboats and snipers on the shores, the *Diana Mine* steamed down the Mississippi River, Big Sam at the wheel, determined to get his gravely injured captain and Kathleen safely home to Natchez. The boat's hull damaged from a rain of Union bullets, the boat limped to the pier at Natchez in the early morning hours of June 26.

Kathleen pounded on the door of Rembert Pitt's home while Sam stood behind her, Dawson, still unconscious, in his big arms.

"Doctor Pitt, open up, please," Kathleen shouted in desperation. "Uncle Rembert, it's Kathleen. Wake up!"

A light appeared in an upstairs window just as Rembert's old servant, Walt, opened the door to peer at the nighttime intruders.

"Walt, get Doctor Pitt, hurry!" Kathleen shouted at the surprised servant.

Rembert was descending the stairs, tying his bathrobe, "See here, what's going on?" he demanded.

"Doctor Pitt, it's Kathleen, you must help us. Dawson Blakely's been shot, he's barely alive." The old doctor looked at Kathleen, bewildered, while she stood in Dawson's white shirt, pleading, "Hurry, Uncle Rembert, he's near death."

"Bring him in my office," Doctor Pitt walked away, with Sam following, carrying Dawson to a clean white table in the center of the room.

Completely awake now, Dr. Pitt rolled up the sleeves of his

blue bathrobe and began scrubbing his hands. Kathleen stood at the table beside Dawson, touching the cold cheek and whispering, "Dawson, Doctor Pitt will help you. Hold on a little longer, the doctor will save you, dear."

Dr. Pitt eyed Kathleen standing over the man who had once been her suitor. She stood there in a man's white shirt, tenderly touching the wounded man's cheek and calling him dear. Kathleen raised her eyes and met the Doctor's, offering no explanation. Refusing to leave Dawson's side, she remained and watched Doctor Pitt remove the bullet buried deep in Dawson's chest. Slowly, methodically the doctor worked, giving rapid fire commands to Kathleen which she hurriedly obeyed. Poking and probing, the skillful doctor at last raised the menacing bullet up for her to see, "He's lucky, if the bullet had been one half inch more to the left, it would have hit the heart."

"Oh, thank God," Kathleen breathed. "Will he make it, Uncle Rembert?"

"I don't know yet, he's lost too much blood. Luckily, he is a big, strong man in excellent health; that will help a lot." He began bandaging Dawson's chest.

"When will he wake up? Will it be a long time?"

"That's impossible to say, Kathleen. He will need to be watched closely for the next couple of days. If he lives that long, he should be out of danger."

"Can he stay here until he regains consciousness? Wouldn't it be dangerous to move him?"

The doctor hesitated for a minute, looked down at the wounded man on the table, then said, "I suppose he'd better stay, but I'm much too busy to watch him all the time."

"I'll watch him, Uncle Rembert, I want to." Rembert was staring at her and she could read his disapproving expression. "Please let me explain," Kathleen looked into Rembert's eyes. "The first thing I want to tell you is that I made it to Vicksburg, I saw Hunter, and he's fine. I love your nephew very much, Doctor Pitt, I hope you believe me.

If you don't, there's nothing I can do about it and it doesn't matter too much because Hunter knows I love him.'' The old doctor raised his eyebrows, but said nothing. ''Hunter and I have worked out all our differences and when he comes home we will spend the rest of our lives together, I assure you. As for Dawson, he saved my life, Uncle Rembert. When Daniel and I left Vicksburg, we had hardly gotten away from the city before we were attacked by some Yankee soldiers. Poor, loyal Daniel was shot and killed, his body still lies where he fell. The Yankee soldiers had me and they were going to rape me and then perhaps kill me, too. Dawson and Sam appeared, don't ask me why or how, but they were there and they saved me. Dawson was shot by a Yankee while saving my life. I shall be grateful to him forever, just as I'm sure Hunter will be.''

''Kathleen, you know why this man saved you, he is . . .''

''Stop! Don't say a word about Dawson Blakely. You have no right. Dawson saved my life and that's all that matters. For his trouble, he may lose his own life and if there is anything I can do to see that he doesn't, I will do it. Do you understand?''

''Yes, I suppose so, Kathleen, but I can tell you right now, people are going to talk. They'll know he's here, they'll know what happened. . . .''

''I couldn't care less what they say. If you do, I'm sorry, and I promise I'll have Dawson moved just as soon as it's safe. But this man is not going to die because of what the gossiping gentry of Natchez have to say about him or me.''

''Very well, I won't argue with you. I'm going to have some coffee, would you care for a cup.'' The doctor headed for the door.

''No coffee, thanks, but please ask Sam to come in.''

Doctor Pitt frowned, but summoned the worried black man. Sam eagerly hurried into the room as the doctor went out, closing the door behind him. ''Sam,'' Kathleen smiled at Dawson's tall friend, "Doctor Pitt has removed the bullet and he said there's a good chance Dawson will live. His heart was not hit, but he lost a lot of blood, as you are well aware. But there is hope."

Sam stood and looked down at Dawson, big tears filling his eyes, "Thank de Lord, thank de Lord."

Touched greatly by the concern written on his face, Kathleen moved around the table and put a hand on his shoulder. "Sam, dear Sam, he isn't going to die. You and I love him too much to let that happen. Stop worrying and go home and get some rest. You saved us Sam, both Dawson and me, and I will never forget it. We'll keep Dawson here until he regains consciousness, then together we'll move him home. You may feel free to come here anytime you like to check on him and I will remain by his side."

"Yes, ma'am, Miz Kathleen," Sam said, blinking back his tears.

"Goodnight, Sam. Come over tomorrow, maybe by then Dawson will be awake."

After Sam left, Doctor Pitt stuck his head back in the room and said, "Kathleen, there's nothing more I can do. I'm going to bed. Do you want to go upstairs and lie down for a while? If you do, I'll stay with him."

"I wouldn't hear of it. Go back to sleep, Uncle Rembert, and . . . thanks."

"Goodnight, Kathleen. Wake me if there's any change."

Kathleen took up her vigil beside Dawson. She pulled up a chair, took a seat, and reached out for his hand. Holding his large hand in both of hers, she looked at his face and whispered, "Dawson, I told you I wouldn't let you die," and she smiled.

When the sun rose, Kathleen still sat at Dawson's side, her eyes never leaving his face. Slowly, Dawson Blakely moved his head a little and the dark eyes opened slightly. The first thing he saw was Kathleen looking down at him.

"Kathleen?" he whispered.

"Yes, Dawson, yes. I'm here." She rose and leaned to him.

"Kathleen, darling," he grimaced, staring up at her.

"What is it, dear?"

"You, you're hurt. Your lip is split, it's been bleeding."

"Oh, Dawson," she laughed and kissed his forehead. "My lip's all right, everything's fine now."

The events of the previous night flooded back into Dawson's now-thinking brain and he grabbed Kathleen's arm, a worried expression on his face, "Oh my God, now I remember. Darling, did they hurt you, were you . . ."

"No Dawson. I'm not even scratched, you got there in time. It's you who are wounded and you must be quiet; don't excite yourself, please. They didn't touch me, Dawson, you stopped them."

"Thank God," he said, smiling.

When Sam came at 10 A.M., he was met by a happy, smiling Kathleen, "Sam, he's awake, he's going to get well."

"Miz Kathleen, let's get him home, there be where he be most comfortable."

"Yes, Sam. He's already begging me to take him there."

Kathleen went to Sans Souci that noon where she was met by a relieved Hannah and Scotty. She hugged her son and held him in her arms saying, "Darling, I saw your father and he is fine, just fine. He told me to give you a big kiss for him," and she kissed the laughing face over and over.

"Honey, what in de world is you doin' in that get up," Hannah stood beside the embracing pair.

"Hannah, you wouldn't believe what I've been through," but she was laughing, happy to have been with her husband, happy Dawson was going to live.

After several more hugs and kisses from Scotty, the little boy went out to play. She turned to Hannah and told her everything that had happened. She embraced her mammy while Hannah cried over Daniel's death, "I'm so sorry, Hannah. I know you two were very close. I loved Daniel, too, and we shall all miss him. He was brave and good and he died defending me."

"He was a good ole man," Hannah sniffled, "we sho gonna miss Daniel. I jest be mighty grateful Doctor Hunter and Mister Dawson be all right."

"Yes, Hannah, now come upstairs and help me get cleaned up."

Hannah helped Kathleen bathe and dress, then fixed her something hot to eat. After the meal, Kathleen rose from the table and said, "Hannah, I must go now. I'm going to Dawson's."

"Honey," Hannah looked at her surprised, "you mean you is goin' over to his house? Why, you know what folk'll say if they see you."

"Since it's broad daylight, I'm sure they will, but I don't care. Dawson Blakely saved my life. He is badly hurt and I'm going to him."

Dawson's card room had been turned into his sick room, a bed brought in and placed by the windows. The green felt tables had been moved out and replaced with easy chairs and couches. Dawson smiled when Kathleen walked in and he patted the bed beside him.

"No, Dawson, I'll have a chair," Kathleen laughed.

"Well, at least pull it up here close to me."

"Aye, aye, captain," she drew a straight-backed chair to his bedside. "Dawson, you're amazing, you're already beginning to look better."

"That's because you're here," he smiled. "You know you shouldn't have come though, what will people say?" he teased.

"Good Lord, you, too? Since when did you start caring

380

what people say?''

''Love, I don't give a damn what they say about me, it's your reputation I'm concerned about.''

''That's terribly gallant of you, Mister Blakely, but save your concern. It no longer matters to me.''

''Kathleen Diana, you are quite a girl,'' he smiled and took her hand.

''Are you just now finding that out?'' she answered and together they laughed.

Kathleen came to visit Dawson every day, staying from early morning until sundown. She read to him from the many volumns of books lining the walls of his big library. She fed him from a tray sitting across his middle. She drew the curtains in the late afternoon so he could rest and doze. She combed and brushed his dark thick hair. She rubbed soothing lotions into his arms and legs. She worried over him like a mother hen, never tiring of her chore, and Dawson Blakely loved every minute of it.

Doctor Pitt came by each day to check on Dawson and he never failed to frown when, every time he came, Kathleen was at Dawson's bedside. Kathleen paid no attention to his looks of displeasure and questioned the doctor at length about Dawson's condition.

''He's doing remarkably well for a man so recently shot,'' Doctor Pitt assured her. ''Perhaps it's all this Florence Nightingale treatment he's receiving from you that is making him mend so rapidly.''

''I certainly hope so,'' Kathleen smiled. ''Goodbye, Uncle Rembert, see you tomorrow,'' and she closed the door behind him to return to Dawson.

On the morning of July 3, Dawson awoke with the sun and called to his servant, Jim, to come and give him a shave.

"Jim, get me out a fresh white shirt, will you?"

"Why? You is still sick, Mister Dawson. You ain't goin' nowhere. You best jest put on clean pajamas for another week or two."

"All right, but get me the nicest pair I own."

Jim brought Dawson a new pair of dark silk pajamas and helped him put them on. He gave Dawson a close shave and plumped up the pillows behind him.

"How do I look, Jim?" Dawson asked his old friend.

"You is lookin' good, Mister Dawson. Won't be long 'til you be as handsome as ever."

Dawson lay propped up in his bed, eagerly waiting for Kathleen to arrive. He was feeling better with each passing day and almost dreaded the time when he would be completely well. It would mean Kathleen would no longer be coming to visit. He must not worry about that now; any minute she would flounce into his room, the blond hair falling around her delicate face, the billowing skirts swaying prettily as she walked. Dawson smiled and waitied for the magic moment.

By mid-morning when she had not arrived, Dawson was irritated and disappointed. It wasn't like her to be late and he certainly didn't appreciate it. He wanted her here, not just for part of the day but all day long. Didn't she know he needed her badly? His poor, wounded body was aching and he longed for the feel of her tiny, soft hands rubbing him soothingly. The long, lonely day dragged on; Kathleen did not come.

Each morning before going to Dawson's, Kathleen went to the square where the casualty list was posted. Her heart pounded in her chest each time she looked at the long list of wounded and dead in battles for the Confederacy. She sat in her carriage and waited for the dreaded list to be posted, then sighed with relief when Hunter's name did not appear on it.

On the morning of July 3, she sat visiting with Becky Jackson, the two friends waiting together for the daily posting. Becky's husband, Ben, was now with General Lee's army at the Battle of Gettysburg. She, like Kathleen, held her breath each day as the killed-in-action were posted. The street was crowded with carriages and buggies as other familes waited for word of their loved ones. Morning after morning, Kathleen and Becky heard the screams that went up from heartbroken mothers, wives, and sweethearts as they found the name of their loved one on the list.

At nine o'clock, the long paper was posted and everyone crowded anxiously around. Kathleen and Becky squeezed each other's hands and went to look. Leading the list was Colonel Hunter Alexander, the very first name. "No, no," Kathleen murmured and swayed against Becky. Becky put an arm around Kathleen's waist, but without a word her worried eyes went on down the list. Ben Jackson's name was there, killed in action at the Battle of Gettysburg. Becky screamed and fell into Kathleen's arms. The two life-long friends had both lost their husbands on the same horrible day. Mindless of the milling crowd looking at them, the two women stood, holding to each other, sobbing; their worst fears had become reality.

Three days later, the two girlfriends stood at the cemetery together in the hot July sun while a memorial service took place for their fallen husbands. While their children held to their skirts and cried, the two pale, brokenhearted women heard the mournful sound of a lone trumpet playing "Taps" as they looked down at markers over empty graves. Denied even the comfort of having their husbands' remains returned to them, the two women and their children mourned their terrible losses and knew the bodies of their husbands would never rest in the graves laid out for them.

Dawson heard the news of Hunter Alexander's death and wanted more than anything to go to Kathleen and comfort her, but he knew he couldn't do it. When his servant told him the shocking new, he turned his eyes to the ceiling and murmured, "My poor tortured Kathleen. My poor unfortunate darling."

The long, sad summer was a terrible ordeal for Kathleen. Overcome with grief, she refused to go anywhere, not even to church. She didn't go to Dawson's, though she did inquire about his condition when Doctor Pitt came to Sans Souci. She spent long, lonely hours in Hunter's room, touching the books he had studied so diligently, lying on the bed where he had slept for five years, looking in the closet where all his clothes still hung. Everywhere were reminders of him, even in the drawing room where the grand piano sat untouched since last he played it. The ache in Kathleen's heart never left and the pain in her stomach was so severe, she was often nauseated and started losing weight.

Scott, too, was despondent over the loss of his father. Many nights after he had gone to bed, Kathleen would hear him crying alone in his room. She hurried to him each time and took him in her arms as together they cried for the dear, kind man who would never again hold either of them.

At dusk on a hot August night, someone knocked on the door of Sans Souci. Kathleen was upstairs in her room, Hannah in the kitchen. Seven-year-old Scott Alexander opened the front door and looked up to see a tall, dark man standing before him.

"Sir?" Scott looked at him.

"Scott," Dawson said softly, removing his hat, "I'm Dawson Blakely, a friend of your mother's."

"I'm sorry, Mister Blakely, my mother is not feeling well, she's upstairs lying down."

"I understand. I just came to pay my respects."

"Come in, please," Scott offered.

"Thank you, Scott." Dawson stepped inside.

Scott led Dawson into the drawing room and invited him to sit down. "Did you know my father, Mister Blakely?"

"I didn't know him well, Scott, but I had met him. I just wanted you and your mother to know that I'm terribly sorry about his death."

"Thank you. My father was a hero, you know."

"Yes he was, son, he was a very brave man and I know you are proud of him."

"Mister Blakely, how did you know my name is Scott?"

Dawson smiled at the dark boy, "I met you once a long time ago. You were much too small to remember." He rose, "I must be going, I hope I didn't impose on you."

"Not at all, Mister Blakely. Do come back to visit. Maybe next time you come, my mother will be well enough to come down."

"You take care of your mother, Scott," Dawson said and started to the front door. Hannah came waddling in from the kitchen when Dawson and Scott reached the hall.

"Oh, Mister Dawson," she came to them. "Scott, darlin', why don't you go on in the kitchen, I have your supper ready for you."

"All right, Hannah. Goodnight, Mister Blakely. It was nice of you to come," and he headed for the kitchen.

As soon as Scott was out of sight, Dawson grabbed Hannah's shoulders and whispered, "How is she? Is she going to recover?"

"Oh, Mister Dawson, I's so worried 'bout her. She won't hardly eat and she won't go anywhere, she won't hardly leave her room. That po' baby sufferin' sompin awful. Jest breaks my heart to see her like this."

"Hannah, I'd give anything if I could go up to her and . . ."

"No, you knows you can't do that."

"Hannah, if I could just see her for a minute, I . . ."

"Mister Dawson, I wishes you could, too, but you know it ain't right."

"I know, of course I can't, I shouldn't have come here, but I just had to know how she is. Hannah, let me give you some money to help out, at least let me do that much."

Hannah shook her head, "No, she won't take it, but you is mighty nice to offer. How is you feelin'? You over your awful wound yet?"

"Almost as good as new," Dawson smiled at her. "I will go now, Hannah, and I'll not be coming back, so, please, take good care of her for me."

" 'Til the day I dies, Mister Dawson."

Thirty-four

The November sky was gray and bleak, threatening to spill more rain on the already-soaked city of Natchez. The two-day drizzle had ceased at dawn, but the sun made no appearance, as though afraid of being chased away by the dark, ominous thunderheads still filling the sky. The dirt streets had turned into mud puddles in many places and the wooden sidewalks were almost deserted of people, save the milling Union soldiers with time on their hands and nowhere to spend it.

Dawson sat in the upstairs office of Crawford Ashworth. He balanced a cup of coffee on his knee and looked out the rain-spattered window. His mood was almost as gray as the day and he yawned, hardly hearing what his attorney was saying to him.

"I tell you, Dawson, if the war drags on much longer, I am going to be out of business. I lose more of my old clients every day. The population of Natchez is dwindling steadily as more of the men are killed and their wives and children flee to be with their families in New Orleans and other cities less devastated by the conflict."

Dawson set his coffee cup on Crawford's big oak desk and folded his hands in his lap. "I don't see how it can possibly last much longer. The south is like a punch drunk fighter, knocked unconscious but refusing to fall down. We were beaten when Vicksburg and Gettysburg fell simultaneously. We should have cashed in our remaining chips then. Thousands more lives are going to be needlessly lost in a war that is, for all intents and purposes, hopelessly lost."

"Well, I don't know, Dawson, we did beat the Yankees at Chickamauga," Crawford's eyes brightened.

"Crawford, at times I think you're as naive as the rest. That much-heralded victory was erased just last week. Hooker's Union troops easily took Lookout Mountain at Chattanooga, a supposedly impregnable position. Face it, it's over. We're outnumbered in every way; I'm telling you, the Confederacy is dead. I knew from the start we would get no help from France or England and now even you and the rest of the diehards finally agree. I'll tell you something else, every trip I make to Europe becomes more treacherous. It's growing increasingly difficult to make it through the ever-tightening blockade. It's just a matter of months or perhaps a year at the outside that we can get any supplies in."

"I know that's true, I've been meaning to talk to you about it. Why don't you give it up? It's too dangerous, you could be killed. Don't you have enough money?"

Dawson smiled his lazy smile, "Why, Crawford, you make me sound like nothing more than a greedy opportunist." He shook his dark head in mock despair. "Did it ever occur to you what I don't do it for the money alone? Believe it or not, wealth, though it certainly is not distasteful to me, has never been my only motive for risking my neck. I, too, love the Confederacy and like to feel I'm doing something to further the cause. I may not be a respected war hero, but I feel I've contributed something."

"Dawson, of course you have. Running the blockade is most important, but I'm worried about you, son. If the cause is lost, as you say, then why keep taking chances? That's all I meant; I worry about you, you could be killed."

"It's debatable whether or not that would be any great loss," Dawson answered flatly.

"Now, Dawson, why do you talk like that? You've everything in the world to live for. You're young, healthy, handsome, and very, very rich. What more could any man

388

want?"

Dawson raised his thick brows and the hooded eyes peered up at Crawford, "I can think of something."

"My boy, when are you going to get that notion out of your head? That reminds me, though, she's coming to see me today."

Dawson immediately straightened in his chair, "When?"

Ashworth looked at his gold pocket watch, "Actually she should be here any minute. She said around eleven o'clock and it's ten 'til."

Dawson's eyes sparkled and he said hopefully, "Do you think I could just stay and say hello? I haven't seen her since Hunter's death. I promise I'll go as soon as I've offered my condolences and had the chance to look at her."

"Dawson, could I stop you?"

"No," Dawson grinned and walked to the rain-speckled window, his hands clamped behind his back. "I better watch for her. Is she coming alone?"

"Unless she brings Hannah, I'm sure she'll be by herself."

"I don't like that; she shouldn't be running around by herself. It's not safe with all the Union soldiers around Natchez."

Crawford sighed loudly, "You are hopeless, Dawson."

When Kathleen rode into Natchez in the covered, one-horse buggy, she was shocked anew at all the blue-coated men lining the streets. The sight repelled her and made her feel uneasy, as though she were in some strange land. Their clean, crisp uniforms were too great a contrast to the poor Confederates stumbling along beside the roads, their uniforms worn threadbare, their bodies maimed and crippled, their eyes dead. They, too, filled the streets as more and more of them wandered back into town from battlefields around the country. Kathleen shuddered as she passed one

389

poor soul, his left leg stiff and useless, leaning on a cane, making slow progress as he trudged through the mud-filled streets toward town, probably to spend his last bit of money on food, or perhaps he had no money at all and hoped someone would take pity on him and buy him a warming meal.

Kathleen shook her head sadly. The sight of the once-proud, immaculate southern gentlemen reduced to wearing rags and begging for food was unbearable to her. She looked away from the man, trying to blot the vision of all the horror from her mind.

She was nearing the Parker Hotel and Crawford Ashworth's office. The streets were deeply rutted and potholes abounded from seemingly never-ending winter rains. The old horse pulling her little buggy was reluctant to venture farther and it took all her coaxing to make the worthless nag continue with his task. Not twenty feet from the hotel entrance, the front wheel of the buggy fell into a deep hole, tilting the buggy to one side. The stubborn horse stopped still and refused to move, though she applied the whip heavily to his backside and pleaded in vain for him to move.

A tall, slim Union officer stood on the board sidewalk near her buggy and, seeing her predicament, stepped into the street, took the bridle, and pulled until the balky horse heeded his sharp spoken commands and moved forward, lurching the tilted buggy, almost unseating Kathleen. Oblivious to the mud quickly covering his shiny black boots, the officer gently guided the horse to more stable ground, dropped the bridle, and strode, smiling, to the side of the buggy. Resplendent in his dress blue uniform with its shiny brass buttons, braid on the cuffs, and grand epaulettes bearing the rank of major on his broad shoulders, he stepped up to Kathleen's carriage and tipped his Hardee hat, smiling up at her. He was a tall, imposing figure, cocky and self-assured, handsome in a craggy, masculine way. His full mouth was turned up into a solicitous smile and his gray eyes crinkled at the corners.

Flustered and half-frightened, Kathleen looked down at him and said, "Thank you, Major."

"Madam, it's my profound pleasure to help a lady in distress, especially one as lovely as yourself," and he rested his hands on either side of the buckboard, blocking her. "If there's anything else I can do?"

"You've done quite enough. Now if you'll kindly step aside, this is my destination, Major," Kathleen said haughtily.

"In that case, I'll help you down," he smiled, not moving, a muddied boot now resting on the carriage near her small feet.

"No, thank you," she almost shouted, "just move, please, Major. I'm capable of getting out of my buggy."

"I'm sure you are, ma'am, but I wouldn't want you getting your dress muddy," and his slender hands moved to her waist as he easily lifted her from the seat and set her on her feet on the sidewalk. His hands remained on her waist and he stood close to her, smiling down, while his gray, flinty eyes ran over her small, well-proportioned body.

"You let me go this instant!" She raised the buggy whip. The sight of the broad, blue-coated chest looming so near her and the possessive hands still holding to her waist brought back all the horror of the fearful night outside Vicksburg when another blue-coated soldier had held her in his powerful hands and torn away her dress. Kathleen felt unreasonable panic rising in her chest and started to bring the buggy whip down on his broad shoulder, but he laughed and caught it in mid-air.

"I don't want to hurt you, madam. I'm here to help you. You're the loveliest lady I've seen in Natchez and I would like to become better acquainted. I certainly mean you no harm, so relax."

Kathleen tried to jerk the whip free, but his strength was far greater than hers. Then, suddenly, the major's hand dropped away from the whip and she could feel it being

391

jerked the other way with a force much more powerful than any she exerted. Magically, the major's hand left her waist and he took a step backward.

"Perhaps you are having trouble with both your eyes and your ears, Major," Dawson Blakely's resonant voice came from over her head. "The lady told you she wants no further help from you. And if you can see, surely you've noticed she is wearing the black dress of one recently widowed. What's your name, soldier?"

"Major Donald Brooks, U.S. Army of Occupation."

Kathleen gratefully let go of the whip, leaving it to Dawson's big hand, and swayed backward a little, bumping into Dawson's hard chest which felt safe and secure to her. Gently, Dawson put a hand to her elbow and moved her to his side as he stepped closer to the major. "I'm Dawson Blakely, Major Brooks. Try hard to understand what I'm saying to you." His dark eyes narrowed and his face was menacing. "Though I'm sure some of our gentle ladies of Natchez are impressed with your stature and are so desperately lonely they willingly accept your invitations to be escorted to dinner, from now on be more careful which ones you approach. This lady is not at all interested in consorting with the enemy and if you ever see her again, be advised you are not so much as to speak to her. Do you understand?"

The major's own gray, flinty eyes narrowed and he said, "Unless this lovely lady is a member of your family, I don't see that it is any of your concern. As for consorting with the enemy, you had best face the way things are, Mister Blakely. We're here and we're going to stay. I have no intention of letting some old-fashioned rules and customs you people are trying so desperately to cling to stand in the way of pursuing whomever I choose. Do I make myself clear?"

Dawson's black eyes filled with rage and his full mouth became a tightly drawn line as he reached out to the blue blouse of the slow-learning major. "I'm telling you for the last time, Major, I forbid you ever so much as to speak to her again.

392

How's that for old-fashioned customs?" and he whirled, took Kathleen's arm, and led her away, bending down to say, "Dear, are you all right?"

"Dawson, I'm fine. Please forget this happened. Promise me. I've enough to worry about without once again putting your life in jeopardy on my account," but she was shaky and gladly let him assist her up the stairs to Crawford Ashworth's office.

Dawson smiled, "I can take care of myself. Now, we'll get you upstairs and get you a glass of water. And when it's time for you to go home, I'm driving you."

"That isn't necessary, I can get home by myself. You've done enough."

"Nevertheless, I'll be waiting at the carriage when you've finished with your meeting." He opened the door to Crawford's office.

True to his word, when Kathleen came down an hour later, Dawson stood with his foot on the buckboard and his big black steed was tied to the back of the buggy. He smiled when he saw her and hurried to her side. Lifting her up, he swung her up onto the seat, paying no attention to her weak protestations. They rode back through the streets of Natchez while Union soldiers, lounging on the sidewalks, cast wary eyes at the lovely blond lady in black and the big, dark man beside her.

"You see," Dawson gestured, "they all look at you. I'm afraid sometimes you are not aware of just how fetching you are. These men are lonely, they drink too much, they're rude, they would love the chance to . . ."

"Dawson, when are you going to stop treating me like a child?" She sounded irritated.

"Sorry. Guess I'm too possessive, but the thought of those Yankees bothering you makes my blood boil. I do wish you wouldn't come into town alone, it isn't safe."

Kathleen sighed and looked at her hands folded in her lap. "Nothing's safe anymore, nothing. By the way, I haven't

393

seen you since that last day I came to your house. How are you feeling? Has the wound healed completely?'' She looked up at him.

Dawson frowned and coughed laboriously while a brown hand went dramatically up to his chest, ''Now that you mention it, I still don't feel well. I think what I need is some care, someone to visit me and stroke my frail, weakened body.''

For the first time in months, Kathleen smiled. ''Stop your foolishness this minute, Dawson Blakely!''

As the months passed, Kathleen began to go out more as she tried to shake the depression of Hunter's death and start to lead a half-normal life once again. She started going to church often and occasionally she went into town to shop, but she was careful to see that either Scott or Hannah went along when it was necessary for her to walk up and down the sidewalks of Natchez. More than once, she saw again the tall, dashing Major Brooks, either riding by on his big bay horse or strolling from the Parker Hotel or a tavern. If she caught sight of him, she immediately cast her glance elsewhere, but she could feel the steel gray look following her and when their eyes did happen to meet on one or two occasions, the Major touched his cap and smiled at her, openly disregarding the advice Dawson Blakely had given him.

The war dragged mercilessly on. In May of 1864, Grant's mighty Union army crossed the James river and the ferocious fighting that took place so depleted General Lee's Army of northern Virginia that he never fully recovered. In the west, General Sherman moved slowly toward Atlanta. The summer in Natchez was hot and humid as it usually was and Kathleen and Scott spent long afternoons in the shelter of the old summer house, the white paint now rotted and peeling away from lack of care. Becky, Johnny, and the red-headed Jenny Jackson often visited, as the two widows sought the comfort of each other's company and understanding in a time that was painfully difficult for both.

The stalemate in Virginia continued throughout the summer and into the fall and the siege of Petersburg turned into slow starvation for the southern defenders. Sherman captured Atlanta and the north went wild with joy, while the south reeled under yet another staggering blow to the "cause". By mid-November, the newly re-elected president, Abraham Lincoln, had victory almost in his grasp as Sherman left Atlanta and marched to Savannah and the sea, capturing the old city on December 21, 1864, while Union General George Thomas shattered the Confederate army at Nashville, Tennessee.

Kathleen sat in her usual pew at St. Mary's Cathedral on a cold December morning in 1864. The priest, grand in his snow white robe, wore a troubled expression when he rose and took his place behind the large pulpit. Apologetically, he told his congregation he was certain they had all read in the *Natchez Courier* that they had received orders from the government of the United States to pray for the health of the newly re-elected president, Abraham Lincoln.

A startled buzz went through the crowd of Sunday morning worshipers and outrage filled the hearts of the bolder ones. Kathleen seethed at such a ridiculous order. If the Yankees thought they could order her to pray for their president in her own church in Natchez, Mississippi, they were sadly mistaken! They were not telling her who she was going to pray for and she had no intention of doing so for Mister Lincoln. She came here to pray for her husband, not some northern president who cared nothing at all for the Confederacy or the suffering south.

Refusing to obey such an order, Kathleen rose grandly, grabbed Scott's hand, and stormed out of the church, her skirts rustling in defiance. She moved out the door with her head held high, her small chin showing determination.

Lena and Lana Hamilton, along with the rest of the crowd, watched Kathleen move down the long aisle, her blue eyes blazing. Without a word, the sisters looked at each other, rose, and followed her out of the church. Lena touched Kathleen's arm when they got outside, "Dear, I knew you would have the courage to leave after that outlandish order." Lena looked down at Scott, "Why, as I've told you, your grandfather was such a distinguished gentleman, so proud and all. I'll just never forget when Lafayette was here in 1825, he was entertained at your home."

Lana interrupted her sister, "That's right, Kathleen. Did we ever tell you there was a twenty-one gun salute?"

Kathleen gently took the arms of the two aging sisters, "Yes, dears, you did tell me. However, I'm afraid we may get a gun salute out of this little episode and it won't be twenty-one."

The sisters gasped and covered their mouths in alarm.

Dawson had just returned from Europe on that cold December Sunday. At sundown, Crawford Ashworth came to his mansion and when he walked into the library to join Dawson, he wore a look of concern.

"What is it, Crawford?" Dawson rose and poured his friend a drink.

"Thanks," Crawford took the glass and sank onto the long leather settee. "Dawson, I debated coming to tell you this." He took a long pull of whiskey and said, "Promise me you won't get overwrought."

"I will not, what is it?"

"This morning at church, the congregation was ordered to pray for the health of President Abraham Lincoln."

"Why, those dirty . . ."

"Some of the ladies were outraged, not that I blame them,

396

and they refused to heed the order and stormed out of the church. I'm afraid Kathleen was leading the pack." Crawford shook his head.

Dawson threw back his head and laughed, "That's my girl! I love it. Her old spunk's coming back, she must be getting better," and he continued laughing merrily.

"Dawson, you haven't heard all I've come to say. I happen to have it on good authority that a certain Major Donald Brooks heard about it and plans to use it as an excuse to occupy Sans Souci first thing in the morning."

The laughter died on Dawson's lips and he rose from his chair, "Over my dead body!"

"Dawson, I know you have some influence with the Union officials. Maybe you could talk to them, I would hate to think of them taking over the Beauregard mansion. You know how they are, last week they occupied the Dover plantation and chopped up the grand piano for firewood. Shall we tell Kathleen?"

"No, because it's not going to happen. Let yourself out, Crawford, I've a social call to make," and Dawson ran up the stairs to change his clothes. Ashworth started for the front door and Dawson stopped on the stairs and called to him, "Crawford, what other ladies were involved in marching out this morning?"

"Those poor pitiful Hamilton sisters followed as soon as Kathleen started out. Then there were a few others, but no one I know."

"Thanks, Crawford."

After inquiring at the desk of the Parker Hotel which suite Major Donald Brooks was occupying, Dawson mounted the stairs and knocked loudly at the door. After several minutes of obvious scurrying taking place inside, the door opened a crack and Major Brooks, sans his crisp blue blouse, stood looking at Dawson, running a hand through his disheveled

397

brown hair.

"Do hope I didn't disturb you, Major," Dawson smiled and pushed the door open and walked by the confused man.

"What is it, Blakely?" the major closed the door and went to pour himself a drink.

"I've heard some distressing news that almost spoiled my Sabbath. I've come here to let you tell me in person that it isn't true."

"I've no idea what you're going on about and if you don't mind, I'm quite busy."

Dawson smiled mischievously, "I'll bet you are," and looked at the half-open door to the bedroom behind the major's head. Without her knowledge, a large mirror hanging in the sitting room reflected the scantily-clad form of Annabelle Thompson standing inside the door, eavesdropping. Major Brooks twisted his head quickly to see what Dawson was looking at, coughed nervously, and went to the bedroom door, shutting it, "Make it brief, Blakely."

"I shall. I understand you have plans to occupy Sans Souci in the morning."

"You're a knowledgeable man, Mister Blakely. You're absolutely correct."

"You aren't going to do it, Major," Dawson grinned at him.

The Major smiled wickedly back, "Hate to disappoint you, but I will indeed take that particular place. I'm sure you must have a rather personal interest in it to have come here tonight, but then I seem to remember you so gallantly defending the lady who lives there against this bad old Yankee helping her out of her carriage one day."

"Whatever my reasons, Major, personal or otherwise, I'm telling you, you will not put one well-polished boot inside that home."

"You keep forgetting who is in charge here, Blakely. You better get your lady friend out of there if you don't want her around me because tomorrow morning at sunup I'm taking

398

the mansion. You may have bought off some northern politicians and greased the palms of some Union generals, but I'm in charge of the Federal billeting in occupied Natchez.''

"Major Brooks, you won't live to see the sunset tomorrow if you set foot on her property."

"Blakely, you're really a fool. I am not personally occupying your friend's home; it's the Union army. Do you think you can stop them?"

"Major, I'm not holding the Union army responsible. It's you I'll hold responsible and if the piano at Sans Souci so much as turns up out of tune, I'll kill you.'' Dawson turned to leave.

The major followed him across the room, "Look here, Blakely, is that a threat?''

"No, Major," Dawson turned, his dark eyes narrowed, "A promise. You will be a dead man if you move in on Mrs. Alexander's mansion. The same goes for the Hamilton sisters'.'' The lazy smile returned to Dawson's face then, "Tell Annabelle it looks like she may have gained a pound here and there, but she's still as lovely as ever. However, I don't think the peach-colored nightgown suits her. She looks much better in gray satin.''

The Major slammed the door shut, but he could hear Dawson Blakely's merry laughter ringing in the hallway.

Thirty-five

Sans Souci was never occupied by the Union troops. At dawn on Monday morning, Dawson Blakely and a group of his men, mounted on horseback, waited along the estate road leading up to the mansion. A Colt .44 revolver resting just under his armpit, Dawson sat atop his big black horse, silently waiting for Major Brooks and his troops to show up. It never happened and by 9 A.M. Dawson relaxed, smiled, and waved his men away. Satisfied Kathleen would have no further problems with the well-chastised major, Dawson and his men departed and Kathleen never knew how close Sans Souci had come to being taken over by the Yankees.

Dawson was correct in his assessment of Major Brooks. He was also right in his prediction of the south's chances of winning the war. The Confederacy reeled under countless defeats and by February of '65, Sherman turned north from Savannah toward the Carolinas. By mid-February, Columbia, South Carolina, surrendered and a day later, Charleston, where it had all began, fell to Sherman's troops. Five days later, Wilmington, North Carolina, was taken, the last open Confederate post. In Washington, Congress had passed the 13th amendment to the Constitution, permanently abolishing slavery.

On April 2, Lee's tired, beaten men departed Petersburg and the next day Richmond fell. A week after the fall, General Lee, weary and heartbroken, rode majestically to the Appomattox Court House, and surrendered to the victor, General Grant. It was over. The south had lost the war. The

400

Stars and Stripes once again flew over the entire land.

On a warm spring day near the end of April, Kathleen, a sunbonnet on her head, was on her knees in the fields in back of Sans Souci. Digging in the fertile soil where once cotton boles had covered the ground, she was planting a garden, dropping tiny seeds into the soft earth, hopeful that her efforts would yield food for the small family to help them survive through the lean times facing them. She looked up, covering her eyes with a soiled hand, when she heard Hannah calling to her from the house. Kathleen rose to her feet, dusted herself off, and started for the kitchen door.

"Dar's a tall man on a horse comin' up the drive, Miz Kathleen. He be wearing a gray uniform, but he be a stranger to me."

"Thank you, Hannah," Kathleen stepped inside and took off her bonnet. "I'll see to it." She washed her hands, smoothed her dress, and started for the front of the house. At the front double doors, she saw the horse cantering up the drive. She stood watching the approaching stranger, wondering who could be coming to Sans Souci. Probably just another Confederate, hungry and thristy, stopping to ask for food. The countryside was full of them since the war ended. All on their way back to their homes, tired and half-starved, looking for a hand, before continuing on their long journeys.

The stranger swung down from his horse and Kathleen could see he was a tall man with gray hair, though his face looked young. He tied his horse to the fence and came into the yard and he was smiling, his pink mouth turned up at the corners. Kathleen stepped onto the veranda and when the stranger saw her, he smiled broader and swept his campaign hat from his head in a grand manner. "Ma'am," he said and came to meet her. "I'm sure you must be Mrs. Alexander. I've heard so much about you, I feel I know you. Let me introduce myself. I'm Cort Mitchell, late Colonel Confederate

401

States Army, a good friend of Hunter's."

"Colonel Mitchell," Kathleen smiled and extended her hand.

Cort kissed her hand, "I'm delighted to meet you. Hope I haven't come at a bad time. Is Hunter home?"

Kathleen disengaged her hand and looked down, "Colonel Mitchell, you obviously haven't heard. My husband was killed in the war. Two years ago in the siege of Vicksburg."

The broad smile left the chiseled features of Cort Mitchell's face and he reached out to the big column of the porch for support. His gray, usually merry eyes quickly filled with tears and in a choked voice he said, "Oh, ma'am, I'm so terribly sorry. I didn't know, I don't know what to say, I . . ."

"Colonel, come inside, I'll get you a glass of water," and she reached out to pat his shoulder, thought better of it, and dropped her hand away. "There's no way you could have known, so don't feel badly," and she opened the door and led Cort inside.

Taking him into the drawing room, Kathleen invited the man to sit down and, seeing tears now streaming down his lean cheeks, felt a lump coming to her own throat, so she turned, saying, "I'll get the water," and fled the room. By the time she returned, Cort had composed himself, took the water from her, and said, "Thank you so much. I'll just drink, then I'll be on my way."

"You certainly will not, Colonel Mitchell. As a friend of Hunter's, you are my friend, also. I insist you stay and have dinner with us tonight."

"Ma'am, I don't want to impose on you, I'll go . . ."

"You are staying, Colonel. I won't hear of you leaving before we've had a chance to visit and get to know one another."

"You're a very kind lady," Cort smiled, "and you are every bit as beautiful as Hunter said you were."

Kathleen sighed, "Thank you, Colonel. Now, I'll bet you would love to clean up, wouldn't you?"

402

Cort looked embarrassed, "I do apologize for my appearance. I've always prided myself on being somewhat of a dandy and now I'm frightfully unkempt."

"Don't you worry, Colonel. We're going to take good care of you. I'll put some water on to boil while you rest. Then you can have a long, refreshing bath and change into some clean clothes."

"But, ma'am, I . . ."

"Colonel, you look to me to be very near the same size as Hunter. There's a closet full of his clothes upstairs. You are welcome to wear any of them and that will give us a chance to wash the uniform you are wearing."

"I can't do that. Why, you wouldn't want me wearing Hunter's clothes."

"Nonsense. They aren't doing anyone any good just hanging there. You may wear them."

"I'm home," Scott Alexander called from the hall and came into the drawing room. The colonel rose to his feet immediately and smiled at the young boy. "I know who this is," he beamed, "this has got to be the one and only son of Hunter Alexander."

Scott smiled at the stanger and came to shake his hand, "Yes, sir. I am Scott Alexander. And you?"

"Son, I'm Colonel Cort Mitchell. I was a friend of your father's in the war. We spent a lot of time together in Virginia."

"If you were my father's friend, then it's a pleasure to meet you, sir," said the well-mannered boy. "You must tell me all about the time you spent with Daddy."

Every member of the Alexander household busied themselves to make Cort Mitchell welcome and comfortable. Hannah brought one of the last hams from the smokehouse, declaring it was a special occasion and they were going to feed Colonel Mitchell properly even if it meant skimping on later meals. A big grin splitting her black face, Hannah happily worked in the kitchen, glad to have a southern gentleman at Sans Souci. She was determined to entertain him in a manner befitting a returning hero who had been a friend of Hunter's.

Scott helped Cort carry kettles of heated water up the stairs to Hunter's old room. A brass tub sat in the middle and when it was filled to the rim with the steaming water, Scott showed Cort a closet where Hunter's clothes were hanging. "Take your pick, Colonel Mitchell," Scott invited. "I'll go back down now and, if it's all right with you, I want to invite my great uncle over to join us for dinner. He was very close to my daddy, so I know he will want to meet you."

"That would be delightful, son. And thanks for everthing. It's been a long time since I've been treated so cordially. I appreciate it more than I can say."

"Colonel Mitchell, we're happy to have you here," Scott smiled and walked to the bedroom door. "Will you do me a big favor?"

"Name it, Scott."

"Spend the night with us?"

"Are you sure it would be all right with your mother?"

"She'd be pleased, Colonel. Besides, I'm the man in the house."

Cort grinned and winked at the young boy, "Indeed you are and I most gratefully accept your invitation to spend the night at Sans Souci."

"Good," Scott returned his grin, "If you need anything, call me."

Cort was still smiling after Scott had gone downstairs. The boy had quickly won his heart and Cort shook his head, thinking how much like Hunter he was, though as opposite in appearance as he had ever seen any father and son. But his manner was much like Hunter's, kind and thoughtful, a very engaging young man. Cort unbuttoned his gray tunic and took it off. He sat on the bed, slipped off his scuffed boots, stood, and removed his trousers. He stepped out of his threadbare underwear and lowered himself into the tub. Sighing with pure pleasure, Cort sunk and rested his head on the tub's rim. He closed his eyes and let the hot water soothe away all the weariness from his body. After giving himself several long minutes just to rest, he then soaped his dirty body and scrubbed until his skin glowed pink. Refreshed and clean, Cort stepped from the tub and toweled himself off.

Clean underwear and stockings lay on the bed for Cort to don. Almost reluctantly, Cort went to Hunter's closet and chose a pair of tan, neatly-pressed trousers and a clean white shirt. Finding them a near perfect fit, he took a pair of shoes from the bottom of Hunter's closet and tried them on. They were a little loose, but felt good after the tight, hot boots he had been wearing. Cort brushed his clean gray hair and went downstairs.

Cort, Scotty, and Uncle Rembert were sitting in the drawing room. Kathleen came in to join them, wearing a clean dress, her hair pulled back from her face. All three men rose when she entered and her eyes went to the colonel. Her hand went up to her breast at the sight of him standing before her wearing Hunter's clothes. Built so much like her husband, the tan trousers fit snugly over Cort's long, lean legs and the white shirt draped over his slender shoulders just the way it had over Hunter's. Cort read the look in her eyes and came to take her elbow, "Mrs. Alexander, ma'am, I know it's somewhat of a shock seeing me in your husband's clothes. Perhaps it would have been better if I hadn't taken the liberty."

Charmed by his good grace, Kathleen managed to smile at the tall, slim man. "No, Colonel, it was I who suggested you wear his clothes. And may I say you look very handsome in them." She turned to greet Uncle Rembert, then said, "I believe Hannah has dinner ready. Shall we all go into the dining room?" She smiled up at her guest and took his arm.

The place of honor at the head of the table was given to

Cort Mitchell and, after pulling out Kathleen's chair, he took his place as though he belonged there. Hannah proudly served the meal, smiling and coddling the tall Texan, hovering close to his elbow most of the time, ready to refill his plate before he could want for anything. Kathleen, Scott, and Uncle Rembert sat almost mesmerized by his easy chatter. He had a gift of gab and the subject he talked most about was one near and dear to the hearts of his table companions. He had known Hunter well and related to them story after story of the time they had spent together in Virginia at the beginning of the war.

"Ah, we were so full of hope then. We were sure the Confederacy would be triumphant. If anyone had told me then how it would have ended, I'd have thought him insane." Cort's gray eyes clouded slightly, "No, it didn't turn out the way we expected. I spent most of my time in and around Virginia with Lee's army. It was my dubious honor to escort the magnificent general to the Appomattox Court House on Palm Sunday, April 9, to surrender to General Grant. It was a sad journey, I assure you. Part of the Union band had remained and as we rode up to the Court House they played "Auld Lang Syne" and I don't mind telling you it was all I could do to keep from crying like a baby. But the proud general showed no emotion at all, he wore his best dress uniform, and he was an imposing figure even in defeat. The Yankees lining the street stared at him with awe and respect. It must have been the most tragic day of General Lee's life, but he bore it like a man and remained the strong, majestic general he'd always been. If I live to be a hundred, I shall never forget that sad day." Cort shook his gray head. "But enough of that," he smiled and rolled his eyes, telling Hannah that he had never eaten such light biscuits in all his thirty-four years. He ate heartily and once again turned the conversation back to Hunter.

"Scott, one of the first things I remember about your father was his saving the life of a young drummer boy. The boy was hardly older than you are now and he had been wounded in an ambush on the Rapidan River. He lay out in the open battlefield and your father, brave man that he was, covered the child's body with his own while bullets flew all around them. The way he protected that child, one would have sworn he was as precious to him as you. He carried the child to safety and operated on him right behind the lines. Saved his life, he did." Cort smiled at Scott. "I had met your father before that day, but that was the first time I really knew what he was made of. Hunter was wounded himself, but he refused any kind of aid until he had taken care of the drummer boy."

"Did the boy live, sir?"

"He sure did, thanks to Hunter. And I'll tell you, that kid fair worshiped Hunter after that." Cort looked to Kathleen. "That was only the beginning. Shortly after that, we were in the thick of the battle in Virginia. I've never seen a man any braver than your husband. He had nerves of steel; I don't remember ever seeing him afraid." Cort took a drink of coffee, then laughed, "You know, I've seen big, tough-looking men brag about how they couldn't wait to meet up with the Yankees so they could tear them limb from limb. Then when the time came, they were faced with the unpleasant fact that they were cowards, fleeing like crybabies in the face of danger. Not Hunter Alexander. Hunter was neither big nor tough, as you well know. He looked more like a poet than a soldier and he never blew his own horn or told anybody how he would teach the Yankees a lesson. Yet, when he marched into battle, he faced the enemy with calm reserve, never outwardly showing any sign of fear or distress. I've seen him in hand-to-hand combat, doing the job he had to do, while the expression in those brown eyes never changed, his nerve never wavered. He was as brave a man as I've ever known in my life."

Beaming with pride, Scott said, "Don't stop, Colonel Mitchell. Tell us more about my daddy."

"Yes, Colonel, we never tire of hearing about Hunter," Uncle Rembert agreed.

Kathleen said nothing, but her eyes never left the colonel. She, too, longed to hear more about her dear, dead husband.

Cort patted his full stomach, pushed his plate away, and said, "Hannah, if I could steal you away and take you to Texas with me, I would do it. That was the best meal I've ever eaten in my life," and he winked at her.

Hannah ducked her head, embarrassed, but very pleased. "Now, Colonel Mitchell, it weren't nothin'. Why, I wish you coulda been here when we really laid out a feast," and she took his plate and waddled into the kitchen.

Kathleen rose from her chair, "Since Uncle Rembert was kind enough to bring a bottle of brandy, why don't we all go in the drawing room and have a drink." She led the way and Cort followed, with Scott at his elbow, saying, "Colonel Mitchell, tell us more about Daddy."

"Sure I will, Scott," Cort smiled and ruffled the boy's hair, "but why don't you call me Uncle Cort?"

Scott smiled at the tall, friendly man and said, "Sure, Uncle Cort."

"And please call me Kathleen," their hostess said over her shoulder.

"If you'll do me the pleasure of using my first name," was the reply.

Seated in the drawing room, Cort lit up the cigar Uncle Rembert offered and took a drink of his brandy. "Hunter and I used to spend hours talking together about the happy day when the war would end and we could get back to living. I'm sure he must have written you about our talks of his coming to Texas."

Kathleen looked at him, unable to hide her shock, "You mean Hunter planned to go to Texas after the war?"

Cort read her dismay and quickly corrected himself. "Oh, ma'am, it was just talk, you know how that goes. I'm sure he never meant to do it, but we used to discuss the move; how

408

he would buy a little piece of land, get a few cattle. I shouldn't have mentioned it. I just figured he had written to you about the idea. Obviously, he didn't, so I'm certain he never really meant to do it."

"Hunter didn't mention it in his letters to . . . he never said anything about it," Kathleen said, flustered. "Cort, surely you knew Hunter was a doctor. I can't imagine him giving up his profession."

"Of course not, Kathleen. When we talked about his coming to Texas, he never considered giving up the practice of medicine. No, what Hunter wanted to do was live on a ranch, but be near enough to a town or community to set up an office. But, as I say, it was just talk, probably more on my part than his, if memory serves. I thought so much of Hunter, I was the one who tried to persuade him to join me in Texas. I told him that Texas is where there is a lot of opportunity and I thought a man like him could do well there. It was just an idea, a dream, nothing concrete."

"Cort, where do you live in Texas?"

"Well, ma'am, it's just a small settlement, one you've never heard of, I'm sure. My ranch is just outside a little place called Jacksborough, the county seat. It's in north central Texas." Cort laughed then, "I'm afraid you wouldn't think it a very pretty place, Kathleen. Not much out there but jack rabbits and mesquite trees, but I love it because it's my home. I've lived around there all my life and I'm anxious to get back, though there's nothing there to compare with the beauty of Natchez."

"Colonel, I'm sure Jacksborough is a charming place and I hope someday we can pay you a visit."

"Could we, Mother?" Scott asked hopefully. "I would love to go. Cort . . . pardon me, Uncle Cort . . . do they have Indians there?"

Cort laughed and drew on his cigar, "Well, Scott, we have had Indians in those parts, but I haven't been scalped yet and I've never known anyone who has. There's talk of building a fort there in the near future. If you decide to visit me, I think I can assure you you'll be safe."

"I don't understand why Daddy never told us about going to Texas," Scott looked puzzled.

Kathleen cleared her throat and said, "Scott, although I know you would love to stay and question Colonel Mitchell all night, it's past your bedtime."

"Oh, Mother," Scott protested, "we're just getting acquainted. I want to hear more about Texas. Tell her, Uncle Cort, I'm too old to be going to bed so early."

Cort smiled at the boy and said, "Tomorrow's a school day, isn't it, son? You'd best mind your mother and get your rest."

"You see," Kathleen smiled at Scotty. "Besides, Colonel Mitchell is tired, I'm sure. He'll be going to bed soon." Cort nodded yes.

"It is getting late, I must be going," Uncle Rembert rose and Cort got up to shake hands with him. "So glad to meet you, Colonel Mitchell. You'll never know what your visit has meant to all of us."

"It's been my pleasure, sir," Cort walked him to the door. "Hunter spoke of you all often and now I know why he did."

After Uncle Rembert had left and Scotty had reluctantly said goodnight and gone to bed, Kathleen and Cort were alone in the drawing room. "Let me pour you another glass of brandy, Colonel," Kathleen offered.

"I'll do the honors," Cort motioned for her to sit down. He poured a glass for them both and came to join her on the long couch. "Kathleen, you and your entire family have been so kind to me. I can't thank you enough."

Kathleen took the glass of brandy and smiled, "Colonel, your visit has been a tonic for us, it is we who should thank you."

Cort touched his glass to hers and said softly, "Here's to

410

better days for all of us.''

Kathleen smiled and took a sip, ''Yes, let's hope for better tomorrows. Cort, you haven't told us about your family. Do you have a wife? Children?''

Cort laughed and said, ''I had a wife before I left for the war, but I don't anymore. She got really angry when I joined the Confederacy and left her there alone. I don't think she ever got over it. She wrote to me for a while after I left and then, within three or four months, the letters quit coming. Finally, I heard from her after I'd been gone for over a year. She said she was tired of waiting for me and she was leaving Texas. Several months later, I got another letter and she said she was divorcing me.''

''Oh, Cort, I'm so sorry,'' Kathleen said kindly.

Still smiling, Cort said, ''Don't be. I wasn't surprised. She was awfully young and spoiled. She was a cute little thing and even when I was home there were always boys buzzing around her, attracted by her beauty and wit. I should have known that if I left her alone, it wouldn't be long before someone else took my place.''

''Cort, how can you take it so lightly?''

''I don't, Kathleen. It hurt me, there's no denying it. I loved that little girl and she made me happier than I ever knew I could be. All I'm saying is that I don't hold it against her. She was too young and pretty to be left alone and I knew it when I left. I hope she's happy, she deserves to be, and I've no doubt she's married again to some man who takes good care of her like he should. I was too much of a wanderer to have settled down in the first place.''

''I wish I could take things in my stride the way you do, Colonel Mitchell. You seem to face life head on and aren't overly shocked by anything that happens.''

''Kathleen, I've had my share of surprises, but then haven't we all? And what choice do we have but to face them. If we let every little problem throw us, we'd be in a devil of a shape, begging your pardon for my language.''

"You're right, Cort." Kathleen fell silent and felt the piercing gray eyes studying her. She coughed nervously and said, "Cort, there's something I want to ask you."

Sensing what she was about to say, Cort said, "Kathleen, Hunter Alexander loved you as much as I've ever seen a man love a woman. I know you had some problems, though Hunter never told me what they were. And I never asked, but I knew him well enough to know that he was suffering inside and it was over you. He felt you didn't love him the way he did you. I used to tell him no woman was worth being hurt too badly over because that's the way I felt about it. I told him if you didn't feel anything for him to just forget you, there'd be plenty of women in the world who would. Hunter would never listen. He told me he had a son he worshiped and the thought of leaving him forever was more than he could bear, but I suspect it was much more than the thought of leaving Scotty that bothered him. If I've said too much, please forgive me. I never saw Hunter again after early '63, so what happened between you two after that is unknown to me."

"Cort," Kathleen looked into his gray eyes, "Hunter and I did have trouble and it was all my fault. I made him suffer for years and for that I can never forgive myself. But it was a misunderstanding between us that took Hunter away and when Vicksburg was under siege, I heard Hunter was there. I went to him and we worked it out, everything was wonderful between us. I looked forward to the day when Hunter would come home and I could spend the rest of my life making up to him for the bad years I had put him through."

Cort patted Kathleen's hand, "Then, Mrs. Alexander, at least your husband died in peace. You and that boy were the only things in the world that mattered to him and I'm happy to hear you worked out your differences before he was killed. Hunter was as fine a man as I've ever known and, now that I've met you, it's easy to see why he could never have forgotten you."

"If that's true, Cort, why would Hunter talk to you about going to Texas? He never told us, so he must not have been planning to take us along."

"I told you, Kathleen, it was mainly my idea. And if he did consider it, it was only because he thought you didn't want him here. Forget about Texas, he never would have gone, and the important thing is you made everything right before he died. Don't be too hard on yourself, my dear. Remember only the good times and discard the bad. Your husband adored you and would have come back to spend the rest of his life with you and Scott."

"Cort?" Kathleen smiled at him.

"Yes?"

"You're a very nice man," and she rose, kissed his cheek, and said, "You must be terribly tired. The bed's all ready for you in Hunter's room."

Cort rose and said, "I'll walk you up the stairs."

Cort rose early the next morning and found his uniform had been washed, mended, and pressed. His boots, freshly polished, sat on the floor at the foot of his bed. Cort dressed and went down the stairs, intending to slip away before anyone was up.

"In here, Uncle Cort," Scotty called and came to meet him. "Your breakfast is all ready."

Cort laughed loudly, his baritone voice booming throughout the house, "I swear you nice Mississippi people are going to have me so spoiled, I won't be able to take care of myself." He followed Scotty into the dining room to have a big breakfast of ham and eggs. Kathleen, looking fresh and lovely, smiled when he entered the room and poured him a cup of coffee.

All during breakfast, Scotty sat close to Cort and asked him more questions about the time he had spent with his father. Cort gladly told him stories that came to his mind, some funny, some poignant, and Scotty and Kathleen clung to every word.

"I've got to go to school now, Uncle Cort. Why don't you stay another day? We haven't had enough time to talk," Scotty said and rose from the table, coming to stand by the colonel.

"Son, I wish I could, but I've been away for over four years. I've a long journey and I really have to go."

Scott hung his head and pouted, "Well, I don't see why you can't . . ."

Cort reached out to Scott's chin, raising the boy's face to his, "Scott, just as you're the man of this house and have duties you must see to, I, too, have duties and I must get to them." Cort moved his arm to encircle Scott's waist and pull him close, "Scott, tell you what, if you don't come to Texas to visit me, I promise I'll come back to Natchez someday to see you. You have my word. Now, I want very much for you to go to school with a smile on your handsome face." Pulling him into his arms, Cort kissed his cheek, then whispered in his ear, "I want you to take good care of your mother and make her life as easy as possible. That's what we men are supposed to do, take good care of our women. Right?"

Scott pulled away, nodded and smiled, then went to his mother's chair, "Bye, Mother, see you this afternoon. Bye, Uncle Cort, I'll see you again."

"You bet you will, Scott," Cort smiled and watched the boy leave. "You've quite a boy there, Kathleen, I know you're proud of him."

"Very," she smiled.

"Well," Cort said, rising, "I can't put it off any longer, I must be going." He extended his hand to Kathleen, she took it, and rose to walk him to the door. "Bye, Hannah," Cort hollered through the kitchen door.

Hannah's smiling face appeared at the door and she said, "Now you take good care of yo'self, Colonel Mitchell, and you come back to see us."

"I'll do both, Hannah," he smiled and led Kathleen to the front door.

They stepped onto the big porch together and stood for a minute, looking out over the huge lawn, now grown up in weeds. "I wish you could have seen Sans Souci in the old days, Colonel. It was lovely."

"It will be again, Kathleen. Everything will be grand again," Cort said and turned to face her. She looked up at the kind gray eyes and a wave of emotion overcame her. She threw her arms around him while tears filled her eyes.

The wise man gently drew her into his arms and patted her back gingerly, saying in a soft, soothing voice, "My dear, the world will right itself again, it always does. You're beautiful and young and there's a lot of life ahead for you. This, too, shall pass," and he released her and went down the walk.

He hurriedly mounted his horse, swept his campaign hat down over his gleaming silver hair, and saluted her. He turned and galloped down the long drive while Kathleen stood looking after him, watching another link with her husband disappear before her wistful eyes.

Thirty-six

"Mother, Mother," Scott Alexander shouted to Kathleen, "it's Hannah, hurry!"

Kathleen dropped her mending and went running out of the library. "Where are you?" she shouted, fear clutching her heart.

"In the kitchen, Mother. Please hurry," Scott answered.

Kathleen flew through the large dining room and into the kitchen. When she threw open the swinging doors, she saw Hannah lying on the floor, her eyes closed, not moving. Scott was on his knees over her, holding her hand and patting her face.

"What happened, Scott?" Kathleen dropped to the floor, "Oh, Hannah, Hannah!"

"Mother, she was fixing a lunch for me and she clutched her breast and fell to the floor. What is it, Mother?"

"Oh, dear Lord, I don't know, Scott. Go get Doctor Pitt. And hurry, please hurry!"

Scott did as she commanded. He was on his feet and out the door, running wildly down the drive and across Natchez to his great uncle's office.

"Dear, dear Hannah," Kathleen whispered, then flew to the back door, shouting, "Willard! Minnie! Get in here!" The only two slaves still left on the plantation were in the fields behind the house, too far away to hear her shouts. She ran through the yard, through the once beautiful gardens, now grown up with weeds, out through the stables and empty slave quarters. She saw the two old slaves far out in the withering cotton fields, bent over, working, trying in vain to grow vegetables in the once fertile soil. Kathleen ran toward them, waving her arms wildly and screaming their names. "Williard, Minnie, come quick!"

Finally, the two looked up and saw her, dropped their hoes and hurried to meet her, running as fast as their aging legs could carry them. "What is it, Miz Kathleen?" Williard asked, scratching his white head. Minnie followed along behind him, her old eyes big and wide.

"Oh, Williard, it's Hannah. She's very sick. You must help me get her to bed."

"Yes, ma'am, Miz Kathleen, I helps you," he bobbed his gray head up and down.

The three laboriously got Hannah to her bed as Scott and Doctor Pitt came running in the front door, the elderly physician puffing and shouting orders. "Get everyone out of the room." He placed his black bag on the table by the bed and bent over the unconscious black woman.

Kathleen paced nervously back and forth outside Hannah's door. Scott watched helplessly, "Mother, please sit down. You'll wear yourself out."

"Scotty, I can't. What would I ever do without Hannah? I can't get along without her, I can't!"

Scott walked to his frightened mother and put his arms around her waist, stopping her pacing. "Mother, I'll take care of you, don't worry."

"Oh, Scott," she put her arms around his slim shoulders, "I know you will, darling. Thank you."

"Mom, I'm almost a man. I'll look after you, I promise."

"Scott, you're so strong and brave. I'm sorry I'm such a coward."

"You aren't, Mother, but you're a woman and you need a man to take care of you now that Dad's gone. I'll be that man."

"Thank you, darling," she kissed his cheek and took the chair he motioned her to.

"I'll be right here if you need me," he said, authoritatively crossing his arms over his chest and leaning back against the wall beside his mother.

"You can go in now, Kathleen," Doctor Pitt said and she rose from the chair.

"Doctor Pitt, is she . . . will she . . . ?"

The doctor shook his head, "I'm sorry, Kathleen."

"Scott, please fix the doctor a cup of coffee or a drink. I'm going in to her."

"Certainly, Mother." Scott calmly invited the doctor downstairs.

"Hannah, dear," Kathleen whispered and leaned over the bed.

Hannah's tired eyes came open and, when she saw Kathleen's face, she tried to smile, "Honey, I'm sorry. I needs to get up and make Scott's lunch." She tried to raise herself, but Kathleen put a hand on her shoulder to stop her.

"No, dear, you must lie still. Scott will fix his own meal."

"Thank you, honey. Sit with me, please."

"Yes, yes," Kathleen took a chair by the bed. "Can I get you anything, Hannah?"

"No, I don't need nothin'. I'm going home to de Lord soon and 'fore I meets him, there's sompin I has to get off my chest."

"Hannah, don't say that! You'll be all right, you'll get well, I can't . . ."

"No, honey, I won't. But I is ready to go, I is powerful tired, this ole body done worn out."

"Hannah, please," Kathleen was crying softly now.

"Now, Kathleen, don't you cry for ole Hannah. It's you I is worried 'bout. There's sompin I has to tell you and I hopes you ain't gonna hate me," the worried black face looked into Kathleen's eyes.

"Darling, don't be foolish. I love you, I could never hate

418

you."

"I ain't so sure, honey," Hannah fell silent.

"You can tell me anything, Hannah, anything." She took her mammy's hand.

"It's 'bout Mistah Dawson and . . . and your father.."

"What, darling? Tell me," Kathleen spoke soothingly.

Tears streamed down the withered cheeks of the black woman on the bed as her words came out in a rush of emotion. "Oh, I ruined yo' life. Mistah Dawson, he loved you so much and he came over that day to ask Mistah Beauregard if he could marry you, jest lak he tol' you he would. And yo' father, he send that young man away. He tell him he never let him marry you." Hannah spoke nonstop, at long last repeating word for word the violent conversation she had overheard so many years before. Kathleen stared at Hannah in unbelieving horror as she listened to the shocking revelations about her father's cruel promises which had sent Dawson Blakely out of her life when all he'd ever wanted was to make her his wife. "I wanted to tell you, honey, but Mistah Beauregard, he woulda kilt me if he ever found out. I was scared and I jest didn't know what to do. I is sorry, honey, I is feeling so bad. Please don't hate me."

"Darling Hannah, you did the right thing. I'm sorry you've had to carry this terrible burden all these years. You've suffered needlessly because it doesn't matter. That was so long ago and so much has happened. It's all worked out, so just put it out of your mind and rest easy. I'm not upset with you." She smiled down into the worried face.

"Well, I wouldn'ta tol' you now ifin Doctor Hunter still be alive. No, suh, I woulda taked it to the grave with me if he be here to take care of you. He was such a good man. But he be gone now and Mistah Dawson still be alive and he still love you so much. He never tell you the truth 'cause he not ever want to hurt you. He be a good man, too, jest lak Doctor Hunter be. Maybe it's not too late. I could die in peace ifin I knowed Mistah Dawson gonna take care of you and the boy after I is gone.''

"Be quiet now, dear, you're tiring yourself. Please don't worry about us. Perhaps I will go to Dawson, I don't know, I just . . .''

"Oh, honey, please talk to him. That po' man wants you sompin awful, he take care of you and Scotty for the rest of yo' lives.''

"We'll see, but now I want you to sleep. Don't worry about any of this, promise me.''

"Thank you, honey. I rest now, I feel real good,'' and the big eyes closed peacefully.

"I love you, dear Hannah,'' Kathleen whispered and kissed the tired cheek, then tiptoed from the room.

Hannah passed away before the sunset and two days later was buried beside the summer house, near Louis and Abigail, at Sans Souci, the only home she had ever known. The place where she was born in the slave quarters in 1790 when the huge estate belonged to the Louis' grandfather. She had loved and served three generations of Beauregards.

Kathleen sat in the library alone while the afternoon sun slid low in the west, its last pink rays streaming in through the tall windows. Wearing the black dress she had worn to Hannah's funeral, she had come to the library to be by herself, telling Scott she wanted him to go to Johnny Jackson's for dinner.

"But, Mother, I want to stay with you. You need me,'' Scott had protested.

"Darling, I need you, of course, but for a while I would like to be alone. You go on and have dinner with Johnny, I'll be all right.''

"I'll go, but I'll be home at nine o'clock sharp. You get some rest while I'm gone,'' the dark head bent and kissed her cheek and the black eyes were full of love and concern.

Kathleen ruffled his hair and smiled, "I promise. Now run

420

along.''

Sitting alone now, she was sorry she had let him go. She felt so alone, so lost. The big old house was so empty, the place that once had been so alive. Now it was quiet, with only memories remaining of the happy times of earlier years.

Sans Souci, like plantations throughout Mississippi and the south, was now little more than a wasteland. Where once hundreds of slaves had worked the fertile fields, only Minnie and Williard were left, patiently grubbing a meager garden from the barren remains. The once beautiful gardens and lawns, bursting forth each spring in a kaleidoscope of color, fragrant with the sweet-smelling blossoms of jasmine and honeysuckle, roses and wisteria, now were grown up with waist-high weeds.

Even inside the mansion, the ravages of war had taken their tragic toll. The high-ceilinged rooms, often the scene of gala balls attended by the elite of Mississippi who gathered in laughter and gaiety to dance on the polished marble floors of the ballroom and drink toasts from an endless bubbly stream of the best wines and champagnes, now stood empty, haunted by eerie silence. Many rooms were shut away, unused, the fine furniture and crystal chandeliers sold to pay the exorbitant taxes.

Sans Souci and its few remaining inhabitants were not the only ones suffering. Becky Jackson, widowed by the war, now rented out rooms in the family estate and cooked for boarders in order to feed her two growing children. Julie Bates and her beloved Caleb, were together and still in love, though Caleb, with both arms lost in the war, was only a shell of the young boy he had been. His sad-eyed Julie watched helplessly while he brooded silently. She took in mending to make extra money to keep them going. Destitute families throughout Natchez, the aristrocacy of the old south, wore threadbare clothes and scrambled for food, all pauperized by inflation that tortured even the wealthiest. Stacks of worthless Confederate money was now good only to burn and keep themselves warm in winter.

Throughout Mississippi, it was difficult to find a family not mourning the loss of a loved one in the war. And of the men who did come home, over half were missing a limb. Such was the devastation of the most brutal war ever to be fought.

The glory was all gone. Their way of life would never be the same again. The loved ones were gone. Hunter. Her mother and father. Daniel. And now Hannah. All gone. Never to return. All but Dawson.

Kathleen thought about what Hannah had told her. She shook her head as tears escaped her sad eyes. Dear, dear Dawson. He had never told her what her father had said. He'd gone away because he loved her. How could her father have done such a cruel thing? Kathleen shook her head again. He never meant to hurt her. He loved her, he thought he was doing the right thing. I can't hate you, Father, you made a mistake, but we all do that. Look what I did to Hunter all those years. I've injured people, too. I'm still doing it. Dawson still loves me.

"Dawson," she said aloud, "oh, Dawson," and she rose from her chair. She took out a handkerchief and wiped her eyes. "No more tears. There have been too many for all of us."

Kathleen went up the stairs, took off her black dress, and threw it across the bed. She filled a tub with hot soapy water and stepped into it. Closing her eyes, she luxuriated in the healing warmth as she slid further down under the suds. She scrubbed her body until the skin was glowing. Smiling, she stepped from the tub and dried off. She rushed to the closet and took out her best dress. For the first time in her life, she had to button it herself and she smiled as she fumbled with the tiny buttons. Dressed at last, she skipped down the stairs and out of the house. Williard gladly brought the one-horse carriage around and said, "I drives you, Miz Kathleen, I be happy to."

Kathleen smiled sweetly, "Thank you, Williard, I can do it," and she stepped into the carriage and waved goodbye.

Thirty-seven

Dawson Blakely sat in the library of his big home high on the bluffs of Natchez, his long legs resting on a footstool in front of his chair. A glass of brandy sat on the table beside him, a long brown cigar was turning cold in the ashtray. A book lay across his lap, his dark head lay back in the chair, his eyes were closed. The sun was setting and Dawson could no longer see the small print on the pages of his book, but he was reluctant to put a light on in the room. He was drowsy and lazily sat in the big chair, considering whether or not he had enough energy to go out for dinner. Deciding he didn't, he smiled to himself, thinking, "I must be getting old," and promptly dozed off.

When Kathleen knocked on the big front door, she was met by a smiling Jim, Dawson's most trusted and oldest servant. "Why, Miz Kathleen," he bowed to her, "come in, come in. Mistah Dawson be mighty surprised to see you here, but mighty glad, I suspect."

"Thank you, Jim. He's home then?"

"Oh yes, ma'am, he be in the library. I get him for you."

"No, Jim, don't bother. I'll go to him."

"That fine, Miz Kathleen. Can I get you some coffee or sompin to drink?"

"Nothing, Jim, thanks," and she turned and walked toward the door. It was open and she walked inside. The last rays of the setting sun filled the room with an eerie glow. She saw Dawson stretched out in his big chair and he didn't move when she came in. She opened her mouth to call to him, but

424

decided against it. She walked softly to him and sat down on the footstool where his stockinged feet were crossed one over the other. She looked at the handsome dark face, its eyes closed in sleep. He looked so peaceful she almost hated to wake him. She smiled and slowly lifted a hand to his face, "Dawson," she whispered softly.

Thick black lashes opened lazily over the dark eyes. He looked at her and a smile came to the full mouth. His hand went up to cover hers and he said slowly, "Have I died and gone to heaven, or are you really here?"

She laughed and said, "It's me, Dawson." He started up and Kathleen stopped him, "No, stay where you are, please. You look so comfortable, I started not to waken you."

He lay back in his chair, raised her hand, and kissed it. "I would never have forgiven you if you hadn't. Can I get you something, dear? Is anything wrong?" he yawned sleepily. "Sorry. You know I can't think of a nicer way to be awakened. Now, just name the task and I will do it."

"How about this? You can be quiet and let me talk, Dawson."

"Sorry, darling, I'm just so glad to see you. I . . ."

"Shhh," she put her hand over his mouth, "I'm serious, Dawson, I've something to say and I want you to listen. Now, I'll move my hand if you promise to remain silent. Will you?" He nodded his head and she put her hand in her lap. "Good. Where shall I begin? Dawson, right before Hannah died, God rest her soul, she told me some things. Things I had never known before. She told me about the talk Father had with you when you came to Sans Souci to ask for permission to marry me."

Kathleen studied his face and saw the surprise and shock in his eyes. He moved his feet to the floor and leaned up in his chair, but he didn't speak. "You see, Hannah was supposed to go into Natchez that day with Mother and me, but she got sick. She stayed home and she was there when you came. She heard your loud voices and came downstairs. She

425

was outside the library, Dawson, and she heard everything that was said, but she never told me about it until now. I couldn't believe it when she did. You see, when you left I was convinced it was because you didn't love me, that you were tired of me.''

"Oh, Kathleen, I . . .''

"Please, Dawson, let me finish. You left without telling me and I was certain you didn't love me, that you never came to the house that day. Dawson, I'm sorry for what my father did to you . . . to us. I know now you loved me as much as I loved you and you were hurt terribly by his actions. I loved my father very much, you know that, and I can forgive him because he must have thought he was protecting me, though we both know it was cruel and a tragic mistake. I want you to know, Dawson, that I don't care at all that your middle name is Harpe or that you spent the first twenty years of your life under the bluffs. I didn't care then and I don't care now. I also want you to know that the Harpe and Blakely blood that run through Scott's veins is just as noble to me as the Howard and Beauregard blood. He's a wonderful boy, Dawson, he's very much like you and I couldn't be happier that he was fathered by a man as handsome, intelligent, and decent as you. Now, I've said most of what I wanted to say, and I have just one question. Why didn't you tell me? Why did you leave so abruptly? Why didn't you take me with you?'' She fell silent and looked at him.

His tense, dark face softened and he grinned, "Darling, that's more than one question.''

"Dawson Blakely, will you please be serious?'' she said, but she was smiling.

"I couldn't tell you, you know that. It's that simple. He had me, Kathleen. I was left with no way out. Your father was a very clever man. Darling, you're forgetting, this didn't happen last week, it happened over ten years ago. You were a sixteen-year-old girl who adored and trusted her father. Would you have believed me if I had told you he was a liar? If

I killed him in a duel, would you have still wanted to be my wife? No, Kathleen, admit it. There was nothing I could do. I wanted so desparately to tell you when you came to the *Diana Mine* and I made love to you. Have you any idea how much it hurt me to let you go away thinking I was an uncaring cad? It broke my heart, darling, just as it did yours." He shook his head, remembering.

"No, you're right," she said. "My poor Dawson," she touched his face again.

"Now you know," he said softly, "But, that isn't all, is it? You said a minute ago that was most of what you wanted to say. What's the rest?"

Kathleen smiled, "The rest is more pleasant, I hope. Do you still want me? Will you marry me?"

"My God, Kathleen, I've never stopped wanting you! I've ached to marry you since the first minute I saw you riding by in your father's carriage."

"Well, Dawson, I'm not going to lie to you. I fell in love with Hunter, I've told you that. But he's gone and we do have a son together. I'm not sure I can ever feel about you again the way I did when I was a young girl. Too much has happened, but if you want me, I'll marry you now."

"Sweetheart," he smiled back at her, "if you'll marry me, you don't even have to love me. Just let me love you." His smiled changed to an impish grin, "Besides, my dear girl, I may be turning gray at the temples, but there's still some life left in me. Eight to five says I can have you wildly in love with me again in just a few weeks."

"Dawson, you're conceited," she laughed, then touched his sideburns. "I love the gray in your hair. If anything, you're even more handsome now than the first night I saw you at Sans Souci."

"Thanks," he rose and helped her to her feet, "now, precious girl, if you'll just accompany me up the stairs, I will get started on my campaign to make you mad about me again."

"Oh, Dawson," she giggled, "you're awful."

"I know," he winked at her, "and you like it, don't you?"

Together they slowly climbed the stairs, their arms around each other, as the long May day came to a close and the sun was completely gone. "You know," he said, his lips against her hair, "for once we don't have to hurry, we can just go about it in a relaxed, lazy way, unlike the desperate encounters we experienced in the past. We can take all the time we want. I'm going to pleasantly drive you crazy, my love, before I . . ."

"You're forgetting, Dawson, we have a nine-year-old son and he'll be arriving home at nine o'clock."

"I did forget," he pulled her closer, "in that case, run up those stairs, girl!"

"Dawson!"

"I'm joking," he smiled and they slowly proceeded up to his bedroom.

"This is still the loveliest room I've ever seen in my life," Kathleen said as she stood at the tall, open windows looking down at the lights of Natchez Under and the boats on the Mississippi River. "It looks exactly as it did when we were here so long ago, you haven't changed a thing."

"I haven't been in this room myself since that night," Dawson came to stand behind her.

She turned to face him, "You haven't been in your own bedroom? Why not, where . . ."

"When I brought you here that night to show you the house, you made it seem like our room. After I lost you, I couldn't bear the thought of being in it without you. I told Jim to have it cleaned every day, but never to change anything about it. Maybe I kept hoping this day would finally come."

Kathleen smiled and reached up to finger the cameo around his neck, "Dawson, you're as sentimental as I am. A hopeless romantic."

"Did you ever doubt it? I plead guilty as charged," he laughed, kissed her cheek, and walked away from her. He sat down on the edge of the bed, his feet apart. "Come here," he said, grinning.

Kathleen walked to him. He put his hands to her waist and pulled her close, his knees tightened on her legs, holding her in a viselike grip. "Dawson Blakely," she chided, "you're hurting me. You don't have to pin me with your legs. I'm not going anywhere."

"Sorry," he grinned, moving his knees apart, "I'm so used to you running away from me, it's going to take me a while to get used to the idea that you won't leave."

"I know, darling, but I promise, you won't lose me again." She bent and kissed him, then ruffled his thick dark hair playfully.

"Since that's all settled, I'm afraid I must scold you, my dear."

"Whatever for?" her eyes widened.

"It's about that dress, love." He clicked his tongue against his teeth.

Kathleen looked down at herself and asked haughtily, "What is wrong with it? It's the best one I have, Dawson Blakely."

"It's lovely, darling, the color suits you, but . . . do you see where my eyes are looking?"

"Yes, they're . . . Dawson!"

"Exactly! The neck is too low, there's too much naked skin showing. Have you forgotten that I spoke to you about that?"

"My Lord, you haven't changed a bit, have you?" she laughed.

"Not where you're concerned, my pet."

"Well, just relax, Mister Blakely. You said I could wear this kind of dress with you. I don't see anyone else in here, do you?" She looked around her.

"Did you see anyone on the way over?" he teased.

"Dawson, I don't have as many dresses as I once did. I can't afford to throw things away anymore, I . . ."

"Yes, you can. You're forgetting, my love, that I've plenty of money and I'm just dying to spend it on you. You can throw away every dress you own, and if you want, you can have hundreds of new ones. I can't wait to buy you everything you want."

"That's fine, my generous love, but for now, may I leave this dress on?"

"No," Dawson, smiled impishly, "you can't."

"Why not?" She put her hands on her hips.

"Because, even though it shows too much of you for anyone else to see, it covers too much for me. Take if off, darling."

Kathleen smiled and whispered, "Dawson, you know how spoiled I am, I'm not used to undressing myself. Can you help me?"

He threw back his head and laughed, "My darling, you'll never have to unbutton another dress as long as I'm around," and his brown hands went to the top of her dress. She watched him, smiling, as he hurriedly pushed it off her shoulders and the laughter left his handsome face as love and desire flooded over him and the dark eyes smouldered.

Dawson lay propped up on a pillow, holding Kathleen back against him. He lazily smoked a cigar, blowing out in slow, deliberate breaths. Completely happy and content, he could remember no other time in his life that had been quite so wonderful. The tortured urgency of their other times together had been replaced by the safe, secure pleasure of knowing he could have her again and again, that she'd be his tomorrow, and the next day, and forever. They'd made love as they never had before, both relaxed and a little lazy, and it was glorious. Dawson Blakely was a happy, fulfilled man.

With the golden head of his love leaning back on him, resting just under his chin, his long arm draped casually around her, he had found paradise at last. Dawson kissed her hair and spoke, "Have you fallen in love with me yet?"

Kathleen grinned and turned to look up at him, "Not quite, but I'm on the way."

He laughed, "And you accuse me of being sentimental."

"I know, I'm worse than you."

"No, you're not. You know what I did?" He started laughing at himself.

"Oh, what, Dawson? Tell me," she sat up and drew her legs under her so she could see him better.

He laughed harder, the tears coming to his dark eyes. "I'm almost ashamed to tell you. You'll think I'm really a fool."

"I won't, honest, tell me."

"Well," he said, drawing on his cigar, "when I planned to marry you, I bought you a lovely three-carat diamond engagement ring and I . . ."

"Oh, Dawson, how sweet. And you've kept it for me all these years!"

"Hold on, that's not it. You haven't heard the best part. The night you came to the boat, I grabbed it and ran up on deck to watch you leave. Then I had Sam take the boat out on the water and I threw the ring into the Mississippi River!"

Kathleen's hand flew to her mouth, "Dawson, that's the saddest thing I've ever heard. Do you think we could find it?"

He pulled her back down to him, "Don't be silly. We were out on the river, Lord knows where. Besides, I'll buy you a handful of jewels if you want them. I just thought you'd think it was funny."

"It isn't at all! It's sweet and I don't want a handful of diamonds. I want one exactly like the one you threw in the river."

"You shall have it, my girl" he said and kissed her. "Tell you what, tomorrow I'll go buy it. Then at precisely 3 P.M., I'll come to Sans Souci with it. I'll be there when Scott gets

431

home from school and together we'll tell him we are getting married. How does that sound to you?''

"It's perfect. Thank you, Dawson." She lay snuggled against his chest, silent for a few minutes, then said, "Dawson, may I ask you a question?''

He laughed and said, "Could I stop you?''

"No," she laughed, "I know it really isn't any of my business, but . . . well, I can't help but wonder. When we were apart, were there . . . did you . . . have lots of other women?''

Dawson laughed and said, "You're right, it isn't any of your business. But I'll tell you anyhow." He turned serious and said, "Darling, I won't lie to you, of course there were other women, lots of them, you could hardly expect me to remain celibate for ten years. But, Kathleen, my heart remained yours alone. I never loved anyone else," and he kissed her tenderly.

She sighed, "Dear, much as I hate to, I have to go."

"No," he objected, his arms tightening around her. "I don't want you to leave."

"I don't want to go, but I told you, Scott will be home by nine and he'll expect me. He'll worry if I'm not there."

"Say, isn't it about time that boy got out on his own?" he kidded.

"Dawson!"

"I'm teasing," he said, releasing her.

She got up and said, "Don't just lay there, get up."

"Oh, Kathleen, don't make me," he begged.

"And I was never going to have to dress myself again. How quickly they forget," she laughed.

Dawson bounded off the bed, slipped into his trousers, and ran to pick up her dress from a chair. "What are you waiting for?''

Thirty-eight

Dawson stepped from the door of Burton's Jewelers. The afternoon sun greeting him was almost blinding. An early morning spring shower had passed quickly, leaving behind a brilliantly blue, cloudless sky and a sweet, clean smell in the May air. Dawson breathed deeply and squinted up at the bright sun overhead. Sighing contentedly, he strode to his fancy carriage waiting in front of the store. Patting his upper waistcoat pocket, feeling the reassuring bulge of the newly bought treasure resting close to his heart, he smiled, put his black hat jauntily on his head, and walked to his carriage.

Jim sat, whip and reins in hand, ready to whisk Dawson to Sans Souci and his three o'clock meeting with Kathleen. The festiveness of the occasion had caused Dawson to instruct Jim to bring out the never-used, ostentatious enclosed brougham with its gleaming leather interior. In front of the grand carriage, two high-spirited, perfectly matched black steeds pawed at the ground and snorted eagerly, ready to be off on their journey. Dawson had owned the carriage and horses for over a year, but had used it only once when he had taken a melancholy ride to Natchez Under the Bluffs one dark night last winter. It had been one of the many sleepless nights he'd spent, knowing Kathleen was now a widow, free to marry, alone at Sans Souci, but unwilling to be courted by him or any other man. It had almost been easier for him when her husband had been alive. Then, at least he knew it was impossible for him to have her and he accepted the dreary facts and went about seeking other pleasures, though all of a temporary nature, meaningless though pleasant, serving only to assuage the hollow loneliness he carried inside for an hour or two at a time.

Then she was widowed and he could no longer find even the briefest distraction in the arms of another woman. He longed for Kathleen and no other and the never-forgotten fact that she was a free woman, alone and uncared for, made the never-quenched flame inside him burst into raging fire. He told himself that at last she belonged to no other, was his and his alone. Though he'd never made advances toward her, he spent long hours daydreaming of the time when she at last would capitulate, would send for him, would agree the bond between them had never been completely severed, that she was no longer restrained by the marriage vows, that she had decided to marry him at last, after all the wasted, never to be regained, years.

She had not done it. Dawson had waited, hardly leaving his mansion except for dinner with Crawford or an occasional game of cards with old friends. So sure he was the day would come when she would send for him, would profess a deep affection, if not love, would bid him come to Sans Souci. His hopes rose so high, he had the fancy carriage ordered built in New Orleans, secretly relishing the fateful day when he would indeed go to Sans Souci, riding grandly in his new vehicle, a huge bouquet of roses in his hand, ready to help her inside and take her for a ride like a young, newly met beau coming to call for the first time on the blushing young maiden, who was ready to rush down the steps and into the covered carriage of her nervous new suitor.

She hadn't summoned him at all. He had hardly seen her and when he did, it was usually no more than a glance at her slim back climbing the steep stone steps of St. Mary's Cathedral for Sunday morning church services. Dawson often stole to a well-hidden viewing place so he could watch her while she remained unaware of his perusal. It was after one of those sightings that he'd felt particularly low and lonely for the rest

434

of the cold winter's day, for on that morning she had turned when she got almost to the top of the steps and he was presented with an unobstructed look at her beautiful face, smiling to a friend coming up to join her. She was wearing a heavy brown cape, completely hiding her slim, well-proportioned frame, but the delicately-featured, sweet face, with its shining azure eyes, was enough to make the heart pound in his chest. The pale blond hair was drawn tightly up on her head, but a few rebellious strands escaped and blew around her cheeks and neck in the cold wind. She turned abruptly, taking with her the light from Dawson's world, and he sighed and stole away, unnoticed.

He spent the rest of that dreary Sunday shut up in his huge library, savoring alone the vision of her lovely face, the picture image of it so indelibly stamped in his mind. It brought, by turns, a warming smile to his face to be followed almost immediately by a furrowed brow and a look of pain. By sundown, he could stand his anguish no longer and summoned Jim.

I want you to get the new carriage out of the carriage-house. Hitch up the black horses and come to the front to wait. I'll be down in half an hour.'' That done, he rushed up the stairs, taking them two at a time, shouting orders to the startled servants as he went. Five minutes later, he lowered himself into an oversized marble tub of steaming hot water and sang off key in a loud baritone voice that boomed throughout the house. Dressed impeccably in a pearl gray waistcoat with a doublebreasted brocade vest, tight trousers, and a snow white shirt, he grabbed a black cashmere cloak and hurried down the steps of his mansion. Jim stood beside the grand carriage, waiting for his master. ''To Sans Souci,'' Dawson said cheerily, and swung up inside the brougham.

''But, suh, I. . .''

''Sans Souci, Jim, and be quick about it,'' Dawson shouted and his obedient servant took his place and coaxed the horses away.

Elation filled Dawson's being as he sat back inside the covered carriage, a large fur wrapper over his knees. He was imagining Kathleen's reaction when he rushed up the steps of her home, seeing the surprise written plainly on her lovely face, further shocked when he swept her into his arms and stated his reason for being there. While he whirled her around, lifting her easily over his head, he would look up at her and tell her in no uncertain terms that he had come to claim her. Then happiness would flood over her face and, resting her small hands atop his shoulders, she would throw back her head and laugh in utter delight while she gleefully said, "My darling, why have you waited so long?"

With the happy scene vivid in his mind, Dawson wore a broad smile as the clip-clop of the horses' hooves took him nearer to Sans Souci and the realization of his storybook dreams. As they neared the big mansion, the smile on his dark, handsome face began to fade slightly, as fear of rejection suddenly reared its ugly, unwanted head. From out of nowhere, doubt had bounded and the closer the carriage got to the big house, the more frightened Dawson became. If she wanted him there, she would have invited him long ago. She had never done it. She would think him a madman if he burst into her home on this cold Sunday evening, tossing her over his head and vowing she was his. What could have possessed him that he could have imagined she would willingly accept his presence, much less offer herself to him with no qualms, like some prize he'd won and had come to claim. He was an idiot, a complete fool. She'd be horrified at such a ridiculous idea, would be repulsed by his brashness, by his total lack of regard for her feelings. Convinced he'd almost made a terrible blunder, he shouted to Jim, "Turn the coach around immediately, don't go another step!"

"But, suh, we's almost there now, we. . ."

"Please, Jim, before anyone in that house sees the carriage, drive off."

"Yes, suh," Jim quickly responded to Dawson's orders.

Where does you wants to go, Mistah Dawson, back home?"

"No, I don't. Take me down to the river. To Natchez Under."

The carriage now retreating, Dawson looked over his shoulder as Sans Souci grew smaller and the occupant inside farther from his reach. The grand new carriage carrying the nattily dressed, lovesick suitor made its way down to the river and the squalor and bawdiness contained on the muddy shores of the Mississippi. Instead of spending a quiet, gracious evening in the drawing room of Sans Souci, holding the tiny, soft hand of the lady soon to be his wife, Dawson Blakely, sans the elegant waistcoat, his white silk shirt unbuttoned, its sleeves rolled up over his brown arms, spent the night at a dirty green felt table, playing poker with an assortment of dandies and river rats, drinking whiskey straight, blotting from his brain the ridiculous plans that had made so much sense earlier in the evening.

That cold night was the one and only time the grand carriage had been out of its shelter. Now, as he rode to his destination, it was at last to be used for its original purpose. To court his lady love, to woo and win back her affection, even if it meant after they were man and wife. Dawson smiled and took out the pink velvet box from his breast pocket. He popped the top open and held the box outside the carriage so that the perfect, brilliant stone could catch and reflect all the light from the glaring afternoon sun. Exactly like the one he'd bought for Kathleen over a decade ago, the beautiful gem caught the sun's rays and cast colored prisms of light into the bright, happy eyes of her fiancé. It was a flawless stone and soon it would rest on the third finger of Kathleen's flawless left hand, to stay there forever, a constant reminder to her of his love for her, a constant reminder to him that at long last she was his.

He drew the ring back inside the carriage, replaced it in its velvet box, and slipped it inside his pocket. He relaxed against the leather seat and felt a great peace settling over his entire body, a feeling of relaxed easiness he'd never known before. The quiet desperation he'd carried with him for years had been replaced with a quiet contentment.

Dawson looked at his gold pocket watch. Only 2:30. He had told Kathleen he would be there at three o'clock. If he arrived early, she might not be ready. Not wishing to disturb her last minutes of preparation for his arrival, he explained to Jim it was a little premature to be heading for Sans Souci, but since it was such a breathtakingly beautiful day, he could just drive around, it made no difference where, he'd just enjoy the ride. The two matched steeds pranced proudly through the streets of Natchez and people turned to look at the grand carriage pulled by such quality beasts. Realizing no one recognized the vehicle as belonging to him, Dawson decided to let the identity of its owner remain a mystery.

Leaving the city behind, Jim headed out to a country lane. He, too, was enjoying the spring day and the ride atop the new brougham and he smiled to himself that no one recognized him since Dawson had insisted he wear the brand new gun metal gray coachman's livery with its fringed shoulder plates. He felt like royalty himself and handling the high-spirited, black horses was a pleasurable challenge to the old servant.

They had hardly left the buildings of Natchez behind when Dawson saw a young boy and a man, walking along beside the road, not more than a hundred yards ahead. They were walking in the direction of town, away from a lane that turned just behind them, leading to the small cemetery. Dawson squinted at the strange pair. The boy had a small arm around the man's waist and the man rested his arm along the top of the boy's slim shoulders. They walked very slowly, the man limping badly, favoring his left leg. Their progress was slow, as the child seemed to be laboriously supporting the man's weight. As the carriage drew nearer to the strange pair, Dawson could see the dark hair of the boy. The man bending over him had gray hair and, though slumped over, Dawson could see he was a tall man. His body was painfully thin.

Kathleen had taken great care in dressing for her three o'clock meeting with Dawson. She chose the best gown she could find in her closet. It wasn't as lovely as she would have preferred, but, though years old and rather plain, it was a pretty shade of blue and it had a very high neck. She giggled to herself as she struggled to button every tiny button right up to her chin, happy to follow the instructions of her jealous, but easy-going husband-to-be. She brushed her long blond hair until it shone with highlights and luster, then parted it down the middle to let it tumble loosely around her shoulders, because Dawson liked it that way.

Kathleen remembered with a shudder the other time Dawson was to come to Sans Souci for their engagement. She'd been so young and desperately in love with the handsome, dashing Dawson Blakely. And he'd been just as much in love with the sixteen-year-old, naive Kathleen Diana Beauregard. Kathleen sighed and sat down on her bed. There was no denying it, the young eager girl so infatuated was gone forever. There was no recapturing what she'd felt for Dawson then. She had adored, longed for, idolized, looked up to, almost worshiped him. Her heart would never beat quite that fast by his simply coming through the big double doors downstairs. She would never again wish the world contained only the two of them so that they could spend all their glorious days making love with a passion too great to have ever been experienced by other mere mortals. Then, with a rush of remembering, last night's hours of lovemaking came to Kathleen's mind. She realized she was blushing and she laughed and said aloud, "So we're not that young anymore, but last night with Dawson was better by far than our other times together and it's only the beginning."

As the grandfather clock in the hall struck three, Kathleen

skipped down the stairs, ready for Dawson to arrive, ready to start a new life, one full of hope and happiness. By fifteen after the hour, she was pacing in the drawing room, becoming increasingly irritated at Dawson's lateness. By three thirty, she was angry.

"Why is he late? He distinctly said he would be here at three sharp. I could choke him!" By three forty-five, Kathleen was furious and more than a little nervous. "My Lord, is this to be like the other time so long ago? Is he on his boat leaving Natchez as I wait here for him? Has he decided he doesn't want me after all? Have I been duped, made a fool of by him again? Dawson, where are you?"

By four o'clock, she was beside herself. "He's not coming! I know he's not. If he were, he would have been here long ago. What is happening? Is my whole life to be one long series of broken promises and misunderstandings? Haven't I suffered my share? Must I pay my life long for mistakes and sins I committed when I was still a young girl? Do I deserve it? Have I been that bad? Dawson, why haven't you come?"

At fifteen past four, Kathleen had given up hope. Resigned and dry-eyed, her nervous pacing had ceased. She sat with her hands folded in her lap as weariness claimed her body and once again she forlornly looked ahead to a cold, uncertain future alone. For whatever reason, Dawson had no intention of coming to Sans Souci today to bring her a diamond engagement ring. She didn't search for his reason, what difference did it make? Tiredly, Kathleen raised a hand and massaged the base of her long neck. She had a frightful headache. It raged with a vengeance and she felt her whole head might explode at any minute. She was hot, the room was stuffy and warm. Slowly, she unbuttoned the buttons under her chin. I guess I can undo as many as I like," she thought, "Dawson will not be here to witness my wanton display of bosom and berate me." She kept unfastening the tight bodice until it was comfortably open half way down.

Still feeling too warm, she rose wearily and headed for the

double doors. As she crossed the hall, another disturbing thought struck her. "Where is Scotty? It's after four-thirty, he should have been home before now. Has the whole world turned upside down again? Has Scotty decided to desert me too, leave me all alone to die a lonely old woman? I've told him repeatedly never to dawdle after school. I shall blister his bottom when he gets home. If he ever gets here."

Dawson recognized the boy. It was Scotty. He started to call to him, but looked at the man before he spoke. Dawson studied the features, the face was strange yet vaguely familiar. Though gray-headed, the man did not look elderly. The left side of his face carried deep scars, from forehead to chin, grotesquely vivid under the afternoon sun. The scars carried none of the redness of a recent injury, they were completely healed, as though they had been there for a long time. The two had stopped in the road, seemingly to rest before going on in what was conspiciously a chore for them both. Dawson continued to study the face of the man holding onto Scotty. The right side of his face was unscarred, though in need of a shave. The man straightened at that minute, bringing himself to his full height, with the assistance of Scotty. The man's head raised and looked up at the grand carriage approaching. The unmistakable eyes of Hunter Alexander!

The breath caught in Dawson's chest. Kathleen's husband stood in the road not fifty yards away. He was alive, though scarred and crippled. He was alive in Natchez, Mississippi, walking along a country lane with his arm around his son. He had come home. Kathleen Alexander was still a married woman.

The crushing blow of Hunter's existence brought with an alarming rush all that his reappearance meant to the lives of Kathleen, Hunter, Scotty, and himself. Painfully aware of where it left him, Dawson quickly told Jim to go past the man and boy without slowing down.

"But, Mistah Dawson, looks lak they could use some help, why the man's all crippled and. . ."

"Apply the whip and go past without looking down," Dawson commanded and sank back deep inside the carriage, saying under his breath, "Damn my luckless soul to hell!"

The black man laid the whip to the horses' backsides and the brougham quickly passed the helpless man and little boy standing in the dusty road. Only when they were safely past did Dawson slowly turn around in his seat. Scott and Hunter were making their slow, steady progress down the road. The tall, thin man and his loving son were heading home. To Sans Souci.

Scott had walked home from school with four of his classmates. The day was warm and lazy, the sun overhead bright and brilliant in a blue, cloudless sky. The children were in high spirits because another school year was nearly at an end. They walked the road from the school house, shouting and yelling like wild animals turned out of their cages. Turning somersaults and running, hitting each other, the young boys were full of unspent energy and looking for adventure as always. They made their way to the nearby railroad trestle, hopeful of seeing the 2:30 train to Memphis, a treat they would be afforded due to classes being dismissed early on this pleasant spring day. They might get to see the mighty locomotive, blowing its whistles grandly, filling their young heads with dreams of adventures in far away cities.

They waited for the appearance of the roaring train and one of the boys shouted to the other, "Hey, look down there! There's an old derelict under the trustle," and following his lead, all ran down the embankment for a look.

The thin, gray-haired man sat in the shade, his right knee pulled up in front of him, the left leg stretched out, his head resting on his arm. Their shouts made him raise a weary head warily and when the boys neared him, one hollered,

"Look, he's all scarred and ugly," and took one of the pebbles he still carried and threw it at the man, barely missing his head. The wretch made a move to rise, but had great difficulty as he crawled from the opening on the far side of the trestle and tried to get to his feet. More rocks were now sailing past his slim form and he did his best to dodge and shield his body with thin arms thrown up. His progress was slow as he dragged his left leg stiffly behind him. Rocks were starting to hit his back and he heard one of the boys say, "Stop it! Stop it! You'll hurt him," and footsteps running towards him.

"Aw, you don't ever want to have any fun," one of the voices said and then he could hear the laughing boys, running in the other direction. All but one. The boy who had told the others to stop throwing rocks was heading in his direction and the man tried to speed his pace, hopping hopelessly, trying to flee. The boy soon caught up with him and came to stand in front of him.

"Are you all right, mister?" the boy said and looked up at him.

Hunter looked down at the boy and something about Scotty's olive face, his dark flashing eyes, brought everything back in a wave of remembering. Staring unbelieving down at his son, Hunter raised a frail, shaking hand and said, "Scotty!"

Not wanting to be touched by the strange, dirty man, Scott moved out of his grasp easily, "How did you know my name is Scott?"

The strange man looking down at him had tears in his eyes and he was choking, trying desperately to speak. Scott couldn't understand why, but he felt compassion for the poor man and finally raised a small brown hand up to the man's arm. "Sit down," he said softly and helped the cripple to the ground. Scott dropped on his knees in front of the crying man and again asked, "How do you know my name is Scott?"

"Scotty," the man said, looking at him intently, "I know you are going to have a hard time believing me, but I'm your daddy."

Scott drew back as if the derelict had burned him, "No, you are not! Why do you say such a cruel thing?"

"Scotty, it's true, I'm your father. I swear to you. I know I look very different, that's why you don't know me, but I'm Hunter Alexander."

Scott's dark eyes were large and luminous, "But . . . no, you can't be. My father is, he's . . . come! I'll show you where my father is," and Scott rose, leaving the cripple to get up as best he could. Wordlessly, Scott led the way to the small consecrated cemetery. The man followed Scott, stumbling along, trying to keep up with the healthy young boy. Tired and gasping for air, the man stepped inside the cemetery gates and followed Scott to a large marble marker. "There," Scott pointed to the headstone, "My father is dead!"

Hunter slowly limped to the grave and bent warily down to read the inscription on the heavy stone.

Here lies Hunter Alexander, Colonel, C. S. A.
Beloved husband of Kathleen Alexander
Beloved father of Scott Alexander
A brave hero of the Confederacy who gave up
his life in the line of duty in Vicksburg, Mississippi
March 30, 1831–July 3, 1863

Hunter read and reread the epitaph. He looked up at Scotty standing over him with his arms folded over his chest. "See," Scott said, rebelliously, "My daddy's dead. He died in the war, he was a great hero."

Hunter looked at Scott and smiled, "Son, do you have a piece of paper and a pencil in your notebook?"

"Sure, but why do . . ."

"Can I borrow it for a minute?"

Frowning at the strange man, Scott nevertheless pulled out a clean sheet of paper and a stubby yellow pencil and handed it to him.

"Thanks. Now, can I use your notebook, too?"

Scott complied and Hunter placed the paper on the notebook, took the pencil in his left hand and wrote, "Scott Louis Alexander is right-handed, though he's always tried to be left-handed, just like me. He sleeps each night with his arms thrown over his head and his right foot hanging over his bed. His lovely blond mother, Kathleen, I'll bet, is waiting right now at Sans Souci, wondering where he is. He remembers me with blond hair and no scars. I remember him as the boy, not five years old, whom I played catch with in the yard on my last morning before I left for the war."

Hunter handed the piece of paper to Scott and watched as he read it. Scott's eyes grew wide and when he'd finished reading, he lowered the paper and looked back at Hunter. He studied the face carefully and slowly his small brown hand came up to Hunter's scarred face. In a half-choking, frightened voice, he said, "Daddy, is it really you?"

"Yes, Scotty, I swear to you. It's me, darling."

"But they told us my father died in the war and we thought . . ."

"It was a terrible mistake, son. I was badly wounded, but I lived."

Scott slowly sunk to his knees, his hand still on his father's face. "Then why didn't you come home? We cried and cried for you. Why didn't you come back?"

"Son, I was shell-shocked from my head wounds. I didn't know who I was, I didn't remember you or your mother. I remembered nothing. I was lost, Scotty, I had no idea where I belonged or who I belonged to. Little bits and pieces of the past have been returning in the last few months, but never enough to tell me who I was. Then, darling, I saw your dear face and it all came back at once. Oh, son, please, please believe me."

Scotty, tears stinging his dark eyes, raised trembling arms around his father's neck, "Daddy, Daddy."

Hunter, dropping the notebook to the ground, hugged Scott with all the strength his frail body possessed and when he felt tears from the boy's face wetting his own cheeks, he pulled back a little, holding his son by his shoulders, "Don't cry, Scott. We've found each other at last. I love you so much and I'll make up to you for all the years I've been away."

"Yes, Daddy, yes," Scott smiled through his tears and rose. "Let me help you, Daddy," and he tugged on Hunter's hands, helping him to his feet. "Just lean on me, I'm real strong, I can get you home."

Hunter stood leaning against his own son, his arm draped around Scott's shoulder. Scott handed Hunter the notebook, then put one arm around his father's waist, the other he brought to Hunter's slim middle.

"Before we go, Scotty, tell me . . . is your mother . . . is Kathleen . . . "

"What, Daddy?"

"Is she married again?"

"Daddy," Scott grinned up at him, "my mother could never love anybody but you. She's never been out with another man since you left. Now come on, she'll be so happy to see you. Just like I am."

Nearing the double doors of the mansion, Kathleen was flooded with relief when she looked out and saw Scotty coming up the long drive. Then new alarm immediately possessed her. He was with a man, a beggar. Hadn't she taught her son better than to bring hungry veterans home with him. They hardly had enough to eat themselves, much less enough for the poor hungry men now filling the countryside around Natchez. Indeed, she had cautioned him about even talking to them, much less bringing them home. Didn't she have enough trouble without her disobeying son dragging some unwashed, half-starved stranger home with him.

446

The poor man was crippled. Scotty was supporting him, his arm around the stranger's waist. The wretch was leaning on Scotty, his skinny arm around Scott's shoulder. His emaciated body was pitifully covered in worn, baggy gray trousers, a threadbare shirt hung loosely from his frail chest. And he was scarred. The entire left side of his face bore scars. He must be an old man, his hair is almost completely gray. No, no, he isn't old, the right side of his unshaven face bears no scars and it's unlined, like the face of a young man.

Kathleen stood staring intently at the man and something strange was taking place inside her body. Every muscle was tense and strained. Unexplained sensations surged through her veins. "What is it? What is happening to me? Why am I looking into the face of a scarred, crippled derelict and feeling an overpowering affection for him? Have I finally gone mad that I would feel a need to fling myself into his dirty arms and stroke the scarred cheek. Why is the heart in my chest pounding with an excitement usually associated with love and desire? I have gone crazy! That's it, I'm insane! I want to embrace that filthy stranger. And I want him to hold me too."

Kathleen stood transfixed, watching Scott and the beggar coming closer until they were inside the yard. Shocked and dreadfully confused by her reaction to the man coming up the walk, she continued looking only at him. Her eyes seemed to be locked on him until she was powerless to tear them away and she knew it was all part of the insanity possessing her. The scarred, gray-haired man looked up and the pulse in her ears drummed loudly, as every piece of the puzzle fell into place. Now she knew why Dawson never came. Now she knew why Scott was late from school. Now she knew why he so willingly helped the beggar. Now she knew why her heart was pounding and she longed to touch the tall, skinny man coming towards her.

"Hunter," she screamed and flew out the doors. She ran down the walk with tears filling her eyes and hysterical laughter escaping her lips. He watched her coming toward him and the full mouth trembled in the gaunt face, then turned up into a smile. The brown eyes turned into the soft ones she remembered so well and he opened his mouth to speak, but she never gave him the opportunity. She threw her arms around his neck and was kissing his lips, his scarred face, his gray hair, sobbing between kisses, "Hunter, Hunter," over and over again. She moved her hands to his back, feeling each protruding rib. She clung to him with such ferocity that he was in danger of toppling over with her on top of him. Speechless, Hunter let himself be embraced, patted, felt, touched, cried on, kissed, and loved.

Scotty stood watching them, tears of happiness sliding down his brown cheeks until, embarrassed by his unmanly behavior, he fled into the house. He turned when he got inside the door and looked back. They still stood together, his mother embracing his father, and at last his father was speaking.

"Darling," Hunter whispered, "I'm so dirty, you shouldn't be touching me."

With her head now resting on his chest and her arms securely around his waist, she murmured, "My darling, do you really think you could keep me from touching you?" And she raised her head to look into his face.

His dreamy brown eyes were swimming in tears and he choked out the words, "I hope not," and for the first time his arms came around her and he smiled, "Hope you'll pardon a few scars, darling."

"Hunter, my love, you've never been so handsome in your life," and she stood on tiptoe and lovingly kissed the deep scars covering his left cheek. "But I do agree, you're a bit soiled."

"I'm so sorry," he tried to pull away, but she wouldn't let him go. "I am so ashamed, I've so much to explain to you, tell you, and if you don't still want me I . . ."

Kathleen put her lips near his ear and whispered, "I love

you, Hunter, I've never stopped. Now come into the house where you belong." Moving underneath his arm, she put her arms around his slim waist and said, "Lean on me, my love," and together they made their way into the house, she supporting him and he willingly letting her. Their son waited with the door open.

After Dawson saw Hunter and Scott, he had Jim drive him directly to the river. Stopping at the wharf where the *Diana Mine* was moored, Dawson walked up the gangplank in no hurry and headed for his cabin. Once inside, he cast aside his fine waistcoat and vest. He unbuttoned his white silk shirt and sat down behind his big desk. He drew out a bottle of whiskey from the bottom drawer and poured himself a stiff drink. Resting his feet atop his desk, he lay back in his chair and slowly drank the liquor while his fingers toyed with the cameo resting on his chest. The full impact of what had happened was slowly registering and he felt a great weariness throughout his large body. He sat quietly drinking, his dark eyes narrowed, morose. Fate had again dealt him a hand to play and, although he didn't like the cards he'd drawn, they were all he had and he must do the best with them. A wry smile came to his lips and he swung his long legs down from the desk and went to his coat. He reached inside the breast pocket and took out the small pink velvet box. He popped it open for one last look inside, holding it close to his face. He sighed, closed the box, and went to the cabin door and flung it open. "Sam," he called up to the pilot house, "Sam, are you here?"

"Yes, suh, Cap'n Dawson," came the sleepy answer and Dawson heard Sam's heavy footsteps coming down to his cabin. "Sorry, Cap'n Dawson, guess I was takin' a little nap. I didn't know you was here."

"That's all right, Sam," Dawson smiled at his friend. "Come in for a minute. Have a drink with me."

449

Suppressing a big yawn, Sam scratched his head and followed Dawson into the cabin. "Cap'n, why is you here? It jest dawned on me, you is supposed to be up at Sans Souci."

Dawson grinned sheepishly and said, "Yes, I know, but looks like my plans have changed," and he told his understanding friend what had happened.

Shaking his big head in disbelief, Sam sympathized, "Oh, Cap'n, I is so sorry, so terrible sorry."

"Well, don't be, Sam, because it's an ill wind that blows nobody good. Here," Dawson held out the pink velvet box to Sam, "Take this, Sam, give it to Ruby or one of your other women."

Sam looked inside and his eyes grew big and round, "But, Cap'n, I can't take this, why it be the most pretty ring I ever did see."

Dawson picked up his waistcoat, rolled down his sleeves, and started for the door. He turned and laughed, "Yes, you can, Sam. It's yours. After all, if I keep this up, the damn Mississippi River's going to be full of diamonds."

Thirty-nine

Dawson went home to his mansion after giving the diamond ring to Sam. When the servants saw the dark scowl on his face, they dared not ask him what had happened to displease him or why he was home when he had announced earlier in the day that he would be at Sans Souci all evening. Pretending nothing was amiss, they greeted him and quickly fled his presence, knowing Jim would tell them later why the master was in such a fowl mood and why he had returned home.

Dawson stomped directly up the stairs to his own bedroom and no one saw him the rest of the day. When a tray of food was taken up at the dinner hour, he refused to open his door, so it was placed on the table in the hall where it was to remain untouched. Dawson paced the floor of his big upstairs bedroom, muttering expletives under his breath and stopping often to pour another drink of whiskey from a crystal decanter. The pacing continued all evening and far into the night. What was even more frightening to the servants was that around eleven o'clock that night they heard the master's door being flung open and what sounded like heavy furniture being moved about upstairs.

Perspiring and tired, Dawson cast aside his shirt at midnight and continued with his work. He was moving every piece of furniture out of his big bedroom and sitting room. Even the heavy blue brocade drapes were yanked from their rods by a cursing, drunken Dawson, intent on ridding the room of all its possessions. Loud, bawdy singing replaced the

451

cursing around three, mixing gratingly with the sounds of heavy chairs, sofas, and tables being pushed and dragged into the hall. By five, nothing remained in either large room except for Dawson's oversized bed. Pulling and tugging, the singing once again turned into loud curses as he sweated and shoved and heaved on the heavy, stubborn bed that would not move. Refusing to give up and let it best him, Dawson continued in vain to try and move the giant bed. Holding to a huge round post, blindly drunk now and desperately tired, Dawson grunted and struggled until the veins on his forehead stood out and every muscle in his broad, glistening back strained under its burden. The bed would not budge and, exhausted and beaten, Dawson at long last sank down onto it defeated, fell over onto his back, and was fast asleep.

At nine that same morning, Dawson, surprisingly sober and immaculately groomed and dressed, opened his door and weaved his way around the stacked furniture lining the walls of the hall. Laughing at his own drunken foolishness as he worked his way around the displaced furniture, Dawson shocked his servants anew as he descended the stairs, humming in a pleasant baritone and smiling to them as though the evening's events had never taken place.

Instructing Jim to drive him to Crawford Ashworth's office without delay, Dawson climbed into the back of the carriage, drew out a long, thin cigar and smoked while a lazy smile played at his full lips.

"Crawford, sorry to come without an appointment, but I've something important for you to handle."

"Sure, Dawson, have a seat. I'm always glad to see you."

Not pausing for small talk, Dawson told his friend and attorney the reason for his visit. "I want to make my will immediately."

"That's a good idea, son, everyone should have a will. I've got a lot going right now, but let's set up an appointment for sometime next week and we'll draw it up.''

"No. We'll do it right now," Dawson smiled at his old friend.

"Just what's the hurry?"

"God, I'm almost ashamed to tell you," Dawson looked at Crawford sheepishly and related the story of Hunter's unexpected homecoming.

Crawford's eyes filled with concern for the man sitting across from him and he started to sympathize, "Dawson, I'm so sorry. . . .''

Dawson waved a brown hand to quiet him, "I'm not here for any of your outpourings of pity and other nonsense. Get out your pen and make up my will. I want to leave everything to Scott Alexander. I want it put into trust until he is eighteen, then it's all his to do with as he pleases.''

Crawford's concern turned to alarm and he said loudly, "Good Lord, Dawson, you can't do that.''

"It's my money, I can do anything I please with it, so write it up.''

Crawford rose from his chair and came around his desk, sitting on its edge, leaning close to his friend. "Dawson, in the first place I'm sure you'll live to a ripe old age so I don't see the urgency of writing your will today. But in the second place, if something should happen to you, God forbid, in the near future, don't you think it would cause a bit of a problem for all your money to go to Scotty?''

"For who? Scotty? I told you, he won't get it until he's eighteen. Then, I'm sure he'd be delighted to inherit a large sum of money. What kid wouldn't?''

"Dawson, I'm not speaking of Scotty. I mean . . . well, what would Hunter think? How would he feel about it? You have to consider other people, why, Kathleen and . . .''

Dawson smiled, but straightened in his chair, bringing himself up to his full, imposing height until his face was only inches from the man standing over him. Very softly, he said, "Crawford, I think I'm a decent man and I've always tried

453

to be very careful of other's feelings. But, I'll tell you something, I am going to leave my money to my son, my own flesh and blood. I fathered him and no matter how many people wish the facts were otherwise, they are not. So, as to how Hunter Alexander would feel about it, although I met him once and he seemed like a very nice man and I am sure he is a good husband and father, you'll forgive me if I tell you I really don't give a damn how he feels about that or anything else.''

"Now, Dawson, you don't mean that. I know you don't, why . . .''

"I do, Crawford. I've lost them both, through no fault of my own, but I'm a big boy and I'll accept it. But I'll be damned if I intend to worry about the delicate feelings of the man who took them both.'' He rose from his chair and said when he reached the door, "Draw up the will, I'll be back in an hour to sign it.''

True to his word, Dawson returned in an hour and, with Crawford and the young assistant attorney as witnesses, Dawson signed the document and said, "I appreciate it, Crawford. I'm going to tell Sam what's in my will, so send him a copy. I'm relying on you and Sam to carry out the wishes of my will should the need arise.'' Then he smiled and added, "Don't look so worried, old friend, I intend to live to be a hundred.''

Forty

The January night was bitter cold. No stars shone down from the heavens and the murky gray clouds filling the sky threatened to bring drizzling rain before the dawn. Chilling winds blew restlessly, cutting through even the heaviest of greatcoats like a sharp-bladed knife, and made an eerie moan as it roamed wantonly around the clapboard buildings, seeking entrance at every door.

Inside the small crowded saloon on Silver Street in Natchez Under, the air was warm and stuffy. A blue haze of cigar smoke hung suspended, moved intermittently by the front door being swung open to allow another soul shelter and comfort from the biting Mississippi norther'. Tinkly piano music greeted any new arrival and loud voices and boisterous laughter made the thin walls of the little room vibrate with their timbre.

At a card table near the center of the room, a dark, slightly dissipated gentleman sat playing draw poker with four men. The tall man, a dark stubble of a beard evident on his lean brown face, sat smiling, a long, thin cigar clamped tightly between his white, even teeth. Coatless, his fine white shirt was open, the sleeves rolled up to his elbows. A glass of whiskey sat at his right hand, a dish of discarded cigars near it. Directly in front of the man, tall stacks of poker chips rested in the circle of his arms laying on the table.

A large brown hand reached out and picked up the five new cards that had been dealt him. Raising them close to his chest, the man studied them while the expression on his face changed none at all, not even a dark eyebrow raised to give his table companions a much looked for clue as to what the consistent winner of the drawn-out game might be holding. Carefully, he looked at the cards in his right hand, spreading them only enough to be sure of what he had. The top card was the King of Hearts, the second, the Queen. The next two cards, barely glanced at by the man, were the Jack of Hearts and the ten. The fifth, the duce of Clubs.

The dealer looked at him as he tossed the duce, face down, to the center of the table. "One card," he said and the dealer shot him a card across the green felt. Covering it with his other cards, the man again spread out the five cards. He had drawn the Black Ace.

At the back of the room, a tall, slim man with a black patch covering one eye, a Union greatcoat pulled up around his ears, stood drinking his whiskey. Unnoticed and alone, he watched the card players, his good eye narrowed in revenge. A slim-fingered hand went inside his greatcoat and when he pulled it out, it contained a derringer. Tossing down his glass of straight whiskey, he wiped his mouth on his coat sleeve, raised his right hand, and fired the revolver one time. He dropped it to the floor and fled through the back door near the bar, out into the night.

The bullet ripped into its target with great accuracy and the man holding the four hearts and the ace of spades crumpled the cards in his hand. Slowly dropping them to the table, his right hand came up to his chest. The bullet had entered his broad back directly under his left shoulder blade, made a slightly upward path through his heart to exit his chest, and hit the low ceiling overhead.

The large brown hand quickly filled with blood and the dark eyes looked stunned and dazed. The man's mouth opened to speak, trying to form a word, but only a tiny trickle of blood escaped the corner of his mouth. His hand left his bullet-torn chest and moved slowly up to clasp a tiny cameo hanging from a gold chain around his neck. Without a groan of agony, he slumped from his chair to the floor, falling over onto his back amid the crowd of gasping, horrified gamblers.

Dawson Harpe Blakely was dead.

Over a year had passed since Hunter had returned home. The warm July air of the late Mississippi evening promised another long sweltering summer. The hour being well past eleven, Scott lay asleep in his upstairs bedroom at Sans Souci, his arms flung over his head, his right foot hung over the edge of his bed. In the nursery next to his room, a chubby, three-month-old baby lay asleep in her crib. Resting on her stomach, a small fist was jammed into her mouth. The downy soft blond hair of her head made a halo around the tiny delicate features of her face. Judith Kathleen Alexander, named after Hunter's mother, slept peacefully, not knowing she was no longer in her father's proud arms where she'd gone to sleep an hour earlier.

In the master bedroom across the hall from the nursery, Kathleen lay propped up in bed, reading a novel, while her husband sat at a small desk, his white shirt discarded, his feet bare, carefully going over the many bills they owed. Hunter, completely recovered and back to his normal weight, bent his grayish-blond head over the long column of figures, rubbed his scarred left cheek absently and frowned.

"Hunter, your face will freeze like that if you aren't careful," Kathleen said, watching her husband from the bed.

He turned and smiled at her, scratching his head with the blunt end of the pencil, "I sure wouldn't want to mar my looks," he laughed. The smile faded immediately and he said, "Dear, I'm afraid I'm not the provider I should be. I've been back at my practice for over nine months and we are hardly any better off than when I first got home."

"You worry too much," she chided him. "Come to bed and forget it until morning."

"Honey, I'm serious." He held up the sheet of paper he had so meticulously figured on, "There's always more going out than I take in. Sans Souci costs a fortune to maintain, even in its sad state. We're going to end up paupers. I don't mind so much for you and me, but what about our children? I can't stand to think about Judith and Scott being poor."

Kathleen laid her book on the night table, put her hands behind her head, and said, "You know, Hunter, I've been thinking, maybe we should sell Sans Souci."

Thinking he'd surely misunderstood her, Hunter whirled in his chair and said, "What did you say, Kathleen?"

She looked at the surprise on his handsome, scarred face and laughed. "Come here," she patted the mattress beside her.

Dropping his paper back to the desk, Hunter hurried to her side, taking a seat beside her on the bed. "Did I hear you correctly?" he looked down at her.

Smiling still, she raised a hand and caressed the scarred left shoulder of his hard, lean chest. "You did, sir. I said 'Why don't we sell Sans Souci.' I've been thinking, it might be a very wise idea if moved somewhere else."

"But where we would go? Any mansion in this city would be just as large a burden as this one. Out of the frying pan into the fire, you know that."

"Oh, I agree wholeheartedly. I don't mean move to another home here, I mean perhaps we should seek our fortune elsewhere." She paused for effect, then looked up and grinned mischievously, "Say, Texas?"

Kathleen watched as Hunter's dreamy brown eyes widened and excitedly he grabbed her shoulders, "How did you know about that?"

She giggled and sat up close to him, "Darling," she said and her finger traced his full upper lip, "Colonel Cort Mitchell came here for a visit after the war ended. He told us all about your bravery and what good friends you became. And he said that the two of you often talked of you coming to

458

Texas after the war was over."

"We did, Kathleen, but that was because at that time I never planned to return to Natchez . . . or to you."

"I know that, darling, but if you considered going to Texas, even without us, you must have thought it held some kind of future for you. Would the unplanned addition of a family change it?"

"Of course it wouldn't."

"Then tell me about it, what did you have in mind when you were considering going there?"

Hunter's eyes sparkled and he kissed her fingers and pulled her hand away from his mouth. "Sweetheart, it's like a new frontier there. Cort tells me things are just beginning to happen there, whereas here, we both know, the best and most prosperous days are in the past. Things can never be the same here, we both know it's true, even if it's a somewhat bitter pill to swallow. Cort tells me in Texas the land is cheap and there's lots of it and . . ." Hunter was talking a mile a minute and there was more excitement shining in his brown eyes than Kathleen had seen in a long time. Laughing wildly, Kathleen threw her arms around her husband's neck and hugged him while he continued with his obvious sales pitch on the bright future Texas had to offer.

"Darling, darling," she said at last, "no more, please. You've convinced me. I've only one question. It sounds to me as though you wish to become a rancher. Are you already weary of being a doctor?"

Hunter took her arms and set her back, "No, Kathleen, certainly not. I'll set up practice in Texas. You know I could never give up medicine. Next to you and the children, it's the most important thing in my life." He had bounded from the bed, walking around the room, the limp now hardly noticeable, healed considerably from the proper care and exercise of the past year. He rubbed his palms together and marched around the room while her eyes followed him. "I'll set up practice in Texas, but at the same time we can own and live

459

on a ranch. Nothing large like Cort owns, of course, but a small spread somewhere with a few cattle and a couple of hired hands and . . .''

"Hunter," Kathleen smiled, "When do we leave?"

Hurrying back to the bed, Hunter once again sat down by her, "Oh, honey, do you really mean it?"

Gathering her happy husband into her arms, Kathleen whispered, "Yes, darling, I mean it," and raised her face for his kiss.

Not a month later, Kathleen closed the door of Sans Souci for the last time. Waiting for her in the drive, Hunter stood beside the carriage. His independent daughter, who'd arrived over two weeks early in order to enter the world on his birthday, lay cradled in his long arm, plucking contentedly at his shirtfront while he patted her full stomach gently and made foolish faces at her. Scott stood at the front of the carriage, the reins in his hands, ramrod straight, but more than a little impatient at the dawdling of his mother. He was anxious to be off and longed to set out on his new adventure in a strange land where he envisioned of himself in buckskin pants and fringed leather shirts, atop his wild stallion, riding the range in wild abandon while strong winds whipped his thick hair around his head and the call of coyotes filled his ears.

Earlier in the day, Kathleen had made her last visit to the graves beyond the summer house where she and Hunter stood quietly side by side and said goodbye to the dear ones resting there. Hunter had sold Sans Souci and though it was harder than he knew for Kathleen to understand how a property once worth well over half a million dollars would bring no more than eight thousand now, he could get no more for it. The packing had been done, goodbyes to all their friends had taken place the evening before at a going-away party at Julie and Caleb's house. Uncle Rembert had been invited to accompany them to Texas, but he'd declined, saying Natchez was the only home he'd ever known and, since it was well past the September of his life, he had no intention of spending the remainder of his days anywhere but there.

Everything had been settled and taken care of and her family waited for her at the end of the long walk; only her appearance was holding up their departure. Dressed and ready to leave, she took one last look at the high-ceilinged rooms where she'd been born and raised. Echos of familiar voices filled each room and Kathleen could almost hear the conversations of the past filling her ears when she stood in the empty foyer. Cold in spite of the heat of the day, Kathleen felt the much dreaded lump rising in her throat, though she had promised herself she would not cry and upset everyone. She closed her eyes tightly for only an instant, opened them, and ran out the door and into the yard.

Hunter and Scott saw her coming and Scott quickly took his place on the seat in back of the carriage. Hunter handed his baby sister up to him and went to meet his wife. He saw the set jaw and the mist behind her big blue eyes threatening to spill into tears. He took her arm and said very softly, "Are you all right, darling?"

Afraid if she tried to speak her resolve would disintegrate, she stiffly shook her head up and down and refused to meet his eyes. Hunter smiled at her, reached his hands to her slim waist, and easily set her up in the carriage. Walking around the horses, he swung up beside her and applied the whip. The carriage moved down the long drive, away from Sans Souci. Worried about Kathleen, Hunter kept stealing glances at her immobile face and finally he said in a whisper, "Darling, do you want to take one last look back?"

The blue eyes lifted to his and, when finally she was able to speak, she said, "No, I don't want to look back. I only want to look ahead," and the trembling lips smiled and she scooted over closer to him and slipped her arm through his.

Hunter laughed, kissed her cheek, and said loudly, "Then

let's head for Texas.'' He cracked the whip over the horses' backs and they quickened their pace, leaving forever Natchez Above and Natchez Below.

''Yippee,'' Scotty shouted, startling his new sister, who promptly cried. ''Here, Mother, take her, she's bawling again!''

Kathleen smiled and took the little girl from Scott's arms. Settling the child in the crook of her arm close to her breast, she cooed down to her and Judith sighed and went to sleep. Hunter looked down into Kathleen's arms at the dear little bundle, so plainly a mixture of Kathleen and himself. He looked from her tiny face to the lovely face of his wife bending over their child. Pride and love swelled pleasantly inside Hunter's scarred chest and he shocked his entire family when, for the first time ever, they heard his resonant baritone voice break into a catchy, happy song, ''Oh it rained all night the day I left, the weather it was dry. . . .''

BE CAPTIVATED BY THESE HISTORICAL ROMANCES

CAPTIVE ECSTASY (738, $2.75)
by Elaine Barbieri

From the moment Amanda saw the savage Indian imprisoned in the fort she felt compassion for him. But she never dreamed that someday she'd become his captive—or that a captive is what she'd want to be!

PASSION'S PARADISE (765, $3.25)
by Sonya T. Pelton

Kidnapped by a cruel and rugged pirate, a young beauty's future is suddenly in the balance. Yet she is strangely warmed by her captor's touch. And that warmth ignites a fire that no pirate's seas can put out!

AMBER FIRE (848, $3.50)
by Elaine Barbieri

Ever since she met the dark and sensual Stephen, Melanie's senses throbbed with a longing that seared her veins. Stephen was the one man who could fulfill such desire—and the one man she vowed never to see again!

TIDES OF ECSTASY (769, $3.25)
by Luanne Walden

Meghan's dream of marrying Lord Thomas Beauchamp was coming true—until the handsome but heartless Derek entered her life and forcibly changed her plans. . . .

TEXAS FLAME (797, $2.75)
by Catherine Creel

Amanda's journey west through a haven of outlaws and Indians leads her to handsome Luke Cameron, was wild and untamed as the land itself, whose burning passion would consume her own!

Available wherever paperbacks are sold, or order direct from the Publisher. Send cover price plus 50¢ per copy for mailing and handling to Zebra Books, 475 Park Avenue South, New York, N.Y. 10016. DO NOT SEND CASH.